SKYS

•

After a time, he turned, a look of pure defiance and determination etched on features suddenly very old.

"You bastards," Dr. Scarborough cried, shaking a fist at the sky, toward the darkness that hid the foul snakes who had stolen his only daughter away from him. "I'll get her back. And you're going to pay! Do you hear me! You're going to *pay*!"

Jake Camden lit a cigarette, took a drag, got Dr. Everret Scarborough back in the car, and drove back toward Las Vegas.

"Something tells me," he said softly as Scarborough stared out mordantly at the desert, "we're not in Kansas anymore..."

ABDUCTION: THE UFO CONSPIRACY

DAVID BISCHOFF

WARNER BOOKS

A Warner Communications Company

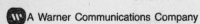

For
Susan Benton

PROLOGUE

The night Harry Reynolds was abducted by the aliens, he was sitting on his toilet with a copy of the *Weekly World News* and a bad case of constipation.

Even so, Harry Reynolds was ready for 'em.

He figured the little buggers would eventually get around to picking him up. Harry *knew* they were around—*had known* since the big flap started in the early fifties. Harry Reynolds had seen a few of their saucers from time to time, zipping over cornfields or rising up from behind trees, but that wasn't what made him sure that creatures from outer space were buzzing around earth, checking out missile silos, playing chicken with commercial airliners, and poking instruments up horror-writers' assholes.

He knew, because he'd heard them on his shortwave radio.

Harry was a ham-radio operator, had been since the fifties, when he'd gotten out of the army with his right leg left behind in Korea. Back then, he'd done a lot of sitting, they didn't have artificial legs as good as what they had now, and he just wasn't real used to his wooden one. So he tinkered with electronic gadgets a lot, built himself a sweet little shortwave radio from a Heathkit, and started broadcasting and intercepting broadcasts like a regular deejay of the night sky, bouncing his handle— Aardvark—through the airwaves. Even then he'd been interested in flying saucers, so when he started getting strange broadcasts, unusual beeps and hums, weird chatterings that sure as hell weren't English or any foreign language Harry'd ever heard—he pegged 'em quick. Regularly, he'd even do special broadcasts for the UFOs, giving them his address and inviting them over for beers, trying to explain this and that—things they might not understand in easy American. That gave him a reputation amongst other ham operators. Pretty soon, he was Klatuu—named after the Michael Rennie character in *The Day the Earth Stood Still*. Harry didn't mind. It got him a lot of attention.

Unfortunately, no little green men in shiny suits ever came by for some Bud and bullshitting.

Still, Harry knew they'd come. They were out there, sure as hell—all the fancy brains in the world had worked hard to prove that there *were* no such things as flying saucers, but they'd failed. Harry still heard their messages on the band, and he believed lots of the people who'd seen them, who'd talked to them. Harry read the UFO journals, and he checked out the UFO books from the Dubuque Library System, so he was up on the latest, which seemed to be that his Long Distance Audience—that was what Harry called the extraterrestrials—had taken to picking people up in the flying saucers, doing tests on them, sometimes even making them pregnant. Fascinating stuff, yes siree, Bob, and too bad that they hadn't made that Whitley Strieber feller or that Maximillian what's-his-name pregnant. Now *that* would be a *story*!

No, Harry Reynolds figured the aliens would get around to him eventually, and he figured that when they did he had a pretty good chance to get some proof that they really existed. Wouldn't that make the other ham radio boys at the lodge sit down with their jaws between their knees!

So, when the aliens finally did get around to abducting him, old Harry was ready for them with a device he'd constructed in the basement workshop of his little house just outside of Dubuque. Harry knew there was no telling when the aliens would take him, so it was no good hauling the thing around in his pocket, or around his neck. 'Sides, they'd see it and take it off, real quick.

Instead, he designed it special, just the right size and weight to fit inside his hollow, fake right leg.

Then, when the aliens came for Harry Reynolds and plucked

him from his white-tiled bathroom right outside Dubuque, Iowa, they had no way of knowing what was in store for them.

As soon as he'd driven home from his printing shop in his '76 Chevy station wagon, Harry Reynolds knew that something weird was going on.

He pulled into his garage, got out of his car and, in the spring dusk went to his front yard checking to see if he'd seen what he thought he had.

There seemed to be some kind of aura around his house.

Now, standing in the grass (that needed cutting—he'd have to fire up the old Toro this weekend) he looked at his boxy cinderblock-and-brick home, squinting real hard at the edges, where chimney and roof and siding and tall radio antennae gave way to grass and trees and the gentle cobalt of the fading sky. Here, he'd fancied he'd seen, as he pulled up in the driveway, a periphery of light—a shifting gentle spectrum of light, as though some pixie had just zapped 3210 Elmore Drive with a magical spell.

"Damnedest thing!" he said, staring a moment longer, then giving up. He was going to have to put this on his shortwave radio show tonight. Course, he put near about *everything* on his radio show, and then would gab into the wee hours if some fellow ham operator was unlucky enough to get buttonholed by his signal. "Mebbe the Centaurans did it."

Harry shrugged, then stumped back to the wagon to get the bag of groceries he'd picked up at the Val-U-Mart, the limp of his false leg only slightly evident. The cats were waiting for him at the side door, meowing up a storm.

"Whoa there, Joker! Hang onto your bonnet, Bessie!" he said, as they performed their evening feline come-ons with Harry's legs. "You happy to see me . . . or you just hungry?"

Both, actually. He kept his cats inside when he was away, letting them roam outside only when he was at the house. It wasn't that he didn't figure they could take care of themselves— he just liked to know where they were when he got back, otherwise he'd worry and ruin the evening. He'd had cats run off when his wife was alive, never to return, and it hadn't been too bad. But now that Carolyn was never going to return, well . . . maybe he just liked to *know* that somebody was home waiting for him.

Harry opened up a can of Figaro Seafood Supreme, and divided it up amongst the black manx and the female striped-tabby, wincing at the awful smell. Then he changed their water dish, and set it carefully down onto the kitty smile-face place mat in the corner where the cats huddled and gorged. Later, he'd spill some Meow Mix into their communal dry-food bowl, but only when they got peckish. Cats appreciate you more if they have to work a bit to get their food.

Then Harry put away his groceries, fired up some burgers under the broiler, and got his mail. Bills, *Fate Magazine*, the latest *Weekly World News*, and nothing from his children, Hattie and Ted, married now and living on opposite coasts. He'd hear from them on Father's Day, and that was about their only spring ritual communication. Oh, well . . . They had their own lives to lead. They regarded their father as a bit of a crank—an unfortunate box of peculiarities, stacked away in the midwestern closet of their childhoods.

Harry ate his burgers with a can of Hormel Hot Chili dumped on them, while he perused *Fate*. Good magazine, but not the magazine that good ol' Raymond Palmer had started up years ago. Too much goddamn psychic nonsense, for one thing. This issue had an article on the lost continent Lemuria, a piece on dowsing and a long previously unprinted interview with the late J. Allen Hyenk which looked interesting, but all the rest was either crystal-brained New Age garbage or Harry's perpetual bugaboo, psychic predictions and the like. Bad as astrology. Goddamn stuff just didn't make sense, but people ate it up like Post Toasties!

Finished with dinner, he put the dish in the sink, and belched loudly. "Beans already workin', cats!" he said, addressing his startled pets. "Better let you out. Goddamn beans are mighty tasty, but they make the only gas I know that *sinks* to lower extremities! But maybe we'll dynamite the blockages and get the mail movin' again, huh?"

He turned to run some water over the dish so the chili stains wouldn't dry (wash the sucker later) and was staring out the back window, when he thought he saw a flash of light in the trees behind his house, and thought he heard a faint confluence of whispers that died away almost soon as they had begun.

A shiver raised the hackles on the back of his neck. What the bejesus was goin' on out there?

He let the cats out, and he followed them into the backyard. The sun was long since gone, and deep Iowa night had set in. It had gone cold with a brisk spring chill already, and Harry shivered as he stepped out past the rusted swing set and the broken barbecue into the smell of new grass.

"Anybody out there?" he called. But the light was gone and the only sounds were from leaves rustling and branches clicking with the breeze. "If it's you Centaurans, come on out. I've been waiting for you and I ain't gonna hurt you, you should know that."

Harry was sure that the extraterrestrials probably didn't come from either Alpha or Beta Centauri, but he liked the sound of the word, so that was what he called them. Up above him now, only a few clouds obscured the stars. Harry Reynolds looked up at them for a moment, and got that shiver again, that shiver of wonder...

"You suckers are up there," he whispered. "I know you are. You may wait to come down and not show yourself until next century, when I'm six feet under... But people that remember me will say, Goddamn. Crazy ol' Harry Reynolds was *right*!"

With only a short-sleeve shirt on, no undershirt either, Harry got cold fast and retreated back into the house.

He was in the mood, no question.

He was in the mood to *broadcast*!

A wisp of acrid smoke coiled up, wreathing the round fluorescent work-lamp for a moment, then disappearing into the cellar darkness. Harry examined his soldering work carefully through a magnifying glass, then fitted the circuit board carefully back into the bulbous box that was his shortwave radio. A minor repair. Had to expect this kind of thing when you built your own radios from the git-go. He applied screwdriver to screws, putting the casing back together.

Around him in his basement hung his tools, arranged like bats hanging from a cavern ceiling. Harry had built all this himself, and he kept it neat and orderly. From time to time, he dabbled with inventions. Nothing serious. Better mousetraps, a new kind of catalytic converter for old cars, an electronic cat-door, stuff like that. Mostly, he enjoyed the electronics, playing with resistors and capacitors, transistors and wire, like a kid with Legos.

Harry hauled his shortwave set up from the basement, balanced it on a knee as he switched off the workshop light, then carried it on up to where he spent most of his widowed time: the attic. When he and his wife and kids had moved here in '59, this had been a normal A-frame attic, insulation between the rafters and all. Above Carolyn's objection that they needed the space for storage, Harry had claimed it, then applied his carpentry know-how to create a study. He'd always found his basement a little oppressive. The pounding of kids' feet and intrusions of his wife for laundry chores, along with countless other bothersome things all intruded upon his concentration and privacy terribly. But up here . . . .

Even now, with everyone gone but his cats—when too late he *realized* those interruptions were cherished reminders of companionship—when he pulled down the folding stairsteps and clambered up into Contact Central, he was in another world.

He put the squat radio down, plugged in the AC, jacked in the mike, and put on his headset. His swivel chair whined metallically as he leaned forward to fiddle with the controls and fine-tune the frequency for tonight's transmission. Signals beeped and slurred at various volumes across the band as he turned the dial, like "Saturday Night Live from Babel." His favorite channel, though, was free.

He switched open the mike, leaned back in his chair and began.

"UFOs, alert! UFOs, alert! All Centaurans and you other human and humanoid hangers-on, listen up! This is Klatuu, broadcasting at a frequency of 51.2 milahertz. FCC License Number . . . shit, I can't remember. Well anyway I'm legal, boys, and you're not!"

He swivelled a bit, leaning toward the mike, hand against his head and a finger in his ear, better to appreciate and adjust the resonance of his voice. It had a tendency to squeak out of its baritone when he got excited. His fellow ham operators used to call him "Klatu the Mouse" back in the sixties when this was a real problem.

Harry was sixty years old, but he'd never smoked, he didn't drink much more than beer, and that just on weekends, and he'd always done his own physical work, so he was in pretty good shape all-in-all. He had a stubby nose and big brown owlish eyes that now sprang open incredibly wide as he talked. When he was younger, he'd worn a goatee, because he'd seen a lot of UFO experts wearing them, but now his chin was bare, except for evening stubble.

"I know you've been sniffin' around my house. I've seen your lights, I've heard you—hell, I *sense* you've been here. I just wanna make sure you know that the invitation's still open, like it's always been, ever since my first broadcast to you from Contact Central. Come on over, and let's talk a while, real personal. I know you don't want most folks to know that you're around, but you can trust Harry Reynolds." Harry looked up at the star-chart he'd tacked onto the tilted ceiling, just one of the posters and maps and photographs papering the room, all related to UFOs. "I've been waitin' to talk to you guys for a loooong time! 'Cause I knnnnnoooooooww you're ouuuuuut there."

That last was his signature... kind of like Jack Benny's "Well..." or Steve Martin's "I'm a wild and crazy guy." The reason the other hams liked him, the reason they listened to his "show" whenever they could, separate from actually *talking* to him, was that Harry Reynolds had a sense of humor. He took UFOs dead serious when tit came down to tat—but in the meantime, he could joke about them, and he did.

"Lemme see... long as I got your ear. Last Sunday night, I was talking about..." he eye-scanned a stack of books on the table before him. "Ooh, yeah! that goddamn new book by that goddamn Scarbaloney goof." He picked the hardcover book out of the stack and read the title. "*Above Us Only Sky*, by Dr. Everett Scarborough. Yeah. Doctor of Quackology! Who does this bozo think he is? You gotta wonder from just the title! A quote from a pinko like John Lennon. Listen, I know this Scarborough jerk, I've read his books, all of 'em. Yeah, yeah, I know he's the doo-doo head who helped convince the government to wrap up Project Blue Book in '69. I know he's today's leading UFO skeptic, kinda the Amazing Randi for us saucer buffs. But ever think about it... This garbanzo bean-head has been making a *killing*, writing and lecturing and consulting... Hell, I hear some loony network is thinking about a TV show based on his so-called UFO investigation work. The dough must be *rollin'* in!"

Reynolds flipped through the book, muttering the doctor's

name over and over again, so that the Centaurans and his other listeners wouldn't think he'd gone away.

"Yeah. Yeah, here we go—this is the kind of attitude that *really* gets me miffed." He began to quote from the book. " 'Credulity. If I could sum up the entire reason for this twentieth century phenomenon, I would simply use the word "Credulity." As a scientist, I use the rigorous standards and methods of my training as a yardstick for all my investigations. These scientific investigations reveal absolutely no shred of evidence that the earth is being visited by denizens from other planets, other dimensions, other shopping malls. People experience what they *want* to experience. People believe what they *want* to believe. And some people simply want to believe in creatures from outer space. Deep psychological problems? Inadequacies? Paranoias? Mental disorders similar to schizophrenia that our doctors haven't categorized yet? Who knows. But the common denominator is simple. Credulity.' "

Harry Reynolds took a deep breath and then continued. "Now this really steams me!" The sentence came out close to soprano. Harry stopped for a second, got control of himself.

"Centaurans, you listening? Course you are. This is the kind of dope who's going to make things hard for you, when you finally decide to announce yourselves to the world at large. I got a real good idea. You know, we earth people, in our literature—we've got this interesting legend. Roman legend... no... GREEK. Yeah. Well, you see, the Greeks, they had a bunch of gods. Uh, like Zeus and Aphrodite and Odin. Yeah. And they made mankind, but they had a real warped relationship with humans and animals... like old Zeus liked to come down and have sex with swans. But if a guy... a guy like this Doctor Scarborough... got a bee up his ass, thought he was hot stuff, the gods didn't like it, they thought he was getting uppity had too much... uhm... *hubcapz*. Yeah, it's like pride and arrogance, only more so. So the gods would take the guy a peg or two down, put his face in the mud. Sometimes they sent the Furries after him. Sometimes they blinded him.

"Maybe that's what this Scarborough guy needs, huh? Pick 'em up in one of your saucers, give 'im a ride. Freak him out just a little bit, so he's not such a uppity snot anymore. Do him some good, I think." Reynolds chuckled. "Course, I want you to come see me first. 'Cause I knooooooow your ouuuuuuuut there!''

He continued his commentary for another half hour, finishing up his devastating book review, touching on a few entertaining highlights on the day at the printing shop, discussing his long-entertained notion of self-publishing his own book on UFOs (it had been turned down by thirty publishers). Then he finally described the aura he'd seen around his house when he'd got home and the lights and sounds he'd heard from the woods.

"Well, gotta go, friends. My bowels are acting up—and it ain't in no comedy!" he said, finishing.

He signed off, figuring he'd do the chat rounds in a couple of hours, get feedback from anybody who'd listened to his show... Maybe even zero in on some saucer broadcasts. Tonight definitely had that touch of weird to it.

Then he went down, grabbed his *World Weekly News* and headed hopefully for the crapper.

"UFO SHOCKER," screamed the headline.

"HEAD BANGERS FROM OUTER SPACE"

"You Centaurans," said Harry Reynolds, rocking on the commode with laughter, as he read about a UFO heavy metal concert in South America, his belt buckle jingling on the tile floor. "What comedians!"

He turned the page, where he started to read about the pregnant hundred year old woman. ("And Dad's a hundred and four!")

That was when he started feeling groggy.

He looked up, and noticed that the bathroom light looked a little funny. He'd been sitting on the can now for about fifteen minutes. About five minutes into the session, he'd noticed the light waver a little. And the house had creaked a bit. It was nothing to get excited about; it wasn't exactly a *new* house, and it made odd sounds from time to time. But the lights—he kept those in pretty good repair, what with his electrician's sensibilities. He felt ludicrous and vulnerable now, his Lee jeans and boxers around his ankles, and the lights going funny—

He put the *World Weekly News* down and moved to get off the commode, when the faint spell hit. It wasn't really like he was paralyzed—it was like the air had suddenly turned to Jell-O, and he just couldn't move real quick. The very act of

simply pulling up his pants was a daunting proposition. He
blinked, and just stayed in that bent-over position, happy to be
able to breathe.

What the hell . . . ?

The sounds were an odd swirling of little feet and little
voices. First, they sounded like they were coming from the
living room. But then they altered subtly in texture, echoing
and booming nearer, like steps coming through a tunnel.

The sounds were coming closer. They were coming toward
the bathroom! Fear like he'd never felt before engulfed Harry
Reynolds. These sounds were touching something deep and
primal—an ancient alarm signal that never goes off in most
people! Sweat popped out in beads on his face, and he strained
again to reach down and pull up his pants. He had to get up!
Had to close that door! Through the fog of his slowed percep-
tions, the ringing klaxon inside him demanded: CLOSE THAT
DOOR! LOCK IT! it screamed. THEY'RE *HERE*, HARRY.
THEY'RE COMING TO GET YOU!

He touched his belt. His fingers curled around the top of the
blue jeans. Even as he felt the fabric on his fingertips, he knew
there would be no time. With all his might, he pushed himself
away from the toilet, toward the door. He sprawled across the
tile floor, hands outstretched toward the door, the pink tassels
of the bathmat looming like a jungle before his left eyeball.
He'd left the bathroom door ajar, and now he had to close it,
lock it!

Through the clear tar of the air, he wallowed, reaching,
reaching for the door.

He fingers were just a moment from the wood, when a hand
reached around the doorjamb.

It came around, below the knob. Harry could see long,
delicate digits move into a slow grip like spider's legs.

Sheer terror stopped him from further movement. Harry
Reynolds could only stare up helplessly as the being entered the
room. All language had fled his mind, so he did not think the
word *alien* or *visitor* or any of the many synonyms he'd used
over more than thirty years of fascination with the UFO
phenomenon. His mind was in pure R-complex now, back to its
prehistoric beginnings, locked in flight-or-fight mode, but unable to jerk out of paralysis.

The door opened, and the being at the other side swam into view.

The creature was perhaps three feet tall, and humanoid purely in dwarfish standards. Its limbs were slender and garbed in a dark blue jumpsuit of some sort that seemed to absorb rather than reflect the bathroom light. Some kind of cap was perched atop a narrow insectoid head, but this was not what caught Harry's attention. It was the eyes.

The eyes were like gigantic onyx almonds. They looked down at Harry with a bottomless strangeness from a grey-tinged skin pulled tight over a delicately boned skull.

For a moment, Harry was lost in wonder at those eyes. They looked like the darkest corner of space. Space beyond time, beyond being, space that was somehow *alive*.

The creature moved further into the room, stopping by the sink. Another one moved in, identical to the first. Beyond the door, out of sight, Harry could hear others, chattering softly.

In the hand of the second was a wand, and suddenly Harry's fear was back again, full force. Because the tip of this wand began to glow, to pulse a cherry red, like the tip of some red-hot poker. And the creature was moving it toward Harry's face.

Suddenly, Harry realized he was screaming.

It didn't sound like him. It came out, unbidden and urgent, like a spike of vomit.

The creatures stepped back, blinking their eyes, seemingly surprised by Harry's reaction. Another one entered the room. The one with the wand leaned over and said something, though its lips did not move. "Please be quiet. You are alarming us!"

Harry could not stop screaming. A tiny part of his mind watched himself, wondering that after thirty years of waiting for just this moment, why he should react this way. That tiny part, though, was fading, fading into the scream . . .

They weren't *out there* anymore. They were *here*!

The wand lifted. It floated as though adrift in antigravity, and gentled down to touch the forehead of Harry Reynolds.

The night flowed in through the bathroom window, swirled around him, and zipped him up into seamless darkness.

Spicy cardboard.

That smell. In the darkness, that smell came first, like a

beckoning finger hooking into him and dragging him out of unconsciousness.

When Harry Reynolds woke up, he wasn't screaming.

He lay, he realized, elevated from his surroundings, on some sort of horizontal cushion that was like an examination table. His eyelids fluttered open fully. His shirt was off, but his jeans were on. He looked around him, first focusing on the array of blinking lights which were hung in screens and panel displays, some on what appeared to be controls—and some embedded in three-dimensional patterns, like floating holograms. Then he realized that he wasn't alone. His company shifted into view.

The ones hovering over him were taller than the ones who had come into his bathroom. There were three of them, and he had the odd feeling that they were female. Their heads were more humanoid, less triangular, and their eyes, though certainly slanted, had pupils. Their jumpsuits were more metallic looking, silver sheaths over slim bodies.

The table on which Harry lay was against the wall of a circular room perhaps twenty-five feet in diameter. He could see, in the dark side of the room, the dim outlines of a round passageway. A door?

"What are you doing?" he said as one of the beings turned to a globular outgrowth attached to the wall.

He could talk. He was still terrified, but he could talk! The return of his tongue—his most cherished physical commodity— reduced his sense of impotence. Everything remained foggy and uncertain, a dreamlike quality draping over the reality, but he had some kind of control.

The closest of the creatures turned to him, curiosity filling its eyes. "We will not harm you," it said, but its mouth did not move. Harry felt as though the words bloomed like audial flowers in his brain.

He lifted his head, but the strain of just speaking exhausted him, and he lay back, still confused. He could only watch what the creatures were doing.

The globular unit at the wall seemed to be an item of furniture. The creature pulled out a drawer from it, and on this drawer rested the gleam of metal, the shiver of crystal. The creature picked up a long, needlelike instrument that seemed to sparkle of its own accord. Carefully, gracefully, the instrument was carried over to Harry. He could see it glitter by his eyes, and caught the reflection of a hypodermic-like end nearing his neck, by the base of his ear.

"No," he said. "I don't want you to *do* this!"

They ignored him. He felt a sharp bite on his neck and could feel the metal going in, as though it were an insect proboscis probing for a vein. Deeper, deeper, deeper... And the pain did not stop. The sensation of the metal intrusion jabbing up into his brain stopped, but the pain in his head screamed and seared. He slipped into unconsciousness once more, and then abruptly he was back awake, the cardboard smell in his nostrils again.

Cardboard and roses, this time.

Two of them leaned over him now. Some kind of tubing dangled down from the ceiling. It was coiled, and had a metal device on the end, like something out of a dental nightmare. One of the creatures grabbed the device, and turned on a switch. The instrument hummed and began to glow a bright green. The creature carefully made a scan of Harry Reynolds, from cranium to abdomen, the device beeping and humming with an unearthly awfulness. The three other aliens in attendance watched the operation intently.

"Would you STOP THIS!" screamed Harry. "Talk to me— don't dissect me."

They tilted up their heads and looked at him, like he was the oddest and most astonishing thing in the universe. Then they started chattering amongst themselves.

"You turkeys! Stop hurting me! Let's *communicate*! For years I been defending you, and now you do this to me?!"

He tried to get up, but found he could barely move.

"What kind of things *are* you?"

All of his life, he'd cherished the odd and unusual. But this wasn't just weird—it was goddamn *scary*!

One of them came and leaned over him. Its breath smelled foul, like machine oil mixed with garlic and strained through old cardboard. "Please be still," it said, its voiceless words filling his head. "You are the Honored One."

"Yeah! My ass!" And then such a wave of dread consumed Harry Reynolds that he thought he was going to die. He felt cold... Cold, and alone... The lights glowed around him like dead diamonds. Cold and lonely... Adrift not just an in uncaring universe... but a *malevolent* universe.

Harry moaned, unable to scream: vocal dry heaves.

Another device lowered from the dark, misty ceiling, like a periscope with claws. The creatures conferred amongst each other, then they turned back to Harry, their tender hands drifting toward his pants. In a few deft motions, they had undone his belt, unzipped his zipper and pulled down his jeans and underpants, exposing his genitals. The cold and fear had shrunk them, and now with this new blast of chill, they dwindled further. One of the aliens took the newly lowered device from the ceiling, and adjusted the cuplike object at the end.

Harry could only stare, horrified, the "No!" caught in his throat like a chunk of gristle.

The sheen of stainless steel, slivers of razor-sharp glass, pinpoints of needles: the end of the thing, opened, was like a robotic porcupine. The creature guided it down so the cup fitted over Harry's penis and scrotum. Harry sensed the sharp parts of the device more than felt them. Still, it was like imminent fellatio from a moray eel!

"No!" he whispered.

The creature touched a section of the shaft of the instrument, and lights—red, yellow, blue—rotated, whispering a soft whir. It started as a tickling that reached and shivered the short hairs of his very soul. Then the penetrating pain began, worse than anything before. It felt as though his privates were being fed to a food processor, resurrected, then fed in again. Somehow, through this blinding pain, Harry remained conscious. Tears leaked from his eyes and his back arched, but otherwise he could not move.

And through it all, he was aware of those dark alien onyx eyes on him, staring dispassionately.

Mercifully, his mind managed to tear away from consciousness, and he slipped again into nothingness.

When Harry woke up again, his muscles were braced as though for pain, he was breathing hard and was aware of the sweat on his face and chest.

The visitors no longer hovered over him. Two were by the nearby control boards, and the others were gone.

Harry realized that he could move—he was no longer in pain. He simply felt very confused and deeply troubled. He lifted his head and saw that his pants were still lowered. He perceived little red dots covering his genitals, but there was no blood. His midwestern modesty winning over his paralysis, he lifted himself and pulled his jeans up to cover himself.

The creatures at the control board did not seem to notice that he was awake. They stared intently at their screens or readings or whatever, ignoring Harry.

Harry shivered on the examination table, getting hold of himself. The pain, dread, and terror still hung on him like a shroud, but somehow other emotions, as well as ego, had reasserted themselves, and were in control again once more.

Harry Reynolds felt ashamed. Deeply, inexplicably ashamed. He knew then, at that moment, how violent a degradation rape must be for a woman. There was pain and abuse here, yes . . . but it was more than that, something deep and unexplainable, and so troubling that Harry did not care to explore it. He focused instead on his other, more familiar feelings.

First, there was outrage and anger. And then . . . then there was *betrayal*.

It had been so long ago that Harry Reynolds had started looking up at the sky and wondering about other superior life forms that he'd forgotten the purity of his initial, almost religious attitude. For so long, he'd reached out, shaming himself in the eyes of people—reached out for them with his radio signals, his heart on his sleeve.

And now, this.

Somehow, though—something, inside him, feared that something bad would happen. Korea and the army had drained Harry's innocence, and the embittered side of him knew that the possibility the aliens *weren't* saintly emissaries from paradise definitely existed.

They had done nothing to assuage his anger and his sense of betrayal.

On Harry's left pants' leg at the inseam, was a zipper. He'd fixed these jeans himself, special—just like he'd fixed all his pants, so he could get at his false leg, if he needed to adjust it or take it off or something, without actually shucking his whole pants. He found the zipper tab and carefully, soundlessly pulled it up all the way to his crotch, laying bare his leg.

Good. The aliens hadn't fooled with it. A quick glance up showed the two remaining creatures involved with their work.

Harry returned to his fake leg. His right leg had been amputated just above the knee by a MASH unit (and he never could watch that TV show) after a Chinese shell had blown most of it off anyway. For years he'd relied on a clunky, VA-provided wooden leg that needed a crutch as a complement. But in the late sixties, he had gotten one of those articulated plastic-jobbies and never looked back. Supposedly, with the new ones you could play basketball, they were so good. But Harry didn't play basketball. He figured out pretty fast how the things worked (and cursed himself for not inventing them earlier) and started perfecting his own type—one with a compartment.

He thumbed the tab, and the springs pushed out a lid that lifted. Harry waited a moment for his fingers to stop trembling, then lifted out his invention.

The smallness of this compartment in the calf was the key to the nature of the device; you could only fit one thing inside, and Harry wished to conceal *several* things. He called it his Swiss Army Camera.

One of Harry Reynolds's consuming life-passions was to get a picture of a UFO. Those first two times he'd seen the things, he'd only had words to recreate them. And should he ever be actually *picked up* by aliens, he wanted to take their pictures. But then, he thought it over, he also figured an *audio* recording wouldn't hurt either. But when he had this secret compartment on his body, the first two things together couldn't fit, so he built a casing that slid in perfectly, and built inside of this a camera and a tape recorder.

Harry assayed the situation. He figured he had time to take a couple of pictures. He took off the lens cap, and clicked off a few shots—the camera automatically adjusted its own f-stop. He took out the roll of film and stuck it into the pocket of his jeans, just in case he ever got out of here—which he rather doubted. What he had planned next, the fucking buggers wouldn't like at all.

In his paranoid nightmares, Harry Reynolds had foreseen this possibility. He'd been following the reports of alien abductions carefully, and knew how upset the abductees were with the experience. Harry's figured that there was two possibilities—either naivete on the part of the Visitors (and hadn't he tried to educate them in his broadcasts), or malevolence. With what had just passed, he had to opt for malevolence. The fuckers were gonna *pay* for betraying his hopes and dreams and

violating his body. Apparently not only the planet earth stank—
so did the whole universe!

In the army and in Korea, Harry Reynolds's specialty was
munitions. He'd built model rockets for his son, but he didn't
go in much for weapons. Still, when he made his decision, it
was easy enough to construct the thing with a safe little ball of
plastic explosive and a firing wire. It had slipped into the extra
space of his camera casing, easy as you please. He'd also made
sure that it was damn hard to accidentally press the button that
would set off the timing device—you had to pull the camera
button up, twist it around just so, and then cock it before it
would engage.

Harry Reynolds did this, anger and outrage still swelling in
him, the pain in his head and his groin still throbbing.

He set the camera-grenade. There was a five second fuse.
Harry carefully studied the panel where the aliens stood. He
could lob the thing right underneath, and the bastards wouldn't
be able to touch it. And when it blew up—Harry had no idea
where he was. He supposed he was in one of their ships. There
was a possibility that the ship was in the air, and his little
present would send it plummetting. His pain and his upset were
such that he didn't care. Maybe this would lob a present into
the laps of UFO fanciers—a crashed saucer, courtesy of Harry
Reynolds!

Wherever he was, he *had* to strike back. Every part of him
demanded it. And if he died—well, from what he heard, if
aliens got hold of you once, they liked to come back and mess
you over some more later on. He didn't want to believe it was
that bad, but now he knew it was worse than he could possibly
imagine. Better to die than to again go through what he'd just
experienced.

He hit the button, and was gratified to hear the timer
engage. He counted.

One second.

Two seconds.

Three seconds.

"Chew on this, spacewarts!" he growled softly and tossed
the camera-grenade.

The device hit the floor right between the aliens at their
posts. They neither moved nor reacted, even though the clack
of impact was loud. They just stood there, staring into their

control panels as the grenade slid into the dark space beyond them, beneath the ledge of instruments.

Four seconds.

Harry, though surprised at their lack of response, did not watch any further. He turned his back on them and curled into a ball, hands and arms wrapped over his head.

Five seconds.

The room shook.

The blast was deafening. A flare of heat blasted Harry's bare back, and then he was pelted by debris.

He braced for a half-suspected lurch of the ship as it lost control and plunged for the ground. Or maybe even for the quick death that awaited him if they were in outer space and the grenade'd cut a hole into vacuum. But neither thing occurred—the floor remained steady.

He waited a few more moments, and then turned to check the damage.

Black smoke coughed from the wall, speckled with sparks from the electrical fires, dying down. But the smoke was sucked away by the hole the grenade had blown in the wall, and above the acrid fumes rode the familiar smell of fresh air and—

No, it couldn't be!

Manure?

It smelled like Iowa farmland! Could the ship have been on the ground all this time!

A flash of hope spurred Harry up onto his feet. His instinct for survival had returned, and now he knew he had a chance. But he had to get out of here . . . He just prayed that the hole he had blown in the side of the ship was big enough to get through.

By the fitful sparks of the dying fire and the lights that still flashed, Harry could see that the explosion had literally blown the heads off the aliens. Whatever satisfaction he felt, though, departed as he realized that the things shouldn't be standing at all—and that a few of the guttering electrical fires actually sparked in them! Fascinated, he was drawn forward.

From charred torsos emerged burnt insulation, the color-coded spaghetti of wires, the blackened shapes of cogs and gears. Were they robot drones? Were the aliens that had picked him up actually mechanical creatures?

Further inspection proved that they were indeed robots. But by the sputtering flickers of the lights, Harry Reynolds's electronic expertise rapidly determined another fact.

These things were robots, all right, and the stuff they were built out of was as American as Radio Shack.

"What the hell is going *on*!" he murmured.

Then he looked down and saw the cable connecting the "alien" robots to the control panel. One of the "alien's" hands twitched in the same pattern, over and over again. Reynolds had seen these kind of things in Disney World! They weren't even legitimate, self-contained robots!

He looked over to the closed doorway, half expecting Allen Funt to come charging in, screaming, "Smile! You're on 'Candid Camera!'"

It was then he heard an alarm finally cough to life. Though muted, it sounded just like the Volunteer Fire Department's siren down the road. The smoke was clearing away from the hole in the wall. The explosion had torn away the instrument panel, revealing guts of cheap forty-gauge wire. This wasn't any alien ship! This was some kind of elaborate hoax.

He stepped forward toward the hole. It was big enough to step through. He could see a smudge of dawn paling the horizon through a copse of nearby trees. Off to his left, he made out the bulky form of a grain silo.

Harry knocked away a splintered section of old wood and corrugated cardboard (so *that* was where the smell had come from!) and then fitted himself through the hole, coughing a little from the smoke. Outside, the grass was littered with blown-out debris, and the morning cold made Harry shiver, but nonetheless it was good to know he was on solid, genuine earth ground!

"Hey!" cried a voice behind him. "Hey! You! Stop!"

He turned around, and saw the door opening up like the iris of an eye. Then he saw a brief flash of suit.

But Harry kept on going. He had the feeling that if this was one of the guys who had kidnapped him, they wouldn't be too thrilled with him, now that he'd blown up part of their grim little play.

A haziness still hung inside his head, and he realized that a lot of what had happened to him was because they'd drugged him. But they'd left his Chuck Taylors on, and the adrenaline from the past couple of minutes was enough to boost him on. He ran far enough away from the building to see that it was a *barn*, but he didn't stop long enough to study it. He chuffed along around it, running from that suit.

Gotta get help, he thought, *gotta find the cops*.

Around the barn, a large farmhouse came into view, but that wasn't what attracted his attention. On a square stretch of tarmac the size of a basketball field was a Bell Air Force helicopter, and beside it was a military jeep.

Harry was seriously considering trying to hotwire the jeep when a man opened the back door of the farmhouse and stepped out toward him. He wore the blue uniform of the air force. His hair was short, gray, and grizzled, and he had a puzzled expression on his face. But he was unarmed, and regarded Harry with such surprise, even shock, that Harry didn't think he could possibly have anything to do with the business in the barn.

"Help!" Harry said, "There's a man after me! The aliens . . . They aren't aliens . . . ! Help me . . . Gotta get out . . ."

"Who are you?" asked the man. Harry could see by the arrangement of the colored bars that the man was a full colonel.

"Reynolds," he returned. The mere sight of a military uniform triggered ingrained responses of respect. "Harry Reynolds, sir! I've been abducted! And . . . And I don't know why!"

A pained expression crossed the colonel's face. "That explosion."

"Yeah. I escaped. But there's a guy, he's—"

Even as he spoke, a young man wearing a suit rounded the corner and ran at full gallop.

Alarmed, Harry turned to run. But the colonel raised his hand and spoke in a reassuring tone. "Stay put, Mr. Reynolds. I'll get to the bottom of this."

The suit stopped a few yards away from them. He lifted a walkie-talkie and spoke into it. "Junior here. I've got him, right by the pad." He was a tall man with short hair and a deeply pitted face that was sallow against eyes alive with blue, reflecting the awakening dawn.

A filtered voice murmured, "I'll be right there." It was a woman's voice.

Harry didn't know what to do, and so when the authoritative

military bass instructed him to stand still, he did just that, until he could figure out something better.

"Mr. Reynolds, I'm sorry about all this. I'm going to put things right immediately, I promise you," the colonel said. "Just stay here a moment—we'll get you out of this chilly morning in a moment." The air force officer turned to confront the man in the suit. "Woodrow. I demand to know what's going *on* in this establishment! This is a civilian, man! With rights!"

The man in the grey suit sighed, rocked back on his feet, getting in control. He actually shook his head and laughed. "I don't believe it. I don't fucking believe it! You must have had a *bomb*. Where the hell did you get a fuckin' *bomb*?" he said to Harry.

A door in the side of the barn opened and a blonde woman in a lab smock walked out toward them, carrying a clipboard. She wore glasses, was in her thirties, very pretty. But her mouth was set into a hard, severe frown.

"I'll get to the bottom of this, Mr. Reynolds," said the colonel. "But you're shivering. Here—" The colonel walked over to the jeep, pulled an army blanket out. "Wrap this around you for the time being while I kick some ass."

What Harry wanted more than anything now was just to get away, but the colonel's tone was so reassuring he figured he was in good hands.

The colonel wheeled upon the woman in the lab coat.

"Well?"

"Big trouble," she said in a small voice, looking distinctly troubled at the man's presence. "Snafu. How could we know— Mr. Reynolds received Treatment Express Double A. Drugs, subliminals, the works—"

"Jesus Christ!" said the suit. "Not in front of the mark!"

The woman seemed to turn even paler, even colder. "You don't understand. It doesn't make any difference *what* he hears now. The process was interrupted midprocedure. We've got an abort situation on our hands."

"Colonel," said Harry, sick to his stomach, but grateful for the blanket. "I don't know what they're talking about. I'm a veteran. I'm a citizen. I've got rights. And as an employee of the U.S. Government, it's your duty to see that I am placed under proper protection!"

"You don't understand, Mr. Reynolds," said a voice from the back of the farmhouse. Startled, Harry turned to see a man standing there in a bathrobe, smoking a cigarette. "We *all* work for the U.S. government." The man, fortyish, gray at the temples and smiling, turned to the young man in the suit. "Justine, Mr. Reynolds is ambulatory. Could you correct this, please?"

"You bet," said the suited man, and before Harry could move, the man ran up to him, struck him at the juncture of his neck and head with the metal walkie-talkie. Abruptly, Harry found himself face-first in the dirt and grass, groaning, his head feeling as though someone had driven a spike through it. He rolled around, groaning. But he remained conscious, and he could hear everything that the people had to say.

"That wasn't necessary!" said the colonel.

"Yeah," said the man in the suit. "But it *felt* good. You should see the mess back there. How the hell—" Harry could feel himself being roughed up, searched. Someone tugged hard on his right leg—and then yanked it off. "What have we here! A goddamn fake leg! Hey, beautiful, a really wonderful research job you did on this bozo. He smuggled a goddamn grenade inside a prosthesis!"

"That's not what concerns me now," the colonel's bass rang challengingly. "Cunningham, can you fix him up? Can you make him forget all this? You guys are the Editors."

"I'm afraid the negative reality-input is too great. I don't even think we can implant a screen." The woman's voice was cold, monotone. "He's seen too much, done too much. Drugs and hypnotherapy, compu-suggestion: far too risky."

"Wha—" groaned Harry through the fog of pain.

The colonel said, "The Publishers will not be pleased."

Harry lifted his head a bit, rolled over. He could see the four of them, standing around him like judges, trying him for a crime he did not commit. "Help," he managed to say. "Hosp—"

The man in the bathrobe stooped down. Reynolds coughed from the gust of smoke the man blew into his face. "Harry, we had high hopes for you. High hopes. You coulda been a star." The man made a tsk-tsking sound, stood, and flipped the cigarette away. "Terminate," he said to the younger man, then walked away.

"Jesus," said the colonel. "Wait! I do not authorize this! I will report that other options were available."

Harry made a superhuman effort to stand. But his leg was gone, and he flopped back onto his back, groaning.

The man in the suit stepped up closer to Harry, while the woman watched, the impersonal expression on her face replaced by a gleam of sudden interest, even enthusiasm in her eye. The man they called Justine reached into his suit jacket, and pulled out a silenced .38 caliber Smith and Wesson automatic.

"It's time for the big sign-off, Klatuu," said the man, a death's-head grin on his face. "Your ratings were just terrible."

The first bullet thunked hard into Harry's chest, driving the breath out of him. He saw a gout of blood splash over the woman's shoe.

The second bullet was just a whisper to him as the darkness set in, and by the time the third and fourth bullets struck him in the head, everything was as black as the nothingness between the night-time stars.

CHAPTER
ONE

Washington, D.C., is perhaps one of the most unusual cities in the world, filled with beauty, covered with paradoxes, and stocked with secrets that could tear the very country apart or heal a wounded planet.

Each April, bright pink-and-white blossoms bloom on trees surrounding a man-made tributary of the Potomac River, gifts from a country defeated by the nation governed by this capital: cherry blossom trees, from Japan. Although categorized in the 1800s by the British Foreign Service as ''subtropical'' duty due to its summer heat and humidity, the city's spring is a beautiful celebration of the flowers and trees and parks strewn amongst the official buildings and stately houses, its temperature moderate and pleasant.

It is a city of facades, Washington, D.C. For behind the marble columns of the Capitol Building, behind the grey doors of the ugly Executive Building growing from the White House like some Victorian tumor, behind the military-drab walls of the Pentagon, secrets and whispers and subterfuges sussurate unheard beneath the press releases and official reports. Power moves here like invisible currents beneath a seemingly tranquil river.

Here, the democratic power of the citizens of the United States of America is legally exercised by duly elected representatives, and officials and their appointees, executive, legislative and judicial.

The power of groups, clatches, and cliques, old and new, are struggling for true control of the country, perhaps of the entire world.

And should the truth ever be unearthed, the secrets revealed, the very fabric of the civilized world of mankind would fracture.

As it happened on that mid-April day, the cherry blossoms were just making their appearance, justifying the Sunday parade that would soon celebrate their arrival. A cold and wet March had given way to a tranquil, sunny April.

The two men who entered Dominique's Restaurant on Pennsylvania Avenue in Northwest Washington, D.C., at 12:10 in the afternoon looked like a pair of the brokers of power in the nation's capital. From all appearances, they seemed to be K-Street lawyers, out for a typical power lunch. They wore tasteful Brooks Brothers grey pin-striped suits, red ties and spit-shined black shoes. The taller one was clearly the older, grey brushing the sides of his razor-cut hair, and a spiderweb of wrinkles just beginning to show below his eyes. The younger looked to be newly graduated from law school, a sparkle to his eye, an eagerness to his smile, as he opened the glass door of the posh establishment for his companion. Yes, here was the prototypical canny senior partner, it seemed of X, Y, Z, and Associates, squiring the cub counselor, showing him the ropes of legal shmoozing territory.

This was exactly the impression the men wished to create. A kind of *Gentleman's Quarterly* camouflage. For these men were not lawyers.

They were brokers of a different kind of power that had nothing to do with legality.

The glass door closed behind them, muffling the roar and horn honks of the traffic outside. Soft strains of Chopin's Preludes played from masked speakers, the piano gently dominated the blur of luncheon conversation, the clink of glass, the clatter of cutlery. The older man took a moment to let his eyes adjust from the sunny-day dazzle of Washington in spring, then he casually surveyed the discreetly lit dining room, filled with the scent of lilies and French cooking. It took him a few moments, and the maitre d' had already approached them and inquired if they had reservations, before he found his quarry.

"Sir, might we be seated over in that corner there, near where that gentleman and the young woman are sitting? I like the feel of that area. Not too close to them, but in the general area.''

The younger man pulled a twenty-dollar bill from his pocket and tucked it into the maitre d's pudgy palm. "For your trouble."

The fortyish man in the tuxedo smiled. "Of course. This way, please."

They were placed at a small table beside a potted palm tree. The older man directed his companion to sit in the chair that had a view of the two diners, while he chose the spot in the shadows, near the palm fronds. He placed the Gucci leather briefcase he was carrying upright on the floor beside him, and took the proffered menus from the maitre d'.

"That is Dr. Everett Scarborough," the greying man told his associate in a low voice. "Our mark, if you will."

The younger man turned his blonde head a moment, and studied the man called Scarborough for a few seconds. "Central was correct. He definitely has a certain charisma. Observe how he charms the young woman."

"Look away," instructed the older man, opening his plush and outsized blue menu. "Listen for a time. Absorb."

The two men studied their menus in silence, listening to the conversation taking place just yards away from them.

"Another thing I'm sure our readers would like to know," said the young woman, a petite brunette with long slim legs and an overbite, dressed in a pale blue business suit. "Don't you think that there's at least a *possibility* that we are being visited by aliens from another planet? This *is* a pretty large universe, after all, and the odds would seem to dictate that if there's intelligent life on the planet earth, there's bound to be lots elsewhere."

"Intelligent life on the planet earth?" said Scarborough brightly. "That's news."

The woman chirped with laughter. "Please, Dr. Scarborough. The magazine that's commissioned me to interview you is perky and upbeat. Let's not be *too* cynical."

"Ms. Ennis, you haven't met the whackos that I've met. In this field of endeavor they literally crawl from the walls!" Dr. Everett Scarborough was a dark, glibly handsome man, slender and fit, with a keen cast of awareness to his hazel eyes. He wore a dark blue blazer, a white shirt, red-striped tie, and dark wool slacks. He had the easygoing air of a professional entertainer, not the aloof introspection one might expect from a scientist of his caliber. On his wrist was a Rolex watch, which he studiously ignored, keeping his attention focused fully on the young journalist before him.

"Please, Dr. Scarborough, call me Kate," said the woman with a sexy chuckle in her voice.

"Only if you call me, Everett, my dear." The doctor paused to clear his throat. Even this sound had the tone of authority, as though an announcement of great import were about to be intoned. "Make sure your Sony's on. I'm about to present you with a sparkling and brilliant answer that may well sound like a monologue. You may break it up with appropriate questions if you like, and then maybe you can tell me something about yourself!"

"The tape recorder's rolling, Everett, and I'm afraid I'm married." The light tone of flirtation remained in her voice, however.

"But of course you are, my dear. All *truly* delightful and beautiful women are."

The woman blushed prettily and allowed Scarborough to continue.

"Yes, of course. Back to the interview," he said, his fork playing amongst the vegetables in his nicoise salad. "You have a point, Kate. Statistically, life should exist elsewhere in the universe, even in this galaxy. I won't bore your readers with the scientific details, but scientists are quite aware of this— hence, legitimate programs such as SETI: Search for Extraterrestrial Intelligence—utilizing radio-telescopes to sweep the skies not only to map the radiation emitted by the stars, but also to pick up signals of civilization, signs of life. We've also been broadcasting ourselves, as well as launching our own testament of civilization, the Pioneer Mission, replete with pictures of our species and the music of Chuck Berry. But then perhaps you should talk to such luminaries as Carl Sagan on that—he's so much more eloquent than I on that subject.

"Alas, I concern myself not with the expansion of human knowledge, but the *correction* of human knowledge. Civilizations have always had their mythologies. I suppose the general population is entitled to thrill to stories of flying saucers, of visits from extraterrestrials bearing crystals and news of peace, or perhaps just channelling their good vibrations across the dimensions. Or even, God forbid, visitors' morbid abductions and laboratory experiments upon human beings. But when a goodly percentage of our citizens actually *believe* that this is the *truth*—well, when it's *not* the truth, it's necessary for someone to stand up and make a few announcements. Necessary for the successful practice and understanding of *science* amongst the populace.

"All of my books, all of my lectures, all of my appearances on television, are for a common goal: to battle the insidious upsurge of pseudoscience and falsehood. Our civilization has its problems, certainly, and industrial and scientific progress has had its backlashes—but the backbone of human hope, I believe, is the practice of scientific principles. We must base our knowledge of the universe on empirical facts . . . that is, everything must be proven. What many call the New Age, is, I believe, actually more of a return to the Dark Ages. And yet those I have sworn to oppose—the UFO-ologists spouting nonsense so fluently—claim to present factual evidence. As I see it, it is my task to explore this evidence logically and intelligently, and show it for the flimflam and fuzzy thinking it truly is.

"In my new book, *Above Us Only Sky*, I not only address UFO sightings and theories case by case, but I also discuss my own investigations. Including my investigations when I was on the air force's Project Blue Book study back in the late sixties. I make the point there—and emphasize it here—that science is a *tool* that has been developed by mankind. We are not naturally inclined to analyze things by the scientific method. This explains, I think, our tendency to be fooled. It is my job to remind people—goodness knows, from time to time I have to remind myself—that the scientific method, based on the sound and functional rules of logic, is to be used as a tool. It is here for our benefit, that our race can grow intellectually and spiritually.

"To get back to your initial question: No. I do not believe that earth has been visited by creatures from another planet, or that it is currently being visited. Of all the thousands of sightings and experiences that have been investigated, *none* have been proven to be the result of extraterrestrial visitation by the tenets of the scientific method.

"Now, as to what these sightings actually comprise—well, that's an entirely different kettle of aliens!"

At the table of the two suited men, the waiter arrived to take the guests' orders. The younger man ordered a simple coq au vin, while his companion requested the special of the day, sea bass au Provencal. When wine was offered, both men declined, asking instead for fresh-squeezed orange juice.

When the waiter left, the younger man listened to a few more sentences flowing eloquently from the table only eight yards distant, and they turned to his companion.

"He is a proud man. I sense a great deal of self-confidence. He clearly enjoys his—work." The younger man's accent was almost midwestern in its flatness, although each word was clearly pronounced, and with excellent diction. The other's accent was mid-Atlantic ... American, with a touch of high British, and perhaps a trace of something vaguely Germanic.

"Yes," said the older, smiling for the first time. "In his calling, he needs such. For a debunker—a negative profession that tends to earn much social enmity, and tends to attract sour, negative personalities—he enjoys much popularity. His books sell well, and he receives large sums on the lecture circuit. He is often invited on local as well as national talk shows, along with the usual UFO-ologists. He takes great pleasure in having been a chief antagonist of the late J. Allen Hyenk, and regularly locks horns with such luminaries as Stanton Friedman, Whitley Strieber, Maximillian Shroeder and Jascque Valle."

"Jascque Valle?"

"Yes. The Francois Truffault character from *Close Encounters of the Third Kind*. You are an excellent partner, smart and skilled—but you have much to learn in the UFO field. In the coming months, you will learn much indeed, I think. Now, let us eavesdrop a little longer. This is vital for your imminent mission."

The interview at the other table had proceeded apace, with Dr. Everett Scarborough expounding at length on his factually based opinions, totally unaware that the two men sitting past the screen and the potted plant were listening carefully to him. He fielded Kate Ennis's questions with expertise and good humor, taking the occasional opportunity to flirt. He seemed particularly concerned with the importance of the American public's attitude toward UFOs.

"You know, I read somewhere that a poll claims over 50 percent of the American public believe that extraterrestrials are buzzing over their housetops. Just as many believe that there's some sort of government conspiracy to keep this knowledge from the public! You remember when Ronald Reagan made those hypothetical comments concerning possibilities of aggressive intrusion of starships from another planet?''

"Oh, certainly. That certainly made for good happy hour conversation at The Front Page,'' said Kate Ennis, referring to a press hangout on Dupont Circle. "An alien attack would bring all the countries of the world—including the Soviet Union and the United States—together, and make us realize that what we all share is our humanity.''

"An innocent enough observation, if quite a bit fantastic— well, the UFOols...my abbreviation for UFO-ologists, Kate...well, they absolutely *pounced* on that one. 'The President is almost *admitting* that he knows there are aliens visiting Earth!' they cried. 'There's been a huge cover-up for years! We've been right all along!' ''

Scarborough tapped his head. "The mind is a complex thing, Kate. It is like a film projector. Most of these deluded people simply do not realize that what they are experiencing is merely a superimposition of their own self-produced movie from Ludicrous Productions.''

"But people do see things in the sky!'' said Kate Ennis. "My brother-in-law saw some kind of hovering light up near Westchester, Maryland.''

"Of course there are things in the sky. I'm not saying there aren't UFOs. But we forget too soon that UFOs are Unidentified Flying Objects—not spinning disks stocked with bug-eyed monsters. Most UFOs thoroughly investigated become IFOs— that is, Identified Flying Objects. They're usually weather balloons, or aircraft or clouds or lots of other normal things like bright stars and planets, warped and twisted by atmospheric effects. What we see, Kate, are not things, but the reflection and refraction of light from things. And our atmosphere— particularly with present-day pollution of various chemicals—is a veritable funhouse mirror show! This is what most people see, and their imaginations run wild. But even wilder run the paranoias of the whacko UFOols who interpret the sightings, and have created a pseudoscience: a folly that will be laughed at by our ancestors for centuries to come, much as we laugh at the phrenologist doctors who believed that a man's intelligence could be interpreted by the number of bumps on his head!''

The interviewer laughed, and Dr. Everett Scarborough smiled smugly as he lifted a tinkling ice-water glass to his lips.

They paid their check, and agreed to continue their conversation at the Devonshire Bar down the street, over drinks.

They took absolutely no notice of the two men who had been listening to their conversation as they left the restaurant.

At the table of the eavesdroppers, lunch arrived.

When the waiter left, the younger man looked over his steaming, fragrant coq au vin and said, "What a persuasive speaker. There is more there, though—I sense the emanations of his power and ability. I can understand now his importance. I look forward to this assignment."

His companion nodded. "Yes. The next few months are of vital importance to our mission, and Dr. Everett Scarborough plays a key role." He lifted his briefcase to his lap, dialed a combination, and opened it. From within, soft multicolored lights winked, as though a small Christmas tree were secreted inside. The man took out a manila folder and handed it to his protégé, shutting the case and placing it back beside his chair. "You'll find the preliminary information needed for your duty inside."

The younger man opened the folder, keeping its contents screened by his head and chest.

The first item in the folder was a picture of Dr. Everett Scarborough, followed by sheets of information concerning him.

"Yes," said the greying man, a frown playing on his thin, sensitive lips. "And the next few weeks will be a time of danger and trauma and fear for Dr. Everett Scarborough. Few man have the mental stamina to bear up to what he will soon go through without a psychological collapse. That is, if he survives at all."

The next item was a picture of a blonde woman—young, smiling, eyes bright and full of life.

"And that," said the older man, as though reading his colleague's mind. "Is Dr. Everett Scarborough's daughter and only child, Diane. Diane Scarborough is the most important person in Scarborough's life."

The younger man glanced over the computer printout following the picture. "Yes. Her mother is dead . . . A physical and intellectual resemblance . . . I believe that we might term this young woman the doctor's Achilles heel.''

''Yes,'' said the other, taking up his fork to address his meal. ''After so many years of dormancy, so many years of subtlety, the project is finally entering a dangerous period of potential violence, . . . perhaps even of cataclysm. And Dr. Everett Scarborough is a man very much in the middle of it all.''

''And if it doesn't work,'' said the other in a monotone, ''that is why I have been trained as I have. I understand now.''

''Do you still accept?''

''I have no choice. I am devoted to the Cause. If Dr. Everett Scarborough veers from this purpose, I shall terminate him.''

The older man plucked the eyeball from the whole sea bass and regarded it placidly for a moment as it dangled from the tine of his fork. ''And his daughter?''

''And his daughter.''

CHAPTER
<u>TWO</u>

Dr. Everett Scarborough, she thought.

Here she was, in a parked car in Make-Out Lane in the middle of the night, with her boyfriend's left hand on her breast, his right one under her dress struggling with her panties in a deliciously slow way, and all Diane Scarborough could do was to think about her father.

''Uh—Tim,'' she said, raising her voice above the rasp of his breaths. Suddenly, she wasn't turned on at all by his dousing of Obsession for Men, a cologne that generally turned her extremities to the consistency of hot oatmeal. In fact, the scent made her feel a little ill. She turned away from it toward the open window, toward the trees beyond, shadows of spring below the moonlight. ''Tim, can we give it a rest.''

The guy came up for air from the smooth juncture between her neck and shoulder, blinking and sputtering. "What—something wrong?"

"I guess I'm just not in the mood, that's all," she said, sitting up a little, pulling her dress down in a time-honored female signal of sexual disinterest.

Timothy Reilly was silent for a moment, his face inert in the red light from the dash radio. The Eagles were droning "One of these Nights" from a soft-rock FM station. Then he lifted his hands up as though an imploration to heaven itself. "*You* drove me out here!"

She tapped the wheel of her '89 Nissan, Tim's ring clicking arhtyhmically. "I thought it would get my mind off things."

"You mean your goddamn father, don't you," he said, words a little heated. "Diane, I'm pretty sick of hearing about the old man, and I'm generally *not* uncompassionate!"

"He's not old, Tim, and you're *hardly* a man."

"He's almost fifty, that's old. I'm almost twenty-five, and that's far enough past twenty-one to be a man. As for the *hard* part—well, I guess I can take a cold shower later."

She laughed. "Sorry. I can be a real bitch. It's just that I'm so *worried* about him."

Tim Reilly sighed with exasperation, looking out at the stretch of Kansas fields and roads that faded into the distance. He was a slender fellow, with a cap of long curly reddish hair, light eyes, wearing Levi jeans and a Sears red-checked flannel shirt, sleeves rolled up. Everything from his gift of gab to his square, clefted chin said "Irish" except for his accent, which was pure middle American.

"The guy's in great health, he's got a book on the Nonfiction Bestseller List of the *New York Times*, he's raking in the dough on a lecture tour, you're going to see him next week for spring break . . . and you're worried about him?"

"He's in danger," said Diane, softly but emphatically. "I know he is."

"He's *not* in danger," said Tim. "Don't worry."

"Tim, the Tarot cards say 'Danger,' his astrological chart is flashing red flags like crazy—and I've got this intuitive feeling . . ."

"God, ever since you talked to that psychic last week, you can't let this go, can you? That's when this started, right?

When that loony channeller started going on about your old man!''

"She wasn't loony, she said a lot of fascinating, truthful things about everything, including us."

"Look, I'm as interested in this stuff as you are, though it's quite apparent that I'm *far* more of a skeptic than you. I've been studying it for years, I've done the ashram trip, I've been to India, I've studied plenty of psychic phenomena—and dearest, you can't take any of it too literally. That's the whole point. One rides with the tao of existence, and all this shit is just frequencies for your personal TV set. You tune them in, you tune them out."

"My father might be in danger, and it's because of what he does—he *has* to be warned. I've decided."

Tim nodded. "Oh, I get it. You just didn't know whether or not to call out the National Guard, or to just tell him and take his abuse, huh?"

Diane flinched a bit inside. Hammer to head of nail. Her father, the eminent Everett Scarborough, Ph.D., was Mr. Rationality himself, Mr. Spock of "Star Trek" without the eyebrows and the flickers of humanity. Normally, Diane delighted in teasing her father about his dedication to the realm of logic. Much of her adolescent life was a rebellion *against* cold analytical numbers, bare brass facts. Her interest in the realm of the spirit world—an interest that had led to participation in the Lifespring movement, a brief tenure as a disciple of Sri Hasha Rodani, a brush with astral projection and trance channelling, to say nothing of the weekend seminar she'd taken taught by Shirley MacLaine—made her father positively livid. He'd spent hours upon hours attempting to reason with her, pointing out the fallacies and follies of her New Age spiritual pathways. But now she felt like the boy who had cried wolf. She really did have a bad feeling about her father's future, with no proof but a turn of the cards, a few words from a psychic, and a bellyful of heavy intuition. Chances were that at the merest mention of the *causes* of her trepidation, therein might lie the actual cause of the danger itself: he'd go purple with apoplexy and die of a heart attack.

Still, she had to warn him.

Something was going to happen to him.

Something *bad*.

"I've got to try, Tim. I've really got to try."

"Great. Lay it on him next week in D.C. when you go back home. I don't understand why it's giving you all this distress. Meantime, long as we're out here—" Tim reached into the back seat and pulled a can of beer out of a foam ice-chest, "let's relax a bit. It's exactly 11:00, the moon looks like a big white pizza with extra amore on, I'm with my honey, and even if she doesn't feel like satisfying my molten, desperate urges, I feel like being with her—" He popped the top off the Coors and offered it to her. "So let's make nice, huh?"

"I'm sorry, Tim. Maybe you should find someone else. I let my moods get to me too much."

Tim finished his long sip of beer. "Sorry, kiddo. I got this terrible problem, you see. I'm stuck on you."

She leaned over and kissed him on his cheek. "Thanks."

Timothy Reilly was a graduate student at the University of Kansas, supposedly working toward a Master's in psychology but actually just humoring his father, owner of the biggest car dealership in Missouri and intent on his son getting an advanced degree. He'd run out of money a couple of years back, after several years of vagabonding around the world. Dear old Pop had given him money on the condition that he finish his Bachelor's Degree. The Bachelor's Degree got finished, but by the time the sheepskin was in his hand, he had met Diane Scarborough. So he'd figured he'd hang around the university a while longer. A stab at a Master's financed that tenure, and delighted the old man in Missouri to boot.

Many guys had gotten their Master's Degrees on much poorer motivation: Diane Scarborough was beautiful, brimful of personality, and had a perverse and disarming sense of humor unlike any Tim Reilly had ever encountered. Her sense of adventure was amazing—and her imagination preferred petting in cornfields to pedestrian bed sheets. Diane Scarborough was the kind of woman that Alfred Hitchcock might have cast in a suspense thriller—and then woe the day. In fact, she had the looks of a young Grace Kelly, blue eyes smouldering with life framed a cool blonde. But beneath this exceptional beauty, a complex and unusual individual, filled with wonder and dread, existed—unconventional and unpredictable.

Diane was the only child of Dr. Everett Scarborough, a Doctor of Physics and Engineering whose career had somehow veered into uncharted areas of science. While still working on his first Doctorate, Scarborough had met and married Phyllis Poindexter, a young Boston socialite. It had been a passionate romance, according to what Diane had heard, anyway, but this she found hard to believe. Her father seemed scarcely a romantic sort to her. As a matter of fact, ever since her mother had died, ten years ago of cancer, he'd been rather a cold fish. Oh, he was *most* attentive to her in odd ways, but he limited his physical contact to simple pecks on the cheek just when she needed to be held the most. His great dream was that she would follow in her mother's footsteps. Phyllis Poindexter, despite a moneyed background that would usually lead to a classical education, had deviated into the computer sciences, specializing in artificial intelligence. But despite a high mathematical aptitude, Diane chose to take the money allocated by the trust fund toward her college education and get far away from dear old Dad, straight into a curriculum filled with liberal arts. To his consternation, her majors and minors had wavered like Washington, D.C., weather from subject to subject, none scientific or mathematical. Last semester, for example, she'd plunged headfirst into art history after a heady fling with Tim through the museums of Europe. It had been their first trip together—they had met a year before—and she had financed it from Mother's trust fund, a source that kept her fortunately independent of her father's academic pressures. They had gone to the museums of Florence—they had visited the Louvre in Paris, and the Prado in Madrid, and her absolute favorite, the Van Gogh Museum in Amsterdam. Mere prints could not match the vibrancy and power of that crazed master's colors, and they certainly could not imitate the depth and relief achieved by his brush strokes. But then, when Tim read her papers describing her emotions concerning art, he had claimed there burned a true writing talent. Diane, who had always wished to draw and paint but knew she wasn't very talented with her hands, exulted in this assessment, immediately plunging into a creative writing major. Now, a few short stories and poems later, she was in the midst of a novel about Kansas at the turn of the century. She called it *The Innocent and the Damned*, and while it contained far too many passionate sex scenes for the tastes of her professors, she continued to write two chapters every weekend on her IBM computer—a Christmas gift from her father. He'd pointedly only supplied computer language and mathematical software, but it had been easy enough to pirate a copy of WordPerfect from Tim's cheap cobbled-together IBM clone and immediately set about forging a literary career.

"I think I'll have one of those," she said, looking at his beer.

"Hey, lady. I heard a rumor that drinking age is twenty-one hereabouts," said Reilly.

"So let me have a beer and then turn me in to the law," she said, giving him one of her classic glares.

He laughed, and got out a can of beer for her.

"Boy, what I wouldn't give to be a bug on the wall to hear you give your speech to Daddy," he said, watching her sip.

"You'd get smushed, I'm afraid. Dad abhors bugs."

They were well into a discussion of the conversational tactics best suited for this onerous task, when *it* happened.

It started as a vibration.

A kind of thrumming seemed to shake the red Datsun, the trees and air around it—Diane could feel it shaking the fillings in her teeth.

"What the hell?" said Tim, looking around for the source of the vibration even as the can propped on the dashboard fell off, sending a splash of beer into his crotch. "Yeow!"

The radio station, halfway into Cat Steven's "Moonshadow," suddenly erupted into a haze of squeaks and static. The field before them, furred with light grass waiting to be turned over by a plow, seemed to ripple like a giant creature, shivering.

Diane's heart started beating wildly and she grabbed Tim's arm, clutching as though he were a life preserver. Beyond the vibration, she *sensed* something. Something imminent, something *terrifying*. It had an otherworldly quality she'd felt when that channeller last week had summoned up that 10,000-year-old spirit from the lost continent of Mu. She felt a deep sense of the numinous.

"Good grief, I don't believe it," said Tim, pointing upwards and craning his neck to peer out the top of the windshield. "Look!"

Diane looked.

Hovering over the edge of the field, right above a shallow forest, was a cluster of lights. As Diane's eyes adjusted, she was able to make out a form, holding those lights together.

The lights were red and blue, the blue were separate pin-
pricks in the body of the object, the red a soft, radiating band
delineating what appeared to be a lower, disk-shaped section
from the upper and smaller bubble-top extension. As she
stared, shocked, she could see a soft fog emanating from the
bottom—a haze that suddenly turned bright orange as the
hovering thing began to lower, past the trees, going out of
sight, but taking its time and leaving no doubt in Diane
Scarborough's mind as to what she'd seen.

"Did you see *that*?" whispered Tim.

"Daddy would shit," she said, staring at where the thing
had been.

"Yeah," said Tim, his tones reverent with awe. "I can't
believe it. I think we just saw a UFO, and it *landed*."

Before even she realized what she was doing, Diane popped
the latch of the door, and got out of the car.

"Hey," said Tim. "Where are you going?"

"I'm going to get a closer look!"

"What?! Are you *crazy*!"

"No. This could be an opportunity of a lifetime!"

She shut the door on him and strode through a tangle of
underbrush out into the field. The moon, though not quite full
and partly obscured by a cloud, bathed the spring grass in soft
light. She could see nothing past the copse of trees beyond
which the object had settled. No lights, blinking or otherwise.
Had she and Tim experienced some kind of hallucination or
mirage? She'd heard her father's monologues on the subject all
her life (though she'd studiously avoided reading his books and
articles—on UFOs anyway), so she was well acquainted with
all the natural explanations available. The thing—if it was not
an illusion—could be some military balloon; some weird weather
blimp; some wacky high-school prank. God knew that astonishing
tricks could be performed with lights these days, now that
lasers and neon were easy tricks in the technical canon. But
Diane forged ahead nonetheless. She *had* to see. Some inner
alarm was going off. Intuition? Perhaps—but whatever it was,
it pulled her toward those trees like a magnet.

"Hey!" cried a voice from behind her. "You wanna wait
up?"

She turned. Tim puffed toward her, tripping on a clump of
weeds, recovering. As he reached her, he grabbed her arm to

recover his balance. "Lose your jitters?" Diane asked, sarcastically.

"Give me a break! I haven't got the instant nose for trouble you do," he said, and she could see a nervous smile in the moonlight. "I have to think about it a bit, and *then* I jump in headfirst."

She grabbed his hand. "Okay, but we've got to hurry. If there's something behind there, it might go away."

"Not such a bad idea," said Tim, but when Diane started toward the trees, picking up the pace, he kept abreast with no complaint. They hustled along for a minute in silence, Diane becoming more and more excited the closer they got to the thick stand of cedars, which were now obscuring their view with new spring shoots and thick spring leaves. As they approached, she began to smell honeysuckle.

Tim was getting excited. "This is just *great!*" he said. "Nothing like this has happened to me before. Thanks for kicking my butt, Diane. Leave it to *you*, to show up a soldier of fortune like me."

"Soldier of fortune," she said. "Sure."

"Even if we *don't* see anything behind those trees, we've got plenty to report. I saw it, you saw it—maybe other people saw it. It'll make the local papers . . . And I'll call Craig at the university rag. And you know what, Diane?"

"What?" Diane mused that Tim had a terrible penchant for gab when he got nervous.

"The *National Intruder*. I've *always* wanted to get into the *National Intruder*."

"Right. I can just see the headlines: 'UFO Wizard of Oz Lends College Student a Brain.' "

"No, I mean it. The reporter they've got on this kind of stuff . . . Jake Camden? I read his book a couple years ago. The guy takes this sighting stuff and makes it *really* interesting!"

"Nothing serves the truth in journalism like an imaginative writing style, huh, Tim?"

"Could you save the cracks for now? I'm *with* you, aren't I?" His voice had a hurt quality, and Diane felt bad. She hadn't meant that barb to really penetrate. Try as she might to repress it, she was her father's daughter. Sarcasm dripped from her tongue like venom from a casual viper. Only in her open-mindedness, her credulity, and her bright good looks did she reflect her mother—she had her father's steel-trap mind, his relentless need to know.

They reached the trees, and as they stopped to puzzle the best path through, Diane could hear the sound of the breeze rattling the branches. It was cool on her face as it touched the light perspiration there. In her excitement, she seemed intensely aware of every sensation now, from the cry of an owl in the trees to the smell of Tim's cologne and sweat, stark and sensually feral against the honeysuckle.

"See anything?" he asked, catching his breath.

She saw nothing. The woods beyond were dark, with only a hint of a break beyond into the next field.

"Damn," she said. "I wish I'd brought the flashlight!"

"Wait a sec . . . What's *that*!" Tim pointed off to the right, toward the thinnest part of the trees, where Diane could make out a cluster of bushes, their berries outlined in the meager glow of the moon.

Diane looked and she saw nothing at first. But then . . . she noticed a brief dazzle of light, like a splash of bright orange airbrushed onto a shadowed canvas.

"Come on!" she said, excitedly, plucking at Tim's shirt and then striking out ahead of him into the underbrush. Twigs and brambles and thorns tugged at her stockings, and she instantly regretted the dress she wore. Actually, jeans were her usual apparel, jeans and Izods, or maybe a blouse. But jeans were damned troublesome when you want to make out with your boyfriend in a cramped car, and besides, how did she know that tonight she was going to be chasing an Unidentified Flying Object in the woods?

"Slow down!" called Tim. She could hear him crashing behind her like a bull in a leafy china shop. No *way* would they be able to surprise anything on the other side. They'd just have to rely on speed, so Diane, who kept herself in shape by playing racquetball, instead of waiting for Tim, sped up. To hell with him—*she* was going to get a shot at seeing what was there.

The bright orange light blinked, then it was joined by a fuzzy magenta glow, radiating up from an incline beyond the trees like an alien sunrise. A faint humming sounded, like a fluorescent lamp being turned on. This was joined a few seconds later by an incandescent blue light that absorbed both—and then

winked out, leaving an afterimage on Diane Scarborough's
retinas. The lights had totally disappeared, leaving only the
moon-swathed wood and field beyond—and silence.

Diane, stunned, stopped in her tracks. Something was
wrong . . . something was wrong inside her head. Where excitement and curiosity had been, there was now fear and dread. It
was as though some *force* had reached inside her head and
twisted a dial on her emotions. Twisted *hard*. She was having
difficulty breathing.

Then Tim caught up, almost knocking her down.

"Diane. What was *that*? Hey—are you okay?"

She was getting control. She sucked in some breath, feeling
less like the world was vortexing in on her. She caught hold of
Tim's arm, reeled him in and held onto him.

"It was those lights . . ." he said, clearly realizing that
something had happened to her. "Look, Diane, I'm feeling
kind of spooked. Maybe we should just get the hell *out* of
here."

"No!" she said. It took a great effort of will, but she pulled
away from him, and teetered in the direction where the lights
had blazed. "Have . . . have to *see* what's there."

Even as she spoke the words, the dread returned threefold.
Every part of her emotional being told her to turn, grab hold of
her lover, and then race away from there, as fast as they
possibly could . . . Then get in the Nissan and put as much
distance as possible between those lights and her soul. But her
mind rejected these instinctual warnings. If there was some
kind of strange flying machine just yards away, be it from
Betelgeuse or Bethlehem Steel, Diane Scarborough was going
to do everything in her power to get a look at it.

A *good* look.

The night seemed to swirl about her. The moon seemed
monstrous, peering through the breaks in the leaves like a
broken, swollen eye. The odor of dead vegetation on the
ground suddenly swatted at her face. The breeze in the branches,
the deep shadows connecting the trees—everything was accen-
tuated, warped, as though her fear had unloosed not just a rush
of adrenaline, but also some psychoactive drug as well. But a
question drove her past the terror she felt, cold at the base of
her spine: *What was beyond the trees? What waited for her
there?*

Then, abruptly, she had a feeling of déjà vu. An ancient *awareness* opened up inside, like a flower of metal and crystal. Somewhere, somehow, she had felt these feelings before.

She had seen those lights, experienced this peculiar mix of trepidation and anticipation. The memory bubbled up now from the dark mix of memory, shapeless yet familiar.

Diane could see the field now, beyond the trees. She could hear Tim behind her, running and calling her name. "Diane! Diane, wait!" And as she approached, she could see that the field beyond the trees deeped down in a steep incline. She could make out a dome—glass—metal. Lights.

Even as she reached the edge of the wood, though, the lights blasted on like the heart of an exploding sun. She was swept through a river of colors, and she could feel herself falling, falling, falling.

"Diane!" Tim called behind her. "My God, I can't see!"

Then the lights blasted off into blackness, and consciousness fled softly but fleetly.

Before she had reached puberty, become less of a tomboy, and begun affecting more feminine roles, one of Diane Scarborough's favorite things was *camping*. She loved the sensations of the *outdoors*, the thrill of wandering through a forest, the taste of pinecones in the air, the smell of rushing rivers, the sound of still and mirrorlike lakes. Her mother, Phyllis Scarborough, had originally been the outdoorsperson, insisting that they take their vacations in tents and canoes and trailers amongst the woods and streams, the sky and the wild animals. Diane's family had explored much of New England, upstate New York, Pennsylvania and eastern Canada, and on one memorable escapade had made it as far as California, dipping into the splendors of the Rockies and Yellowstone National Park along the way. Everett Scarborough merely acquiesced—as far as he was concerned, he was happy taking vacations in a midtown Manhattan fleabag hotel, as long as he had his books and his equipment along with him. He objected that he really couldn't take off time from work, but the objection was only token. Aware of her father's interests as far back as she could remember, Diane's great hope was that some night, after they had pitched their tent and were roasting marshmallows for that traditional trail-treat, S'mores, the great

theater of the stars would unroll a proscenium before them and
a Ooo Foo would spin down to dance for them in a bath of wild
lights. (That's what she called Unidentified Flying Objects,
Ooo Foos—to the delight of her father, who dutifully reported
her interest in the subject to his readers. Later, when she was
older, Diane wondered if the Great Debunker didn't secretly
wish for such a celestial show himself, all his logic and venom
in the cause of disproving their existence, a little boy's
disappointment that they didn't come down and show him their
ray guns.)

One of Diane Scarborough's favorite sensations was *waking
up* at a campsite. Yes, waking up, snug in your down sleeping
bag by a dead campfire so you had that lovely charred smell
stirred into the invigorating briskness of air *alive* with maple
sap or grass smell, or even the lovely scent of creek. Coming
awake inside could be awfully dreary and gloomy—too easy to
just nod right back off again. But springing awake in the
outdoors—ah! You were instantly roused to awareness, and
your blood was up and you felt like eating a stack of pancakes,
sweet and sticky with syrup.

That was the way Diane Scarborough felt now, waking up.

Only now she wasn't in a sleeping bag, nor was she in a tent.

The smell of dew on leaf and grass was in the air. Dawn
washed the sky with a pink and blue, moody clouds swirled
into the mix. The taste of cinnamon was in her mouth. She
stirred and yawned, stretching out. Her hands hit a steering
wheel. Blinking, she realized that she sat in the driver's seat of
her car, and that the car was parked well off the road, situated
between a couple of large oaks, the splendid view of a Kansas
field before her, grass rippling with the tug of a morning wind.

She felt a sense of calm, of perfect peace. She felt one with
the sky and the trees and the sweeping Kansas grass, as though
she'd just been in some meditative trance.

Someone moaned beside her, and then the moan turned into
a snore. She turned and saw that it was her boyfriend, Timothy
Reilly, his seat back, mouth open, zonked out totally. She
looked at him, his sandy red hair a mess, his handsome
freckled features boyish and innocent, and she loved him very
much. She was happy that he was here, and she reached over to
touch him—and then the peace shattered like a gossamer
bubble.

What were they doing *here*?

She had no memory of getting into a car. Her last memory was sitting at her desk, studying for a grammar class, figuring out the deep structure of a sentence and being very bored. After that—nothing.

Now, she was sitting in a car—*her* car. She instantly recognized the usual refuse near the stick shift, the gum wrappers, the comb, the empty coffee cup. Stuck in between the passenger seat and the emergency brake was a crumpled Coors beer can. In the rear seat was Tim's battered, trusty beer cooler. Had she and Tim gone out drinking last night? Had they gotten drunk? Had she gotten drunk, and had a blackout?

Unlikely. Diane drank beer with Tim, but she rarely got drunk. And if she'd drunk a lot of beer, she'd be able to taste it in her mouth, to say nothing of feeling a hangover. No, physically she felt just fine. Awake. Alert. And semi-amnesiac.

What had happened last night?

She had the feeling that whatever had happened was terribly important, *vital* even. And now she was consumed with frustration that she hadn't a clue as to what it *was*!

She shook Tim's arm. "Hey! Tim, wake up!"

He snapped awake. He blinked, looked around him, a kind of dazzled wonder in his eyes. Then, as he focused on his surroundings and got his bearings, he looked over to Diane and said, "Wow!"

"Tim, what are we *doing* here?"

Tim shook his head. "Diane? I don't know—I was going to ask you the same question."

"Why did you say 'Wow'?"

"Did I? I don't know. . . I just have the impression that I've just been someplace *really profound*!"

"How do you feel?"

"Terrific! Never better."

"Me too. What's the last memory you have . . . ? Mine's of sitting at my desk in my apartment, being bored, studying."

Tim thought about this for a moment. "Lights," he said with suddenly finality. "Yeah, colored lights. And . . . people. Really far-out people, like I'd never met before . . . But so filled with life, so *electric*. I don't know, it had a dreamlike quality . . . It could have been a dream."

He shook his head, then turned, pulled the top off his cooler, then pulled a Coors out of the icy water, tiny fragments of ice tinkling. He popped the top and took a pull.

"Beer. In the morning?" she said.

"Doesn't feel like morning . . . Hey . . . Beer in the back seat . . . And I remembered it. We must have gone out last night. Parked here. Why? To talk . . . No, to make out! That's right, you were tired of making out in bed, and you said you needed fresh air. You're a fresh-air fiend, and you wanted to go out and fool around and listen to the radio under the stars."

It sure sounded right. Sounded characteristic of her. She was an impulsive sort, and hauling Tim out like that was just the kind of thing she was likely to do. Why couldn't she remember a goddamn thing?

Tim drank more of the beer. And then, in midgulp, his eyes frosted over, and the stuff started foaming down his mouth, onto his jeans.

"Hey," she said, pulling the can out of his mouth. "What's wrong with you?"

He swallowed, and without looking at her said, "I remember, now."

"Remember what?"

"We were sitting her. Kissing, fooling around, but you couldn't concentrate . . . So we just talked . . . And then we saw it. We saw it, coming over the field. It was incredible. A saucer-shaped object, with spinning lights. It landed past the field, past some woods. Looked like it landed, anyway, so we got out . . . Yeah, we got out of the car . . . *And we went to check it out!*"

Not exactly believing, but not disbelieving, Diane said, "And then . . . ?"

"And then . . . lights. That's all . . . just lights!"

Diane sighed and closed her eyes. "I don't remember . . . I just don't—" But as she closed her lids, a whole explosion of lights seemed to go off in her mind, like remembered fireworks. She recalled not as memory usually plays itself out, but as a ragged series of sensory impressions. The smell of cow manure as she hurried across the field, the *dread* of wondering what lay beyond the trees, the thrill of wanting to find out, the *desire* to grab hold of something with her mind . . . some kind of *proof* to give her father, to get his attention.

"Daddy!"

"Jeez, is that *all* you can think about? We wake up in a car with a partial amnesia, and all you can think about is your tight-assed father..."

"No. Sorry. I just realized, Tim. It's coming back. Some of it...enough," she looked over to him, staring at him with awe and horror. "We've got to talk to my father. Tim, you've heard about all that business my father's been investigating lately. That Budd Hopkins, Whitley Strieber, Maximillian Shroeder stuff...Missing time. That thing we saw...Tim, we must have been abducted by a UFO!"

Timothy Reilly did not dispute her. He just finished his beer, then immediately got himself another.

CHAPTER
THREE

Later, after the shooting, the people that had sat beside the man in the balcony of the auditorium where Dr. Everett Scarborough gave his presentation described him as a "man in black."

That was what Alfred and Gertie Hopper remembered mostly, that the man was dressed entirely in black: black tennis shoes, black polyester chinos, black belt, wrinkled black banlon shirt, black coat, even a black hat, that he didn't wear, but carried crumpled in one hand with nails bitten down to the quick.

"A *raincoat*. I thought that was weird. It was a nice night outside," said Gertie Hopper later. "I definitely thought that was weird. But then, I guess I expected to see weird people there. I mean, flying-saucer speeches bring 'em out, don't they? I've seen some odd-lookin' people before at some of the symposiums, so I guess that guy kinda blended in. Maybe he just wore that long black coat to hide the gun. And you know, funny thing, now that I think of it...*that* was black too!"

Alfred and Gertie Hopper were from Charles County, Maryland. Alfred had a liquor store in Waldorf, and a motor boat docked at Chesapeake Beach, with which he liked to go out crabbing in the bay on nice Sundays or Saturdays. Gertie worked in the store, and was very active in the local Baptist church. They had two sons, both grown, and shared an interest in flying saucers. They had both seen UFOs years before. Gertie's had been hovering above a tobacco field. Alfred's had been during a late evening fishing trip. They belonged to MUFON and avidly read all the magazines and books on the subject. They were not at all obsessed, nor did they hunger for contact with aliens from distant planets. They just agreed that it was damn interesting stuff, that people should pay more attention, and that the government should start up some kind of sequel to Project Blue Book to investigate the phenomenon. Alfred had somewhat of a reputation as a letter-hack to the flying-saucer publications. One of his favorite authors was Doctor Everett Scarborough. While he didn't agree with Scarborough that *all* UFO reports were hokum, he savored the way the man skewered the wild and wacky fringe weirdos that UFO study attracted. When they'd heard that Scarborough was speaking on the campus of the University of Maryland as the beginning of a national tour to publicize his new book, *Above Us Only Sky*, they'd decided to go. They'd seen him twice before, once at the Prince George's Community College, and once at the Sheraton Park in Washington, D.C. at the MUFON National Convention. They both agreed that Scarborough was a fascinating speaker, and besides, he gave a damn good show.

This "man in black" by whom they had sat had one other feature they'd noticed and recalled easily. "Pop-eyes," Alfred Hopper told the police later. "You know...bugeyes? Like, what's the term? Oh, yeah. Hyperthyroid. You know, you've seen them, it's like their brains are too big and pushing at the backs of the eyeballs." Otherwise, he was nondescript enough, with a limp, long hair, dark eyes. Late thirties, maybe early forties.

"Sat through the whole show, quiet as you please, still, listening to Dr. Scarborough's talk, watching the slides, listening to the music, maybe stirring a bit when Scarborough did his demonstrations. Wasn't until the end, with the question-and-answer period, when Scarborough was talkin' 'bout the Zeta

Reticuli Connection—that was when he started gettin' twitchy. And when that guy came up on the stage and started arguing with Scarborough, that, of course, was when he pulled out the gun.''

Dr. Everett Scarborough stood at the podium, letting the applause wash over him, savoring the fruits of a most successful lecture and demonstration. God, he loved this! When he started doing the speaking engagements, fifteen years before, after the publication of his very first book criticizing the UFO phenomenon, he'd reluctantly accepted that first lecture offer before a library reading group, only to wet his feet. He'd been nervous then—and, in fact, a touch of stage fright always occupied those first minutes before a lecture—but as soon as he'd launched into his song-and-dance, as he called it, unsuspected wings of oratory had unfurled and he'd flown off into a most successful side-career.

''Thank you, thank you,'' he said into the microphone, the words booming out over the auditorium like the pronouncements of some demigod over his minions. ''But the best is yet to come. I understand we have some saucer clubs in our midst. The Believers are amidst us!'' He smiled out over the audience, a taunting cast to his head. ''Surely you Ooo Foo freaks aren't going to take my words of wisdom, logic, intelligence, and truth without lobbing some pseudoscientific offal and ill-reasoned opinions into the pure and unsullied waters of this evening's discussion!''

His biting delivery and self-mocking diction sent a wave of laughter through the audience—but it also performed its other function splendidly. It ticked off the fuming U-FOols royally. Doubtless stunned by the sheer intensity and weight of his talk that evening, they would be speechless for a time. It took a nice slap across the chops, a challenge, to make them rise to the bait.

A young man wearing thick eyeglasses stood up from near the front, waving his hand for attention.

''Yes! The first question of the evening. In case you all haven't noticed, I'm just *full* of answers!''

Light laughter. The audience was in the palm of his hand. They'd loved the innovations in tonight's show—the lasers, the magic exhibition, the new jokes, the specially commissioned music. His hunch was paying off. Broaden the entertainment value of his lectures, and he'd broaden his audience. More people would hear his arguments, and he'd make more money speaking—to say nothing of selling *lots* of books in the lobby after the show.

"Dr. Scarborough, on the Carson show last week, and even tonight, you've been addressing the recent phenomenon exclusively, particularly the sort of UFO contact experienced by such people as Whitley Strieber and Maximillian Schroeder— namely abduction. But you've not addressed the fact that throughout history and especially since 1947, mankind has experienced a rash of UFO experiences of various kinds. *Something* is going on, Dr. Scarborough, and I really can't buy your slick and glib explanations."

"Something is going on, all right," Scarborough said, pausing to time his punch line properly. "People are just high-teching broomsticks and black cats!" Chuckles. "I'm serious! Some brains in this vast sea of humanity are still bobbing and drooling in the Dark Ages. Aren't you *listening* to me, numb-nodes?" He raised his hands as though to direct a symphony orchestra, keying his already established refrain of the evening. He started to recite, and half the audience—his faithful, and those he'd just won over—echoed along with him: "People believe because they *want* to believe." He pulled the mike from its holder and walked forward to the edge of the stage, smiling at the young man, who was already withering with embarrassment.

"Were you out buying popcorn when I went over this . . . When I did those magic tricks the Amazing Randi taught me, and then showed you how they were done, were you out visiting the little boy's room? Let me summarize just for you . . . the power of suggestion. I say to you now: Hey, wouldn't an ice cream sundae taste good after the show? Maybe vanilla with some hot fudge and thick rich whipped cream! And don't forget some crunchy nuts and a tart maraschino cherry. I guarantee you that a healthy percentage are going to *forget* I made that suggestion to you, walk out of here, drive past a Baskin-Robbins and be damn tempted to wheel in for a treat. And I'm no hypnotist, and I'm no dairy flack either . . . I'm just pointing out the hidden currents that can run in our minds. The human mind is a lot more than just the thoughts you have. It can play some damn odd tricks on you, and it's the thing that's attached to your eyes, your ears, your whole sensory apparatus! For instance, ever just lay on your back and stare up at cloud formations? Hmm? Sure, everybody has. Some people see ghostly galleons of white and grey coasting through the sea of a sky. But if you're a horny young male—or even a distinguished older man with a taste for feminine company like yours truly—you tend to see naked female bodies!''

He let the laughter play itself out, and die to silence as he dramatically stared out at the audience.

"I admit, I've been talking a lot about one aspect of the UFO phenomena tonight. But as a surgeon of logic and truth, it's my duty to cut out the biggest cancers of contemporary thought first. In case you haven't noticed, sir, abduction is the hot ticket these days in the UFO sweepstakes!''

"Hey, pal! You're not hurting in this business!'' a heckler called out in the audience.

Scarborough shrugged. "I guess you're right. But still, when I heard about a one million dollar advance for *Communion* and *two* million for Max Schroeder's *Star Son*—well, I walked out into my backyard, and held my arms up to the starry sky and cried out, 'Please ETs. Take *me*!' ''

The audience loved that one. They roared. Nothing like money jokes to get a U.S. group going.

Everett Scarborough smiled upon his congregation benevolently. He was a tall man, (six foot two) with dark hair and beautiful dark eyes which he'd gotten from his Italian mother. His chiselled good looks though, were from his father, a descendant of English settlers in Massachusetts. Some people said he looked like a British Roy Scheider, but Scarborough preferred to think of himself as an Italian Cary Grant. Regular bouts with free weights kept his stomach trim and his shoulders and chest big. He cut a striking figure tonight in his London-tailored three-piece suit. The jacket was long gone, and the vest was unbuttoned, now. It was said that at some points in his fiery oratory Everett Scarborough resembled nothing less than a superb preacher of the Gospel. Only in this case, the god proclaimed was Isaac Newton, and *Scientific American* the bible that was thumped.

"Seriously,'' he said, the picture of solemn sincerity. "I address all aspects of the UFO phenomena in my books, and I want to thank you, sir, for pointing out the heavy contemporary obsession of this evening.

"Nonetheless we stand now at a point in history where we can look back and easily see just how relevant my comments this evening on suggestion *are*!

"Let me give you two quick examples," he said, pacing the stage, to keep more movement in the act, a trick he learned from watching Jimmy Swaggart before that evangelist self-destructed in his own sexual juices.

"In my book, *History of a Delusion*, I cover not only modern sightings, but ancient evidence of Unidentified Flying Objects as well. Now, we all know that the Wright brothers made the first engine-driven vehicular flight in 1901 at Kitty Hawk, North Carolina: a feat which had been called an impossibility less than a quarter-century before. But did you know that there were a *rash* of UFO sightings in 1897 and 1898? Now, a lot of opportunistic writers on the phenomena *jump* on this fact, much as they jump on all those biblical quotations about wheels of fire and such. But let's take these sightings in context.

"First of all, they dealt with flying machines not at all saucer-shaped. In fact, they allegedly looked more like boats of the air. The favorite story was about anchors dropping from the sky and men in Victorian outfits climbing down from vessels straight from Jules Verne novels. No little men in shiny suits, no bald heads and slanty eyes, and *certainly* no free proctology examinations!"

They laughed at that one too, and Scarborough permitted himself a smile. He realized that his underarms were soaked in sweat.

"But we can't take these experiences—mostly American, by the way—in a vacuum. In fact, flying machines were starting to become a *possibility*. They were the stuff of dime novels, and while science fiction was in its infancy at the time, plenty of writers imitated Verne, and the young H.G. Wells was just beginning to write his famous scientific romances. A lot of international tension existed—doubtless the denizens of these wood-and-bolt UFOs had German accents.

"But consider—the average American's subconscious mind was just absorbing these fantastic scientific endeavors. There must have been a great deal of psychoprojection at the time.

Now, as we all know, it's a scientifically proven fact that the sky and the world, to say nothing of the universe, is simply full of weird phenomena. In fact, as I always say at these occasions and as I'll say again, if people were merely looking for odd facts, they'd be quite content with the continued study of natural science, to say nothing of the other realms of scientific pursuit. And if you *really* want to get bizarre, just get involved with what's going on in quantum mechanics. Indeed, in my opinion, a few of my colleagues are *far* weirder than your average alien contactee who's had tea with the king of the Rings of Saturn—and they're dealing with scientific fact! But as Alexander Pope said, the proper study of mankind is man. People are interested in other *people*. This is why, when people observe the many possible natural phenomena of the skies, they superimpose subconscious information onto the occasion."

Scarborough sketched and elaborated for a while, detailing the history of UFOs, threading in his theme of suggestion. When he finished, he made a joke about saucer clubs, which earned a rousing round of laughter.

"Look," said Scarborough, winding things down. "I have had a lot of fun with the people called UFOols, granted. I must be pretty fascinated with the whole subject to study it so much, right? I guess I don't have much room to talk. We've all got to explore this mysterious world we inhabit and I applaud *everyone* who does. Curiosity is a wonderful thing. But I guess if I have a single message that I'm trying to drive into the international consciousness, it's that we have developed an absolutely wonderful and useful tool with which we can study the unknown. It's called the *scientific method* and it's derived from *logic*. This is the yardstick we can use to measure what we know. It's the sword that can separate knowledge from ignorance. And if I can communicate the value of this incredible tool to the masses by applying it fiercely and unmercifully to the modern mythology of flying-saucer hokum, then I can feel that this life has been worthwhile."

Thunderous applause met those words. People actually stood up, clapping wildly. Not more than a handful, but it was enough. Scarborough stood, accepting the accolade, wearing a serious and somber expression.

"Thank you. Thank you very much. But as time is running out, let's have another question, at the most two. And then you can all rush out to the lobby where presigned copies of my new book, *Above Us Only Sky*, awaits your purchase.''

He returned to the podium, poured a glass of ice water. Ice cubes tinkled, and he could hear the murmur of the crowd. He took a long cool drink, then took the linen handkerchief from a shelf below the podium and wiped the perspiration off his brow. One of these days, he thought, they're going to invent stage lighting that doesn't turn a suit into a steambath. Still, he wondered if he cared to give up the effect that simple sweat contributed to a performance. It was like a soggy underline of passion—a much needed complement to a message that was, after all, meant to be cold and clear reason.

Scarborough was reminded of the story that James Randi told him about the revival-tent preacher who would paint a cross on his forehead with a special type of invisible paint. When the preacher got to sweating hard toward the end of his sermon, the cross would begin to glow a fiery red, and the congregation would proclaim a miracle of God.

No such tricks tonight. Oh, certainly, tricks and subtleties of persuasion and argument and rhetoric—but all in good cause. Science. Logic. Even that good old American staple, simple *common sense*.

Putting the half-empty glass down, he looked back at the audience. Several arms were raised, but he was immediately attracted to the hand raised by a young female student in jeans, standing out in the aisle toward the front. She reminded him of his daughter, Diane, and so on a whim he called on her, remembering that spring break was just around the corner and Diane would be visiting soon.

"Yes! The lovely young woman in the front! You look like an intelligent person. You have a question?"

"Yes, I do!" she said adamantly. "You know, Dr. Scarborough, you're a most entertaining speaker, and you're a very intelligent and learned man, and I've enjoyed myself very much tonight. In fact, I understand you're single—"

"Please . . . I like to keep these speaking engagements purely business. I am very flattered, miss, but—"

"Actually," she said, her voice loud enough for most of the hall to hear. "I was thinking of introducing you to my widowed *mother*!"

Scarborough affected a Jack Benny "Well!" stance, staring

out at the audience with contrived exasperation. They erupted into laughter. Excellent! Everett Scarborough had learned to use all kinds of humor to his advantage, and gentle self-mockery without loss of dignity was absolutely classic. The laughter lasted hard and long. He'd learned very quickly that the public figure who could not make fun of himself was soon called "arrogant" and "obnoxious." Everett Scarborough knew that he certainly had his moments of both qualities—but thanks to Phyllis, he'd at least learned not to take himself *too* seriously. His scientific opinions, of course, were sterling—but being human, he knew he had a few foibles.

When the laughter had died down a bit, he said, "My dear, I'm sure your mother is as beautiful as you, and I'd love to meet her, as long as she has a book for me to sign. Now, if we can return to the less serious business at hand—flying saucers!"

"Sorry. But really, Doctor, has it ever occurred to you that *you* believe what you want to believe too?"

"It's not a matter of belief, my dear, nor faith. I use a system constructed specifically to deal with empirical *facts*."

"Okay, you won't accept that...Let me ask you another one. You've been talking a lot about the recent abduction experiences. I was watching a film on the late show the other night. It had James Earl Jones in it and it was about a couple who were abducted in *1961*!"

"Yes. That would be *The UFO Encounter*...A TV movie from the seventies, I think."

"Right. But even the movie was made before all this business...And Dr. Scarborough, the things that happened to the Hills...They were *a lot* like what's been described in the past few years! Maybe this has been going on for a long time, and it's just coming to light!"

Scarborough stroked his square, clean-shaven chin for a moment. "I'm glad you brought that case up. Don't think that I'm not familiar with it. The book to read on the subject is John Fuller's *Interrupted Journey*. And I address the matter from chapter five through chapter ten in my second book, *Unidentified Flying Oddballs*. It just focuses further on my previous theory of suggestion, actually.

"But for those who aren't familiar with the case, let me summarize it briefly."

He turned to face the audience fully.

"Betty and Barney Hill were returning from a vacation in Canada to their home in Portsmouth, New Hampshire. They observed a UFO. For some reason, Barney Hill pulled into a side road. The next thing they knew, it was several hours later.

"They tried to continue in their normal lives, but were deeply troubled by that night, both of them, and they sought professional counseling. When the matter of the observed Unidentified Flying Object was brought into the forefront, Dr. Benjamin Simon, a specialist in hypnotherapy who enabled his patients to relive forgotten experiences, was brought in. Dr. Simon hypnotized the Hills and this was the story that they relived—with a great deal of angst and melodrama, actually."

Scarborough paused for effect. The great thing about discussing saucer tales was that even though they were generally the sheerest gobbledegook, they made for *great* storytelling. Most of the audience had been persuaded tonight that UFOs were the stuff of fairy tales—but still, he could see their eyes trained on him in fascination, leaning forward slightly in their chairs, listening to the suspenseful tale unfold.

"According to the Simons, a group of humanoid creatures about four feet tall intercepted them, and used some kind of hypnotic method to make them get out of their car and accompany them to their vehicle—a landed saucer-shaped vehicle, of course—deeper in the woods. Inside the saucer, the Hills were subjected to a number of tests. Skin was taken from Mrs. Hill's arm. Mr. Hill claimed that a semen sample was taken from him. At first, the Hills were quite frightened, but then they began talking to the visitors and calmed down somewhat. Then they were released and returned to their car, and told they would not remember the experience.

"Now, this is the first documented case of creatures doing biopsies and taking sperm and perhaps egg samples, and we don't get a great deal of that through the late sixties and early seventies. But notice—immediately after that film was shown on nationwide television to millions of people, these cases of alien physical tamperings after abductions began to be reported. You know, that makes me wonder if I shouldn't do a private study of just how many of the people who report this kind of experience *saw that TV film*.

"Of course, we can't just blame that particular film. For thirty years you haven't been able to get through a grocery line without being regaled with tales of alien sexual encounters and kidnappings. Maybe that Julie Brown song 'Earth Girls are Easy' is a galactic hit!''

The audience laughed. But then a man walked down the aisle, holding a book in one hand. He stood patiently near the stage until the noise died down, and then cried out, ''You edit your stories for your *own* purposes, Scarborough.''

Scarborough recognized the man and cringed a bit. The fellow had accosted him earlier. He was a plump man with short hair, and thick, horn-rimmed glasses through which myopic eyes glared like those of an angry turtle. He had a Roman nose, and classic nerd-garb, all the way from untied shoes to white short-sleeve shirt and a plastic pocket-protector crammed with pens. This was a man far past the UFOol stage—he was what Scarborough termed an Unidentified Flying Oddball. He couldn't remember his name, but he knew that the man held some position with the local office of MUFON, the flying-saucer investigation organization.

''Oh dear. What did I leave out?'' said Scarborough, giving a martyred expression to the audience.

''The most *important* part of the Hill abduction case. How can you have forgotten! The Zeta Reticuli connection!''

''Oh my goodness,'' said Scarborough, ''The Zeta Reticuli connection! How could it have slipped my mind!''

Someone from far back in the audience cried out, ''What the hell is a Zit Ridicule connection?''

''I'll tell you what it is!'' said the man, holding a book above his head. ''It's one of the most important proofs that exist that we are being visited by creatures in ships from some other planet! If you'll just let me use your overhead projector, Dr. Scarborough, I'll be glad to prove my point.''

Scarborough shrugged. ''By all means, Mr. . . .''

''Tamowitz. Jacob Tamowitz, vice president of the local MUFON group.'' He started up the steps to the stage while Scarborough used the mike to make sure that the audience didn't think his knowledge of UFOs was less than encyclopedic.

''According to Betty Hill, when she asked the creatures where they were from, they showed her a three-dimensional map depicting a constellation of stars. Some of these stars were connected by thick lines that the aliens claimed were 'star routes' between the stars. When this fact came out during hypnosis, Dr. Simon asked if Mrs. Hill could reconstruct that map. She did. It wasn't until several years later, after the publication of Fuller's book on the Hills' experience that anything came of it—and I believe Mr. Tamowitz here wants me to show you a picture of that map.''

Indeed, Mr. Tamowitz did. He was standing by Scarborough, glaring balefully, his face an indelicate shade of red, clutching the book, opened, to his chest. He was so close that Scarborough could smell a cloying mixture of Right Guard and Brut emanating from the angry saucer-freak.

Scarborough took the book and placed it atop the lens of the overhead projector, then switched the machine on. The star charts appeared on the screen: a collection of dots, dotted lines, and solid lines in various configurations, labeled at the bottom respectively, ''Betty Hill's Original Sketch,'' ''The Fish Interpretation,'' and ''The Atterberg Interpretation.''

Tamowitz grabbed the mike and proceeded to talk, explaining.

''It's funny how you twist the facts to your own means by simply leaving out certain key information, Scarborough. The Betty Hill Star Chart is perhaps the most important fact about the Hill abduction. It not only confirms the validity of the Hills' story—It *also* proves that the visitors from these flying saucers are from other planets in our universe.''

Scarborough threw up his hands, mugging to the audience. No problem, he thought. Things were still well under control. He signaled to the wings, and one of the student assistants posted to him ran out with a wireless microphone, ready and waiting for just such an eventuality as this. ''Proves?'' he said. ''This is a new one on me! Would you elucidate, please, Mr. Tamowitz?''

''I'd be happy to! In 1968, after seeing Mrs. Hill's chart, Mrs. Marjorie Fish—a member of MENSA—took the map and compared it to Dorrit Hoffliet's *Catalog of Bright Stars*. She recognized this as the first possibility of astronomical evidence of alien visitors. She built a three-dimensional scale model of the Hill chart. After six months of searching and aligning, she discovered stars *in the exact same positions*! This work was continued when a new book was published, *The Catalog of Nearby Stars* by Wilhelm Gleiss. Mrs. Fish continued her work, built more models, and discovered that the view presented by the Hill map was from a few light years past the stars Zeta 1 and Zeta Reticuli, looking back toward our sun. The star 82 Eridani is also included. But the really startling aspect is that *this pattern exists*! Astronomers agree that these systems contain planets that could hold living beings, Dr. Scarborough! Mrs. Hill *must* have been shown an actual map! What do you say to that?''

"Well, I'd say that since there are *billions and billions*," he smiled at the applause for the Carl Sagan catchphrase, "of stars out there within range of our telescopes, chances are pretty good that there'd be a pattern similar to the one Mrs. Hill drew.

"This, Mr. Tamowitz, is hardly what I would term scientific evidence. It's more like connect-the-dots for *MENSA* members.''

That infuriated the man. "I'll have you know that I am a member of MENSA, and it is a valuable and distinguished organization for people with far above-average intelligence.''

"I've got nothing against intelligence at all! I just wish people would use it on more constructive projects than looking for extraterrestrials where there *aren't* any!''

"I'm not finished," Tamowitz said, jabbing at the illustration with a forefinger, shaking the screen. "After Mrs. Fish published her account at a Mutual UFO network convention and it was subsequently printed in *Astronomy Magazine*, an aeronautical engineer and amateur astronomer named Charles Atterberg—''

Scarborough wondered why Tamowitz was bringing up Atterberg, who claimed that there was another possible area of stars that could have been charted in the Hill map. It played right into the points he had made about superimposing patterns and meaning over random facts. What was that called? He'd have to use that word in his rebuttal, if he could remember it.

But he never got the chance.

Because that was when the shots broke out.

The first shot sounded like nothing more than a backfiring truck from the parking lot. The shot echoed around in the faulty acoustics of the auditorium.

Before the echoes, though, the top of podium exploded into splinters.

In 1987, a comedian named Dick Shawn died onstage in the middle of his act, of a heart attack. He lay prostrate in front of hundreds of people who waited patiently for him to get up and continue his routine; his style of performance was such that people thought falling down and looking dead was part of the act.

The audience at Everett Scarborough's lecture at the Tawes Auditorium on the University of Maryland took only a few seconds to realize that shots and an exploding podium were not part of the show—but since the demonstrations had included some startling magic tricks, it was understandable that for a while they were quite confused and did nothing, watching the events unfold in stunned silence. Dr. Everett Scarborough, however, certainly knew that exploding podiums were not a part of the act. Split seconds after the gunfire and the sting of the wood pieces against his cheek, he was down on the floor, less of a target.

The second bullet sang over Scarborough's head as he crawled away for cover, smashing into the overhead projector, sending a shatter of glass across the floor. "Get down!" he cried to the paralyzed Tamowitz, who stood transfixed in the same position, like a startled deer caught in auto headlights.

"What—?" the man managed before the third bullet caught him full in the chest, knocking him down and sending a splash of blood onto the white screen behind him.

By the second shot, the Hoppers knew that it was the man dressed in all-black clothing who was doing the shooting. They had been so immersed in the proceedings on that stage, though, that they had not noticed the man getting up and going to the intersection of the balcony railing and the right auditorium wall. He stood there now, just squeezing off the third shot from his long-nosed .44, his longish, limp hair parted in the middle and hanging down the sides of his face. He held the gun with both hands. There was no expression on his face at all.

"Hey!" Alfred Hopper cried, getting up.

Gertie Hopper screamed and clutched at her husband frantically, pulling him back in the seat, not wanting to be the widow of a dead hero.

At the sight of the MUFON official's blood on the screen, several other people in the audience screamed, others cried out, pointing up toward the direction of the shots.

Everett Scarborough struggled to control the panic that gripped him. His instinct told him to just get up and *run*, but he'd had enough time to judge the angle of the bullets, and knew that the assassin had him pinned. All he could do was crawl to the base of the podium, which provided some cover. As he reached it, he realized that he was trailing blood. He lifted a hand to his face, and his palm came away scarlet. The splinters had gouged into his face. Nearby, was the shuddering body of the man with the star charts, lying on his face. A pool of blood was slowly collecting to his left side, then rivulating down the proscenium. "Turn out the lights!" Scarborough heard himself yelling. With the lights on, he still presented a target.

The man in black clothing fired one more shot from his automatic—the bullet thunking into the wood floor just to the left of the podium—and then vaulted the balcony railing like a practiced acrobat. His raincoat belled out like the cape of Zorro as he fell, and he landed on his feet in the red-carpeted aisle fifteen feet below.

More people screamed.

"Stop him!" a man cried.

"Are you crazy! He's got a gun!" another answered.

If he'd hoped to have a better shot from the ground floor, then he'd made the wrong move. But the man simply took one look at the stage, waved his gun threateningly at horrified nearby onlookers, and then slammed his body hard to the right, hitting the latch of a fire-exit door. There was the breath of night, the sound of cars passing by outside, and the faint flap of raincoat—and then the man in black was swallowed up by the lamp-touched darkness of trees and parking lots.

The door whooshed closed behind him, slamming hard.

From his cover behind the base of the podium, Scarborough managed to glimpse the man jumping from the balcony, like some modern day John Wilkes Booth. Unfortunately, the man did not break his leg, but escaped easily.

Scarborough could feel the panic about to break through the audience. He understood group psychology all too well—if people freaked, they'd start running for the other exit sign as though someone had yelled "Fire" at them. Swallowing his own initial and reflexive fear, aware that another killer might be just waiting for him to poke his head up to take another shot, he nonetheless took the risk. He stood, found the microphone, and began to speak to the audience, trying to calm them.

"Please! People, calm down," he said above the tumult,

making himself an easy target, but counting the lives of others as more important. "Stay in your seats!" he ordered. His authoritative baritone bellowed above the crowd, and the noise died down. Heads turned his way, as though expectant of an announcement of a hoax. Instead, he turned to the side of the stage and glared. "Haven't we got any security around here! And a doctor. We need a doctor, a man's been shot. Call an ambulance—now!"

His commanding tone quelled the rising panic in the crowd and they stayed in place. No one rushed for the exit. There were no fights, no trampling. They all seemed to wait for what Scarborough had to say next.

"This," he said, wiping some blood from his face, "is real, but don't panic. The man who fired the shots is gone."

A pair of men moved from the side of the stage and knelt down over the fallen man. Another came out and said something to Scarborough, which he kept from the audience by muffling the mike under an armpit.

Scarborough nodded at the man. Then he spoke again to the audience. "The police are already pursuing the attacker, and we've got a rescue squad coming. I have been asked by the people in charge that you please stay in your seats for the time being, until proper authorities arrive to tell you what to do."

He stared down at the fallen man. One of the stage hands dragged a length of canvas out, and covered the now-dead body and the spilled blood.

Scarborough turned back to the audience. "Ladies, gentlemen—friends," he said, his eyes glistening a bit as realization set in, his voice choking with emotion. "I've received death threats before, but I never thought it would come to this. I am very sorry."

The wail of a siren sounded outside.

CHAPTER
FOUR

Everett Scarborough's house was a big colonial off River Road in Bethesda, Maryland, surrounded by large oak and maple stands, and several cherry blossom trees. He'd bought it in the midsixties when he'd moved to Washington to take on the position as Chief Scientific Consultant for Project Blue Book, and had stayed on after the project had shut down. Washington was full of consulting positions for a bright and personable scientist like Dr. Everett Scarborough, and Scarborough lived well off these while he started to build his side-career as a writer of nonfiction articles and books. He and Phyllis had fallen in love with the sturdy brick house to the northwest of a city they found to have just the right mixture of cosmopolitan culture, interesting people, and attractive countryside. They decided that it was here that they would start a family.

It was very late that night of the shooting, when Scarborough pulled his Mercedes into his macadam driveway.

He had been treated at Holy Cross Hospital for superficial facial cuts, and several thick splinters had been extracted. He wore a bandage, and carried a packet containing adhesive tape, cotton, and a fresh bandage for tomorrow, along with a disinfectant. The hospital did not keep him long; the police, after questioning him, let him go. They would have preferred that he stay with a friend or at a hotel for the night, but Scarborough had assured them that he kept his place of residence highly secret, due to all the crank activity that buzzed around him. Still, the state police promised to notify the Montgomery County cops to keep a watch on the house.

Scarborough shut the door of his blue Mercedes, sighed, and

looked up at his house, at the night lights glowing from the windows.

If only Phyllis were here. If only she were still alive and waiting for him, he wouldn't feel so leaden and lonely inside now. His wife had died seven years before, and while Scarborough had been dating regularly for the past four, he'd only had one relationship that had lasted over six months. Plenty of women were attracted to him. He was a man of vast charm and appeal, perhaps even charisma. But when they actually got to know him, if they cared to make the relationship more permanent, they rapidly realized that they were competing with a ghost— the memory of his wife.

Generally, Everett Scarborough *liked* living alone. He had plenty of friends all over the Washington area, all over the *world* for that matter, and the Scarborough house often had guests, or dinner parties or just pals over for poker. Scarborough liked to control the influx of visitors, and preferred to have the option of being alone when he cared to be, so that he could finish a book, or write an article, or just immerse himself in his vast library and his record collection.

Tonight, though, he knew he didn't really want company. He wanted Phyl.

As he walked up the stone pathway to the front door, he trod upon cherry blossoms that the front tree was just beginning to shed. The April season for them was very short, but they were so beautiful when they bloomed. Phyllis had them planted when they first moved in—she always associated Washington with cherry blossoms, she claimed, and wanted a couple trees for her very own, so she wouldn't have to jostle with the tourists for looks around the Tidal Basin. Still, every year, Phyllis *had* to go visit them, tourists or no tourists, especially when their daughter Diane got old enough to appreciate them. Scarborough never cared much about the trees until Phyllis had died—and then suddenly they were very important to him.

Slotting the key into the lock, opening the front door, he immediately had an overwhelming urge for a drink. After the lecture tonight, and the horrible events afterwards, he was positively speeding with all the adrenaline pumping through his system. Now, although pure sadness and depression had slowed him down some, he still felt very ragged, very on edge. One of Scarborough's vices was his fondness for good, twelve-year-old Scotch, and he could almost taste the wicked, bracing sting of a neat three-fingers' worth as he opened his door.

As soon as he entered the house, he sensed that something was amiss.

There were no odd sounds, no odd smells—everything was in order. Clean, neat—maybe that was it. Yes, he decided, putting his briefcase down on a table near the staircase, remembering. Today was Mrs. Morgan's cleaning day, and as he'd been over at the university since ten A.M. this morning, preparing for the lecture—the first of a planned nationwide series keyed to tie in with last month's publication of *Above Us Only Sky* by Quigley Publishers—Scarborough had not run into her. The older woman, who'd been cleaning almost as long as he'd owned the house, had her own key with which to let herself in and out. The house *felt* different because it was all straightened up, vacuumed, dusted, mopped. There was a touch of Pine Sol to the air, a taste of Lemon Pledge.

Besides, Scarborough was not a man who dwelt on unsubstantiated feelings. He believed that such human properties as intuition were merely primitive sub-neocortex forms of mental logic, developed as defense mechanisms in early primates. Any hunches and such that he experienced were quickly brought to light, examined with his trained mind, and then acted on, or discarded. He counted this *feeling* of wrongness inside his house now as the paranoid result of the evening's events. He knew that if he didn't get a grip, he'd be checking under his bed for boogeymen.

Scarborough laughed gently to himself. "Good evening, boogeymen, the wounded soldier is home!" he called out to the silence.

His voice echoed through an empty house. There was, of course, no answer.

He hung his jacket in the hall closet. Now, about that drink. His face still ached. The stinging was gone, but still, a good solid drink would numb the ache, and relax him. Maybe he'd even be able to sleep tonight, though that was an iffy prospect.

He went through his living room, into the porch that he'd converted into a study. The louvered windows still remained, which made the study very bright and cheerful during the day. As he switched on his light, the most prominent feature of the breezeway/study was immediately displayed: not his old IBM

PC huddled in his corner, nor his desk, piled with papers—but a huge walnut bar that ran half the length of the brick wall, filled with Victorian bric-a-brac and mirrors, populated by six stools, a copper footrest-railing, and English-style taps connected to kegs of Bass Ale, Watney's Red Barrel, and John Courage, the only British beers he could get in the United States in that form. This was the centerpiece of Scarborough's social events, and had been dubbed by his poker buddies as "The Bar That ET Built," since it was the result of an abundant royalty payment from his third UFO exposé bestseller, *Cultural Profiteers and Alien Visitors*, a study of how mass media affected the mythology of weird phenomena, with a large part devoted to the famous Steven Spielberg blockbuster movie, *E.T.*

Scarborough went behind the bar to where his spirits were neatly racked. He scanned his selection of Scotches, and selected a half-empty bottle of Dewars. From the overhead glass-rack, he pulled a long-stemmed glass. He uncapped the bottle and poured himself a liberal dollop, which he sipped slowly, savoring the woody aroma as though it were the finest of wines.

Like alcoholics say, thought Scarborough as the knot in his interior slowly untwisted, the thing about a drink was it worked every time.

He was about to go to his stereo and put on some Chopin, or something similarly restful, and stretch out on the divan across from the bar, when he heard the noise.

It sounded like someone moving around in the basement.

Adrenaline pumped again. He froze, his hand gripping the glass so hard he almost crushed it. He put the drink down and listened. The sounded continued—someone was *definitely* in the basement. Then there was a clatter and crunch of something falling and scattering.

His heart racing, he went to the fireplace. He pulled open the bottom drawer, and moved aside a cloth concealing a loaded .38 revolver. He wasn't a gun person by nature, but after his second searing indictment of UFO fanatics, he had started receiving hate mail, including death threats. As these threats were usually indirect, promising retribution from the skies in the form of death rays and disintegration, he did not take great notice. But since he'd had a family at the time, he thought that the logical thing to do was to get a gun—just in case. And make damn sure his place of residence was kept a secret.

But there *was* someone in his basement, and it was almost two o'clock in the morning.

He thought about calling the police, but then realized that they couldn't get here quick enough. He'd have to deal with whoever it was downstairs himself. After watching that poor Tamowitz fellow get gunned down this evening, he almost welcomed the intrusion. It would be a way to deal with his frustration at being able to do nothing before. Now, he held hard cold metal in his hand; now he could deal with things.

Cautiously, he made his way into the foyer, not turning on the lights, treading on the rug and avoiding the side table with the fake flower arrangement by simple touch and memory. From the foyer, a flight of carpeted stairs led to the second floor. Beneath these stairs were the steps that led down to the basement, where Scarborough kept his library. He eased quietly through the darkness to the closed doorway, carefully turning the knob and looking down the steps.

There was a light on in his library.

He hadn't left a light on, had he? He searched his memory. Mrs. Morgan generally never ventured down there, unless he specifically asked her to. The library was the one place he allowed his tendency to clutter full reign. This was also where he kept the bulk of his record and CD collection, and there were always new stacks of recordings waiting to be shelved, which he did *not* want the cleaning woman to tamper with.

There were no other noises. Had one of those stacks simply toppled over? A possibility, though unlikely. He had to check.

The basement steps were not carpeted, so he took them one-by-one with care and quiet. He kept his breathing controlled and silent. Holding the gun up, he clicked the safety off, and continued the descent.

His blood hammered in his ears, and he felt his heart thumping away with tension in his chest.

At the bottom of the steps, he paused.

Another sound. A squeak. It sounded like his Eames chair— he never got around to oiling it lately, and the damn leather monstrosity tended to squeal like a wounded cat when you swivelled. Scarborough hardly needed his training in logic to come to the conclusion that there was somebody sitting in his chair.

He took a deep breath, made the final step onto the landing, swinging around for a full view of the library, holding his .38 out in front of him. He barely noticed that his hand was shaking.

The entirety of the large basement room's walls were lined with shelves, and upon these shelves were thousands and thousands of books. Old books, new books, paperbacks, magazines. More books and journals sat on the two coffee tables and the large Oriental rug on the floor. On the far wall was a fireplace, the room smelled of the uncleaned flue and the charred wood still lingering on the grate, mixed with the tobacco smells from Scarborough's pipe collection and his humidor, which lined the walnut mantel.

Scarborough immediately noted that the lights of his Fischer stereo system were on. A coiled wire stretched from a jack to behind the Eames chair, turned away from him. Scattered by the chair was a pile of his latest CD purchases. From the chair to the footstool stretched a pair of legs wrapped in jeans, shod in black Reeboks.

"What are you doing here?" he demanded, after a heavy sigh and a shake of his head. He lowered the gun.

There was no answer. He noted the toes moving back and forth in rhythm with some unheard music. Scarborough put the safety back on the gun and placed it on a free space on a nearby shelf. Whatever she was doing here, it wouldn't do for her to see him coming toward her holding a gun. Besides, the possibility of scaring her also played havoc with her image of him as an unshakeable stalwart man. He checked to see if his hands were still shaking. They were. Mentally, he ordered them to cease. After a few seconds, and a few more deep breaths, they did.

Scarborough went to the stereo amplifier and hit the power button to the Off position.

The result was immediate. The Eames chair swivelled around, bearing the surprised blonde face of his daughter Diane, framed by a set of Koss headphones. She focused on her father, her shocked expression rapidly changing into a big, happy smile.

"Daddy!" she cried, taking her headphones off, getting up, and rushing to him. "Dad, you're home."

She was about to hug him, when she noticed the bandage. "My God, what happened to *you*?"

"Tell you later."

Scarborough wanted to hold her. He wanted to grab her and

hold her a very long time. But instead, as he did ever since she had reached puberty and filled out, he confined himself to a peck on her cheek. When she put her arms around him, and hugged him, he tensed up. She was too much like a young Phyllis. Besides, he simply wasn't a physically warm man; he hadn't been brought up that way by his parents. He let his daughter hug him for two seconds, and then he gently pried her away. "You've cut your hair," he said. "I liked it long. But what are you doing here? I thought you weren't going to be here till next Monday?"

"Change of plans." She backed away from him, reaching out and touching the white bandage gently. "There's something I have to talk to you about. Something *very* important. But that can wait. I want to know what happened to you! You're home so late! I'm still on Midwest time, so I just thought I'd sit down here awhile and listen to your wonder box here."

"What . . . You're into jazz and classical now?" he said, startled.

"Naw . . ." she said, pointing to a CD carrying-case, lying amidst a sprawl of Wise potato chips, onion dip and a half-empty bottle of Classic Coke. "I brought my own."

He went over to the CD player, and picked up the empty jewel-box. "Depeché Mode, huh? Sounds fashionable."

"Electronic pop, Dad. Do you want to hear some?"

"No thanks, Diane. I just hope that my Fischer hasn't been hopelessly offended by youthful garbage." He smiled when he said it—they always playfully sparred about their different musical tastes. It was safe territory for a release of the many tensions between them.

"Well, if it can take the dying cat howls of Mingus and Coltrane, then it can probably bear up to D. Mode. Although, this *is* a very sonically full recording, Daddy dear. I just hope I didn't blow any tubes or anything." She picked up her Coke and sipped it.

Scarborough was pleased to see that she was wearing the red blouse, and the necklace that he had given her this past Christmas. She was also wearing Opium perfume, her mother's favorite. Scarborough wasn't so happy about that.

"No, really, Dad, what the hell happened to your face?"

He sighed. "I guess you'll hear about it eventually. I don't want you to worry, though." The tremors again, inside. He went to the table where he kept a couple bottles of Scotch and poured some Glenlivet into a clean glass. "It's an isolated incident, and I guess I knew that it was bound to happen sooner or later."

"Whatever are you talking about? Out with it, Dad! You hem and haw so much when you've got something important to say. I can't stand it."

He took a gulp of the amber stuff. "I had a lecture today. University of Maryland. Some nutcase took a couple potshots at me."

"Daddy!" She nearly dropped her bottle of Coke, her expression changing entirely. She was staring, horrified, at his face.

"Oh, none of the bullets actually touched me," he said, reaching up reflexively and touching his wounds. "Splinters from the podium. Very superficial. Unfortunately, a man who was on stage was hit by one. Killed, too."

"That's awful!"

He drank the rest of his Scotch. "Yes."

It was clear she wanted to go to him and hold him again, but he countered the possibility by turning away to his bottle and pouring himself another drink. "I'm okay, though. A little shaken up . . . more by the shooting and the death than by this little wound here."

"Well, I just thank God you're okay."

"If God had anything to do with it, I'd probably be in the morgue now," he said, a touch of bitterness in his voice.

Diane said nothing. Religion was one of the touchy points of their relationship, and she clearly didn't care to deal with her father's thoughts on God. Awkwardly, she put the Coke down and wrapped her arms around herself, as though she were cold. "You must be really wired now, Dad."

"Yes. A bit paranoid, too. I heard you knock that stack of CDs over from upstairs. Thought you were some assassin, out to finish the job!"

"Did you call the police?" she asked.

"No. Maybe subconsciously I figured it was you. You do, after all, have a tendency to knock things over." He looked at his glass, thinking about taking another sip. But he could already feel the whiskey singing in his veins, and clouding his mind a touch. He decided he'd had enough for now. "Anyway, everything's okay now, Diane. But I want to know what this important thing is that you *have* to talk to me about?''

''Maybe we should wait till tomorrow,'' she said, looking doubtful. ''Maybe we both should get a good night's sleep first. It's been a long day for both of us and—''

Suddenly, she wasn't twenty years old anymore. To Scarborough, she was just eight years old, in pigtails, gap-toothed and guilty. ''Diane!'' he said in a deep, commanding but fatherly tone. ''Tell me *now*!''

She cringed a bit, and looked away. But then, recovering she stood up straight, took a deep breath and became more herself— damnably independent, frightfully like Phyllis at her most appealing.

''Dad, I've had the most incredible experience. And you're the only one who can help me come to grips with it. Actually, Tim and I—we had it together. You can help us both—Tim thinks so too. But you're going to have to grow for us . . . reach into the unknown . . .''

''Oh no, I see it coming . . . What new religion is it this time . . . the Quakers . . . the Mystical Nabobs of Narcissism?''

''Dad, I'm very serious. Tim and I—well, we saw an Unidentified Flying Object.''

''What?'' It was like a Kennedy child telling Papa Joe they were turning Republican.

''And there's more, Dad. We think that we were abducted by creatures from the UFO. Abducted, and then released—but somehow . . . changed.''

He was stunned. Scarborough couldn't believe his ears. His own daughter—spouting this *garbage*!

''This is a joke, right?'' he said, shaking his head as though she'd just struck him across his face. ''You *know* how I feel about this subject, so you and your Irish hooligan have concocted a grand April fool's joke for the old man!''

She shook her head no, standing her ground firmly, staring him straight on. ''No, Dad. I wouldn't joke about something so very serious. Two nights ago, Timothy Reilly and I were in our car. We saw a saucer-shaped vehicle, covered with odd lights landing beyond a field. We got out to investigate, and walked a ways, we think.''

''You *think*? You don't *know* for sure?''

''No. Because the next thing we knew, we were back in the

car and it was dawn. We had no memories of what had transpired the night before, Dad. Tim is arranging for a hypnotist to take us back through whatever experience we had. I knew I had to reach you right away, to talk to you about this. I figured you would want to share in our exploration of this . . . well, this whatever it is."

Everett Scarborough felt dizzy. For a long moment, his brain seemed to simply freeze up, unable to engage. He stared at Diane, and saw for the very first time, not his daughter, but a *stranger*, someone he didn't know, didn't understand, didn't *want* to understand. All this New Age religiosity was hard enough to take. He knew that part of it was a normal rebellion against parental disposition. He'd humored her as much as possible, indulging in arguments with her as much for her sake as his own. If he agreed with her, her penchant for perverse rebellion would not be satisfied. Meditation was okay. Crystals? Harmless enough. Channelling and rebirthing? A bit outré, but he'd humored her. But abduction by beings from a flying *saucer*?

"How sharper than a serpent's tooth," he whispered, going to his Glenlivet bottle.

"What? Dad, are we going to talk about this? Are you going to look at me even? Have you forgotten I *am* your flesh and blood. Don't you care about me?"

He poured the Scotch into the glass, he drank two swallows' worth, knowing that a *barrel* of the stuff would be insufficient. "We'll talk about this in the morning, all right, Diane?"

She looked down at the floor, her shoulders sagging, a moistness appearing in her eyes. "All right, Dad," she said in a disappointed tone.

"Go to bed now. Mrs. Morgan's already prepared your room. You know where everything is."

"Yes. I'll go. But there's more, and we're going to have to talk in the morning, okay? We never talk, and this is really something serious, something important that needs to be discussed by you and I, just you and I." She said it in a flat voice, as though it were a previously prepared speech that she now recited simply by rote.

He mumbled a disgruntled "Yes," and she started away, climbing the steps, while he finished his drink and watched her go, hearing her feet ascend.

He went to get another drink, then selected a Deutsche Gramaphone CD of Beethoven's Ninth, knowing he'd not be able to sleep for awhile yet.

He knew Diane would get the message. He always played Beethoven's Ninth when he was royally pissed.

Scarborough turned on the Fischer, and started the CD, sitting back in his Eames chair. Beneath him, a spill of potato chips crunched.

Maybe, he thought, it would have been better if that assassin, that guy in the black raincoat, *hadn't* missed.

CHAPTER
FIVE

When the phone call came at seven in the morning, he was working out in his home gym.

Woodrow Justine pushed the two hundred pounds' worth of barbell and Olympic weights up, eased them down again, feeling his pectorals strain at the load. He could already feel the lactic acid accumulating in the muscles, and now he was just pushing past the burn-point . . . the place where strength training did the most work. That was the extraordinary trick that the truly cut, truly bulky guys had learned: Take the reps up to where you can't go any more—and then, somehow *go* farther. Stripping, pyramiding, rest-burning—there were several methods, but the effects were the same. Hypertrophy to the max.

So when the phone rang, it annoyed Woodrow Justine terribly. He'd just gotten home last night from a whole week in the middle of the country, and he was looking forward to some R and R. If it hadn't been his special, restricted line—the one from Headquarters, the Company Line, as he called it, he wouldn't have answered.

With an expulsion of breath, Woodrow guided the barbell

back, and let it drop into the cradle of the Weider bench's extended arms, where it clanged to a shaky rest. He got up and padded over the mat-strewn wood floor of his gym, across the carpeting in his den, past the hamster cages, to his desk, upon which one of the three phones was ringing, flashing a red light.

He picked up the phone. "One-one-oh-six," he said, his voice still breathless from the exertion. "Bananas for lunch!"

"Hold the mayo," said a terse voice. "Number Two here, Woody. Sorry to bother you. Gotta call you back to duty."

He blinked. He knew it had to be important, they usually liked to give him enough rest so that he'd be in maximum shape when they needed him. So, he didn't say, "But I just got off a solid week of work!" which was what he felt. No, that wasn't Woodrow Justine's style at all. Besides, he didn't know what they had for him. It could be something worthwhile!

"Okay. What's the scoop?" He took the end of the towel around his neck and he patted off the perspiration from his forehead and temples.

"We've got a one o'clock Pan Am flight for you to Washington National. Tickets are at LAX. We'll meet you at the airport with instructions and equipment. Just bring your muscles and your brain."

"Yeah, sure," he said in his usual monotone voice. "Tell me, though, what do I got."

"You're gonna like this, Wood. You've got a Code Four."

Woodrow Justine took a deep breath, let it out, feeling a delicious shiver play along his back.

Code Four. Woody's Fave, as people in his section called it. Termination with extreme prejudice. Plus the possibility of a little preliminary persuasion thrown in, if possible. Read: torture.

"Yeah," said Woody. "Yeah, okay. Those things come along so seldom, I'm *always* ready for 'em. What's the make?"

"Tell you the full story when you get here. But it involves Scarborough."

Woody grinned. "That jerk! Great!"

"I'm personally going to be there to meet you, Woodrow, and you'll get the full details then." The man hung up with no farewell, as usual. Business, with no à la mode. That suited Woodrow Justine just fine. He checked the clock, decided that he had time to do a few more sets before he had to get ready to go. Good to get pumped up, man. *Primed*. He could go out like a light on the plane, take a nice nap, and be ready to go all night, if necessary. But first, he had to get primed.

Primed.

On the way back, he stopped at the hamster cages. Obviously Conchita, his maid, had filled the water bottles and the food bowls yesterday. The sunflower seeds in the three cages were plentiful, and the carrots and lettuce, half-nibbled away, looked almost fresh. In the central cage, Albert, the great-great grandson of Woodrow Justine's first breeding hamster, Sniffles, was racing pell-mell in the cage's circular running-track. The central cage was a traditional wire affair. The left cage was actually a large glass aquarium, where Justine kept the bulk of his hamsters. The right cage was a colorful and complex modular affair, consisting of tunnels and skywalks and cupolas for the creatures' amusement. Justine had twenty-two hamsters now, with a new batch on the way, now that Mildred was pregnant.

Woodrow Justine loved his hamsters.

"Code Four, Al," he said to the running hamster as he peered into the cage. "Sorry to leave, you guys, but I got a Code Four. Conchita will take care of you, don't worry."

Albert just kept on running to nowhere, but some of the others looked up and twitched their whiskers at him, their round dark eyes popped cutely from their golden fur. April Bluesbuster yawned, showing a cute set of incisors. In the corner, Grandpa Bluesbuster slept in his pile of newspaper shreds, snoring. Grandpa was going a little grey around the edges, but he still ran a mean wheel, yes sir. Justine blew a hard puff of air onto the hamster, startling it awake. It spun completely around, revealing the soft white fur on its stomach, its little claws held up defensively, its eyes wide and confused.

"Just a joke, Grandpa!" said Justine. "Just a joke!"

Chuckling, he wiggled his fingers toot-a-loo to his hamster brood, then fairly skipped back to his weight room, where he commenced a spirited workout, including leg extensions and another set of bench presses, along with lateral curls and squats.

Woodrow Justine was twenty-nine, and he'd worked for the U.S. government since he was eighteen years old, when he'd joined the marines right out of high school. An exemplary first two years mastering a number of different technical trainings, as well as a startling expertise at martial arts and weaponry, promoted him quickly. He'd been stationed at a number of hot spots around the world, including the Philippines and Beirut, where he just managed to not get blown up, but his real showing came during the invasion of Grenada, when he stormed that Caribbean island with the elan and determination of a young John Wayne. Soon, a special branch of the Central Intelligence Agency came knocking at his door. A number of interviews and a battery of tests later, Justine was invited to work for his country in a different capacity—an operative for the CIA. He was trained another six months before he was put into the field, where he quickly became known for his dependably ruthless and efficient methods to deal with potentially unpredictable situations. After three years of first-rate service, not just in the United States but in various other parts of the world, doing what he laughingly called his James Bond service, he had been contacted by yet another affiliated branch of the CIA. A highly secret branch . . . so secret that it was unclear if it was truly a branch—or the tree itself.

These were the Editors.

In just three years, Woodrow Justine had become a Junior Editor, assigned to Special Project, Codename: Skylark. He was entrusted with highly classified secret information, and the power that it imbued. He reveled in the power, and was openly amused about the secrets he knew. Amused, because, as a controlled psychotic personality, it fit in perfectly with his paranoid purview of the universe. He ate his medicine like a good boy, got his checkups regularly—and in turn, the U.S. government paid him, taxed him, and assigned him people to kill. All for a good cause, of course. Justine was nothing if not a patriot. His victims were enemies of democracy—even if they didn't know that they were. All in all, Woodrow Justine was extremely grateful to his country, and the intricate surprapower structure that *really* ran it. Justine was a dangerous psychotic killer. If not for the marines and the CIA, he'd be a *criminal* psychotic killer. The difference was spelled out in rank, prestige, salary and perks—which included this beautiful suburban home in Venice, California, just a half mile from World's Gym. A beautiful home in the city he loved, El-Ay, Cee-Ay—mellow city without a soul. But with lots of distractions.

When he was finished with his abbreviated workout (usually, he preferred two to three hours), Woodrow Justine flexed a bit in front of a full-length mirror. Justine kept himself muscular and sinewy, but not ostentatiously muscle-bound, like a lot of weight lifters. He kept a perfectly symmetrical body, geared to work well with his training in karate and aikido. He loved weight-training because it gave him such *control* over his body. People said that he looked like the rock 'n' roll star Bryan Adams—all the way to the pockmarked face. Justine knew they probably wondered why, as an Angeleno with easy access to plastic-surgery clinics, he didn't smooth out his face a bit. Not that it was deeply pitted or anything—just that it didn't fit with the rest of his body. Justine rubbed his face now, frowning at his visage. What they didn't know was how important it was to him to keep his face rough, to keep the memories of his teenaged years when the acne had erupted, just one more nail in the coffin of a social outcast. No, he wanted to remember, he wanted to savor that pain still burning in his soul. It gave such fire and immediacy to his purpose. Maybe his victims weren't his classmates, or his principals or teachers back in that Houston, Texas, suburb . . . but they were just the same. People were all the same, they were just pieces of shit bobbing in this cesspool called earth. Yeah, old Charlie Whitman\ back on that Texas tower had the right idea . . . but he wasn't as smart as Woody Justine. A psycho can kill just as many people as he wants, as long as he has the law on his side.

Justine admired his biceps and his delts and his traps one more time, loving the way the bright California sunlight created a sheen over the patina of sweat on his skin. He loved the smell of his musky sweat, full in his nostrils. He could feel his cock getting hard in his gym shorts, just looking at himself, and he rubbed it, feeling a tingle of urgency.

Maybe he could call Conchita, he thought. The wetback was always looking to make a few more pesos. Or maybe Candy.

But no, he was on the way to deal with a mark, and it wasn't good to shoot a wad within a day of a kill.

"Hands off, pal," said Justine, slapping his own wrist playfully. "Cold shower, bud. Gotta be *primed*, Woodrow Justine. Can't have that lightning comin' outta your *balls*!"

After his shower, he packed some light articles into his flight bag. He didn't have to take any weapons . . . That was the nice thing about working for a widespread government network. They always had just what he needed, waiting for him. He went on airplane rides clean as a newborn. And if perchance he needed to carry heat—well, they'd give him a license and a badge to boot. Justine felt well-cared-for by his bosses. And to work for such great minds—knowing that destiny was within the grip of intelligent, molding hands . . . Yes, he had found his ecological niche, he knew. He was proud to be a Junior Editor. He was proud to kill for his country.

He parked his luggage by the door, along with a note for Conchita, who would be in on Monday morning to clean and feed and rewater the animals. Just in case. Who knew, he might be back by then.

He had a few errands to run, so he was leaving early. But there was one more thing to do. Justine went back to his den and kneeled before his hamster cages.

"Hey, kids," he said. "Sorry to have to leave you so soon, but I've gotta job to do. You all know what Daddy does, don't you? And that's one of your reasons to be here, to help him, right? So whose turn is it to show your love?"

None of the hamsters volunteered, but several responded to the sound of his voice, wiggling their whiskers and sniffing the air, coming forward to the perimeter of their worlds to peer out at the Great Being who fed them. The cages smelled of fresh *Los Angeles Times*, rodent urine, and that elusive perfume of *life* which dangled over all animate beings. Justine filled his nostrils full of the effluvia, and held his hands beneficently out to the creatures before him. "Lo! Behold your maker and your benefactor," he began to intone. "Your feeder, your father, your god. Bow down and worship me, my children, for I am a jealous god, and will have no other gods before me!"

The hamsters twitched. One yawned and went about his business, chewing on a carrot stick. Another sniffed a female tentatively.

"This morning, I seek a Chosen One," murmured this muscular Jehovah as he hovered over the hamsters. "A Chosen One, to perform the ritual of Love. Let it be known amongst your number—I need a volunteer!"

For several long minutes, Justine watched as the hamsters went about their business. Then, one young male—Earnest, as he recalled by the dabs of colored paint marking the rodent's back—got on the wheel and began to exercise.

"Ah!" said Justine, smiling. "The Chosen One."

He opened up the cage, stopped the wheel with his hand. He reached down and gently grabbed Earnest around the midsection, pulling him out of the cage.

The hamster squealed in protest, squirming and kicking. But when Justine started to stroke the back of his neck, the hamster's hackles went down, and he became calm under the familiar ministrations of his master.

"Good, very good, Earnest. You are my beloved. Come, and I will show you my bounty." Gently petting the hamster, Justine carried him through the hallway, through the cool and dark dining room, tastefully decorated in a modern style, into the kitchen, brightly lit in the California sun. Stainless steel gleamed, and newly waxed linoleum glowed, smelling of a gentle pine scent. Though he seldom used it, preferring to eat out, Justine kept his kitchen extremely clean and well-equipped with the latest in can openers and Oster food-processors. His earliest memories of kitchens were wretched—gas fires and garbage and heat and spattering grease. *His* kitchen was immaculate.

"Here, Earnest, look," said Justine, opening the door of his refrigerator. "Nice, huh. Food. We can drop the me, God; you, servant line now. It's just you and me, Earnest. Want some lettuce, pal? Let's get you some lettuce."

Justine opened the crisper and tore off a leaf of lettuce from the head inside. He closed the door and carried the lettuce and the hamster over to the counter by the sink. He put the lettuce down, and let the hamster go right beside it. The hamster tested the air with a few sniffs, and then settled down to nibble at the green, crunchy leaf.

Justine leaned over, his head propped on his hands, watching his pet. "That's right. Enjoy, Earnest." He looked over to the sink for a moment, smiled, then turned his head back. "You see, pal. It's like this. I need you. I'm about to go on a Code Four . . . Yeah, really exciting, huh? And I'm not ready yet. Oh, I worked out, and I packed—but a guy in my position—well, he's gotta get ready in a different way. He's gotta get *primed*. And that's how you can help me."

The hamster just chewed and chewed obliviously, happy with his fresh meal.

"That's right, Earnest. Another few bites. Enjoy, enjoy."

Justine took a deep breath and closed his eyes. He visualized the man that Two had mentioned, Dr. Everett Scarborough. For three years, Justine's life had hovered around Scarborough's. He knew Scarborough, he'd read all his books, he'd seen him lecture many times. He'd never actually shook hands with the man, or spoken with him, but nonetheless, Woodrow Justine knew his type. Arrogant, haughty, charming—a member of the invisible ruling social class of this country. Justine hated the man for this, and other reasons.

As though preparing his mind Samurai-like in Zen meditation, Woodrow Justine focused on his mental image of the popular scientist. "Scarborough!" he whispered.

With one quick motion—with reflexes trained for incredible speed—Justine grabbed the hamster, stepped over to the sink, and stuffed the squirming rodent into the drain, past the rubber guard that stood above the garbage disposal unit. The hamster squeaked shrilly in protest, scrabbling to get out. Justine topped the drain halfway by its rubber plug with his left hand. With his right, he reached over to the electrical switch.

"Yeah!" he said, and he turned the switch on.

The rodent was able to emit one last shriek before the grinding began. The unit gargled and coughed and sputtered on the bones and the fur, but in the end it chewed the thing up as though it were just the latest hunk of garbage pushed into its maw.

A small gout of blood splashed from between the rubber plug and the metal, landing on Justine's fingers. He reached over and turned off the disposal, then he took a deep breath of the fresh blood-smell that hovered over the sink.

Yes, he was primed now.

Woodrow Justine was ready for his assignment.

He was ready for Dr. Everett Scarborough.

CHAPTER
SIX

"You know," said Jake Camden to the Iowa farmer, "you look to me to be like the most honest man I ever met." The reporter for the *National Intruder* took a drag of his Camel and blew out the smoke, without taking the nearly consumed butt from his mouth. He squinted at the hayseed through watery blue eyes and started scribbling something on his long yellow journalist pad, its torn manila flap hanging precariously from the coiled wire at the top. "Yeah, I see an angle. Clyde Whitcomb, honest farmer from the land of Honest Abe Lincoln tells his UFO story of terror!"

"Mister," said the stolid-faced man in the crew cut, his face wrinkled from the sun. "Lincoln was from Illinois."

"Oh yeah, too bad!" Camden sucked another lungful of smoke from the cigarette, dropped it onto the ground and stamped it out. He reached for the fence post, grabbed the cup of coffee the farmer's wife had made for him, and took a bitter gulp, regretting the previous evening's carousing in the Iowa City college bar, where some students had shown him their superior liver power. But then, if he hadn't gone to Dirty Harry's, he wouldn't have gotten to talk to that nude dancer, Carrie, either; and if he hadn't talked to Carrie, he wouldn't have gotten laid last night. Oh, well. Chalk up another night of grist for the journalistic mill. Besides, halfway through sexual congress, (with a condom, natch—the tabloid he worked for had been VD-conscious long before the AIDS crisis) a story had occurred to him: "UFO Exotic Dancers Steal Sperm From Customers." He intended to investigate *that* story thoroughly!

"So anyway, how tall were these creatures you saw coming out

of the landed flying saucer?'' His voice was hoarse and rough
with hard living, but it had a peculiar, comforting effect on
most interviewees. Camden figured they probably subconsciously
felt they were jawing with a regular at the local tavern.

The man—a taciturn fellow about fifty years old with broken
teeth, wearing grass-stained overalls—stared at Camden quizzically.
''Mr. Camden, I just seen some funny lights, and maybe the
outline of some kind of air-ship earlier this year. I reported it to
the police, and the local paper gotta hold of it.''

Camden nodded as though the farmer had just imparted a
fact of the greatest consequence, and jotted a note onto his pad.
''And where did you say you actually *saw* the alien UFO, Mr.
Whitcomb?''

''I was in the south quarter-fields, yonder,'' the farmer said,
pointing past the sagging barn and a farmhouse badly in need
of paint to where the horizon dipped into corn-fringed haze.
''Just finishing up laying down some fertilizer. It was after
dusk. I hear a buzzing kind of sound, I look up. There's these
lights—red and purple—and they're streaking along about five
hundred yards away. The thing whisks along real quick, then it
stops and hovers—and then it zips away, even quicker. Scared
the hell outta me—never seen nothin' like it.''

Jake Camden sucked on the eraser of his pencil, regarding
the silo and the fence that ran off from it. A motley collection
of farm animals were strewn along the landscape, a couple
cows, a pig behind a fence, some chickens pecking away
behind the house, and finally a mangy tan-and-brown mongrel
that crouched near its farmer, perspiration dripping from its
tongue. The farm had that manure-and-mud, urine-and-hay
smell that every American farm had to one degree or another.
Camden knew; he'd been to plenty of farms. He was considering a book called *Old Macdonald Had a UFO*, which would
detail farmers' adventures with extraterrestrials.

''Had any animals die on you recently, Mr. Whitcomb?
Die . . . or maybe . . . disappear?''

''Well, old Gertie, a milk cow . . . she passed on in the
winter. But that weren't no surprise.''

Camden jotted down ''Gertie—cow—cattle mutilation victim.''

''I see. Now tell me . . . how have you and the Missus been
sleeping since you saw that UFO?''

''Well, Peg, she sleeps like a mule . . . But me, I've got a touch of the lumbago, and I've been waking up lately in the middle of the night.''

Camden scribbled, Abduction . . . Late night awakenings . . . Screened memories.

"How about dreams, Mr. Whitcomb. You have any unusual dreams lately, like about little men with dark, almond-shaped eyes and fingers with only one knuckle?''

"Well, I don't rightly remember many of my dreams, Mr.—''

"Camden. Jake Camden, the most famous UFO journalist in the world.'' Camden pulled a crumpled pack of Camels out of his rumpled light blue linen jacket, sleeves rolled up Miami-Vice style to expose skinny forearms. "You ever see *Close Encounters of the Third Kind*?''

"Nope. Can't say I have. That a movie?''

Jeez. This was going to be a tough nut to crack. He'd hoped to get a full story out of this guy, but he'd be lucky if he could use it as a paragraph in his monthly UFO-Roundup column. What he needed was as an angle, something unique to hang his story on. But what? This bozo was pure-bred midwestern boring, and about as talkative as a tree stump. Camden supposed he just had to go fishing.

"Ever heard of Mothman, Mr. Whitcomb?''

"Don't tell me . . . that's a comic book, right?''

"How about Men in Black . . . Any strange-looking guys in black suits roll up here in black Cadillacs, asking you questions about the unidentified flying saucer?''

"Nope.''

Camden plucked a set of cards from his back pocket. His good old prompt cards. If *these* didn't work, this was a lost cause and he should have just stayed in bed. "Mr. Camden, I want to thank you for bearing witness to the facts you've just related. I'm a dedicated journalist, sworn to dig out the truth in this vital and mysterious field. Can I ask you to just give me your *opinion* about what you saw . . . And about flying saucers in general.''

"I told you what I saw. I ain't got no opinion on it. 'Cept that it might not have been no alien flying saucer. Shit, I seen some air force and army vehicles around here these last years, and there ain't no official United States Armed Forces' base within a couple hundred miles of here.''

Camden was already dealing out the five Alien Identification Cards, marked with drawings of various types of reported extraterrestrials, and was considering sliding in the picture cards of Richard Nixon and Elvis, just in case Whitcomb might choose to fixate on one of those midwestern cultural icons. "Elvis Moons Farmer in UFO," might be an okay headline. Or maybe "Richard Nixon's Flying Saucer on Top Secret Political Junket in Midwest." But then Whitcomb's words penetrated, and Camden's head jerked up and he smiled, taking a quick slap at a huge horsefly that just started to strafe him.

"What did you just say, Mr. Camden?"

"I said, I don't have no opinion about those lights . . ."

"No, about there being no official U.S. air base nearby." Camden stopped a moment, then took out a white handkerchief and gently mopped his forehead. He relaxed. This was the angle. His mistake had being going straight through with the outré stuff. Your average farmer might speak in tongues or handle snakes at his weekly religious meeting, he might see the Beast of Revelations squiggling through every worldwide headline, dragging the date closer to Armageddon. But God forbid you should talk about strange things like extraterrestrial visitations happening in scratch-ass county . . . Things that might be Of The Devil. No, a much more practical subject would doubtless unlock the floodgates.

Camden pursed his lips. "You know, you got a real nice place here, sir. I hear that the U.S. government hasn't been much help to you farmers in the last few years."

Whitcomb stiffened noticeably. "Help! The bastards! I almost *lost* this place! My daddy gave it to me, and I almost lost the mortgage! Had to sell a few of my best acres. Listen, Mister, you want a story, you write about what this here administration in Washington's been doing to us, the *backbone* of this country."

"Yeah. I'll mention it. But tell me—you think these lights you saw . . . you think maybe they were from some government flying saucer or something?"

"I tell you, that would be a hell of a lot easier for me to believe."

"Maybe the government is spying on you Iowa farmers, huh? From a secret base in the middle of the state?"

"Could be. Wouldn't put it past the sons of bitches!"

"And then again, maybe these flying saucers are from outer space—and they're working for the CIA, checking up on you farmers."

"Yeah!" Whitcomb's face was getting red, and his eyes were glowing now with fervor. "You know, come to think of it, Mr. Camden—"

"Jake! Please, just call me Jake."

"Jake. I guess you're right. Something *damn* funny's goin' on, and I wouldn't be a bit surprised if some superstitious agency in Washington, D.C., weren't behind it."

"Surreptitious, you mean. *Surreptitious* agency of the government—like the CIA, or the NSA, or the FBI, or some branch maybe of the military!" Camden cleared his voice and lowered his head in a confidential manner toward the farmer. "Just between you and me, Clyde, this is a secret project I'm working on right now. Did you realize that there's been a top-secret cover-up project going on with, at the very least, the CIA and the air force ever since a flying saucer crashed in Roswell, New Mexico in the late forties?"

"No!"

"You bet. A regular cosmic Watergate. I have UFO-ologist friends who have been trying to get at the papers concerning that, as well as vital papers through the Freedom of Information Act. And let me tell you, even those papers have been radically censored! Washington is hiding something, and goodness knows, part of that insidious project might be based— *in your own backyard*!"

Whitcomb blinked and jumped back a full foot, his eyes darting about as though looking for government officials hiding behind his rotting fence posts. "You know," he said, working his jaw as though literally chewing on his thoughts. "I *have* heard tell, there's been some mighty pee-culiar things going on at the old Bennington farm, about thirty miles north of here. I never paid it no mind . . . Lots of folks round here got nothing better to talk about 'cept ridiculous gossip. But I been hearing stuff about the Bennington place for about six, seven years now—ever since ol' Rick Bennington sold the place and moved to Sun City, Arizona."

"Like what?"

"Oh, lots of activity. Noises. And, like, helicopters! Now what would helicopters be doing in the farming business!"

"How interesting." Jake jotted down a note in his book. "I'm definitely going to check up on this, Clyde. But right now, I want to get back to you and your UFO. Clyde, like I say, you're clearly an honest man, so I'm going to have to ask that you don't tell a living soul what I'm about to tell you."

Whitcomb's eyes were big and round, and he fairly oozed perspiration under the growing heat of the sun. The man was rank by now, as a matter of fact, but Jake could take it a little longer. His final hook was just sinking in. "You have my word, Jake," said the farmer, licking his lips with growing excitement.

"Clyde, you're just one of a growing number of farmers in the Midwest who've had a series of frightening, horrible experiences with UFOs. And after talking to you, I'm starting to believe there's growing evidence that extraterrestrials are being employed by the United States government to scare farmers off their beloved land!"

The man's jaw dropped. "No!"

Jake shook his head up and down, pure sincerity burning in his eyes. "And you're the man who's going to help me to *stop* this loathsome practice!" He pulled up the cards, removing the Nixon and Elvis pictures, and mixing in a few other renditions of aliens, some with long necks, some with big noses, some with pointed ears. "You may not realize it, Clyde, but I can just smell it coming off of you . . . You've had direct contact with aliens from a flying saucer! Now, these buggers have great powers with which they can control minds. They do things like make you forget you talked with them . . . They put up, what we call in this business, screen memories. You think you just went out back to take a dump in the crapper . . . when actually, what you did was to talk to an ET! Now I want you to look at these official artist renderings of the types of aliens that have been encountered by normal Joes like you over the years. And I want you to tell me *which picture* strikes a familiar chord in your memory."

Wide-eyed, the farmer agreed and studied each of the pictures carefully.

Readying his camera for a shot of Clyde and the alien he picked out, Jake Camden had already started to write the story up in his head: "Government UFO Slaves Terrorize God-Fearing Farmer."

Yeah. Perfect!

CHAPTER
SEVEN

Everett Scarborough awoke, the ringing of his telephone slicing through his headache. He groped for the phone, picked it up, and muttered into the receiver, "Yes?"

"Good morning, Mr. Scarborough," a voice began. "This is Lieutenant James Daniels of the Montgomery County Police. We were asked to make sure you were okay. We've had a patrol car pass your house at half-hourly intervals last night, and we saw no irregularities, but we're calling this morning for courtesy's sake."

Scarborough looked at his alarm clock. Five minutes before eleven o'clock. He had a headache, but he suspected that it was as much from his facial wounds as it was from the Scotch. Still, it hurt.

"Yes, Lieutenant, thank you so much for calling. I'm just fine. In fact, I'm sleeping in."

"Don't blame you, sir, and sorry to wake you up. We'll be checking in this afternoon. You'll be there?"

"That's right, and I really appreciate your concern."

"Just doing my job, Dr. Scarborough," said the lieutenant, his voice betraying an air of hard-boiled self-importance.

Scarborough hung up the phone, dragged himself out of bed and into the bathroom, where he opened the medicine cabinet and pulled out his supply of Veganin. He punched two white tablets through the foil and took them with a glass of water. Every time he went to England, he made sure to stock up on the pain reliever, which consisted mostly of pure aspirin, but also contained trace-elements of codeine, a nonprescription drug in the United Kingdom in small amounts. They erased his

Scotch headaches in a matter of minutes—and perhaps, that was what they'd been designed specifically for. He imagined some Scot chemist with a morning hangover, experimenting for just the right cure for the headache...Well, anyway, they worked for him.

Scarborough took off his bandage, and he took a short, hot shower. Short, because he wanted to get downstairs as soon as possible, to talk to Diane. He still couldn't believe what she'd told him the night before, but he realized now that he'd overreacted. He wanted to make amends and hear out her story. There was more than one way to skin a cat. And this was one *hairy* cat! By the morning light, however, his self-confidence had returned, and he knew that since such a thing *could not* have actually happened to Diane, it logically followed that he could prove to her, carefully and patiently, that she must have had some kind of illusion. Drug-induced, perhaps. He didn't like to think about Diane taking drugs, although he knew she probably did. A lot of bright kids dabbled. Why not Diane? Phyllis had tried LSD in the sixties, as a college professor, and although he didn't brag about it much, Scarborough had actually had a period, after he'd met Phyl, that he'd let her prod him into smoking marijuana, though truth to tell he'd never cared much for the stuff.

That was it. After he discussed her "experience" with her patiently, wisely, and thoroughly, he would tender the subject of her possible ingestion of illegal substances that might have tilted her mind toward this "delusional complex," as he had dubbed the psychological phenomenon. He would *not* be disapproving or even patronizing. He would simply offer it out as a possibility.

Scarborough examined his wounds. No stitches had been necessary, fortunately; and already the several wounds had scabbed. He put on the bandage anyway, making sure that it was loose enough to allow enough air on the wound. Then, he put on a flannel shirt and a pair of faded jeans—his usual Saturday attire, since he usually did some garden work on Saturday—and went downstairs.

Even from the steps, he could smell the bacon, the muffins and the fresh-perked coffee. He smiled to himself, and felt much better. Even alien abductions and potshots from wackos could not stop Saturday morning breakfast.

Diane was sitting in the dining room, reading the *Washington Post*, drinking coffee. In front of her was a stack of freshly baked blueberry muffins, jam, and butter.

"Hi, Dad," she said contritely. "How are you feeling?"

"Better," he said, leaning over and kissing the top of her head, his one expression of affection that had stayed the same since she was a very little girl. He went to the side table, and poured a cup of coffee from the electric percolator. He added some milk and sat down beside her.

"I fixed some bacon. How do you want your eggs?"

"Scrambled," he said, smiling. "Just like this poor old head."

She touched his arm. "Yesterday *was* bad, wasn't it. And I didn't help much. Sorry." She looked away, sipping at her coffee. Then she got up to go fix his breakfast, and stopped in her tracks. "This man who shot at you—I forgot to ask you, did they catch him?"

"No. Not yet, as far as I know. But I'm sure they will. By all evidence, the fellow was not a professional. He fired an automatic handgun from the *balcony*, for God's sake! The guy was a nut, whom I upset. In case you haven't noticed, I upset a lot of nut cases, a lot of loonies. I've been getting more threatening letters lately, too. I just put it down as an example of the growing mass psychosis in this country. But I never thought that someone would actually take a shot at me!"

"Well, I just hope that they get the guy."

"There's never security at these things . . . Never the need before. Now, I guess there will be. Too bad. But I meant to ask you . . . how did you get here last night? That flying saucer land you?" He smiled, but she grimaced at the lame joke.

"I flew, but in an airplane. I took a cab from the Bethesda Metro station."

"I figured as much—but there was always the possibility that one of your local friends picked you up at the airport."

"No. No one knows I'm here so soon—except for you. And Tim, of course." She touched his bandage gently. "I'm afraid for you, Dad. Maybe you shouldn't go on this lecture tour."

"Got to, dear." He sipped at his bracing coffee. "I have to push my book. There's got to be some antidote to this whole new UFO upsurge . . . Which reminds me, we have to talk." He cleared his throat. "I'm sorry for the way I reacted last night, but you have to know I was under a lot of strain. Diane, I will listen to this odd story of yours . . . And I will help you and Tim in whatever way I can."

"Oh, Daddy!" she said, her face suddenly lighting up. "I knew you'd come through." She hugged him hard, then bounced away happily. "I'll just fix your eggs, and then I'll tell you the whole crazy story."

"Crazy is the word for it, all right," Scarborough said, getting up and dragging his coffee over to the phone. "We'll straighten the whole thing out, I promise you."

He dialed Abe Novak's home phone number by memory. Better talk to him as soon as possible, and arrange for special precautions for the upcoming speaking tour. Abraham Novak was his speaker's agent—he worked in conjunction with the publishers when Scarborough had a book to push. In the past years, Novak not only had gotten his fee up—Scarborough pulled down a healthy 10,000 bucks for a simple speech, and much more for his special show, which was more expensive to produce and needed ''roadies''—he had also been successfully booking Scarborough for several years, book publicity or no book publicity. In fact, Dr. Everett Scarborough had become a national figure, a symbol of logic and science to match Isaac Asimov or Carl Sagan, although much more handsome, much more charming and witty. Last year, in fact, he'd even received movie offers . . . which he'd turned down. What he really wanted, was a PBS show. Scarborough had more than enough money to suit his chosen lifestyle. What he craved was a place in the history of science—perhaps in history, period. Besides, he enjoyed immensely his role as gladfly to the perpetrators of scientific folly, archvillain to the champions of pseudoscience.

"Yes?" a voice answered.

"Abe. This is Ev Scarborough. I guess you heard about last night."

"Everett! Everett, man, are you all right?"

"Sure. A few scratches."

"Yeah, I was just going to call you. Sheesh, if Henry hadn't of called me, I would've seen it in the papers! Who would've thought!"

Abraham Novak lived in Long Island and worked out of a Manhattan office. He and Scarborough knew each other socially before Scarborough had hit the lucrative lecture trail. It was only natural that the curly haired, frenetic booking agent and he should hook up. They had always known that they would make a great team in work, just as they made a great team in bridge.

"They're starting to crawl out of the woodwork, Abe," said Scarborough.

"You've mentioned the letters you've gotten. Any of them ever hint of what happened last night?"

"A few, but nothing I took seriously."

"Babe, you're in a scary new world here. I guess we've just been lucky so far."

"We'll just tack on security measures, right?"

"Sure, eventually. Right now, though, we postpone the speaking tour."

"What? Abe, we can't do that! I've got to push my book!"

"Why not? You got your radio and TV tour out of the way two weeks ago. Your book is on the lists, what more do you want?"

"I need to get out and speak with the people, Abe. That's what I need."

"You need it like you need a hole in your head. C'mon, Ev. You're the vaunted man of reason. Give it some thought. First, we ain't got time to do up security right for all the dates. Second, every psycho saucer-nut in the country is probably going to be inspired to copycat that goof last night. Third, I don't want to lose a goose that lays golden eggs—and can match me drink for drink at any bar. Sorry to get all blubbery here, pal, but I don't want to lose you."

"You said postpone. How long?"

"Couple months. We're just talking a little time-displacement here. All your dates will understand after what happened last night. Besides, they're not going to really *want* you until you're properly prepared, anyway. They don't want dead bodies littering their stages."

Scarborough had a disquieting thought. "They're not going to think I'm *afraid*, are they?"

"After last night? I understand that you got right up and kept the crowd in control, Ev. That's a hero. It's an *idiot* who goes in knowing there might be bullets waiting for him."

A very reasonable suggestion, although truth to tell, Scarborough hated the idea of having geared up for this, his most elaborate lecture presentation, only to have to wait a couple of months to place it on the track. Still, it made a lot of sense. Maybe he could do a few more TV and radio dates to make up for the lost publicity. Although come to think of it, if the incident had made the national papers—well, *that* was publicity, wasn't it? He suddenly felt much better about the whole thing.

"When you put it that way, Abe, I guess it sounds much better. But you'll deal with all the hassle involved."

A sigh issued from the other end of the phone. "That's my job, Ev. So you take it easy, guy, and I'll be in contact."

They exchanged final pleasantries and Scarborough hung up. His public relations people could handle all the other stuff, he supposed. He'd release a simple statement to the press, and then do just what Abe suggested: lie low for a while.

Lie low, and deal with this odd business his daughter had dragged in.

He went back to the table and sipped at his coffee, considering how he was going to handle Diane. It took but a few thoughts; he'd consider her claims in the way he dealt with everything else in his life: rationally.

She brought in his bacon and eggs, along with a side of buttered toast. He thanked her and started eating while she settled in a neighboring chair. "So, should I start in on you now, or do you want to finish your breakfast?"

Even the few mouthfuls of food he'd managed to get down had improved his spirits tremendously. "Go ahead, I'll listen while I eat."

She reiterated what she had told him the night before, filling in details. As she spoke, Scarborough found it difficult to remain his usual rational self. He realized that he felt betrayed. That his *own daughter* should have one of these silly experiences— but then, when he thought it out, it actually made a kind of skewed sense. Diane's consciousness had always been drenched in rather mystical things. Even as a child, she lived with invisible companions, had her own private fairy world. And after all, at its core, alien abductions were simply the mystical experience du jour. Really, it wasn't that surprising for Diane to come home with this story.

Not only that, but this was apparently a different *kind* of alien adbuction. Not at all as bizarre. Neither Tim or Diane boasted stigmata from their experience—no scars, no holes in their necks or heads—that seemed the general rule in these abductions. Come to think of it, neither were they as upset or frightened or confused. It seemed a very *positive* thing, this UFO experience, more like a Maslovian peak-encounter shrouded by amnesia, leaving only vague lingerings of ecstasy.

Scarborough pointed this out.

"Yeah!" said Diane, excited. "Tim mentioned that as well. That's why we're not really sure what happened."

"Where's Tim now?"

"He's spending the weekend looking for a good hypnotist in Kansas City. I'm going back on Monday. Daddy, now that you're not going on this speaking tour—"

"You eavesdropped on my conversation with Abe, huh?"

"I overheard it. I caught the gist—and I think you *should* wait awhile before you go out again."

He nodded. "That's what's happening. So, I suppose you want me to go out with you and your beloved, chasing the wild extraterrestrials . . ."

"Oh, Daddy, would you? You're the *best* . . . And you know, you haven't been out in the field for a while." She sparkled with enthusiasm, her blue eyes shining as bright as her beautiful light hair. For a moment, Scarborough was almost swayed. But he'd made up his mind, and even the power of his daughter's personality could not persuade him otherwise.

"I was in the field for work on *Above Us Only Sky* last year, Diane. And the results were just the same as always, from the first time I started investigating UFO sightings twenty-five years ago. No conclusive evidence. *Nada.* Zip. And I don't care to waste my time on another case, even though my daughter is involved, because I know I'll find exactly what I've always found . . . nothing."

"Daddy. You're so stubborn! Just give us a few days . . . if only to *be* with me. This could be very important and exciting."

"Diane, you're the princess of self-dramatizers. Every waking moment is the most exciting part of your life. Even though I'm not going on my tour, I have a lot of other work to do. I can't waste it hunting snipe."

She stood up, her eyes suddenly molten with fury. "Oooh! I *hate* it when you're so patronizing!"

"Look, there's no reason to get upset, Diane. This is just a phase you're passing through like all the rest! Don't you think I've been around these twenty years to watch them all, from diapers onward! I'm sorry. And by the way, it really wouldn't look very good if this ever leaked out to the press. I can just see the *National Intruder* headlines now: 'UF-NO! Investigator's Beautiful Daughter Raped by Aliens!' ''

"A lot you'd care if I was!" she said, still fuming.

"Okay, let me run over this with you, Diane, since you refuse to read my books on the subject. I apologize if I sounded patronizing. I apologize if I overreact to these things sometimes—but you have to admit that this is even wilder and a lot more personal than when you thought you were a resurrected astrologer from ancient Lemuria."

"Oh, Daddy, I was just a junior in high school then! I'm a mature woman now! With every bit of your intelligence—and Mom's to boot! Give me some credit, okay?"

"Credit extended." He pushed the breakfast plate away, only a slice of toast uneaten. "To the matter at hand.

"In 1969, my four years of work for the air force on their Project Blue Book finally closed the case; the conclusion was that earth was *not* being visited by flying saucers holding beings from another planet in our galaxy, another galaxy—or even another dimension. I have personally investigated almost three hundred of the strongest sightings in the last twenty-five years. You are welcome to examine my files on every last one. The most significant ones have been written up in my books on the subject. In all these years, all these cases, not only have I not found anything resembling extraterrestrial artifacts, I have also discovered that virtually every bit of evidence has either been hearsay, unprovable—or simply hoaxed."

"But all the people who've seen them—experienced them! Dad, you can't deny that *something*'s out there! Now, I can prove nothing in my case. And I can't really actually prove I *love* you, scientifically. But I do love you . . . And something did happen to me!"

"Wait a minute. I'm not finished yet. I'm not saying that nothing actually happens to people. But I think that every case can either be explained by natural causes, psychological causes—or, most commonly, a combination of the two.

"Weather balloons, large stars . . . planets . . . clouds . . . ball lightning . . . fireballs . . . Goodness knows if we really understand all the meteorological phenomena that can happen on this planet. Diane, I've heard accounts of them all. And people won't go for the natural explanation. No, in general, they see something weird, and wow! They've seen flying saucers! Culturally, we're predisposed. Naturally, all the hoaxes just compound the problem. This whole Billy Meier thing in Switzerland, for example—a guy hangs a model of a saucer in front of a Super-8 camera, then tells the world some female ET has taken him back in time to talk to Jesus! I mean, come *on*!''

"But this doesn't have anything to do with that, Dad. I've told you my story. And you don't believe it. It's as simple as that!''

"Let me tell you a story, dear,'' Scarborough said, grasping at a last straw. He spoke gently and sincerely, his tone promising love and understanding to his daughter. "Last year, I went to one of those New-Age conventions—incognito. I had a mustache, a wig—I wore scruffy clothing, and even changed the color of my eyes with colored contact-lenses.''

"Daddy! You never told me this before!'' she said, clearly quite amused at the notion.

"Well, I guess I wanted to find out what the credulous were really like. I guess you're aware of the phenomenon that quantum physicists are talking about these days: even observation changes the observed. Well, I know that when these saucerites see me, they have immediate reactions—I wanted to see what they were like without my sour face interrupting their fun.

"Anyway, I went to see a speech by a lady who ran a UFO magazine. You'd think you'd get lots of information about sightings at such a speech, wouldn't you? Well, no such luck. What I got was a shy lady who spoke about feeling 'not of this earth' since she was a child. She spoke of feeling 'odd' in a physical body. Naturally, when she learned of the possibility of creatures from the stars, she was fascinated. Did she even question the possibility that there *were* no visitors from the stars! No, of course not. She was not only ready for them, she sought them out.

"Now, I thought that someone in the audience would point out the fallacy of this as a basis for intelligent and responsible journalism. But no one did. In fact, the predominant attitude of people was not only a fascination with the subject . . . but a predisposition toward belief, even a preparedness for the general announcement that aliens had contacted the government!

They were all involved in an almost religious belief-system which they reinforced amongst themselves."

"Daddy! That's wild! If they'd known you were there, they would have *crucified* you!" Diane seemed very intrigued at the whole notion.

"That's not all. I sat in on a lecture by none other than Dr. Fenton Leiberman."

Leiberman was one of Scarborough's archenemies—a UFO-ologist with a scientific degree who self-published his work and made a living touring and speaking about UFOs and the government cover-up. A good speaker, who used facts in a clever way, he was, nonetheless, in Scarborough's opinion, an overweight geek in bottle-bottom glasses with a psychological paranoid hang-up that needed psychiatric treatment.

"Daddy! Leiberman!" Diane was aghast and thrilled. Fenton Leiberman had once challenged Scarborough to a fistfight after one of their debates.

"Yes. And he happened to be talking about then-President Ronald Reagan's several remarks about a united earth, should aliens invade. Well, of course, being a UFO-ologist, he lapped this up! He didn't see it merely as the mental meanderings of an old president going senile—he saw it as proof positive that "YES!" the president himself admits we are being contacted by extraterrestrials!"

Diane shook her head. "That's all very interesting, Dad, but what does that have to do with me?"

Scarborough sighed. "Don't you see, dear? Your father is a noted UFO debunker. First, it's natural that you would want to rebel against the authority figure in your life . . . I guess it's part of the urge of achieving independence.

"Second—and maybe I'm being paranoid here, but I have to be careful of these kind of things—people *know* who you are. People who would like to have me put up for ridicule. Suppose someone set you up for this . . . Suppose it's a hoax, meant to make me look very, very silly!"

Diane looked stunned and hurt. "You think . . . you think that I would *trick* you! That I would do anything to hurt you? You *know* I'd never do anything like that, Dad!"

"Of course you wouldn't—not *consciously*, anyway. But believe me, there are plenty of people in this country, in this *world*, at this time, who would like nothing better than to have me held up as a laughingstock. And what better method than to fool a credulous, spacy daughter, and drag the noted scientist and debunker into his discrediting? Mind you, I'm not saying that this is the case. I'm just saying that it's something I have to consider. I've a reputation to uphold.''

''And your reputation is more important than your own daughter, your own flesh and blood?''

''No. But like I say, you've merely been the victim of a hoax—or you've suffered a delusion of some sort.'' He cleared his throat uncomfortably, about to move on to a touchy subject. ''Uhm, dear, I don't want to pry into private matters concerning you and your Irish hooligan—'' It was a long-standing fact that Scarborough did not approve of Timothy Reilly. ''But have you two been indulging in psychoactive drugs lately? This is a matter that I'm going to have to explore in my next book, since it's coming to my attention more and more that the age of UFOs coincides with the age of psychedelics . . .''

''Daddy, you know what!'' Diane said, standing up and pacing, throwing dramatic gestures about. ''You're simply impossible. Tim was right. He said that it would be useless to talk to you, that you'd never come back to help us out, that you're too much of a tightass, that probably suppositories don't melt in your rectum!''

Scarborough laughed. ''Diane!''

''I should have listened to him! I should have just stayed in Kansas, explored this with Tim. I shouldn't have bothered to come home to you.''

''That's not *true*, Diane. You know I enjoy seeing you. You know I don't mind giving you advice.''

''And you know what, Daddy dear,'' she said, her own face reddening. ''Here's how much you can trust me—and you know that you *can* trust me. Because I know that there's something in your past . . . something in Mom's past . . . God knows, something in *my* past . . . Things you won't admit. Strange experiences, maybe even missing time. Mom told me about that business in Massachusetts you refuse to acknowledge, she told me before she died. I'm confused . . . but maybe the hypnosis will bring that out too. But I'm not blabbing it, am I? I have the most damaging bit of information . . . maybe the key to the very reason that you're so *obsessed* with disproving UFO existence. I didn't want to bring this up, but you've forced my hand!''

Scarborough was stunned. He had no idea that Phyllis had mentioned that nonsense to their daughter. It could only have been when she was very ill with the breast cancer, when she was out of her mind. He struggled not to show alarm to his daughter as he responded. "I've made no secret of the reason for my interest in UFOs. It's in my very first book, for all to see. I may have seen one myself, and I have a proven psychological disposition toward experiencing cultural archetypes. But I deal with it all in a scientific, logical manner. And my mission is to prove it to others, Diane. You know that!"

"Admit it. The one thing that scares the great Dr. Everett Scarborough more than anything else is that there *are* extraterrestrials visiting this planet. Because that would open a whole can of worms . . . Maybe a whole closet of skeletons . . . And you want everything tightly sealed and catalogued and explained and well-lit. No room for mystery in the life of the Eminent Authority. No room for the mystical, the spiritual—because these things might just arouse some emotions in the Great Cold One, the Dean of Scientific Inquiry. Dr. Scarborough might just have to *feel*—really confront his emotions and, oh, that's the most frightening possibility of all."

"Diane! How can you say these things to me! I feel—and right now you're hurting me!"

"I doubt it. You've been ready for this for years. You know exactly the words to say, the things to do—and your logic protects you. But Dad, I was here, I remember what it was like with you and Mom. Those days when you didn't even speak with her or with me—those times when you were so aloof I didn't even know I had a father. And the only time you really paid any attention to me was when I did something wrong . . . Or worse, something that annoyed you. And heaven forbid that I should bring home a report card showing that I was less than Daddy's little genius in math and science . . ."

"Your IQ is something I'm proud of, dear. Your aptitude in both math and the physical sciences show great promise and naturally I want you to take advantage of them—"

"Bullshit." Tears were dripping down from Diane's eyes. "You just want me to be your little clone! Your little robot creation. Well, let me tell you, Mr. Wizard, I'm *not* a clone of you. I'm my own self. I know what I saw, and experienced. And I'm going to discover what happened to me. And if your precious position in the golden Academy of Science, your vaunted reputation in the annals of letters is besmudged a bit . . . well, too fucking bad!''

Turning, she started running for the steps.

"Where are you doing, Diane?" he said, struggling to remain calm.

"I'm packing. I'm taking a cab. I'm going back to Kansas!"

"You can't do that!"

"You keep on forgetting, don't you? I've got my own money, Daddy. You don't have my strings on that score. Mom left me enough to choose my own college and be independent while attending—and when I'm twenty-one, I'll get the rest. You can't control me, you can't control my mind—I'm sorry I'm not the daughter you want me to be, and I'm sorry if I'm *embarrassing* you by having an open, exploring mind. Maybe if you weren't so uptight about your standing in the scientific field, your precious reputation in the eyes of the public, your sterling career, then maybe you'd remember what science is really about, Dad. To learn, to venture, to discover. And you don't have to worship a man who had an apple fall on his head to have a seeking heart, a questing mind!"

She turned and rushed up the stairs, sniffling back her tears and rage.

Scarborough followed her up a few steps, and then stopped when he heard the door of her room slam. He listened to the familiar sounds of luggage being tossed around.

"Damn you! You're just like your mother—at her worst!" he cried up at her. "Do what you like, Diane. Say what you will about me to whomever you want, you ignorant, willful child!"

Suddenly, the door flung open and she was standing on the landing above, clutching her old giant panda bear, Colonel Blimp, its left eye still missing. "Oh yeah! Well, I've got a bit of news for you, Daddy, and you can choke on it. Guess who Tim wants to contact on this story? I told him no, but now that you've given me carte blanche, well, maybe I'll reconsider."

"I don't *care* who! I stand on my achievements, my reputation—and they're all on the hard bedrock of science, of the proven."

She screwed her face up almost comically, reverting to a rebellious, bratty girl. "Can you say, 'Jake Camden,' Daddy dear?"

"Jake *Camden!*" The name stopped him cold.

"I knew you could!" She threw the stuffed bear at him, and it knocked him down two whole steps. He looked back up, and she was gone, throwing luggage around again.

His mind went wild with a terrible fatherly rage he hadn't felt since she'd run over his prized tulip-bed with her bike when she was nine years old. He wanted to run up the stairs and strangle the insolent whelp—or, at the very least, take away her allowance for a month. But he quickly caught himself. He knew he could do neither. Frustration welled up in him like a physical thing as he visualized what a man like Jake Camden would do with a story like this. Oh, Diane knew his vulnerable spots all right, and when she was mad, she would zero in like a dive bomber.

He took a deep breath.

"Just don't catch any *disease*, all right, Diane?" he cried, then stomped back down, stormed to the basement door, flung it open, stamped down and put on his CD of Beethoven's Ninth Symphony.

Loud.

CHAPTER EIGHT

Jake Camden zoomed the rented Toyota Corolla down Route 80, topping the speed limit by thirteen miles per hour and blasting his Bob Seger tape just a notch past endurance. He would have preferred a convertible on this bright, sunshiny spring weekend. But this would have to do, awful blaring-red paint and all. What the hell, he thought, singing "Ramblin' Gamblin' Man" along with the Jensen speakers. Plane leaves tomorrow afternoon, and, hey, I'm free as a bird!

Camden, after all, had his story now.

He'd lined up several possibles for this Midwest UFO

investigatory jaunt, but like Farmer Whitcomb, they were all just vague sightings. He could do them all by phone and ask the more gungho people to send in snapshots of suspicious footprints or burnt landing sites, like when he was back in Florida, working out of his office.

Nope, he had the rest of the weekend to himself and he'd be damned if he was going to do any more work! These sightings were all the same anyway, he could generally predict what the rubes were going to blather on about. No imagination whatsoever! So that was Jake Camden's job, imagination! Yes sir, he had imagination to spare—and all in a good cause. Expanding the minds of the *untermenchen*! "P.U." Journalism, Camden dubbed it—pretty unusual. It provided a kind of meta-education to the great unwashed. Hey, Betsy Shoppingcart may not know Monet from Mozart, but she sure as hell knows that there are other planets in this galaxy that are probably sending spaceships to buzz the earth's atmosphere. It may not hit the Carl Sagan Cosmos bull's-eye of edification, but, hey, it was in the same solar system!

The wind blew back Camden's long, greasy hair from his Silver Ray-Ban sunglasses and he smiled as he thought about how easy this story was going to be. Hell, in a flash of brilliance he'd not only done a weekend's work, he'd headed off into a delicious new tangent of *Intruder* inquiry . . . And possibly created a foundation, a thesis for his new UFO book. He had reason to celebrate! Just a few more miles to the motel—take a nice siesta and a dip in the pool and then hit the Iowa City night-spots. His hangover was history, and he had to forge ahead, writing his name in beer and whiskey. All research, anyway. Couple more years it would be time to investigate the aliens who actually ran the Betty Ford Clinic anyway!

Camden smoked a Camel and grinned all the way down the highway.

After picking up a bottle of Jack Daniels Kentucky-Fried Whiskey at a neighboring liquor store, Camden pulled into a parking slot at the Comfort Inn and carried his notebook, camera, and plain brown bag to Room 124, where he was staying, eyeing a couple of teenage cuties frolicking by the video game-room. Whew . . . he thought. Maybe it's time to check out the old hand-eye coordination.

One of the perks of his job with the *National Intruder* was

the travel. Normally, Camden wasn't a travel nut and the only
thing that got him through flights was heavy pill-popping—but
it was a damn sight better than squatting in the middle of
Nowhere, Florida, where the *Intruder* was headquartered. As
part of his job, he had to regularly head out anyway, beat some
stories from the bushes, and maybe do a little UFO investigation work as well—but mostly, he did the work quick and dirty
and he used the time to just party, meet people, have some
laughs; hell, he got half his story ideas from drunks and
bartenders. It was all part of the research!

Camden fumbled for his key in his jacket, and opened up
124. Immediately he was hit by a blast of air-conditioning and
the smell of old beer and dead cigarette butts. The TV was on,
muttering and flashing a basketball game. He walked into the
carpeted motel gloom, closed the door, and opened up a
shade.

"Hey!" cried a groggy voice. "Don't do that!"

Camden grinned and put the brown paper bag on a table and
sat down beside it. "Didn't think you'd still be here, Carrie!"

"Corey. The name's Corey, and would you *puh-leze* turn off
that light."

"Sure, babe," said Camden. He leaned the chair back onto
his rear two legs, reached up and pulled the shade back down,
so that the room resumed its previous subterranean darkness.
Then he opened the radiator compartment and turned off the
air-conditioning. From the debris on the table, he pulled out a
used glass with a soggy cigarette butt floating in a half-inch of
Budweiser. He dumped these contents into a full ashtray, pulled
the Jack Daniels bottle out and filled the glass up halfway.

"It's one-thirty in the afternoon, Corey," he said after a
quick snort. He spat out a glob of ash. "When do you start
dancing again?"

The pile of blankets and sheets and pillows—with a trail of
long red hair peeking from them—coughed, and then replied,
"Saturday, right? Not till 10 P.M. We're open late."

"So, you decided to sack in at my digs, huh?"

"No decision," she said, pushing herself up. "Just never
woke up." Green eyes smeared with mascara stared at him
blearily as the covers rolled off of her, displaying two ski-jump
breasts, young and perky as you please. She was a pretty girl, in
the cornfed tradition. Her Swedish and Germanic heritage had

stamped out a predictably snub nose, high cheekbones, and square chin, all features of a smooth peaches-and-cream complexion. Corey was a student at the University of Iowa, who danced parttime at the bar. She was a business major, and, as far as Jake Camden was concerned, she could do business with him anytime.

The perfume and musk rolled off her in delicious waves, and Jake found himself aroused, remembering certain highlights of last night's thrashings. He grinned even wider. "Yeah, that's okay. Stay as long as you like."

She collapsed backwards, her breasts flattening and jiggling like Jell-O. "Besides, Jake," she said, rubbing her eyes. "You promised to tell me about flying saucers. You *are* the world's authority—that's what you told me last night, anyway. The next thing I know, I'm drunk and getting humped, and I came here to listen to UFO stories! You weren't just using a line, were you? You *are* a newspaper reporter."

"That's right, sweetheart." He got up, trotted over to the dresser drawer, opened the briefcase sitting there, and pulled out a recent copy of the *National Intruder.*

The tabloid was a definite offshoot of the *National Enquirer* school, its cover a noisy riot of color and screaming headlines. This particular issue promised juicy articles about Liz Taylor's liposuction diet, Barbra Streisand's sword-swallowing lessons, and an astrological guide to fast-food eating. The *Intruder* took its key from the *Star* in terms of graphics and look, but as far as contents went, it was an extreme version of the *Weekly World News* with a patina of respectability. It hired respectable reporters who needed money. Its writing was top notch, its photos were ace, it was a fast, entertaining read for Mary Oprahwatcher or Joe Drinkbeer and at least 75 percent of what it printed was true, which made it top of the line, in the way of grocery-line papers.

"Here you go," said Jake, displaying the newspaper in front of her face. He rifled through the pages, and found his article in that issue: "Russians Play Chess with Vodka-Swilling UFO Crash Victims." He gave it to the naked girl, tapping his five-point byline. "I get even bigger letters for my monthly column."

"Wow!" she said. "My mom reads this! Dad says it's all garbage—but you know, come to think of it—he's *mentioned* you. You're *the* Jake Camden! I think my father's got one of your books!''

''Well, I can't autograph his book for him, but give me a pen and I'll be glad to sign his little girl!'' He felt a stirring as he looked at the way her breasts draped over the pages of the *Intruder*. ''On second thought, who needs a pen?''

Corey apparently did not hear what he said. She was absorbed in the article. ''Gosh—a UFO in Siberia, talking with the Russians,'' she said, looking up finally. ''How did you get this bit of news?''

''Top-secret resources. I can't divulge that information.'' He sat back in his chair, pleased with the way she was impressed. Some people were openly derisive when they found out that he worked for the *Intruder* . . . but they were generally the kind of snobs he didn't care to associate with anyway.

''How did you get into this stuff, anyway?'' Corey wanted to know, as she got out of bed and stretched her lithe curves that had impacted so much on Camden last night. Her pubic hair was blonde and silky, like the top of a baby's head, showing her true hair color—but that red was perfect with those emerald eyes.

''Long story,'' he said, not really wanting to go into it.

''I got time. Just let me use the powder room.'' She wobbled forward, leaned over, and kissed him on the forehead, her breasts dangling like ripe fruit in front of his face. ''And maybe the valiant gentleman would care to buy a poor little girl some breakfast from room service.''

''Dumps like this don't have room service,'' said Jake. ''But I think I can rustle up something fun for breakfast.''

''Yummy,'' she purred, her natural grace overcoming her sleepiness as she slipped into the bathroom and closed the door modestly behind her.

Jake Camden went to his luggage. He rooted through his socks and underwear, which he'd never gotten a chance to store in the dresser, and pulled out a Snickers bar, a package of Fritos, a half-empty container of Oreo cookies and a pack of Juicy Fruit gum. Then he dug in deeper, pulling out an ordinary-looking prescription-drug bottle. These things, along with his shaving kit, he dragged over to the table. From the drug bottle, he pulled out a standard gram-container of cocaine. From his shaving kit, he pulled out a mirror and a razor blade.

Crunching on an Oreo, he poured a small amount of the pure white stuff onto the mirror and began chopping it up. Good stuff, this—from a direct source in Florida. Stepped on not at all, a little bit of this delicious fruit of the coca tree went a long, long way.

A few bathroom sounds later, Corey joined him. She wasn't so thrilled with his offered breakfast, but she smiled when she saw the neat, long lines on the little mirror.

"Better than coffee!" she said, snorting one through a rolled-up dollar bill.

"I don't know about that," said Camden. "Coke is a luxury. Coffee is a necessity." She hadn't put any clothes on yet, and he wasn't in any hurry for her to. He'd other ideas—hence this unusual generosity of cocaine to a near stranger.

"So," she said, leaning her head back and sniffing throatily. "You were going to tell me about how you got into the UFO business."

He drank some more of his whiskey and considered. Why not? After today, he'd never see the chick again, probably. She was an open, pleasant sort, about as guileful as a friendly cocker spaniel. He was a well-known reporter, sure, but it wasn't like he had a reputation to sully—no one was looking for a scoop on his life story. Besides, it was all spelled out in the subtext of his first book, *The National Intruder UFO Investigator.*

"I was a journalism major at Princeton," said Camden. "Shit, I had some high aspirations—I was gonna be the new Tom Wolfe, I was gonna be the new Woodward and Bernstein, I was gonna be absolute tops. But all I could get hold of was a job on a Maine newspaper, writing obits and reporting on county social events. Christ, I tried and tried on the biggies . . . could not get in the door, and couldn't afford to take on mail-room jobs, I had this huge college loan to pay off."

He pulled out a cellophane bag partially filled with dry vegetable matter and a pack of Top Jobs. "Roll us a joint, huh?"

"Sure," she said, still quite chemically happy.

"Yeah, so anyway, I'm working the *Monitor* a few years and dying, *dying* . . . I wrote a novel or two and they didn't sell. I go through a couple of girl friends, but I was an unhappy S.O.B. and they couldn't take it. So you know, each year, there's these recruiters who came through Portland, and I'm getting these calls from editors of newspapers. The fucking tabloids were reading my stuff, and liking it, and they wanted me! But shit, I wanted the *Washington Post*, the *New York Times* to call . . . not the *Enquirer*! But the money they were offering me—hell, it was three times as much as I was making in Maine—plus perks.

"Finally, they just wore me down. My old Buick threw a rod, my cat Puddles died, the twentieth publisher in a row rejected my novel—so I said, hell. Why not. I took the next offer—the *Intruder*, natch. I moved to Florida, and never looked back!"

She was sucking on the roach, which gave Camden definite ideas. She took the completed number from her mouth and handed it to him. "But UFOs! That's what I want to hear about."

Camden sighed and lit the marijuana with his Bic lighter—funny, here he was unburdening a bit of his soul to the woman, and all she wanted to hear about was flying saucers. He'd figured her different, thought maybe something of him had rubbed into her last night, maybe she wanted to get into his head a little as well as his pants. But nooooooooo . . . Clearly, what he had here was a Saucer Groupie. Oh, not your garden-variety Saucer Convention Trekkie with pointy ears and a lifelong desire to mate with Mr. Spock—but a space case nonetheless. Hell, though, Camden thought. This one was worth a show.

"Oh, yeah!" he said, shifting gears. "I'd seen some funny stuff in the sky when I was a kid, and I knew this guy in college who claimed that he'd ridden in a saucer—been abducted by people from Beta Centauri, or something. And I'd read a few books on the subject. So when I talked with the editor, he told me I had a natural affinity for UFO investigation, what with my journalistic background and all. So I started working with Pete Hubley, the UFO reporter for the *Intruder*. He taught me his—uhm—investigative methods, gave me lots of books and papers and reports to read, took me to a few UFO conferences. And then—bang!—the great mother-ship of the sky came down and scooped him up with a heart attack. I inherited his position, just as the *Intruder* was squeezing into the book business. I'd been doing some work on the book anyway, so I just finished it and got my name on the spine, and suddenly, here I am, chasing critters from the Pleiades!''

''Have you ever actually *seen* any?!'' said Corey, her young eyes glowing with enthusiasm.

''Not personally, but I've seen things and heard things you wouldn't imagine . . . a lot of which hasn't seen print and maybe won't ever! And I've heard some stories that would curl your toes! UFOs are *real*, Corey, don't you let anybody tell you different. There's something absolutely *paranormal* happening!''

Corey took another line of cocaine, and turned back to him breathlessly. ''I hear that flying saucers come down and take women away and force them to have incredible alien *sex*!'' She was visibly aroused at the very notion, her pink nipples hardening and darkening.

''Uhm . . . er . . . yes! Yeah, babe. Some incredibly kinky sex. The Pleiadans, I've heard, have got these orgasmatrons for one thing. They stick women in these things just for starters, to get 'em warmed up. The chicks I heard tell me they came for thirty minutes straight! And then aliens whip out their sexual organs. And for little guys, these Pleiadans have got dongs the size of *horses*!''

''Really!'' She grabbed his knee, and squeezed hard. A dainty red tongue flicked out of her mouth, tracing the curve of her lips. She half closed her eyes, fading away into her private fantasies. ''More,'' she said breathily. ''Tell me *more*!''

Camden had encountered the alien sex-fetish before, but never had it been embodied by such a fabulous babe as this. Jeez, the odd shit that went on inside people's heads! But he wasn't one to turn down something like this, sizzling just inches from his lap.

''One woman gave me the whole story,'' he said, making it up as it came to him. ''According to her, two of the males attended to her, and they had penises like thick antennae that could protract such a distance that they could have fucked her from across a room! Penises that *vibrated!* And they exuded this kind of perfume that just drove her into a sexual frenzy.''

Her fingers drifted up to his crotch, and long, red-painted fingernails stroked the bulge in his jeans. ''Oh!'' she said. ''Yes, I somehow *knew*, psychically, that it would be like that!''

''And that's not all! There were two ganging up on this

chick, one for her front, one for her back door; and because
they were small—their bodies, that is—they contoured in, real
sexy-like!''

Her lithe fingers tugged on the zipper of his fly, and he
almost lost control, right in his pants, this visage before
him—the naked girl, framed in red hair, big chest heaving,
enthusiastic passion personified—was so exciting.

"Oooooohh..." she crooned. "How...how long did they
do it!'' She had the belt and button undone now, then his zipper
was down, and she moved her face into his crotch, her breath
hot on his Fruit of the Looms. "Tell me! You have to tell me!''

"Hours!"

Suddenly, she fell back onto the floor, legs open, arms
reaching up, eyes open and flashing with lust as her body
contorted and writhed like a spastic gymnast. "Take me, Jake!
Take me *now*! You're my alien lover, Jake. Do it for *hours*!''

He didn't know about the hours bit, but he could try—and he
could always apologize afterward. Grinning, he took one last
pull of the marijuana cigarette, one last snort of cocaine, and
one last gulp of whiskey. Then, grinning still, he began to pull
down his jeans.

The phone rang.

Later, when he got a chance to reconstruct the moment, Jake
Camden was able to figure out why he picked that phone
receiver up at all, and had not just let the sucker ring. It was
because of all the time he spent at the goddamn office desk. It
got so you heard that ringing, and you thought, this could be a
big story, or it could be some key witnesses calling in with
information, or it could be accounting, telling him they had his
biweekly check for him early.

Anyway, still just stepping out of his jeans, Camden automatically reached over and picked up the receiver.

"Yeah?'' he said in his usual unfriendly phone manner.

"Camden!'' the unmistakable voice burst from the earpiece
like thunder from Olympus. "Camden, this is Kozlowski, here.
We got some talking to do, guy!''

Oh geez. "I'm sorry—you must have the wrong number,''
he said in a squeaky voice. "My name's Bob Smith!''

"I know it's you, man. You hang up that phone, I feed your
balls to my alligators!''

The blood in his veins seemed to turn to ice. Howard

Kozlowski was the editor and publisher of the *Intruder*. Jake Camden was in absolutely no financial position to get fired. He owed that Colombian coke dealer from Miami his next month's salary, and those boys from South America had deadly ways of dealing with people who reneged on debts.

On the floor, Corey moaned a bit, then flashed Camden a sultry pout.

"Just messin' with your head, Koz. What's up, buddy!" Camden said, disguising his panic with his usual throaty rasp.

"I want you in my office nine o'clock sharp, Monday morning, Camden!" said the boss. "I want you in there, and bring along some explanations!"

"What for, Koz?"

Corey started to tug at his half-removed jeans, flashing him bedroom eyes. Camden shook his head violently, then jerked his thumb toward the door, holding his hand over the receiver and mouthing the words, "Get the fuck outta here!"

"What's going on, Camden? I hope you're working on your story!" rattled the voice from phone. "You better be working on that story, let me tell you, fella!"

With a hurt expression, Corey got up and proceeded to pick up her clothes from the chair on which they were strewn, and put them on. Jake Camden did not watch. He was too busy gripping the telephone and sweating. Christ, this could be damn serious. He didn't like the tone in Kozlowski's voice . . . It wasn't just editorial . . . Something else was going on, and he was afraid he knew exactly what it was.

"Well, actually, Mr. Kozlowski, I'm happy to say that I did some excellent investigatory work this morning, and I was just on my way out to do some more."

"Sure, Camden, sure," the voice was screeching out over the receiver so loud that Camden had to take the receiver from his ear. "I bet you're in your hotel room with some whore, aren't you! Drinking, screwing, and God knows what else! That's your usual investigation methodology, isn't it!"

Corey heard the outburst. Just buttoning her shirt, she flashed Camden a horrified and angry look, and grabbed her shoes. "Asshole!" she yelled, and headed for the door.

"Who was that, Camden?" his boss wanted to know.

"Uhm—the maid, Mr. K. I'm afraid this room's a real mess

and she's very upset." He winced as the door slammed. So much for an afternoon of hot alien sex.

"Camden, I gotta tell you—if I didn't need you, you'd be history at the *Intruder*. History!"

"I thought you were pleased with the job I was doing, Mr. Kozlowski!" Uh oh. Camden's worst fears were coming true. The boss had found out about him and Cynthia.

"Never anything more than substandard, Camden ... but that's not what I'm talking about. No, my daughter got very ... well, drunk and drugged up last night. And she told me ..." Kozlowski's voice cracked a bit. "She told me about what you did!"

"I can explain, sir. Cynthia's got a few very deep problems, Mr. Kozlowski, and I think maybe she needs some kind of psychological help. I told her so, and I meant to discuss it with you. I care very much about your daughter, sir, and ..."

"Care! I bet! She's barely seventeen years old, you lecherous hooligan! Why, I oughta have your tail thrown in jail!"

"Sixteen's the legal age, I should remind you. And Cynthia is a willful young lady," said Camden in way of defense. "I can't tell you I'm not a weak man, Mr. K. But your daughter wanted her own way with me ... I just couldn't, in good conscience, continue."

There was silence from the other end of the line.

"Sir? You still there? When I get back, we'll have a good heart-to-heart on this, I promise," said Camden. "And you'll like what I have for my next story."

"What?"

"Uh—er—" Kozlowski's demand had been so abrupt that Camden momentarily lost his train of thought. What was it? Abduction? Giant three-eyed creatures from a saucer? No, of course not. He remembered now! "I'm tracking down a government conspiracy with extraterrestrials whose purpose is to scare farmers off their land!" The words gushed from his mouth willy-nilly—he just hoped they were understandable.

"Another government conspiracy!" said Kozlowski. "That story's almost forty years old!"

"A different slant, I told you! Farmers! I've found the exact hook for all that farmer work I've been doing and—"

Kozlowski's voice turned cold and dead. "Camden, I was going to save this for Monday morning, but I might as well tell you now. I'm pretty sick of the bullshit you've been turning in lately. Your column has gone to hell, and the stories you've been writing are just old retreads from the sixties and seventies. I'm giving you a month to come up with a killer story—a story that will do something for our circulation. The goddamn New York posh publishers are getting better saucer stories than you! If you don't give me that story—you're gone, Camden. And just consider this a stay of sentence, in light of this recent development with my teenaged daughter!''

"Right, Mr. K. I'm on the trail of something really exciting! In fact, like I say, I'm on—"

"Don't forget, Camden. Monday morning. And I hope you like assholes, Camden, 'cause you're going to have a brand new one Monday afternoon!''

Click! The connection was broken, and Jake Camden was left standing, his pants around his knees and his job in mortal jeopardy. He hung the phone up, pulled his jeans back on, rebuckled his belt, and zipped his fly. He looked around at the wreckage of the room where the naked Corey had lain, and his lust—so aroused only minutes before—was just ashes in his mouth.

Camden sighed and sat down. He pulled out a Camel and started to smoke it.

That little bitch Cynthia! He *knew* he shouldn't have let her insinuate her little butt into his life!

"The boss's daughter!" Camden said. "Jakey, you nitwit!'' He'd been plowing her for months now, and when last week she'd demanded that he marry her, he naturally had just laughed in her face, thinking she was kidding. She *had* to be kidding! But she'd gone running away in tears—running to Daddy, apparently. Big Howie Kozlowski, owner of the *Intruder*, an orange grove, a TV and radio station—and the biggest alligator farm in Orlando County. The beans were spilled now. The dominoes were collapsing.

Jake sat down and poured himself some more whiskey, thinking feverishly. Within minutes, he'd finished the glass, and poured another one. He stubbed the cigarette out in the ashtray, visualizing headlines.

"Tabloid Tycoon Throws UFO Reporter into Thrashing Pool of 'Gators.''

Camden sipped whiskey.

"Nubile Newspaper Heiress: "I Cut Off UFO Reporter's Genitals and Gave Them to the Saucermen!"

Camden sipped more whiskey.

"Extraterrestrials Beam Threatened UFO Reporter onto Hovering Craft, Rescuing Him From Irate Boss."

"Yeah," said Jake Camden, staring up to the ceiling and beyond. "Yeah, please. Come and get me, for pity's sake. Now!"

He finished the whiskey.

CHAPTER
NINE

"There you are, you old son of a bitch!" growled the man in a deep bass bellow, as he stood up from the lobby couch, splashing some of his beer onto the old rug. "Didn't think you were gonna make it, Scarborough, you absentminded skunk!"

Everett Scarborough extended his hand to shake the meaty paw proffered him, and grimaced as Captain Eric MacKenzie put his usual enthusiasm—and manly pressure—into his grip. "Well, Mac, like I told you on the phone, I'd almost forgotten all about dinner with you tonight. Whatever statistical laws of misfortune there are have ganged up on me."

"Yeah! I heard about last night, that goon and that gun at your tent meeting . . . Like to get that shithead out in the field. Just him and me and Betsy, my trusty twelve-gauge." MacKenzie pointed at a spot on the couch. "Just get your ass down there and relax. I'll rustle up a brewski for you. A darkie, if you promise to be good, and let me in on all the details."

"Sure," said Scarborough. "That'll be fine, Mac. I could use a beer and a friendly ear."

"Comin' up," said the gruff man agreeably. He strode off for the bar.

They had met in the reception area of the Tabard Inn because it was one of their favorite Washington hangouts. Just a few blocks from Dupont Circle, the inn was old, with much history, and an almost palpable sense of *quaintness* clinging to its wooden rooms. Scarborough sat back, relaxing now, enjoying the serenity of the setting. A fire burned low in an old-style brick hearth before him, crackling and muttering a breath of heat onto the plush and comfortable old chairs and couches in the lounge. Atop the mantle stretched a series of ancient bric-a-brac and pictures. From a nearby, dimly lit room, subdued sounds of diners and cutlery emerged. You could almost pretend it was a hundred years ago, and that was what made it so attractive to Scarborough when he and Phyllis had first been taken there by MacKenzie, in the midsixties when they'd first arrived in town. It was something you might find up in New England, this overwhelming charm . . . only it was smack dab in the middle of Washington, D.C.

It also had great food and wonderful beer, thought Scarborough, taking in the scents leaking from the dining room. When Eric MacKenzie returned, bearing two brimming English-style imperial pints of Watney's Red Barrel, Scarborough was more than happy to see him.

Scarborough accepted his drink, and sipped some of the froth off the top. "This place doesn't change much, does it?"

"Hell, no, and thank God for that. Can't hardly ever get one of the few actual rooms they offer—but hell, plenty of room to eat! 'Sides, I like the Hilton just fine!"

Captain Eric MacKenzie was five years older than Scarborough, well into his fifties—but Scarborough thought he looked about five years *younger*. He was a broad-shouldered, bluff sort, with a vibrant head of Scottish red hair and a ruddy complexion from the many hours he devoted to his hobbies, hunting and fishing. Only the wrinkles below his eyes, the grey hair on his long, out-of-style sideburns, and the slight wattle below his chin attested to his age. Blue eyes looked out cheerfully onto the world, infinitely amused at what they observed. A bushy mustache underlined their vibrancy.

"Eric, you know you could have stayed with me," said Scarborough. "You're always welcome."

MacKenzie took a long pull of Watney's, wiped the foam from his mustache, burped, grinned, then slapped Scarborough's knee. "Hell, Doc. I spend time enough at your place, what with those goddamn bacchanalian poker weekends you throw. 'Sides, the conference is at the Hilton, and it's much more convenient, since it's just a weekend here. Still, haven't seen you for a few months, so I thought we could sit around and swap lies for a while, just like old times—with no goddamn women dragging at our coattails!" MacKenzie took another deep draught. His wife—Tama—had left him six years before. Ran off with a sensitive poet with a professorship in English at some comfortable midwestern college. Tama and Phyllis had been close friends since they'd met in 1965—the year Scarborough had moved to Washington to work with the air force. MacKenzie had worked with Project Blue Book awhile as well, and had taken it upon himself to make the new scientist-recruit feel welcome in the strange new city. They'd only actually worked together closely on a few UFO investigations—but they'd seen each other often at the Pentagon and at Headquarters in Virginia, and they'd socialized frequently. MacKenzie had retired a few years after the closing of Project Blue Book, and did something that he'd always swore he wanted to do, which was to become a professional fiction-writer. Secretly, Scarborough envied him. Part of what had driven him toward nonfiction was the allure and glamour of being a *writer*. Unfortunately, though he had tried, and though MacKenzie was always trying to collaborate with him on some oddball project, that was one thing the scientist found that he could not do. Maybe his critics were right, and maybe this was what made him such a top-flight debunker: he was devoid of imagination.

True, MacKenzie wasn't exactly Saul Bellow. He was more of a poor man's Ernest Hemingway, specializing in men's adventure series filled with guns and babes, cars and boobs. Just for variety's sake, he did the occasional article for men's magazines on some nicety of the Uzi machine gun, or better yet, the merits of the color orange on dry flys for river trout fishing. But when the man wasn't out tracking deer or casting lines into fresh water, you could bet your life he was tap-tap-tapping behind a hot word processor and listening to his favorite writing music, John Philip Sousa. Eric MacKenzie loved to write, and his prose had all the bravura and excitement—and alas, all the finesse—of his personality.

"What conference, Mac?"

"Oh, just some dreary magazine journalist stuff," MacKenzie pulled out a big cigar from the pocket of his tweed coat. "Came to talk to some editors—hell of a lot better than trooping up to New York City where most of them are. God, I hate that place. And it's funny, though I'd like to see all that scum and concrete just tip into the Atlantic, I'd be screwed if it did. That's where my goddamn money comes from." MacKenzie lit and puffed on his Ortega y Gasset cigar, then tossed the wooden match into the fireplace. "Hope you're hungry. Our reservations are for fifteen minutes from now. I thought you'd enjoy just sitting here awhile, for old time's sake." Pause. Puff. "So. Pretty hairy, gettin' blasted at, huh? I had my share of that in Korea, believe you me. I guess my series *The Immolator* has got enough bullets per page to ammunitionize a World War II and a half, but shit, I ain't dumb. I may like guns, but hell if I wanna get shot at."

An expression of sympathy and concern was about as close as MacKenzie was able to get to admitting how upset he was that his friend had almost been killed. Scarborough understood, and it touched him, as many things about this bear of a man did. Back in Project Blue Book, there had been an unspoken bond established, and though neither man was demonstratively affectionate, there was the unspoken agreement to keep that bond alive.

"It was damn awful, but it was worse to have that saucer-nut shot, right in front of me." Scarborough sipped at the faintly bitter, full-bodied brew. "You know, Mac, I may damn all their eyes, the UFOols and their brain-damaged ilk. But the bottom line is that they're a form of humanity too . . . And I don't like to see them *hurt*, much less killed."

"Ah, you old softie. Don't give me this 'form of humanity' crap. You're a crusader for science . . . You're just as bad as Jerry Falwell or Billy Graham. You're a fuckin' *evangelist*. You wanna see the UFO freaks come trippin' down the sawdust trail of science and kneel at your altar of logic. You want to save them from the darkness of fuzzy-thinking sin! Yep, Reverend Evvie Scarborough stands at the pulpit with his invitation for all the lost to come forward and be washed of their sins in the blood of Isaac Newton and Albert Einstein!" Cigar sticking out obscenely from his mouth, MacKenzie raised his hands into the air and waggled his fingers. "Hallelujah!"

Scarborough chuckled. Mac was about the only man he'd allow to get away with such a lampoon. Still, it rankled a bit. "Oh, right. A blood-porn hack criticizes his better!" he said, riposting with a traditional insult.

MacKenzie wiggled his eyebrows. "Least I get my facts straight."

Scarborough looked away and picked up his beer. Let *that* one pass. Clearly, Mac wanted to get onto *The Subject* again, and that was the last thing Scarborough wanted. Not after the kind of weekend he'd been having. "Oh yes? As long as *Gun World* doesn't make any typos. But seriously, Mac. I'm a little rocked, and not just because of the attempt on my life last night."

"So tell me exactly what happened."

Scarborough gave his friend the details. MacKenzie listened carefully, nodding and grunting, and when the story was over, he said, "No, I wouldn't worry too much about it. Sounds like an isolated crazy. And not professional at all. A handgun from so many yards away? He was lucky to get the bullets over the stage prompter!"

"Well, Abe's got me in mothballs for a while. Just in case."

MacKenzie shrugged. "Better safe than sorry, I guess. But I wouldn't worry. In fact, I'm surprised this hasn't happened to you sooner. I've always told you to pack heat!"

"Now who's evangelizing, oh, ye disciple of the American Rifle Association!" Scarborough leaned back in the chair, tapping his half-empty glass, staring off into the air. "But there's more. And it's just between you and me, right?"

MacKenzie's voice turned serious. "Sure, Doc. You know you can trust me."

"This one's a lulu. And if it gets out to the media . . . whewee. Won't hurt my credibility, but I don't want this kind of publicity." In terse words, MacKenzie told him about the UFO encounter that Diane claimed to have had with her boyfriend, Timothy Reilly.

"She wants me to investigate," he said. "She really thinks they were abducted. I told her no, that she must have been on drugs or something. We had a terrible argument and she flew back to Kansas U. Going to investigate it herself, find someone else to help."

MacKenzie sucked on his cigar a moment, then blew out a

thick plume of smoke. "I can see why you had that reaction, Ev. Christ, Diane's been a loose cannon on the deck of the U.S.S. Scarborough for years. But maybe you should just, you know, humor the girl a bit. I don't mean patronize, I mean just take a trip out there, look around, pronounce your negative verdict and leave."

"No!" said Scarborough. "She's *not* going to bring me down. How do I know, for instance, that she's not the unwitting accomplice in a plot to ruin my reputation? Someone took a shot at me last night, some others may be plotting my downfall. Mac, it didn't take me long in the debunker biz to realize that I've garnered some serious enemies for myself."

"Yeah, I see your point." The big man blew some more smoke, drank some more beer. "Okay, but I still think you should go out there. She *is* your daughter. But then, you don't listen to your good pal Mac, much, do you? And I really wish you would."

Oh, dear. *The Subject* again. Well, thought Scarborough, might as well get it out of the way—he knew MacKenzie wouldn't let him go tonight without a little wrestle at the very least.

"Mac, I got your packet last month, and I'm sorry, but I really haven't had a chance to examine it closely."

"The other one I sent close to six months ago, and you still haven't given me an adequate answer on that one."

"I'm very sorry, Mac. I just have other priorities. And something that happened over twenty years ago is just not a priority."

"Boy, you've changed," said MacKenzie, his whole body seeming to fall into a frown. "You used to be a top-notch investigator, Doc. You know what I think—I think you just don't want to face up to the possibility that we were working for a bunch of scummy crooks back then. And you *still are!*"

Scarborough clucked his tongue. "A conspirator behind every bush, Mac. To paraphrase the Bard. You know what your problem is? You've been trying to imitate Robert Ludlum far too long. Your fiction is seeping through those holes in your head and getting all mixed up in your poor drink-sotted brain!"

It had all started about a year before, this argument, when MacKenzie had accepted an offer to do a series about his participation in Project Blue Book for *True Magazine*. Eric

MacKenzie was never known for his thorough research, and
when he'd announced the assignment, Scarborough blithely
agreed to help out, expecting only the occasional phone call.
But he hadn't read his friend properly, hadn't noted the signs
that Mac betrayed all too well now—the ex-captain was restless. Slaughtering wild fowl and fauna, and snagging scaly
creatures from rivers no longer fully satisfied his lust for
adventure. MacKenzie yearned for bigger game, like in the old
days when he hunted communists in Vietnam or Korea, or
UFOs in Nebraska. He'd also read a great deal too much of the
pro-UFO-ologists' publishing of the past few years. Oh, no, he
didn't buy the idea of little men from other planets abducting
people, or any of that garbage. But somehow, the idea that
some government agency—or combination of government
agencies—might be covering up some facts concerning their
touted UFO investigations had taken root. Doubtless, it intrigued
him to think of hidden puppet-masters behind oaken doors in
Washington, burning papers, dispatching agents to destroy
files, pulling strings on FBI or CIA operative minions. But
mostly it galled him, even outraged him, to think that, as an
employee of the U.S. government, the wool had been pulled
over his eyes.

Essentially, MacKenzie had reread the official Project Blue
Book reports, including the write-ups of the investigations that
he had worked on, with and without Dr. Everett Scarborough.
Then, from his old mammoth and battered file cabinets he'd
stolen from Fort Meyer, he'd pulled out the actual files concerning those cases. Something had bothered him when he'd
reread the official reports. Little details about this and that.
He'd remembered them . . . differently.

The details *did* turn out to be slightly different. Colors of
lights described by witnesses on the flying objects . . . numbers
of people claiming to have seen the vessels. Nothing major on
most of the cases, but still they niggled on MacKenzie's mind,
according to his letters to Scarborough, anyway. Two investigations in particular were skewed in the final report. One of
which MacKenzie had participated in himself in North Dakota.
Top-secret stuff, since the sightings had occurred near Minutemen
Missile Silos—with subsequent electrical problems in the military equipment. And one investigation they'd both worked on
in Iowa. The Higsdon Farm business.

He'd Xeroxed his file reports and sent them to Scarborough for his comments. Scarborough had glanced at them. There was nothing terribly out of whack, as far as he was concerned. It had been a puzzling case anyway, and the principal witness— one Charles Higsdon—had given different versions of his story to different people. Nonetheless, Unidentified Flying Objects had been reported over the fields of southern Iowa by a number of people, and Project Blue Book people had been called in to investigate. Final conclusion: meteor showers had formed the UFOs, along with astronomical phenomena intensified by rare atmospheric conditions. And psychological difficulties were at the heart of the UFO abduction of Higsdon. The farmer had admitted that he'd reread the *Look* articles concerning the Betty and Barney Hill abduction by John Fuller. Doubtless, they'd impacted on his mind, since the "abduction" he described also included a medical examination by little creatures. Nonetheless, despite the conclusions of that investigation back in 1968, the original sensational story had gotten out and spread like wildfire. What MacKenzie had noted were the inconsistencies between his notes and the published account of the investigation. He'd requested that Scarborough take a look at his own files on the subject. But, of course, Scarborough had never gotten around to it. He tried to order his life in terms of priorities, and checking on the Higsdon Farm business for sleazy UFO articles was very low on the list. Besides, you always had to account for small and insignificant mistakes in these kind of field missions, especially when they were written up by bored bureaucrats who'd not participated in the operation. History was rife with clerical mistakes. You just had to accept it.

MacKenzie drained the glass and grinned. "Yeah. Maybe. But I'm not gonna let this one go, buster. If only because I want to bust your chops back into shape. Look at those goddamn notes, huh, Doc. At least give me a quote on them—so I can quote you as a government *stooge!*"

Scarborough sighed. "Okay, okay. I'll look at them."

MacKenzie leaned over confidentially. "Yeah, and maybe you can dig up something from old Dolan. You can bet I didn't call *him*. We never got along very well. Still, you see him from time to time. Maybe you can pry something out of the old turkey."

"Well, I can't promise you anything on that score, but I'll look at those files. I think I've even got some of my own, on the Litton case, anyway. I'll cross-check, Mac. As long as you stop calling me a government stooge. You know that's the battle cry of the UFOols. My employment with the government ended with Project Blue Book itself—my contacts in the past years have been purely for my benefit and elucidation. And Colonel Dolan has been especially helpful to me."

Colonel Dolan had been their section chief back in the Blue Book days. Scarborough still maintained contact with the man, ensconced now in a Pentagon office—socially as well as professionally. He did not tell this to MacKenzie, though, for fear of further razzing. MacKenzie had always been an air force maverick—and he and Colonel Walter Dolan had butted heads more than once.

"Deal!" said MacKenzie. "I knew I'd browbeat you eventually, guy!" Scarborough again had to endure the muscular, manly handshake.

"Well, maybe you'd have gotten results sooner if I wasn't so busy. As it is now, what with the postponement, I've got some time on my hands. I'll get down to it Monday. Satisfied?"

"Yeah. Now let's go in and chow down. I'm starved!" They stood and MacKenzie slapped his friend on the back in a good-natured way that almost knocked the scientist over the table.

"I'm sure glad you're my friend, Mac," said Scarborough. "I'd hate to be on the wrong side of that hand in a fistfight."

"Well, Doc, believe me. You've come awfully close sometimes, you stubborn bastard."

They went to the hostess to get their booth.

CHAPTER
TEN

The Pan Am Boeing 707 jet landed at 9:43 P.M. at National Airport, Washington, D.C.—almost half an hour late. Woodrow Justine was used to planes being late. He flew a lot in his business. Still, it didn't mean that, after awhile, cooped up in the pressurized cabin with dozens of other cramped, sweaty people, the inevitable bawling baby, and the snot-nosed kids, he didn't feel extremely claustrophobic and twitchy and in the exact kind of mood to kill somebody.

Tonight, maybe he'd be able to release his tensions in the course of duty.

Carrying only a flight bag, he didn't have to go and collect any baggage. Justine, relieved to be on the ground, fled the main concourse, past the filed taxicabs and the milling people and into the fine spring Washington, D.C., night. He walked past the specially designated parking lot for VIPs such as senators, congressmen, and diplomats, then past the short-term lot. Across from this stood the station for the elevated Metro-line. Beside a concrete stanchion, across from the Metro, in the long-term parking lot, exactly where it was promised to be, waited a black Williams Motors stretch-limo.

Justine smiled to himself. In most other cities, that auto would stick out like a sore thumb. But here, in National Airport in the country's capital, where power cruised in splendor, it was just another set of wheels. The sound of a jet taking off over the Potomac River sheared through the air as Justine stepped past the barriers and up to the back door, which opened for him immediately.

"Get in," a terse voice said.

Justine gently put his bag in first onto the plush floor. The smell of upholstery polish, a French cigarette, and English cologne, the faint touch of air-conditioning, and the gentle squeak of a radio surrounded him as he stepped gracefully in and settled into the leather cushions. The barrier between front and back seat was opaque; Justine could not see the driver, or determine if there was an agent riding shotgun. This made him faintly uneasy. Even on friendly territory, he liked to know the gun emplacements.

"Flight okay?" asked Brian Richards, the man Justine knew as Editor-in-Chief. This polite inquiry surprised Justine. He supposed it was Richards's way of saying, "Sorry to pry you out of L.A. on such short notice."

"Made me antsy," said Justine, grinning.

"Tired?"

"Got some sleep on the plane. Slept like a baby last night. I feel good."

"Excellent. Then you feel as though you can operate tonight."

"Shit, Chief, if it's fucking Everett Scarborough you want snuffed, I can do it *last* night!" The very thought made Woodrow Justine tingle with anticipation.

Richards's voice grew an edge. "I told you, Woodrow, never call me Chief. It makes me feel like Perry White of the *Metropolis Daily Planet*, speaking to cub reporter Jimmy Olsen."

"Yes, okay, sorry," said Justine.

"You want some soda? I stocked some A & W for you, and there's ice. I know you don't drink alcohol, which is just as well," Richards's voice softened to its usual mellifluous tenor. "And you must have misheard me. Everett Scarborough is not on the ticket tonight. You're going to have to muzzle that for a while . . . Scarborough's a delicate situation, but the Top still need him."

Justine could not hide his disappointment. "Damn." He leaned forward and picked out a glass, which he filled with ice and root beer.

"I realize your reasons for hating the man, Woodrow. Maybe you'll get your wish someday. But that's not a wish I can grant," Richards leaned forward, smoke from his Gauloise rippling up and cascading past his serious and thoughtful face. "If you'd have listened properly, you'd have realized this is a Code Four that *involves* Scarborough—to protect him, not eliminate him.'' A gentle smile of derision touched the corners of Richards's pale and naked mouth. Justine realized that the chief had been toying with him. A slight jab of emotional sadism—just the kind of thing that Richards enjoyed so much. But Justine said nothing, choosing to suppress his anger, if not his disappointment. Richards was the man responsible for everything in Woodrow Justine's satisfying and rewarding life of money, happiness, and legal murder. Editor Richards had been the man who'd tapped him, trained him, and kept tabs on him. When Brian Richards said ''Kill,'' Justine killed, and when Brian Richards said ''Heel,'' Justine heeled.

''Protect him, huh? What man of good taste wants the bastard gone?'' Justine took an ice cube in his mouth and began to suck on it.

''Last night, at one of Scarborough's lectures, a man took out a handgun and tried to shoot him. From the balcony of Tawes Auditorium, University of Maryland. Another man was killed, Scarborough only suffered minor wounds. The assailant escaped.'' Richards puffed thoughtfully. ''However, due to the sensitive nature of Scarborough's place in the Editorial Panorama, a few subagents were in the audience. It was the debut of Scarborough's new presentation. Much more showbizzy . . . Sleight of hand, magic to prove various points. Lasers, music, slides—quite entertaining, apparently, and a hit with the audience. At any rate, the subagents pieced together a composite on the assassin—and our associates in the FBI have successfully tracked down the identity of the man, and his place of domicile. We in turn requested that there be no records of this exchange of information. This morning, after careful consideration of the facts on hand I decided that it would be best to simply erase this particular threat to Scarborough.''

''Aha. And that's where I come in,'' said Justine.

''Yes. An extreme measure . . . but I studied the man's records carefully. No previous criminal record, no ties to subversive or potentially harmful groups. Not a professional, certainly.''

''Sir, I need more concrete information if I'm to perform my function properly.'' Justine crunched the ice between his teeth.

Richards raised his thin eyebrows and winced a little at the sound. ''Yes. Sorry, Wood, I'm just still musing over the matter. Strange chap, this guy. We've got no character description or psychological profile, but from what we can piece together, he's a sociopath.

"His name is Arnold Klinghoffer. Age: forty-one. He works as a night janitor at Catholic University." A paper crinkled. Justine realized his boss was reading from a crib sheet he had taken from the jacket pocket of his suit. "Lives in Takoma Park, Maryland. Address is right here. It's an old house, which his mother left him when she died two years ago. He's apparently lived there all his life, and he's unmarried. High school dropout—Northwestern High. Hmm . . . what else. Subscribes to a lot of outré magazines, including every UFO periodical available. Neighbors report he keeps to himself, but causes no problems; sort of the neighborhood hermit."

"Why should this bozo take a shot at Scarborough?"

"As you know, the good doctor gets a number of death threats. He upsets the saucer aficionados a *great* deal." Richards smiled ruefully. "He certainly upsets you, Woodrow."

"What, you mean this asshole Scarborough is so important in the Panorama that you're going to waste my talents, taking out every saucernik who looks cross-eyed at the great man?"

"No. I considered merely having Mr. Klinghoffer put away for a while. But still, I like to keep things simple—and utilizing your excellent talents is quick and immediate. This way, we won't have to worry about Klinghoffer trying to blow a hole in Scarborough at the wrong time, ever again."

"I thought you said that Scarborough's gonna have to go *sometime*!"

"Sometime, Woodrow, may be tomorrow—but it may be next century as well. What we *must* have, however, is control over the situation. We are the Editors, man. We exercise our ability to keep the script trimmed, properly plotted and paced. Absolutely no extraneous detail. And most important, it must be kept in absolute control." The smoke hovering about the man thickened as he became more excited and sucked harder on his cigarette. "We are the Fates, Woodrow, spinning our web—and snipping it where it gets too tangled. That is our job—but remember, we merely interpret directions dictated from other quarters. And as much as you hate Scarborough, those 'other quarters' find Scarborough and his activities much to their liking."

"The fucking Publishers," Justine said, shaking his head

and chuckling to himself. "One of these days, maybe they'll come down from on high and explain to me the real reason they're doing all this shit." He shrugged.

"Yours is not to reason why, Junior Editor. The Panorama is for the best interests of our country, and make no mistake about that!" Deep wrinkles etched into the man's face as he spoke, as though reciting a deeply felt creed. "There are forces that would have the greatest nation on earth destroyed. It is our sacred trust to use whatever methods necessary to protect the United States of America!"

"Sure, I guess I shouldn't complain much. I like my job."

Well, he was going to get his kill tonight, anyway, even if it wasn't Scarborough like he'd hoped.

"Yes, I know you do. I trust you've been taking your medicine Ms. Cunningham has been giving you, like a good boy?"

"Sure." Justine pulled out the pale brown prescription bottle from his coat pocket and rattled the loose pills. His thinking tablets, he called them. A light dosage of thorazine, laced with a soupcon of other psychoactives, all delicately formulated to specifically adjust his biochemistry. "Matter of fact, I'm due to take one tonight. I'll wash it down with my root beer."

Richards laid his hand on Justine's forearm, and shook his head. "There's more. We have no indication that this Klinghoffer nerd is associated with other parties. But we can't be too careful, Wood. Find out. No sodium pentathol. Old-fashioned methods."

"Ah. I take it you want me raw, tonight."

"Let's just say you can take your medicine afterwards." Richards gestured outside the window. "We've provided a nondescript Chevrolet station wagon, registered, but essentially untraceable. On the passenger seat you'll find the usual suitcase of goodies. Included are bags of marijuana, crack, and PCP. Plant these on the site of your operation. Prince George's County is just a stone's throw away. Hundreds of people are getting blown away every year. Drug-related feuds, bad deals, what have you. The Montgomery County Police won't know much about Mr. Klinghoffer. We want them to assume this was a drug-related death. Once someone actually *finds* the body, that is. Keep the noise down to an absolute minimum."

"Sure. Then what?"

"You've got a room booked at the Crystal City Mariott. Courtesy of the Editorial expense account. You sleep late tomorrow, leave the car in the hotel parking lot, and take the Metro down here for a five o'clock afternoon flight back to L.A. Take it easy for a few days!''

Justine held out his hand. ''Keys?''

''In the ignition.''

''What's on tap after my days off? More Panorama Abduction Project work?'' Contempt filled his voice.

''You don't much prefer this sort of thing, do you, Justine?''

''I guess I'm a pretty straight shooter, man. I'd much rather kill enemies and obstructions than mess with regular people's heads.''

''Justine,'' said Richards solemnly. ''Our names will probably appear in no history books, but be assured—we are wrapped up in a program designed not only to preserve and protect our country, but to carry its people to a glorious destiny, a shining future. The Project is vital to our goals, and is working splendidly already. Consider yourself a privileged individual, a Soldier of American Integrity.''

Justine reached over and took the sheet of information from his boss, noting that a grainy photograph was clipped to its bottom. ''Yeah. Better go get on my horse and *ride*.''

''You're a good man, Justine. You can expect your usual bonus.''

Justine opened the door, and softly smiled back at the man in the back seat of the limo. ''Hiyo, Silver.''

CHAPTER ELEVEN

Dear Captain MacKenzie,

Something is rotten in Iowa.

My name is Walter K. Mashkin. I've been a semiprofessional UFO investigator for several years.

Perhaps you've heard of me. I've enjoyed your series in *True* magazine very much, which is why I'm writing you, as well as to the other people in the UFO investigatory world whom I respect.

I try to keep in contact with a network of fellow individuals interested in uncovering the truth about this 40-year spate of UFO visitations of this planet. A correspondent and friend of mine is a Mr. Harry Reynolds of Dubuque, Iowa.

Captain, Harry Reynolds has disappeared.

It is my fear that Harry has been kidnapped by aliens. It is my greater fear that Harry has been the victim of those who run the UFO conspiracy in this country. Whichever the case, I am trying as hard as I can to drum up interest, if not outrage and indignation, amongst those who might help me investigate this matter.

Harry Reynolds made regular shortwave broadcasts. Harry was particularly interested in UFOs and the possibility that forms of extraterrestrial life may be attempting to contact this planet. He often challenged the occupants of the reported flying saucers to come down and speak personally with him. I spoke to Harry regularly via shortwave, occasionally listened to his amateur "program," and corresponded with him. Twice, I met him at UFO conferences, and I was impressed with his warmth, sincerity, and friendly humanity. So, when I did not hear his broadcasts for two days straight, I was naturally concerned and called his house. When there was no answer, I called the police, who promised me they'd check on him. A later call revealed that the Dubuque police had found the house deserted except for some hungry cats. Harry's car was still in the driveway, his wallet and identification were still in his bedroom.

I am making arrangements to personally visit Dubuque to look into this matter. However, I have to deal with some personal business first. In the meantime, I thought that my fellow warriors in the effort to discover the truth about the activities of UFOs—and the frightening cover-up on the part of the U.S. government, perhaps *all* the world governments.

Perhaps, since you are a midwesterner yourself, and you take an interest in these things, you can actually visit Iowa and do some investigation. If not for Harry, then for the basis of what might be an excellent magazine article.

I look forward to your response, and I hope we have the opportunity to meet.

Yours sincerely,
Walter K. Mashkin

Everett Scarborough put the letter down and looked across the table at MacKenzie. "You're not taking this seriously, are you?" The remains of a good solid meal of roast beef, baked potatoes, and Caesar salad lay around them, waiting to be picked up by the waiter. In the dining room of the Tabard Inn, candles flickered warmly by their booth.

"Of course I take it seriously, Ev!" said MacKenzie. "In fact, I took the liberty of calling the Dubuque police. Everything that Mashkin says is true. This guy Reynolds—he's gone. No trace. *Marie Celeste* time too—dishes on table, unflushed commode, lights and radio on. If it's an alien abduction case, I've not heard of one like it. They usually only last a few hours, don't they? This one's over a week long."

"The Travis Walton business during the 70s in Arizona . . . right, 1975 it was. That guy was gone for five days! And it was a fairly phony case at that, I might add. I've done several chapters in my books about that character. Apparently, he was associated with a business that had contracted with the government to thin out small trees in an area called Turkey Springs. The crew was behind on the job, and the business would be docked if the work didn't get done on time. I came up with proof of all this by the way . . . And Mike Rogers, the crew-chief admits that he'd seen that UFO-Encounter show several weeks before his disappearance. When Travis Walton disappeared, it was very close to Turkey Springs. And the search for him not only gave the Rogers crew an excuse for not getting the job done—it gave the members an excuse for not wanting to go back into the area . . . and cause for an extension of the deadline. Thanks to that, the job got completed. Apparently, the crew worked, despite their fears of getting sucked up into a flying saucer.''

"Yeah, I remember your reports on that in your books," said MacKenzie. "But dammit, man, what does that have to do with *this* case?"

"Just offering up a previous case, Mac, of a long disappearance.'' Scarborough sat back wearily and sipped at the last of his wine. "I think you'll probably find that Mr. Reynolds disappeared for a reason other than UFO abduction. Maybe he was just a lonely guy who wanted some attention. Lots of possibilities, Mac. The thing that disturbs me is how you, of all people, when a guy disappears, should shout, 'Maybe he was zapped by a flying saucer and carted off to Pluto!' Mac, I just think you're starting to get too credulous! You remember that Francis Bacon don't you? 'A credulous man is a deceiver.' ''

MacKenzie frowned. "You calling me a liar, friend?"

"No, no, no. Lighten up, Mac. I think what Bacon realized is that if you swallow everything you hear enthusiastically, then you're bound to cough up lots of untruths equally enthusiastically. It's our duty as intelligent beings to bring our own experiences and faculties to bear, our powers of analysis. God, man, we talked about this during Blue Book. And come to think of it, you were the guy that dug up that quote!"

MacKenzie wilted a little. "Yeah. I remember now. Sorry to get upset at you, Ev. Maybe I am a little too eager to jump at things. Maybe I just want a little more action in my life, a little more excitement." The big man scratched his bushy mustache. "But really, Ev. I'm asking you to have a slightly more open mind. *Something* weird is going on. The reason I gave you that letter is that something just occurred to me, something that you may be able to help out with."

"Which is?"

MacKenzie flicked his eyes about the dim dining room, as though he half expected someone to be listening in. He lowered his voice confidentially as he leaned his elbows onto the table.

"You've got some time off now. Come on out with me to

Iowa. Let's do a replay on the 60s. Let's do some great investigation together. At the very least, you'll dig up more grist for your debunking mill. And who knows what else you might come up with! Let's check into these stories . . . the Higsdon Farm stuff . . . the Reynolds case . . ."

"God, you sound just like my daughter!"

"Yeah, and I still think you oughtta make a stop in Kansas, too," said MacKenzie, a fleck of steel in his gaze. "C'mon, man. Let's *work* again. Let's get out there and dig up some dirt before we get too old. There are heads to butt, and secrets to uncover! Just a week, Ev! That's all I ask. I want it to be like old times."

Scarborough nodded. "The old times *were* good. Things seemed . . . well, I guess the cliches are true . . . much simpler then."

The big man brightened. "So you'll do it? You'll try to get what you can from Colonel Dolan, and then come and investigate with me. You're the *best*, Ev. Or anyway, at least you used to be. I need you."

Scarborough sucked on his front teeth for a moment, considering. Maybe he *should* get out into the field for a time. Mac was right, he did have some days to spare. He could think of it as a working vacation. Get the blood roaring again. The game's afoot, eh, Watson? and all that.

But his thought-flow struck an immediate barrier.

To accept his friend's invitation would be tantamount to admitting that everything he'd stood for since the Project Blue Book days, everything he'd written in his books and lectured on countless times, could be wrong. It would be almost the same as Doctor Everett Scarborough saying, "Hey, maybe there *is* some kind of cover-up. And by golly, perhaps there *are* flying saucers buzzing about piloted by little green men." No, it just didn't work. It was entirely too much to risk.

"I'm sorry, Mac. I'll look into the discrepancies you've mentioned . . . discreetly. But at this point in my career I just can't chuck the stand I've taken. At least not on the evidence of a few mixed-up facts, or on my spaced-out daughter's experiences. . . . Or on the evidence from a part-time UFO investigator who in all likelihood is a full-time loon." He handed the letter back to his friend.

MacKenzie banged his fist on the table. "Jumping Jesus,

what the hell has happened to you, Everett Scarborough?'' he said through gritted teeth.

Scarborough was chagrined to see that a few of the diners and a waiter turned to see what the commotion was. ''Not so loud, Mac.''

''I'll be as loud as I goddamn please, man! And I'll tell everyone that the Everett Scarborough that I used to know is *dead*! The Scarborough who was tough-minded and open, a maverick who tracked down facts and truth with a hunter's skill and instinct is gone. And what's left? I'll tell you what's left . . . A fat, corporate-minded, government-toady! A fucking ostrich with his head in the sand, getting his asshole crammed with thousand-dollar bills! Fame, fortune . . . God, that's what you're after, Ev, not the truth. You've sold out man! I've never thought to see that day, but you've fucking sold out.''

His face red, the big man got up and threw his napkin down on the table. Scarborough was so stunned, hurt, and embarrassed that he could find no words to answer with.

''I don't think we have anything more to talk about, Dr. Scarborough, sir,'' said Mac. ''Good night.''

The older man stalked from the room.

Shocked, Everett Scarborough could do nothing but sit and blink. Was the whole *universe* coming down on him? Just because he took a stand that other people didn't care for? A maniac with a gun, his daughter, and now one of his very best friends—they'd all taken their own particular potshots.

What the hell was wrong, anyway?

A waiter approached hesitantly, ''Is everything all right, sir?''

No, it wasn't, but Scarborough assured the waiter that he was all right.

''In that case, sir,'' said the man, pulling out the long check, laden with scribbles and prices. ''Here is your check.''

Scarborough sighed. ''Why don't you put one more drink on it, huh? A Glenlivet Scotch. Double. Neat.''

The waiter nodded. ''Very good, sir.''

Scarborough got out a credit card, and stared glumly at its holograph.

CHAPTER
TWELVE

The dark form of Roosevelt Island swept along to the right of the station wagon, giving way to the sight of the city, leaning into the Potomac like a frozen, glistening ooze of civilization.

Across from the Parkway, on the other side of Key Bridge, Georgetown blazed with nightlife. Woodrow Justine could imagine the college students clogging its cobblestone streets, navigating boozy paths from bar to bar, past the quaint shops, with rock and jazz music squeezing out into a spring-soft night. Washington, D.C., drinking age was eighteen, a full three years below that of nearby Virginia and Maryland. The Georgetown drinking establishments—open to the unbelievable hours of three A.M. in the patrician capital—attracted them like magnets. Justine liked Georgetown, he liked rubbing shoulders with young people, making conversation, and was forever startled and thrilled over how naive and stupid and *inferior* these biological sausages of the privileged classes were. It was a hobby of his to imagine how easy it would be to simply take Joe College, in his penny loafers and smart pleated pants, or Jane Sophomore, in her mascaraed face and Guess Who distressed-denim jeans, out into the alley and waste them. He never did, of course. Justine was much too professional for that. He got his share of even-ups in the course of duty. Still, he did enjoy imagining what it would be like.

No time for Georgetown tonight, though. His grey Chevrolet rolled under the bridge and up on George Washington Parkway. Justine admired the view across the river of Georgetown University's lighted spires. He supposed he could have driven up 295, past the Tidal Basin, and on up the Baltimore Washington Parkway. But this way, if not more direct, was at least more relaxing.

He turned onto Route 495—the Washington Beltway, after a pleasant ten-mile cruise overlooking the Potomac, then took that four-lane highway across the American Legion Bridge into Maryland. At eleven o'clock, traffic was light for a pleasant spring Saturday night. Justine slipped past Glen Echo and Bethesda and Kensington easily, gearing his mind up for what lay ahead. Beside him was a nondescript tan suitcase. He'd checked it before he'd left National. It held, of all things, a pretty clunky .38 Special, along with one of the new silencers that didn't mark the bullet. Justine much preferred better handguns—he wished he had his Walther PPK or Baretta automatic with him, two prized members of an extensive gun collection. But this was consistent with the impression that the Editors wanted to make—a death wiped of professional finger-prints. Also in the pack was his usual bag of tricks—certain instruments that would do a Nazi Death Camp commandant proud. There was also a map of Montgomery County, with Klinghoffer's road explicitly marked. This lay on top of the suitcase, and the secret government operative examined it as he approached the signs for the Georgia Avenue exits.

He took the south exit. It took him another twelve minutes of lights and stop signs to get to the heart of Takoma Park. On the map, the town looked like a large wart on the Northeast side of the tilted square that was D.C. In the flesh, it seemed a gentle and old suburb, filled with ancient houses, more than slightly frayed at the ages, but not subject to the kind of decay brought by poor inhabitants who had recently moved in. No, Takoma Park had an old, 1920's-neighborhood-gone-slightly-to-seed feel. One of the things that always impressed Justine about the Washington, D.C., area was the number of *trees*—big trees, small trees, oceans and seas and rivers of trees, streaming beside buildings. Takoma Park seemed particularly wealthy with thick oak and poplar, and their spring leaves crowned them now, creating almost a canopy over the neighborhood in places.

Klinghoffer's house was on Greenbriar Road, quite near to where Piney Branch Road intersected with Flower Avenue (even the goddamn streets were named after plants! thought Justine), and Justine found it with no difficulty. It was a single-family unit—old and faintly dilapidated from the evi-

dence provided by a pass-by—and fortunately not very close to
its neighbors. The lights burning in the living room and
basement reassured him. The mark was indeed home. Just as
Richards had promised.

Justine turned a corner, and parked on a side street down the
block. He pocketed his weapon and his bag of tricks, and then
he looked at the grainy photo of Klinghoffer one more time under
the illumination of the dashboard light. Underneath was printed
the words, *MARYLAND DEPT OF VEHICLES, 1986.* The picture
showed a man with dull, faintly bulging eyes, who was losing his
dark, limp hair. He was not smiling. His cheeks were slightly
puffy. Guy was overweight, thought Justine. Out of shape. Simpler and simpler. Still, that leap over the balcony edge showed
some agility and power. Best to be cautious at the very least.

Locking the car door behind him, Justine pocketed the keys and
proceeded to walk toward 1345 Greenbriar, checking the neighborhood. All the houses were old, though a few looked as though
they'd been refurbished somewhat. A few lights were on, and
from one of the houses the sound of Mozart sweetened the air. No
parties, no activity—good. A quiet neighborhood. It would be
even quieter much later that night, when Justine was finished.

The Klinghoffer residence itself was old, and the grass and
hedges that surrounded it were in want of trimming. It was not
a big house, but a large open porch gave that impression. As he
approached it, Justine could see that the dull green paint was
coming off in strips, revealing an even duller grey undercoat—
and sometimes just brown, rotting wood. Even past the sweet
scent of honeysuckle from the underbrush that surrounded this
house, Justine's faculties sensed a sourness, an *offness*. His
hackles rose as he stepped up onto the porch, past an old swing
whose left chain had broken and lay rusting on the chipped
floorboards. There was a distinct *wrongness* here.

It gave Justine the willies. This was not a sensation he was
used to.

He stuck his hand inside his pocket to seek the comfort of a
gun in his hand. The grey steel was cold and solid, and made
him feel much more confident as soon as he touched it.

A definite moldy effluvia hovered over the porch, an earthy,
fungoid smell, touched with the perfume of the hyacinth
bushes nearby. A shiver touching his spine, Justine made a
complete circuit of the house, padding silently in the overgrown

grasses. Brick foundation, wood frame. A bit of shingle fallen from the tattered roof crunched under his shoe. Basement windows peered up from rusted wells, and light leaked through, but he could not see anything for the dirt and dust that smudged them. Around the back, a dilapidated swing set grew from the ground like a metallic tree, next to a clothesline with clips hooked to nothing but air. Justine checked the back door. Locked. Easy enough to break in, if necessary. He could hear nothing from inside the house—but he sensed that someone was home. He walked around the north side of the house, observing that the windows there were just as heavily curtained as all the first-floor windows were.

Getting the door open would be easy enough. A knock, a flash of an official badge, a request for a few questions . . . but all that depended on the door getting answered. He stepped onto the porch, and the wood groaned beneath his weight. Rotted. Justine just hoped he didn't fall through. Whew—that fungus smell again. Suddenly, he just wanted to get this business over with.

There was a storm door, but the front window was gone. He could see no sign of a doorbell. Justine braced himself and knocked four times on the wooden door. The knocks echoed hollowly beyond, but there was no answer. Justine knocked again, with the same result.

He reached down and tried the old doorknob.

It turned easily in his grip, and he pushed open the door with a faint wheeze.

"Hello?" he said. "Mr. Klinghoffer?" He thought better of announcing the presence of government authority. That ploy might have worked at the door, but there was the possibility the man might be holed up here, just waiting to plug the first cop to walk in. However, the living room showed no evidence of preparation for a standoff. And no one answered him, either.

Justine's nose twitched at the rank stench of sour garbage. A faint light from the dining area illuminated a living room piled high with stacks of newspapers and Hefty bags filled with trash, some cinched at the top, some not. In one corner, by the grate of a hearth was an old RCA black-and-white television.

Keeping his gun gripped in his pocket out of sight, Justine skirted the piles of trash and walked into the dining room. "Mr. Klinghoffer?" he called softly.

More stacks of newspapers lined one of the dining-room walls, all the way to the ceiling. The other wall was solid bookcases, crammed with musty old books and magazines. In the center of the room was a table covered by a filthy tablecloth. On the table were rows and rows of Fruit Loops cereal, some open and empty, some still sealed. A carton of milk sat in front of a half-filled bowl of cereal dotted with color. The whole room smelled of milk gone bad.

"Jesus," whispered Justine to himself.

To one side of the cereal boxes were a spill of books and magazines and tabloids. Justine examined them. *National Enquirer. Star. World Weekly News* and *National Intruder* all were there, opened, and violated: stories had been clipped from the pages. Also there were copies of *Omni*, opened to the red "Anti-Matter" sections, as well as science magazines, the *Washington Post*, and other national newspapers. All had been worked over with scissors. The stacks of books were all UFO-oriented, many written by Dr. Stanton Friedman, and most had the sloppy look of primitive self-publishing. There was one whole pile devoted to *Fate* and *UFO* and *California UFO* magazines. Next to it was a stack of old and yellowing *Flying Saucer* magazines from the fifties.

Justine walked over to look at the bookshelf. More UFO books, but a great deal of science fiction as well, from Piers Anthony to Roger Zelazny, but not alphabetized. As he stepped away, he trod on a pile of paper, and he looked down to see the remains of a book. Scarborough's new book, *Above Us Only Sky*, ripped apart with a knife or razor blade. Amused, Justine picked it up and immediately dropped it as soon as the smell hit him—the destroyed book had been smeared with excrement.

"A critic," whispered Justine. "Definitely a critic."

Question was, where *was* was the critic? Basement? Attic? Put him *away*, Woody, he told himself. Put him down quick, and get the hell outta here.

The kitchen was a smelly jumble, a repeat of the dining room, with a greater variety of food and food stains. A great mound of rotting matter lay in the sink, making Justine ill at the sight and smell. God, it was worse than when he was a kid. Much worse. Oh, jeez, *bury* this guy.

Justine decided to check the upstairs first. Only if he had to, would he deal with what might lie in the subterranean part of this sewer. He eased into the hallway, intending to go back through the cluttered living room and then up the scuffed and tatty stairway, senses alert, when suddenly the cellar door flew open. The big door banged against the wall, and a man jumped up from the gloom below, screaming at the top of his lungs and holding the sides of his head as though they threatened to explode.

"Arwhhhhhhhhhhh!" screeched the man, bashing into the wall. "Arwhieeeeeeeee!" he cried, slipping first to his knees and then slipping to the floor in a paroxysm of agony.

Startled, Justine stepped back two paces, pulling out his gun. If instinct had had its way, that gun would have fired, but the assassin's iron will and years of training held his own panic in check, and allowed him a split second of detached observation before a decision was made.

From the picture, Justine recognized the man who lay on the floor as Arnold Klinghoffer. His knees were tucked up into his chest in almost a fetal position. Spasms wracked his body. He smelled of old and new sweat, and his limp hair was pasted down by a patina of moisture. Around his head was an oddly constructed helmet, apparently made of aluminum foil and coat hangers. Two bent wires stretched out, wobbling, like the antenna of some demented insect.

Justine put his gun back in his pocket. It was a shame he couldn't just waste the crazy now, but Richards had specifically requested an interrogation. He put his pack down against the wall, and leaned over the still-shuddering man, still on guard. He reached into the specially constructed pocket on the side of his pants and thumbed on the tiny recorder.

"Arnold Klinghoffer," he said, touching the man's shoulder.

The man abruptly swung his head around, so quickly that his amateurish helmet fell off. The effect was immediate; Arnold Klinghoffer blinked at his visitor outlined in the light from the dining room, and opened his mouth like a beached and gasping fish. "Anteres . . . message from Anteres . . . We will cure cancer . . . We will cure AIDS. Help from the stars. The Friends of the Universe have landed! Make ready for the Pleiadans! Jesus shall return in a flying saucer!"

"I'm a friend," said Justine, softly. "I'm here to help you."

The eyes—bulging, hyperthyroid—shifted their focus from infinity to Woodrow Justine. They seemed startled for only a moment, and then . . . accepting. "Yes," said the man. "You. You've come. They said you'd come tonight. Tonight. I was talking to them! The helmet worked again. Only once in awhile does the solarnarium-crystoid nexus catch their broadcasts." He turned his head toward the mangled helmet. The aluminum foil crinkled as he picked it up and looked at it as though it were the Holy Grail. "I have their message, and will act!"

Klinghoffer was dressed in black chinos and a dirty white tank-top undershirt. He wore no shoes, and his black socks were filled with holes, so that many long-nailed toes stuck out.

"Mr. Klinghoffer, I hope you'll help me," said Justine, choosing a gentle tack for now. "I'm sorry to bother you, but I've been sent—" He decided on a different, wilder story. "—by the Pleiadans you mentioned. They're very puzzled. They want to know, was it the people from Anteres that told you to shoot at Everett Scarborough?"

At the name, "Scarborough" the already-buggy eyes almost seemed to pop all the way out. "Enemy!" he whispered harshly. "Liar! Danger!" He floundered his way to a kneeling position. "Must stop him!"

"Who told you to shoot him, Arnold?"

Klinghoffer lifted himself to his feet and regarded the man curiously. "You don't know? Then you're not from the Pleiadans! You're from the Moon People!"

"Oops. Sorry, pal. I get them confused all the time," said Justine.

Klinghoffer nodded with great gravity. "The Moon People said they would send you tonight . . . send you to receive the solarnarium device I constructed that their ship needs to fly. But you're human . . . I did not expect a human."

"I'm their friend."

"Yes, they do have human friends." Klinghoffer looked around nervously. "No one followed you, did they?"

"No. I'm alone."

"Good. I have taken off most of the week to finish this work for your friends," said the man with the utmost seriousness. Suddenly, Klinghoffer leaned closer, scrutinizing his new visitor in more detail. "But how is it that you know of the incident with the infidel Scarborough?"

"My . . . er . . . Moon People pals gave me the scoop. Yeah. And like I say, they were real puzzled why you did it."

Klinghoffer suddenly gave a phlegmy cough, and Justine caught a blast of halitosis that made him cringe. But he did not move. "Inspiration, my friend. Pure inspiration. Before the lecture, I felt the Call, and I put on my two-way wrist radio. The Consortium told me that I should take my gun to the lecture, and that I should sit on the first balcony row—the loge, actually. Yes, the loge!"

The Consortium? What the fuck! Justine hoped that the miniature tape player was getting all this down!

"Did this Consortium tell you to kill Scarborough?"

"No. I was—upset. I lost . . . control. I haven't been well. Ever since my mother died two years ago, things have not been good." He gestured to a portrait of a fleshy elderly woman gazing down with that eternal maternal frown of disapproval at the mess in the living room. "But my work here . . . it sustains me."

"Ah yes, the Consortium," said Justine. "Would you tell me some more about them. The Moon People were so sketchy. And I'd love to see this two-way wrist radio of yours."

"Later. First, I want to give you the solarnarium device I constructed." Klinghoffer gestured for him to follow downstairs.

Justine was faintly disappointed as they moved into the cool humid shadows of the basement. The rube was freely dispensing with his information—no bag-of-tricks incentives were necessary. Just as well, though. The sooner he could get out of this creepy place, the better.

The basement, if anything, was worse than upstairs, even though no garbage was strewn about. It was a finished basement, with carpeting over the cement, and tile in the washing-machine-and-dryer area. The place was one large room, with the furnace squatting in the corner like a hulking metal beast hiding in a plywood cave. Justine noticed overhead fluorescent lights in a paneled ceiling, but none were on. Instead, what little illumination there was came from naked 40-watt bulbs, glowing softly in various parts of the room.

One part of the basement seemed to have once been an entertainment center. An old couch and some chairs surrounded a stereo-and-color-TV hybrid. This area was now populated by naked store-window mannequins and several inflatable female sex-dolls, mouths open in permanant Os of gratification. These figures sat and lay in bizarre and contorted combinations—

perhaps a very alien concept of an orgy. Beside the TV-stereo was a VCR, about which lay several porno films; and on a coffee table were several mason jars, covered by Saran wrap fastened by rubber bands. The jars were filled to various levels with a milky substance. Two had gone green with decomposition. The smell as Justine walked past was indescribable. He held his hand up to his mouth and stared at the jars.

Klinghoffer, noticing, sidled up to him and nodded down at the jars. "Yes. I am a fruitful contributor. Star seed!" He looked up with awe toward the ceiling stretching out his arms toward the universe. "My children populate the galaxies now." He looked back down and shook his head. "I'm due for a pick-up." He looked at Justine with sudden comprehension and smiled showing a set of rotting teeth. "You! You bring them back with you to the Moon People. And they can distribute—"

"No!" said Justine, his stomach turning as he looked away. "I mean, the device. That's all I can carry."

Klinghoffer shrugged. "Okay. It's over here, on the workbench. I just put the finishing touches on it."

The man beckoned and Justine followed.

The workbench was the featured spot of the larger work area, which took up most of the basement. On the walls stretched a full complement of tools, from hammers and chisels to screwdrivers and awls. A number of drawers apparently held electrical components. A power-saw sat to one side, along with a number of hand-held saws.

On the edges of the area were bulletin boards. Tacked on these were clippings from newspapers and magazines—principally dealing with UFO phenomena and other paranormal occurrences. A huge blackboard hung nearby, filled with odd equations and even odder diagrams. Scattered on the floor were various half-completed projects, trailing wire, topped with transistors and vacuum tubes. Justine did not have the vaguest idea what they were supposed to be. They looked like the guts of the mutated children of robots—but on closer look, they were just pieces of everyday appliances stuck and soldered together at random. There was the smell of burnt insulation and solder in the air, along with something old and rotting.

The centerpiece of the workbench was a larger version of the oddities strewn on the floor. It looked like the picture tube of an old Zenith TV set, with transistors and resistors, circuit breakers and wire soldered on its base willy-nilly, and then covered with ropes of crumpled-up aluminum foil.

"This is it!" said Klinghoffer, a fevered, distant look clouding his eye. "This is the device the creatures from Anteres instructed me to make for their ship."

"Uhm...what's it supposed to do?" Best to keep the weirdo talking—God knew what might flow out in the way of information along with the verbiage.

"I believe it's a part of their star drive. It ionizes the exhaust and converts it to reusable fuel. The key," he said, tapping the aluminum foil. "Is the solarnarium. You have to convolute it *just so* to obtain proper magnetic harmonics. Solarnarium is the *key* element to my communications helmets. It creates a harmonic field that will pick up messages from their saucers." He petted the device lovingly. "You *will* be careful with it, won't you?"

"Oh, yeah, sure, and the Moon People...well, they're *real* good with this kind of mechanical stuff."

Klinghoffer nodded, staring at the useless contraption, falling into a deep meditative silence.

"So tell me—these solarnarium helmets...Is that how you communicate with the Consortium?" asked Justine.

The effect was immediate and swift. Klinghoffer swung on him, eyes bugged and forehead creases deep. "Of course not, you idiot! The two-way wrist radio! I use the two-way wrist radio for the Consortium." A speckle of drool drifted down from his lips. He ground his teeth.

"Sorry," said Justine. "Yeah, you did mention you were going to show it to me. But tell me, Arnold. The Moon People contacted me just last year, and I don't know much about the extraterrestrial side of life. How did you get involved? And how did you meet this Consortium?"

A dry cough escaped the man's mouth. Another. Justine suddenly realized Klinghoffer was laughing. "Since I was a little boy, I've always known that there were people up in the stars...And then the Consortium came to me, and they said, 'Yes, you're right, Arnold. Learn about them. Study them. Perhaps one day you too can join our number.'

"And so, I study them. I know all about the Star People. There are many different races you know—some good, and some evil. I, Arnold Klinghoffer, only help the good ones, like the Anterans and the Pleiadans and the Moon People and the Golden Ones. And one day soon they will reveal themselves to the rest of the world and sail down in the ships of silver, and bring down the Lord and Jesus Christ and all the good dead people like my mother. And there will be a time of joy and celebration upon the earth.'' Klinghoffer made a fist and dug long fingernails into the palm of his hand. "But first, the Bad Ones must be overcome."

"Yes, absolutely, Arnold. But the Consortium. How do I get in touch with the Consortium? Do I use the two-way wrist radio?" This Consortium could be a group of similarly bent weirdos that the Editors should definitely know about.

"Why do you want to know about the Consortium?" asked Klinghoffer.

"Well, I only know the Moon People. I want to help the whole cause!"

Klinghoffer studied the man for a moment, squinting. Justine felt as though he were some paramecium being scrutinized underneath a microscope. This fucker was really off the edge! I may be borderline psychotic, thought Justine. But I'm not *crazy.*

Finally, after a long silence, Klinghoffer licked his lips and nodded. "Yes. Yes, I will tell you about the Consortium. You need to know. But first, tell me your name."

"Samuels," said Justine, using one of his several aliases. "Peter Samuels."

The bugeyed man nodded as though he had suspected just such a name. "Excellent. It all makes sense. Have you ever noticed how things flow together? Coincidences? Synchronicity? The Golden Ones—they have told me that this is part of the inner mechanism of reality. And this is where the Consortium enters the picture, Peter Samuels." Klinghoffer turned away and walked to a set of battered metal file cabinets. He rolled open a drawer.

"Is this Consortium affiliated with a government?" Justine asked.

"All governments . . . and none! Their agents work in all the countries of the world! Peter Samuels, did you know that they want *me* to join their number? I work toward that goal, but it is hard. Very hard. The sacrifices! The mental energy! Astonishing!" He shook his head wearily, and then lifted something from the drawer, and carried it over to his guest. "But you wished to see the radio. Here it is."

Justine took the device, and Klinghoffer turned back to the filing cabinet, starting to take something else out. It was a large silver band, covered with a zigzag of both naked and insulated wire connecting several cannabilized watch-faces and topped with a tiny speaker and receiver, attached to a nine-volt battery. All this, swathed in that magical material, solarnarium: aluminum foil.

Justine stared at it for a moment, shaking his head. Another bogus device. The guy actually had him going for a while. This Consortium was just another figment of a twisted imagination, just like the Anterans or the Moon People or the Golden Ones. This sucker sure talked organization, but clearly the Arnold Klinghoffer conspiracy numbered exactly one!

Still, he had to make sure. He started to play with the toggles to see if he could turn the thing on.

"Yes! The Consortium! The Men in Black! A worthy aspiration. You, too, would make a good candidate," said Klinghoffer, turning around.

"Huh?" said Justine.

Suddenly, Klinghoffer was on him, and Justine felt a sharp stinging jab his left bicep. He dropped the two-way wrist radio, stepped back and pushed Klinghoffer away from him. The man's rank body odor clung to Justine nostrils. Horrified, the government agent saw that Klinghoffer was holding a large hypodermic needle in his hand. Its contents had been plunged into his veins.

"Don't worry, Peter Samuels," said Klinghoffer. "It doesn't hurt. You, too, shall be a candidate now! You too can join the Consortium!"

"What did you put in me!" screeched Justine. "You maniac! What did you shoot me up with?"

Klinghoffer gestured to a bottle of clear liquid by the cabinet. "Star stuff! It will clear your mind! It will prepare you for contact with the Consortium. And they will tell you what you must—"

"You fucking loony!" Fury overwhelmed judgment in Justine's mind. He stepped over and grabbed the chubby man by his neck. "What is that shit! Really!"

"I told you! Star stuff!" gurgled Klinghoffer. "Stop it. You're hurting me!"

Justine hurled the man toward his workbench. Klinghoffer struck it hard, knocking over the Anteran starship device with a crash, and flopping onto the floor. Justine ran over and kicked him hard in the side. "What was that crap!" he shrilled, holding the still-smarting arm. *"What was it?"*

Another blow to the head knocked out teeth and brought forth a splash of blood. "You . . . you're not from the Moon People!" cried Klinghoffer. "You're not my friend. You're from the Bad Ones!"

"You bet, asshole," said Justine, watching as the crazy crawled away. "I'm from the big bad fucking United States government. Now tell me, *what did you stick in me?!"*

Klinghoffer's eyes were glazed as he grabbed up the fallen two-way wrist radio. A bubble of saliva, blood, and snot grew from a nostril as he fumbled at a switch and began to mumble hoarsely into the receiver, "Help me. Please! Help me!"

Something snapped in Woodrow Justine. He was no longer the cool assassin. The raging berserker, the marine who had charged the beaches of Grenada, took over. He took out his revolver and stepped to a straddling position over the whimpering man. Screaming, he fired point-blank into Arnold Klinghoffer's head. He emptied his gun, the bullets thunking and splattering blood, skull, and brain matter over the basement floor. When he was finished, Klinghoffer's face and head were almost sheared from the rest of his body. A vast pool of blood leaked out from the twitching dead man onto the rug.

By the time Justine regained control, the firing pin was clicking against empty cylinders. Justine put the gun back in his pocket, and stepped away from the flowing gore, annoyed to see that it had splattered onto his pants legs. No matter. He was going to have to go to ground anyway. He had to get back to Operations Central immediately, and get checked. He didn't have the faintest what this nut case had squirted into his arm. Fucking hell . . . And it was probably a fucking *filthy* needle as well.

Quickly, Justine picked the hypo from the limp hand of the dead man, wrapped it in an oily rag. He grabbed the bottle of solution that Klinghoffer had pointed to. The boys in the labs were going to have to analyze this. Fortunately, he could feel no effects from the injection. If it had been some kind of sedative, he'd be at least feeling groggy by now. But all Justine felt was the screech of adrenaline in his system. He wrapped the bottle in another cloth and went back up the stairs to where his black bag waited for him. He stashed the bottle, then took out the cellophane baggies of drugs that had been provided for him to plant. He did not care to go back downstairs, so he simply tossed the stuff onto the dining room table, amongst the stacks of books and magazines.

Woodrow Justine took a deep breath. A strong and long shudder wracked his body.

It took every bit of his willpower, every bit of his training, to keep in control, to keep his mind clear.

These clothes, these gloves—he was going to burn them all. And he was going to take a long, long shower.

With a whispered curse, Woodrow Justine got the hell out of there. It was a very hard thing indeed not to run all the way to where his car was parked.

CHAPTER THIRTEEN

For centuries, strange things have been seen in the sky.

However, it was not until June 24, 1947 that the modern age of UFOs began. That was the day that a Boise Idaho businessman named Kenneth Arnold took off in a private plane from Chehalis, Washington, heading for Yakima, Washington.

Arnold apparently did not notice Rod Serling leaning against the hangar, draped in cigarette smoke, narrating.

That day, a marine corps transport aircraft had apparently gone down near Mount Rainier, the highest point in the contiguous forty-eight states. Arnold, an enthusiastic pilot, eagerly joined the search, rising up past 9,000 feet and cruising past the snow-topped peak, checking the ridges and canyons for debris and survivors.

He found no wreckage, but saw something far more spectacular than anything the marines could offer.

It was a day of crystal clarity, and Arnold was cruising his small craft near the splendid scenery provided by the fabulous mountain when he noticed the flash of a reflection on the steel of his airplane. When he could see no light source for the reflection in the immediate area, he scanned the horizon. North of Mount Rainier, at an altitude of approximately 9,500 feet—perhaps twenty-five miles away—he saw a line of flying objects approaching the mountain quickly. Nine objects. At first, he thought that they were conventional aircraft, perhaps a grouping of the newly developed jet-fighters from the air force. But careful observation noted no wings or tails, nor any sign of vapor trails. Utilizing a device known as a Zeus Fastener—or cowling tool—he estimated each craft to be about two-thirds the size of a DC-4. His calculations also produced the speed of the aircraft, as they flashed and wobbled along in perfect formation, like a group of speeding geese. They were traveling at a speed of 1656.71 miles per hour—far faster than any airplanes produced by the United States in 1947.

Each of the vessels moved "... like a saucer skipping on water..." Arnold noted later to reporters; and the image of a tea saucer skating through the sky, powered by mysterious beings, immediately took hold of America's imagination.

Thus, although there had been odd aerial sightings before, including the bizarre "Foo fighters" that followed B-52 bombers in the Second World War, Arnold's was the first sighting of "flying saucers." The term quickly became a part of the English language, and the phenomenon immediately became a part of the American consciousness.

The air force immediately categorized the sightings as a "mirage." Smooth, crystalline air conditions often contribute to a stable atmosphere necessary for inversions, as well as increasing the refraction index that creates mirages. But the air force explanation fell on deaf ears—the American public thrilled to the notion of weird objects tweaking officials' noses, and the era of the flying saucer was born.

And a very odd era it is, the number of sightings of UFOs

growing proportionally to the public-at-large's interest in the phenomenon.

Dr. Everett Scarborough's problem as a historian of this era—and a debunking historian at that—was that much of the facts concerning Unidentified Flying Objects was anecdoctal. And because so many of the records were kept in popular literature—such as the books by Daniel Keyhoe and Frank Edward's *Flying Saucers, Serious Business*—there were often no hard facts to work with, a must for concerned and qualified historians. That the facts in most pro-UFO books were often canted toward credulity and were journalistically underlined with unprovable observation and theory, muddied the waters terribly. Thus, when Scarborough wrote about flying saucers, his concerns were just as much with UFO-ologist literatures as with the actual sightings of the objects themselves. This was why he kept such extensive files and records on the subject— including the files of his own extensive investigations, both on the field and in the library.

Because the field of study was swamped with such a wealth of nonsense, hoaxes, public misunderstanding, and government mix-ups and vagueness, it was extremely difficult to write clearly about it. This was where Everett Scarborough excelled. Any halfway-intelligent reader could understand perfectly what he was discussing in his books, his sense of organization and clarity were almost unswerving. Unlike the UFO-ologists who wrote about flying-saucer incidents with screaming speculation and blathering exclamation, Scarborough wrote clear factual prose, stating explicitly what was fact, what was supposition, and what was pure fiction, leavening it all with wit and eloquent style.

Readers of Scarborough's books concerning the UFO phenomena—although he had written other books, the UFO material was the most popular—had a working knowledge of the basic outline of UFO history. They knew not only about the Arnold sighting and the "Foo fighters" during World War II, they also knew that "ghost ships" had plagued Scandinavian and European skies in the 1930s, and that not long after Pearl Harbor, a stationary craft drifted slowly along the Santa Monica Bay coastline, observed by thousands of Los Angeles residents, an event that was reported to President Roosevelt himself by General George Marshall. They knew that after more sightings

of supposedly metallic, circular craft, the air force set up its
first investigative probe into the subject, Project Sign, in 1947.
And they knew that on January 7, 1948, Captain Thomas
Mantell's P-51 Mustang jet crashed while pursuing strange
metallic objects climbing through the clouds.

They knew the air force was very concerned that these
flying-craft sightings could be the work of the new communist
enemies of the Soviet Union. They knew that in 1949 Project
Sign was changed to Project Grudge, after a slew of rumors
about alien saucer crash-landings in Roswell, Arizona, and
Aztec, Arizona, which produced burnt alien bodies, were kept
absolutely top secret. They knew that next came Project Blue
Book, and the involvement of the Central Intelligence Agency
working in tandem with the air force to investigate the possible
threat of UFOs to the national security of the United States of
America. They knew that it was Edward J. Ruppelt, the first
director of Project Blue Book who had coined the term UFO—
for Unidentified Flying Objects—which succeeded the mislead-
ing term "flying saucer."

However, most important, Scarborough's readers realized
how the flames of interest in the phenomenon were kept fanned
by a number of crackpots, opportunistic reporters, and media
czars looking for exciting copy. His methodical dissection of
the events leading up to the near mass-hysteria of the early
fifties, when it was even rumored that Presidents Truman and
Eisenhower personally had conferences with alien beings, remains a textbook example of classic social analysis—although
his background was in physics and mathematics, college sociol-
ogy teachers often assigned his book, *Anatomy of a Stellar
Hysteria*, to students to read, particularly for its expert discussion of the 1951 movie *The Day the Earth Stood Still*'s
influence on media and social behavior. His readers knew that
after the crisis died down, it was the work of such fanatics as
the loony dwarf Raymond Palmer—he of the infamous Shaver
Mystery—and his publication, *Flying Saucer*, that kept interest
in UFOs alive.

Scarborough's readers also knew the intimate details of the
work of a methodical UFO investigator, and they were treated
to an almost day-by-day account of his consultancy work for
Project Blue Book from 1966 until the Project was officially
closed in 1969, bannering the conclusion that no conclusive

evidence had been uncovered to prove that any UFO bore extraterrestrial life-forms.

Each of his books updated the trends and fads of the UFO field, so Scarborough's readers were kept updated as to the latest weirdnesses. He took great delight in devoting whole sections of his books to kooky publications, groups and cults fostered by the UFO phenomenon, inviting readers to send for subscriptions to *Saucerian Magazine*, or *California UFO*, or other fringe groups, chortling in his prose at their ludicrous articles.

The most engaging thing about Dr. Everett Scarborough's books, and one of the principal characteristics that separated him from other debunkers, was his admission that the reason the whole UFO phenomenon was so popular—and indeed, why he was able to make such a good living discussing it—was that it was so entertaining. Thus, Scarborough's readers also knew that when they studied the facts of this odd phenomenon they weren't just looking at hard cold data—they were peering into the warped netherlands of human eccentricity.

Nonetheless, those who read Dr. Everett Scarborough's publications knew that the books were extensively researched, and that the facts were always straight. Scarborough often spoke during lectures and interviews of his extensive library on the subject, and of his extensive files of data, culled from his own investigations of UFO sightings, as well as from those of others.

It was for this reason that when Scarborough went to his filing cabinets, looking for his version of the documents that his friend Eric MacKenzie had requested, what he found—or, rather, what he did not find—was quite a shock.

Scarborough kept his filing cabinets in his furnace room. It was the unfinished part of the cellar, separated from his library and stereo room by a woodframed dryboard divider. The bank filing-cabinets were situated against this divider, five big, bulky grey ones, scuffed and marked and banged. Unlike MacKenzie, who had "borrowed" his from the U.S. Air Force, Scarborough had picked these up legitimately at a government auction for very little money. He shuddered to think about all the years of bureaucratic service they'd put in, but they were serviceable enough for his purposes: namely, to store documents that he very rarely examined, but that he didn't care to throw away.

It was a Sunday afternoon when Scarborough went down to dig through the files, and his mood was as grey as the sky that had moved in over the D.C. area, dragging with it a cool spell and the taste of rain. He'd slept late that day, a rarity for him—and when he awoke, his face hurt worse than ever. He dragged himself out of bed, changed his bandage, happy to find no signs of rot or gangrene, and then fixed himself a pot of coffee, trying to kill the Sunday blues with his Sunday ritual of reading the fat *Washington Post* and the fatter *New York Times* back-to-back. One of the many nice things about the *Post* and the *Times* was that there were hardly ever reports of UFOs in their august pages. Reviews of his books he suffered gladly—but when he read the two best papers in the world, he knew his mind could relax from dealing with the barbarities of flying saucers and plunge into the cold waters of nuclear treaties, drug epidemics, disease discussion, business takeovers and *Calvin and Hobbes*. Ah, sweet reality!

But finally, after staring just a little longer at the *New York Times* Non-fiction Hardcover Bestseller List with *Above Us Only Sky* seated securely at Number Eight, he poured another cup of coffee, added some 1 percent milkfat Lucerne, wrapped himself up in his heavy blue cotton robe, and traipsed downstairs to deal with those goddamn files.

He put a Sir Neville Marriner and The Academy of St. Martins-in-the-Field Mozart CD into the stereo, found the packet of Xeroxes that Mac had sent him, and examined them for a few moments, so that he knew just what the hell he was looking for. This Iowa investigation—that was what Mac had the bee in his bonnet about... It should be easy enough to locate his notes on the subject.

He had to admit that he was very hurt by the way his friend had acted the night before, but it was not the first time that the two had argued. And it was always the same. Mac with his Irish temper, and him with his obstinate stands on things. They'd argued about politics, women, even the best kinds of whiskey—often coming close to blows. But still, it had never gotten this personal before, always it was a manly, bluff kind of argument, a defense of facades rather than of inner territory. Last night, though, they'd apparently hurt each other, and Everett felt pretty bad about that. So, after a drink or two more, he'd decided, hell, it wasn't worth it. He'd have to look at the files, talk this over with Mac in a civilized way, and they'd get their relationship back on track.

The guy was way off base, of course, but Scarborough supposed it was best to humor him, maybe even patronize him, rather than jeopardize their buddyship.

They'd always been friends. They'd always enjoyed talking, and playing cards. Scarborough had been surprised when he'd actually thoroughly enjoyed the fishing trips that MacKenzie dragged him on, although he drew the line at hunting. He had a diehard liberal's viewpoint on firearms, favoring rigid control of handguns and harboring a general distaste for all kinds of guns. He regretted deeply having to own one—even though it was registered. He'd even written a soul-searching article on the subject. A favorite uncle of his had died in a hunting accident when he was just eleven, and he'd immediately thrown away all his boyhood gun-toys. Although he'd worked with the armed forces, he'd never actually joined them, shunning them by avidly pursuing his academic career at Harvard and then MIT, and thus being deferred from any possible draft.

Nonetheless, the bond between the men had started when they discovered they had the capacity for deep and meaningful conversations about anything under the sun—or, for that matter, far beyond it. Their conversations were often marathon—they sparked off each other, there was a magical alchemy of words between them, often fueled by alcohol, but that addition wasn't necessary. Whole worlds had opened for both of them in merely knowing each other—MacKenzie's fiction often featured characters . . . mostly heroes, though the occasional playful villain popped up from time to time . . . modeled on Dr. Everett Scarborough. And Captain Eric MacKenzie's world of action and adventure infected Scarborough's books with a sense of excitement. Indeed, it had been MacKenzie's work with Scarborough's prose in the late sixties and early seventies that had shown the scientist how to stop writing for a stuffy world of academia, and construct clean, vibrant, masculine sentences that grabbed a reader by the scruff of his neck and said, "Hey you! Pay attention!"

They'd always been buddies, true, but the relationship had deepened radically when Phyllis Scarborough had become ill. Eric MacKenzie had been there for both of them during those long, cruel months. He'd even moved his typewriter to their house for a whole month while Phyl was in the hospital, helping with Diane and fixing meals and generally serving as a lifesaver in the time of Death. But the breast cancer had metastasized down to Phyllis's liver, and not even Mac's verve and bravado and crude jokes could keep her from eventually slipping away. He had stayed on awhile for the funeral and afterward, playing gin rummy with Scarborough, getting him to critique his latest novel in manuscript, and demanding some first-class research on entomology from the scientist for his next, *The Immolator Meets the Insects*. Of all Scarborough's friends and family, only Mac understood just how threatening this death was to Everett's mental health. Only he somehow instinctively understood, as Phyllis had, that all the logic and science, the mathematics and rigid structure in Everett's life was his attempt to organize, catalogue, and *cope with* the seemingly meaningless chaos of life, a chaos that had just torn the very soul from his body, his beloved wife. Of course Mac never mentioned this, never even brought the subject up. Everett Scarborough's brilliant talents of logic, deduction, and scientific inquiry were the constant butts of his jokes, but he never ventured into the touchy psychological causes, though he knew them. Phyllis had told Mac about Everett's childhood and adolescence—and though Scarborough would never have mentioned the painful background of his youth, he did not mind Mac knowing.

Yes, in those days of IVs and medicine smells, gritted teeth and murmured comfortings, even Eric MacKenzie had no idea of just how close the great Dr. Everett Scarborough had come to that edge he had so closely skirted in his youth. But it was the MacKenzie's presence—along with his love for his daughter, and sheer, stubborn willpower—that kept him from tumbling into the chasm. For Captain Eric MacKenzie sensed the inner storms that raged beneath the rigid control. Mac did not question his friend's lack of tears at Phyllis's funeral, nor his seemingly stoic acceptance of his loss. He knew that with Scarborough's psychology, cold control was absolutely necessary, for if emotion were allowed to reign unchecked, there was the possibility that it might never stop.

Yes, thought Scarborough as he approached his files. There was that bond between him and Mac . . . That bond of understanding and compassion. And, in turn, Mac had let him peripherally know of his own deepest fears, griefs, and feelings—the raw stuff which fed the mighty writing machine that powered out that stream of books.

Each of the drawers were labeled with cards slipped into the slots above their metal handles. Scarborough turned on the fluorescent above them, and as the strip light flickered to life, he began to scan the drawers. It had been a long time since he'd used those files documenting his work with Project Blue Book. Not since he'd written the book about his years working with the air force. He'd forgotten where exactly the files were. Thank goodness for records and libraries and files—his memory was not getting any better with age.

He found the drawer in the fourth filing cabinet, second one down. It was labeled simply, PROJECT BLUE BOOK, in IBM courier-type. He smiled to himself, remembering the faithful cataloguer who had typed those letters. Phyllis Scarborough. He touched the yellowing card.

"Yes, Phyl. I guess I owe it to crazy old MacKenzie to have a look at my stuff on the Iowa case."

He opened the drawer.

The documents were filed in manila folders, with labeled tabs proclaiming their contents. "The Lights in Massachusetts," one read. "The Rexton Family Incident" read another. "The Hill Report" was Scarborough's investigation of Betty Hill's further sightings of flying saucers, a case which had convinced him of her mental instability, after her husband had died in 1968. As he recalled, though, the folder appropriate to MacKenzie's concerns was a hefty one, simply marked "Iowa."

Sure enough, there it was, properly alphabetized and everything.

Only something seemed very odd about it. Scarborough picked it out from its fellows, and the difference was apparent immediately: it was much too thin.

In fact, when Scarborough opened it, it proved to be totally empty. That was funny, thought Scarborough. Had he gotten the documents of the Iowa investigation somehow mixed up with other files? Surely if he'd taken the file out, he'd have replaced the papers if he replaced the folder.

He spent the next half hour methodically paging through the entire drawer, but he could find no sign of the missing papers.

In fact, he found two other folders similarly empty but which should have been stuffed: the "Tujunga California" sightings, and the "Hudson Valley Report."

He took the empty folders out and went upstairs to his office, where he made an immediate call to MacKenzie's hotel.

"I'm sorry," said the operator. "But Captain MacKenzie has already checked out."

"I see," said Scarborough. "Thank you."

Well, he'd call tomorrow night. Just as well, anyway, because now Everett Scarborough knew what he was going to have to do.

He was going to have to go to Colonel Dolan, the big man himself. Mac was right. He was the only man who might have the answers on this one.

Troubled, Scarborough poured himself another cup of coffee, went downstairs and proceeded looking through his other files.

CHAPTER
FOURTEEN

"You fucking, rotten bastard," said the balding man with the nose like W.C. Fields, only not as smooth. "You're damn lucky we're in the twentieth century. Otherwise I'd have your head on a pike and your balls pickled in a jar!"

The balding man was Howard Kozlowski, Jake Camden's boss, the publisher, editor-in-chief, and owner of the *National Intruder*. His hairy fingers were wrapped around Jake's lapels, and if his face were any closer, Jake knew that he'd either be kissing him or chewing off his lips. Jake could smell the scent of the man's onion-and-lox bagel breakfast still lingering about his mouth.

"Yes, sir," said Jake Camden. "I'm sorry about the whole mess, sir. I hope you'll give me another chance."

Kozlowski pushed Camden back so that he fell onto a couch,

rattling the pictures of celebrities, framed awards, and an antique Coca-Cola clock with soda-bottle hands reading 11:32.

"And there your damn lucky too, you slimy piece of sewage!" said Kozlowski. "I'd fire your ass outta here in a minute if I didn't need some good stories, quick."

Howard Kozlowski looked like a Polish sumo-wrestler, his muscles bulging from his grapplings with the business and journalistic world. His head looked like a bowling ball with horn-rims, and he was infamous for his outdated three-piece polyester leisure suits. He sat now in his Eames office chair behind a well-waxed mahogany desk, which was cluttered with expensive knickknacks: a diamond-studded cigarette lighter and a gold-embossed pen and pencil set. The man came from purported mob connections, and had started the *Intruder* in the early seventies in New Jersey, during the upsurge in respectability and popularity of the supermarket tabloid-format. Almost two decades later, any connections with organized crime were mere whispers and tenuous possibilities—Camden suspected that his boss was out and independent . . . He made a point of never going to New York City, despite it being the hub of the financial world, possibly because he feared for his life in that territory. But respectability had not mellowed Kozlowski's business manner—he ran the *Intruder* and his fortune and his alligator farm with all the savoir faire of a demented banana republic dictator, and he enjoyed seeing his minions kowtow even more than he enjoyed his famous afternoon ginseng enemas, a noisy bathroom tradition that echoed through the shoddy air-conditioning ducts of the single-floor building.

Jake Camden did not doubt that the fuming megalomaniac meant everything that he said. He also knew that—if he could—he would have quit at the drop of a panama hat, grabbed his guitar, typewriter, and blender, and headed for Jimmy Buffet's Margaritaville. But there were those troublesome debts he still owed to troublesome people.

It was time for some definite brownnosing, even though he despised ginseng.

"I told you, Koz, I've got some great leads," he said, sitting up. "We're entering a new phase of the UFO era, man—and I'm in the forefront! Do you realize the amount of interest the New Age is blowing back into the same old stories? Instead of green two-headed creatures from saucers, we have green two-headed creatures from saucers *who channel to Shirley MacLaine*! The stories that are going to break soon, are going to be incredible, I promise. I've been talking to our Hollywood snoops, and was close to breaking a story that Rock Hudson got AIDS from Pleiadan leather studs. The amount of interest is just building—and it's all going to explode into a golden era for the *Intruder*!''

Kozlowski stared impassively at Camden, holding an expensive South American cigar in one hand. He never smoked them, he just clutched them—probably for effect. Once in awhile, he broke them in half for dramatic exclamation points.

"Yeah, and Koz, look, mea culpa on this stuff with your daughter. But, you know, Koz—look, I'm just a lonely, weak man, and she's a vivacious, sexy, *beautiful* young lady. I—''

Howard Kozlowski broke his cigar in half, and tossed it at the reporter, showering him with shreds of tobacco. "You say another word about my daughter, and I'm going to forget my stay of execution, Camden.''

"Okay. I understand.''

"I catch you anywhere near her again, you crumb-snot, and the next issue of paper is going to be inked with your blood!'' He fell back into his reclining chair, bloodshot eyes looking wearily at his employee. "She's promised me to be good, and you're really going to have to help, Jake. I want her with nice boys, boys her own age that go to church—or, heaven help me, even a good decent synagogue! She's my baby, Jake, and I guess I'm extremely *hurt* that you would do this to me!''

Camden nodded penitently.

Kozlowski sighed, and shifted in his chair, which squeaked softly. "Seriously, Jake. Circulation is down this year. We gotta start giving readers what they want, and you're right—they seem to want UFO stories with personal twists. I can't fault you for the job you've done. The *Intruder* was the leader for years on the latest in UFO stories. But some of the other tabloids are stealing our thunder. Get me that perfect story within the month, and you can keep your job. Otherwise, you're outta here, amigo.''

"Sure, sir. Maybe if you can clue me in on what kind of stuff you want.''

The boss leaned forward in his chair, and took off his glasses. Little grey eyes stared hard at Camden. "I want a story that will make everyone in those shopping lines buy a copy of the *Intruder*. I want a story that everyone will not only be shocked at, but will *believe*. Something personal . . . something intense, but startling. Something that will make John Doe stop hauling his Cheerios from his cart, and blink and say, 'Hey! Maybe the earth *is* being visited by creatures from another planet!' '' The shiny, freckled bald pate wrinkled with his intensity. The grey eyes shone above the tortoise-shell rim of the glasses. Globules of sweat were forming on his temples. ''And Jake, I want this story to be backed by *facts*!''

Camden blinked. This maniac was *serious*. Maybe he was really in dire need of a break-out issue. The tabloids did scratch and claw for rack space and the attention of the American populace like bratty kids, looking to be noticed. Only what was at stake wasn't kid stuff: it was the green stuff, the moohlah, the legal tenderloin of life that made a rich man rich and a poor man desperate.

''Sure,'' he said. ''I'll get you that story,'' said Camden, feeling a little more self-confident. ''And if I do it within a month, I keep my job.''

''That's the score,'' said Kozlowski, crabbed hand scrabbling at a humidor for another pacifier.

''Chief . . . and if I get this big story, can I have a raise? Cost of living and all . . .''

''You unmitigated asshole! Get the fuck out of my office and get that story or I'll take back *last month's salary*!'' The boss was turning a dangerous red.

''Okay. But how about just a onetime bonus then!'' Camden said, grinning hopefully. ''Of course, the story's gotta be real good!''

''Out!'' cried his boss, and Camden had to duck a thrown copy of *Iacocca*, Kozlowski's favorite book. He'd bought a thousand remaindered Bantam hardcovers for a song, and gave one to everybody who came into his office, whether they wanted it or not. ''Just be lucky you didn't get it up the fudge canal!'' Kozlowski bellowed as the book splattered into a signed picture of Lyndon Baines Johnson.

''Right,'' said Jake Camden, getting out.

From the plush pile-carpeting and leather-and-teak furniture of Howard Kozlowski's private office, the *Intruder* building immediately deteriorated into the pure newsroom tacky of yellowed linoleum floors, cheap desks, and cranky fluorescent strip-lighting. Most reporters, copy editors, and editorial assistants were stationed cheek to jowl, like workers in an assembly line. The lucky editors and reporters were assigned to tiny glassed-in cubicles with their typewriters, or, if they cared to bring them in, their own personal computers. The *Intruder* still hadn't made the switch to a computerized system yet, despite the complaints of the employees. The boss just didn't want to pay out the money when the old system worked well enough. True, the *Intruder* was only a forty-eight-page rag and the stories tended to be so short and bereft of detail that they barely needed editorial attention beyond their initial approval and scrutiny by Joe "the carnivore" Donohue, the *Intruder*'s lawyer, whose job it was to worry about libel suits and such. But a computer system like many papers had would make the whole process *so* much more streamlined. Jake Camden, early in his career here, had bought an IBM personal computer with which to write his articles, but last year he'd sold it to help stake a large cocaine deal. The deal had gone sour, and Jake had never been able to get another, but he really didn't care—the crotchety old IBM correctable the office supplied him with was good enough.

First thing Jake did after getting thrown out of the chief's office was to hit the coffee cubicle. He's been pouring down the stuff all morning, and he needed another cup. He'd gotten in at 8:00 sharp after a sleepless night, and Kozlowski had, in his inimical fashion, kept him waiting until 11:15 for his dressing-down, so that Jake had to wriggle on the barbed hook awhile. During that time, Jake had managed to drink five cups of coffee, urinate three times, and write and rewrite the first page of his report on his Iowa findings ten times, all wretchedly.

Jake plunked a quarter loudly in the Maxwell House can, then pulled the half-filled community pot from the Mr. Coffee Machine and poured himself three-quarters of a Styrofoam cupful. He poured in a steady stream of sugar, dumped in two spoonfuls of Cremora, stirred, and sniffed the heady concoction. Despite his urge to gag (although it was a Maxwell House can on the counter, the secretaries who supplied the thing generally bought generic grind), he took a swallow. It didn't make him feel any better, but it didn't make him feel any worse. Jake looked around to make sure no one was watching, and then silently retrieved his quarter, as well as another, and pocketed them.

He then plastered his trademark devil-may-care grin on his unusually well-shaven face and strode down the aisle toward his desk, ready to field the curious questions.

"Hey, Jake," called Quentin Marshall, the celebrity editor, pushing his designer glasses back with a manicured finger. "Serious rumblings in there. Will you still be parking your saucer in the lot outside?"

The activity in the immediate area all but halted, typewriters no longer clacking, voices stilled above telephone receivers, as ears leaned in Jake's direction. The air-conditioning rattled and cleared its throat, and the smell of ink and paper hung in the air like an ever-present apparition. Jake leaned casually against a UPI wire machine, and winked at Sheryl Stippens, an assistant photo-editor whose desk was covered with pictures of Michael J. Fox in the company of various women. He sipped at his bitter coffee and gave a sly smile to his waiting audience. "Does Liz Taylor go down on Malcolm Forbes?"

"C'mon Camden," growled Bill Walters, the occult-and-astrology editor, scratching a serious beer gut. "Intruding minds want to know!"

"Well, the old man was a mite upset with me, I suppose. Circulation has been down and he wants a killer story... And not a lot that sensational has been going on in the UFO field these days." Jake shrugged blithely and peered over a desk, spying on a list of story ideas, hoping to swipe one.

"Get off it, Jake," said Sadie Diamond, a fiftyish woman with bluish blond hair and a face like a road map, a cigarette bobbing between her lips as she pulled a piece of paper from her typewriter platen. "You've been shtupping his daughter, and everybody knows it. Did you get the can or not?"

Camden sauntered over to the woman's desk, picked up her pack of Chesterfields and stole one. "Actually," he said, fitting the cigarette between his teeth. "The old man just wanted a few sex tips. How about a match, sweetheart."

"My ass and your face," said Sadie. "Gimme my damn cigarettes back, Jake. I'm sick and tired of you bumming cigarettes. I was hoping the old bird would railroad your bod outta here, covered with tar and feathers!"

"Now, now, claws in, oh, my esteemed and professional co-workers of this august and distinguished publication." He turned and addressed all those listening. "I am well aware of the envy all of you have for my position as chief reporter on the most important stories of our century. But be assured, Jake Camden's star is not only still rising, it is discharging all sorts of fascinating life-forms to our planet, all of which deserve front-page coverage! In fact, I predict that very soon a fleet of Pleiadan light-ships will descend on Kiss Grits, Florida, specifically to quell the infighting and bring peace and tranquility to the troubled *Intruder*."

Uneasy laughter greeted his words, and the workers turned their attention back to the tasks, their question answered.

Jake tossed the Chesterfields back on Sadie's desk. "Thanks kiddo. I'll buy you a tobacco farm in Maryland when my ship comes in."

Sadie shook her head, going back to her task of weeding through the world news stories for strange human interest stories. "Jake Camden, you're what the Surgeon General warns about on the packs."

But Jake was already gone, breezing past his co-workers toward his office near the back, mouth frozen in a rictus around his unlit cigarette. He hummed "People Who Need People" as he walked, nodding or winking to anyone who looked at him. Finally, he stepped into his cubicle, where he placed the Styrofoam coffee cup beside a pile of unanswered mail and messages, and then collapsed in his chair and buried his face in his arms.

A sensational UFO story, backed by facts! Where was he going to dig up one of those? And he had only a month? What the hell was he going to do? Johnny Plentenos was settling for intallments on the money due, but if his salary dried up next month, unemployment insurance sure as hell wasn't going to keep that Cuban machete from lopping off certain necessary appendages.

Camden sighed wearily and rummaged through the mess on the desk, as though somewhere within that heap was hidden treasure. He found no gold, but did find a pack of matches labeled "Gino's Go-Go—Girl's Galore." He lit his stolen Chesterfield and blew a stream of smoke toward the ceiling.

"Jake, sorry to bother you, but that Tim Reilly fellow is

calling again," a voice said from behind him. Jake looked around wearily and saw that it was Betty Norton, the secretary/assistant he shared with three other reporters. "He claims to have a UFO story for you." She blinked at him myopically through huge, blue-framed glasses, and Camden was hit by a wave of too much Chanel Number Five.

"That Kansas student, right? Shit, he was calling on Thursday and Friday too. I don't *need* a Kansas story... I got Midwest stories coming out of my wazoo!"

"Looks like a routine abduction, too," Betty chomped on her double wad of Bubble Yum as she stared down at her notes. "Out parking with his girlfriend near some Kansas field, sees some hovering lights—they go to check it out, they wake up back at their car the next dawn. By the way, the *girlfriend* called earlier. Named Diane Scarborough. They must *really* want to talk to you, Jake. Whatcha want me to do?"

"Take down the phone number, tell 'em I'll get back to them..." said Jake.

"Yeah. Okay." A flutter of pink skirt, and she was gone.

"...about the year 2020," muttered Jake Camden under his breath, as he stared back morosely at the piles of stuff tilting precariously on his desk.

That was the problem with this goddamn UFO reporting. One original idea gets into the general populace's mind, and whacko! Instant Xerox copies. That's why you had to stretch the truth some—and often almost fabricate it—to get good copy out of the goddamn phenomenon. But despite his cynicism on this subject, in his heart of hearts, Jake Camden wasn't entirely sure it was all a pile of brain guano—there were just too many reports that were unprovable, and just too much evidence that something was really going on.

Exactly what was very hard to say, but *something*.

He sat in his cubicle for a long time, ruminating. As he thought, he scribbled out ideas on his yellow notepad. As he was writing out "Project Blue Ball: Sexual Scandal Amongst UFO-ologists," he began humming an old English folk song that he'd liked so much on an old Simon and Garfunkel record, finally softly mouthing the words.

"Are you going to Scarborough Fair. Parsley, sage, rosemary and thyme. Remember me—"

He stopped in midsong.

Jake Camden shook his head. Naw, it couldn't be . . .

Still, he was a reporter, and sometimes the damndest things happened.

And if it were true . . .

He rolled his swivel chair out of the cubicle, leaning back and forming a megaphone with his hands.

"Yo, Betts! What did you say the name of that Kansas guy's girlfriend was?"

CHAPTER
FIFTEEN

Diane Scarborough was trying to meditate, but it wasn't coming easily.

She sat on a huge yellow pillow topping a Persian rug near Tim's balcony, where a jungle of flowers in pots obscured a few marijuana plants. The Kansas sunshine was bright, and puffy cumulus clouds rode above the flat plane like breaths of white mystery pasted on blue cosmos.

Diane took a long breath through her right nostril, paused, let it out, all the while focusing on a small milk-quartz crystal she cupped in a palm. She took another breath through her right nostril, this time attempting to shift concentration on a more receptive chakra. From the stereo, the soft drones of Ravi Shankar's sitar, underpinned with tablas, encouraged her onward.

Still, she could find no peace. Inside, she still raged at her father.

Damn the man! she fumed, wiping out any sense of inner peace she'd managed to collect on any plane, spiritual, physical, or emotional. Couldn't he, for once, act not like a scientist, but a loving, caring father? She wasn't an experiment he'd cooked up in a lab! She wasn't some complex equation that he had to solve utilizing only modular quadratics! She was flesh and blood and soul, and he was her daddy, and oh! Shit!

"Shit!" she said, standing up and tossing the crystal back into the basket that held a pile of the things. "Shit, shit, shit!" she said, going to the turntable, taking off Ravi and Company.

Tim looked up from the desk where he was sitting, hunkered over an open book. Stacks of other books and piles of magazines tilted precariously on the desk before him, threatening to collapse on his half-eaten bagel and a cold cup of chamomile tea. The odor of yesterday's marijuana clung to him like a dream. "What's wrong, kiddo?"

"Oh, I just can't get into my meditation, and boy, I really need it!" she said, taking out another record and planting the stylus on vinyl. "Birth, School, Work, Death!" by the Godfathers commenced to blast from the Fischer speakers, a grinding explosion of resentment.

Diane did a few pogos, and punched the air a few times to the insistent and snarling beat. There was a tap on her shoulder and she turned around to find Tim Reilly's solemn face regarding her. "Hey, Joanna Rotten. Maybe you can help me research, huh? We don't need your old man to figure this one out." He offered her a copy of *Missing Time* by Budd Hopkins.

She took the paperback, but didn't open it, still bouncing to the music. She leaned a kiss onto his mouth, and then stepped away, teasingly. "I know. I guess it's just the principle of the thing."

"Yeah, I guess it's like a surgeon refusing to take out his daughter's appendix!" said Tim, nodding with understanding.

Diane looked at the garish cover of the book and grimaced. "No actually it's more like an M.D. refusing to do chiropractics, but you've got the right idea."

"The rotten, selfish bastard!" said Tim, smiling.

"The cowardly, self-righteous asshole!" cried out Diane, punching the air. "Hey, boyfriend. Wanna slam-dance?"

"I can think of a more appealing body contact," Tim said, turning his Irish good looks back to his desk of research. "Seriously, Di. We've got to wade through this ourselves. Your father won't help us, the people I've called won't help us—and the authorities I've talked to look at me like *I've* just stepped off a UFO! No, maybe once we've read all this documentation, and taken that hypnosis session I set up with that shrink later in the week, we'll be able to figure out what happened to us.''

"You talked to that Joe Camden guy, the UFO specialist?"

"Jake Camden. And he's not returning the calls. I've left a bunch of messages for him at his paper, and a killer phone bill for my trouble. Fuck him. I think we can probably get more reputable help than a reporter from the *National Intruder*."

"I'll say. Boy, though. My father just about shit when I mentioned his name."

"I'll bet he did. After that grade-Z film came out last year. Jeez. *Close Encounters of the Sleazy Kind*. But is he sure that it was Camden who created that character?"

"Well, no, but he's just assuming . . . Still, it wasn't close enough for a libel suit. Daddy's just going to strangle the guy if they should ever meet."

A year or two before, a film entitled *UFO Investigator* had been released by a Roger Cormanlike low-budget film company. It had been supposedly based on *The National Intruder Books of UFOs,* and the credits had listed Jacob Camden as special consultant. In this film—remarkable for its soft-core depiction of weird sex between humans and alien beings from flying saucers—a UFO debunker named Titus Wound was featured prominently, shown as a fool of the first water. The sort of character who refuses to believe there's a monster on the space ship, and gets his brains sucked out in the second reel. The character had clearly been based on Dr. Everett Scarborough— particularly on his flamboyant stage and TV presence—and Daddy had been furious that his serious scientific work had been degraded so. Later, he allowed that the publicity hadn't hurt at the bookstore, but still, his pride had been tweaked. He'd always been irked by Jake Camden's mere mention of him in his trashy rag. But now, he really wouldn't mind if Camden was found wearing iron underwear on the wrong side of a lake.

"Well, the guy's had experience, and if nothing else, maybe he can put us into touch with someone who can really help us."

"What about this guy?" Diane tapped the cover of the book under the author's name.

"I called, but there's such a backlog, we won't be able to talk to anyone associated with his group for a while. But I must say, one of Hopkins's associates did recommend a reputable psychologist in Kansas City, and that's where we're going for hypnotic therapy! So we haven't exactly struck out."

Diane tossed the paperback back on the stack, went over to the bed in the middle of the room and flopped down, covering her blonde head in an almost protective fashion. "No, no, I guess not."

"Hey, babe," said Tim softly, sitting by her and stroking her back. "We just have to have *patience*."

"I know, Tim," she said, mopily. "I just want to know what happened to us. These books—I just *know* there's nothing there that's comparable to our experience. I know..." She looked off dreamily at the mandala poster. "I know that something truly wonderful and unique happened to us!"

Tim scratched his stubbly face. "Yeah, I know what you mean. It's kinda exciting. All the alien-abduction stuff in that lot—it's either horror-story material, or it's clearly the work of kooks and mental cases. We're not crazy, Diane. We're a couple of the saner people I know." He smiled and touched her pert nose. "Well, I am, anyway."

"Turkey."

He went over to the record player and turned down the music a bit. "Right. That's the weird thing about this whole business. We both see a UFO, we both have a missing-time experience—and yet, we both feel pretty good about it. I know with your Dad and everything, you're pretty tied up inside . . . But shit, I feel like I've had a weekend of primo drugs, rolfing and immersion tanks, topped off with some shiatsu massage for good measure. I feel like I had some kind of Maslovian peak-experience that night—but I don't recall it, I'm just feeling the afterglow of a massive charge of cosmic consciousness." His eyes fairly glowed with enthusiasm as he turned back to look at her. "And I'd like to do it again!"

Diane said nothing. She felt much the same way, but there was more of the sour feeling now. She'd thought about this all day yesterday, and she knew exactly what the cause of her problem was. She wanted to share this with her father, she wanted him to join her in this search. Deep inside, she felt that Everett Scarborough revealed a deep psychological need in his ranting on this whole business. Somehow, he desired to touch something deep and meaningful and cosmic in the universe, yet he hid this yearning with his polemics of logic, his stone-hearted slavery to science. He was a tight-ass because he was afraid to let go, afraid to surrender himself to an existence of love and joy, for fear of being hurt again so bitterly. Diane wanted somehow to *reach* him. And in his rejection of her plea for help, she knew that he wasn't merely rejecting her—he was rejecting something potentially wonderful and spiritual in the empty shell of his hang-ups.

Tim went back to her. "Hey! Don't you feel the same way, Diane? You were pretty excited just after it happened!"

"Oh, yeah, I guess," she said, not looking at him. "And I'm going to move heaven and earth to find out what happened to us, Tim. I just have to get through my disappointment with Daddy."

Tim shook his head. "Sounds to me like you just set yourself up, Diane. Daddy shoots you down, and damn if you don't just dust yourself off, and sit right back in the shooting gallery. Hurt me, Dad, you cry. If you don't love me, at least show me some kind of feeling, even if it's *pain*! God, what a primo dunderhead old Doc Scarborough is!"

Diane shot off the bed, furious. "Don't you *dare* call him that, Tim. Everett Scarborough is a great man! He just has a few... well, emotional problems sometimes!"

"Yeah. Like a hole where there should be a heart!"

She grabbed a copper vase that held a dead flower and threw it, splashing smelly water all over everything. "Shut up! Shut up, Tim! My father *loves* me!" Tears were leaking down her cheeks and her voice started cracking. "He *loves* me very much."

"Hey! I'm just trying to humor your mood, Diane! Don't get violent, huh? I love a feisty lady, but really!"

Diane collapsed on the bed, sobbing. It was all breaking out now, all of her disappointment she'd felt this weekend, linked with the heartache she'd known as a child. She didn't know how to hold it in anymore, so she just let it out into one of Tim's prized downfilled pillows. It just poured out in sobs and tears and hiccups.

"Hey!" Tim said, leaning over, touching her, comforting her. "I'm sorry. I guess I'm kinda a baboon sometimes too, Di. Sorry to step on a tender toe."

She turned over and regarded him. He was a handsome guy, no question—that showed easily through the scraggly haircut, old jeans, and tie-dyed neosixties look. The way he dressed was a big problem with her father, who had encouraged her early pretty look. Daddy always dressed tastefully and neatly. The sixties revolution had affected him only in his anger—his politics were always liberal, but Ivy League look-down-your-nose liberal. Tim's wild ideas were hard enough to take—the knowledge that more than just the ideas were getting into his daughter doubtless was what swayed him to his very negative opinion of the young man. But of course Dad wouldn't be able to see what she saw: namely, the qualities in Timothy Reilly that were far beyond neatness and taste in clothes, or his radical ideas on politics, religion, philosophy, and drugs.

And to top it all off, he was as intelligent as she was—if not *more* so.

"I guess he deserves it sometimes," she said softly. "The way he's treated you, the way he acts."

"Yeah, but he's your old man. You love him and he's earned your love. He's a good guy. Salt of the earth and all that, Di. I just get rocked off at the way he treats you sometimes, I guess. But maybe I can understand that too." He touched her fine long hair, then traced a tingle along the line of her jaw. "You're a provocative individual." He tilted her chin up and touched his lips to her, a whisper of the erotic in the momentary touch. A breath of yesterday's Old Spice mixed with marijuana and Pepsodent lingered from the kiss.

"I am, am I?" She laughed, reached down, and cupped the basket of his jeans. "What makes you think that."

She could feel the electricity snap through him, arching up into a flash in his eyes. Almost instantly, his crotch lost any softness, and the muscles in his face tensed. "Experience," he rasped.

She chuckled throatily, teased the tight denim bulge a moment with her fingertips and then moved away from him, getting up and sitting on the edge of the bed. "You know, it's too bad I have this awful headache. I'm feeling terribly randy."

"Uhm—can I get you an aspirin?" he said. He moved behind her and kissed the nape of her neck. The stubble of his beard sent chills down her spine.

"No. Perhaps some other kind of oral medication."

"Can you be more specific?" He traced the outline of her side with the fingers of his left hand.

"Gee—the word escapes me. It was just on the tip of your tongue!"

He laughed. "Say no more, madam. We have a fine selection of cunnilingus in today. We have a wonderful slab of hard cold tongue, a gourmet's delight in hot spicy tongue, and the merest slice of tender, juicy soft tongue. What is your pleasure." He reached around and put his hand on her left breast.

"Oh . . . wrap it all up and put it in the freezer for later. I think I need the main course . . . now!"

"Ah, but of course, madam. The man-sized Kansas City prime. Aha! I believe it has just been cut and dressed. Shall I unwrap it for your inspection?"

"Sure. And then you know just where you can put it."

Chuckling, he sprang from the bed, and kicked off his Keds. "We certainly can butcher the fine art of seduction, can't we, Diane?" he said, struggling with his jeans.

She propped herself up on the pillows and slid her tongue across her lips, giving him her half-closed bedroom-eyes look in reply. He moaned a bit, and managed to get his trousers off. In a moment, he was on her, fumbling with her blouse, kissing her lips, her neck, and the tops of her breasts.

In a short time, he had her out of her the red-striped top (she hadn't put on a bra today, so there was no awkwardness about unhooking and pulling it over her head). Her bright, firm breasts were soon under his hands and his mouth, being licked and kissed and otherwise exquisitely physically adored. Tim had this rare and exciting quality of being wanton, yet at the same time delicate. Other men might have mauled her breasts being so mannish and rough, and yet somehow Tim's touch hovered at just the right spot between the barbaric and the erotic. Sometimes, when he was in this kind of mood, she felt like she was being raped by the most exciting lover in the world, totally out of control and yet enjoying it.

As he sucked on her nipples, his left hand busied itself with the button and fly of her jeans. Soon, she was only wearing her black silk panties. Tim grunted with pleasure at their touch. He'd given them to her—his sensibilities were such that he adored silk, and while his wardrobe consisted mostly of denim and cotton, he made sure that his girlfriend had a full complement of sexy teddies, garters, chemises, chamisoles, and such.

No time for extra sauce now—he'd settle for his staple. His breaths coming quicker now, he played connect-a-dot between her breasts and her crotch with wet, lingering, exciting kisses. She watched this march of the lips down her narrow stomach, his head bobbing and weaving between her erect nipples. Spiderwebs of pleasure shot along her skin at his touch, and when he reached her panties, she thought she might very well explode then and there.

But before she had the chance to push herself insistently into his face, he stopped and lifted his head, smiling.

"Oh, yeah. Right. The main course. I forgot."

She felt liquid inside, hot and wet, and she could only nod. Other times, they could do foreplay for an hour before they got to the fucking. So tender and rough, so exquisite . . . Now, she just wanted his comforting fullness inside her, pushing and thrusting her over the edge into the minutes of oblivion that he'd shown her she could achieve.

He rolled off the bed, and pulled off his jockey shorts, his penis jerking up like a salute. A dribble of moisture sparkled at its head. She reached over and touched the shaft, softly but firmly. Tim flinched, caught his breath and closed his eyes. "Whoooo," he said, "Whooooooo." Like a cat being petted, he stayed still and let her fingers coax his cock into full hardness—and then let them drift down playfully, teasing his balls.

"Diane," he whispered, getting back on the bed. "Diane."

Her mouth was dry, but her pussy sure wasn't. She could feel it dripping juice down to the crack of her ass. She opened her legs for him, and helped him guide the perpendicular part of him toward the gaping heat.

"Yes," she said.

"Yes," he said.

"Ring," said the phone.

They froze with astonishment, Tim just short of penetration. He looked at Diane with a "Tell-me-this-isn't-happening," expression. As for her, her ardor evaporated like dew in the desert. All she could think was that maybe it was her father, calling to apologize, calling to tell her that he was on the next plane, that he was going to take care of everything, that he believed her now and was terribly sorry to ever, *ever* doubt her.

"Oh, hell with the thing," Tim said, moving down.

But Diane pulled herself up, and Tim missed his shot, painfully stabbing the hard mattress instead. Lithely, she pulled herself away from him, hopped off the bed, and went to the phone on the desk.

"Di . . . *ane!*" he said, groaning with the pain and disappointment, but mostly with the outrageous humor of his predicament.

"I'm sorry, love. You know how important this phone call could be!" she said, reaching over for the receiver.

"Yeah," he said, face in a pillow muffling his voice. "Yeah. I know."

She picked up the phone.

"Hello?"

"Hey! Hello! Have I reached the Reilly residence . . . I'm returning a very vital call!"

Her heart sank. No, it wasn't her father . . . The scratchy voice on the phone was a far cry from Daddy's baritone splendor.

"Yes, that's right."

"Great. I wouldn't be talking to Diane Scarborough, would I?"

She was surprised. "Why, yes you are!" In the buff, yet, she thought.

"Well, it's my lucky day, I guess, since I need to speak to both of you about this incredible event you recently experienced. But let me explain—my name is Jake Camden, and it would be a great pleasure to help you both out as much as I can!"

At first she was nonplussed. The name struck an off-key chord in her mind. Jake Camden, one of Daddy's adversaries. But then she remembered how much she and Tim needed assistance from experts in this business—and how little help they were getting from Everett Scarborough.

"Oh! Mr. Camden! Of course! We didn't think you were going to call back."

"Yeah, I'm real sorry—but I was away for Friday and the weekend, and things have been pretty hectic around here. Listen, Ms. Scarborough—do I have this correct? You say you and your boyfriend—this Timothy Reilly fellow—were abducted by beings from a flying saucer?"

She looked over at Tim, who was sitting up in bed now, still looking a little chagrined over the interruption, the sheet wrapped around his midsection, reaching out for the phone and mouthing the words, "Let me talk to him!"

She pulled away from Tim, dragging the phone toward the window and shaking her head. "That's right, Mr. Camden. Or it would seem that way."

She gave a very brief description of their experience.

"Yow! That sound's pretty intense. Are you all right! Any marks or psychological trauma? Oh, and please, call me Jake."

"No, no pain or marks or anything. Just curiosity, I guess. Intense curiosity... uhm... Jake. And I guess what we could really use is some kind of help. Someone who *believes* us, who can help us discover what happened. Someone who's dealt with this kind of thing before."

"Well, I've dealt with plenty of UFO abductions, Diane. I know my stuff. Yours sounds quite different. No feelings of fear or dread associated with the experience, huh? Hmm. This could be a breakthrough for the whole field. But I've gotta be candid, Diane. Aren't you the daughter of Dr. Everett Scarborough?"

"That's right."

"Well, pardon my intrusion into intimate family matters... but even if he's a debunker, he's a top investigator. I take it you're afraid to tell him about what happened."

"No, Jake. I told him. He refuses to get involved. He rejects even the possibility that this could have happened to me. I personally asked my father for help, and he rejected me."

"Gee, I'm sorry, Diane." A moment of silence. "Look, I guess you know how your father feels about me..."

"Yes, Jake. But we need *somebody* to help!" Oh God! Was Jake Camden going to turn them down too?

"Oh, kiddo, hey! I'll do what I can. This sounds too good a case to pass up... I mean, like I said, it could be a breakthrough. A benevolent UFO-abduction. Wow. No, I just don't wanna hurt you, Diane. I just wanna be in the clear with you that bringin' *me* on will tick your pop off something fierce!"

"That will be his problem, won't it, Jake?" Diane Scarborough said, coldly.

"Yeah. Yeah, I guess it will be. Listen, sounds like I should meet you and this Reilly guy, go out and check the place where you say the saucer landed. By the way, anyone else see the thing? Any reports to the cops, anything in the papers?''

"Not that I know of . . . 'Course, we haven't really checked, I guess. Didn't think to."

"That's okay. That's my specialty. We'll interview the neighbors, we'll do lots of good stuff. We'll get to the bottom of this business, Diane. I promise. You just relax and feel good, because you're a very special person, and you're going to get the help and attention that you deserve."

What a nice guy, she thought. Not at all the sleaze-ball whom her father described. Just talking with him seemed to lift a weight from her shoulders. "Thank you, Jake. When can you come out?"

"Tomorrow. Will that be okay? I've got some stuff to take care of at the office, but I can fly in tomorrow, rent a car, and come and see you. But you're going to have to give me some directions."

"I'm not very good at that sort of thing," said Diane. "But my boyfriend is. He'll set it all up. And Jake—thanks so much for your help. I guess the hardest part of this whole business is the way people look at me when I talk about it."

"Part of the syndrome, kid. You're not alone. See you tomorrow, Diane."

She pulled the phone back to the bed and handed it to Tim Reilly. "It's Jake Camden, Tim!"

"No kidding," Tim said, taking the receiver. "Hello, Mr. Camden. I'm so happy you returned the call."

As Tim spoke to her father's nemesis, Diane slipped back into her underwear, blouse, and jeans, feeling curiously empty.

When Tim hung the phone up, he was smiling. Diane had picked a book from the stack on the desk: *The National Intruder Book of UFO Investigation*, by Jake Camden. She was sitting in an old reclining chair, flipping through the pages. Tim went over and knelt beside her, rubbing her back.

"Well, he'll be here tomorrow morning," he said. Tim still had the sheet wrapped around his midsection, but it was clear he wouldn't mind taking it off and proceeding with what they'd been doing before. Diane, however, was not at all in the mood anymore.

"Good. We better get back to boning up," she said.

"Uhm—I think I'm already there, lover," he said cheerfully.

"Tim, love of my life and trusted companion—there are more important things in this life than expressions of pure carnality."

He laughed and kissed her on the cheek. "Yeah, I guess you're right." He grabbed a book and lounged back on the bed. "The sucker called! I can't believe it, but the sucker actually called! We got ourselves a qualified UFO investigator. We're going to get the bottom of this business!"

"Did you tell him about the hypnosis appointment with that psychologist?" asked Diane, looking up from artist renderings of almond-eyed aliens.

"No. Why, should I have?"

"We can tell him tomorrow, I guess," she said, tapping the picture for a moment, then abruptly holding up the book for Tim to see. "Timothy. Does this picture jog anything in your memory?"

Tim looked over and chuckled. "Yeah, it looks a lot like the cover of *Communion*."

"No, I mean . . . do you think we saw creatures like this during our memory lapse?"

Tim shrugged. "I don't remember a damn thing, Diane, but that is supposed to be the prototypical alien. Many people have identified it. It's like part of the collective unconscious on the subject."

Diane Scarborough looked down at the picture of the almost insectlike eyes, the triangular face, the expressive mouth, and the delicate nose.

"Tim, I don't remember anything either . . . but my intuition tells me we saw absolutely *nothing* that looked like *this*."

CHAPTER
SIXTEEN

Everett Scarborough stopped at the Vietnamese refreshment-stand on the Pentagon grounds, and waited his turn to buy his ritual spring roll and iced jasmine tea from the oriental couple who ran the concession booth and sold not only the usual hot dogs, Cokes and chips but also a small array of Far Eastern treats.

Scarborough had calculated once that the spot which the stand occupied was precisely Ground Zero for Russian nuclear missiles; and the first stuff to go in the flash would be a lot of minted fried rice, then the fire storm would seep through this gigantic five-sided monster of military bureaucracy, and afterward across the Potomac to deal with the rest of the government buildings.

"Thanks, Anna," he said to the dark-haired woman as he accepted his purchase.

"Dr. Everett!" she said, smiling. "We not see you much lately! Three, four week since you been here!" Anna and Trung Dai had been business people in South Vietnam before the communists had taken over. They'd fled to the States, and lived in Clarendon, Virginia, a section of Arlington that soon came to be called "Little Saigon" because of all the immigrants. The Dais had used what little money they had to start up this booth. Now they owned two more like it and were once again prosperous business people—but they still insisted on running the lunch hour here themselves.

"I've been very busy lately, Anna."

Several years ago, doing work on one of his books, Scarborough had almost camped out at the Pentagon. This was when he

frequented the Vietnamese food-stand so often that he'd gotten
to know the friendly owners. They'd taken him up one night to
a restaurant on Wilson Boulevard, where they'd feasted on
what Trung called "slow Vietnamese food"—spicy soups and
delicious satays, chicken with lemon grass, and marvelous fried
rice with a touch of fish sauce. Now, he made sure that they got
autographed copies of all his books.

"Trung, look who is here!"

The grey-haired man greeted Scarborough cordially. "I read
your book with great interest, Dr. Everett. But I swear to you, I
see a flying thing some miles from Saigon, and it was no U.S.
helicopter!"

"Trung, you've got to admit, there's a hell of a lot of swamp
gas in your part of the world!"

They laughed, and insisted on giving him an extra spring roll
for free.

He took the afternoon treat and sat on some nearby stone
steps in the afternoon sun, enjoying the light breeze rippling
from the trees in the general direction of Arlington Cemetery.
He took a sip of the cold tea, enjoying the crunch of the shaved
ice, and then dipped the first spring roll that was on the tray
into the small container of duck sauce that the diminutive
Vietnamese lady had given him.

He looked up at the monolithic expanse of the Pentagon, and
he whispered, "Dolan, I'm comin' to get you."

That morning, he still couldn't raise Mac, so he'd called
Colonel Walter Dolan, his liaison with the Air Force, whose
office was located here amongst the hundreds of other Department of Defense, Army, Navy, and Air Force offices holding
over 23,000 workers. He'd told Colonel Dolan about the
missing files. Dolan's response was warm but disbelieving, and
he'd ended the conversation with an abrupt excuse, promising
to get back "later on in the week." That date, of course, was
much too late for Scarborough. He wanted his confrontation
with the man, and he wanted it *now*.

Your normal citizen, of course, would have to wait. Fortunately,
because of his constant visits here, Scarborough had a permanent pass. Dolan's inner offices might be a problem if he'd
thought to warn the Pentagon MPs. But Everett Scarborough
was a calm, law-abiding man, wasn't he? There'd be no
problem with Scarborough.

Scarborough smiled at himself as he chewed on the batter-coated shrimp and vegetables. The colonel's estimation of him was what he was counting on.

He finished up his snack, wiped his hands with a napkin, drank down the rest of the tea, and then chucked the refuse into a waste-bin.

Then he headed for the office security checkpoint, pulling his name-badge from his pocket.

The Pentagon was built on a mud-flat called "Hell's Bottom," and it was this difficult site that dictated its unusual shape. General Brehon Burke Somervell, the Army's supply-services director during World War II, came up with the idea: why not house all the essential offices of the U.S. military establishment in one large building, to expedite communication and cooperation? The architect's design—five pentagonal structures arranged in concentric rings around an open court and connected by ten spokelike corridors—had no elevators, afforded little silhouette, and conserved structural steel, since metal was in short supply during the 1941–43 building period.

During the Second World War, and the Korean and Vietnam wars, it seemed to work fine. So what if a well-placed nuclear weapon would take out some of the highest officials in the government in a snap. There were plenty of other military sites more than happy to lob a few missiles at the bad guys. In matters of world destruction, there were megatons to spare. However, it wasn't the cold war or the threat of nuclear obliteration that was dragging the Pentagon down—it was the simple disease of bureaucracy, complicated by corruption, fraud, and bribery. Scarborough had watched it all happening with a kind of detached horror. A longtime liberal, he didn't care much at all for the military, and he simply despised the Republican regime that ran the Executive branch for eight years. He let his steam off in his lectures and books, and it was for this reason that no critic could accuse him of being an establishment sort, a fat cat protecting the fatter cats, helping in a conspiracy. As far as Scarborough was concerned, the bureaucrats of the past and present, whether they be CIA, NSA, or FDA, were far too dull and stupid to properly cover-up crashed flying saucers. And the military! Whew! They didn't call marines jar-heads for nothing, and marines tended to be the smartest of the sorry, gun-crazy bunch! He counted his dealings with the Air Force in the Project Blue Book as unfortunate but necessary, which was just how he felt about his further contacts. Somehow, though, the country had muddled through, despite everything, and Scarborough was happy about that— he kept his cynicism about the government at an amused and witty level, an attitude that most military and government sorts could not only tolerate, but could actually privately sympathize with as well. "The saving grace of this whole convoluted mess," Scarborough had once written in a book, "is purely and simply the process of democracy and this nation's lovely and vital Constitution."

Scarborough's pass got him all the way through several checkpoints stationed along dull linoleum and Hellenic passageways in the mammoth complex. In fact, it got him all the way to Colonel Dolan's secretary, a severe-looking WAVE in starched blues and horn-rims who registered surprise to see him.

"Doctor Scarborough, what are you doing here?" she said in her nasal Queens accent. "You haven't got an appointment."

"That's right," said Scarborough, "but I need to talk to the colonel right away. I know he's in today, I talked to him on the phone."

The secretary's hands clenched above a mass of paperwork. "I'm sorry, but the colonel's having a meeting now. You'll either have to come back later—or make an appointment later in the week."

"Hmm. I see," said Scarborough, looking around at the spartan office, complete with aerial photographs of Washington, D.C. and portraits of several recent presidents and famous U.S. generals. "Well, in that case, maybe I'd better make an appointment. The colonel didn't seem to have time to do that himself, so perhaps you can tell me when he'll be free this week."

The secretary—Corporal Ellen Nichols, Scarborough knew from past meetings and from the plate propped on her desk, if he'd forgotten—relaxed visibly. She leaned over, pulled open a drawer, and removed the colonel's appointment calendar. "Yes, I think that I can take care of that for you, Doctor," she said in a monotone, turning her attention away from him.

Scarborough used the opportunity to scoot past the desk, turn the knob on the glassed door and walk into Colonel Walter Dolan's office.

"Dr. Scarborough!" cried the secretary.

Colonel Walter Dolan, USAF, sat at a large walnut desk, a phone cradled at his ear, pudgy neck, and blue dress-shirt. His tie was undone, and his sleeves were rolled up. His much-decorated blue air force jacket hung neatly on a coatrack, right by his stiff drumlike blue cap. His seat squeaked as he swiveled to see who this unscheduled visitor was, and his dark eyebrows—particularly pronounced against his mane of white hair—rose with surprise.

Scarborough walked forward and slammed the desk with the heel of his hand, "Dolan, I demand that you explain what the hell is going on with my files!" He leaned over and glared at the officer, who blinked and grinned stupidly.

"Captain, can we continue this conversation later? I've got an unexpected guest. Yes, a half hour will do." Calmly, he cradled the phone and leaned forward, folding his hands in a fatherly gesture of relaxed authority. "Ev, I don't remember telling you to come down here."

"He just stormed through, sir," said the corporal, looking nervously at the tall, overbearing sight of Everett Scarborough in fighting stance. "Do you want me to get Security?"

Colonel Dolan shook his head adamantantly. "What? No, of course not! Ev Scarborough's been in this office plenty of times. But I must say, never without an invitation." He directed a disapproving look at his colleague.

Scarborough did not flinch from the cold expression. "I'm sorry, Walter, but I don't like to be brushed off. I've got an important matter to deal with here, and I demand an answer."

For a moment, Dolan looked as though he was going to change his mind and summon Security; a flash of anger, chagrin, perhaps even a touch of fear went through his usually friendly grey eyes. But then he looked down at his desk for a moment, took a breath, and looked back, cracking a wry grin. "Hell, you don't take no for an answer, do you, boy!" he said, affecting the bit of the East Texas drawl he grew up with.

"That's why you hired me back for the Blue, that's why we've kept in touch, Walter. You've got to know that if I'm acting like an ass on this, it's got to be something that merits that kind of behavior."

The colonel gestured to his secretary. "He'll be okay, Corporal. Don't call the Mumps." Dolan sat back into his deep, yielding chair. "'Course, this bozo better have something important to chew about, or you'll have to call the medical corps."

Not quite totally satisfied, but nonetheless obeying orders, the woman marched stiffly out. Scarborough waited for the door to close, then turned back to the older man. "Colonel Dolan, you know why I'm here. We didn't speak long this morning, but I gave you the gist."

"Ev! What's this 'Colonel Dolan' business! For the past fifteen years it's been 'Walt'—here, sit down. You wanna cup of coffee?" Dolan hefted his girth up and strode to a Mr. Coffee machine, where he commenced to pour some brew into a mug labeled "Sirly." "How 'bout I sweeten it up just a tad," he said, pulling out a whiskey bottle from a drawer.

"Just coffee, Walt. We've got to talk. This is serious."

"Okay, fella. Talk is cheap enough. Here you go." Dolan settled the mug of steaming coffee in front of Scarborough, and then sat down. "I really couldn't gab this morning, Ev. Damn busy. You know, I only got a couple of years before mandatory retirement, and I think the government wants to squeeze every bit of juice outta this pour dried-out husk before they let the winds just blow me away."

"Colonel—Walt—" Scarborough took the folded Xerox copies of his relevant file-papers that Mac had sent him. "You remember Captain MacKenzie, don't you?"

"'Course I remember the crooked bastard. Cheated me out of a huge poker-pot back in '68." Dolan leaned forward in his chair, pointing to the side of Scarborough's face. "You okay, Evvie? I heard about that business on Friday night at your revival meetin'. We don't want to lose you pal. You take care, now, hear?"

Scarborough touched his bandages. "It's nothing. I'm sure you know all that needs to be known about it." He tendered the papers to the colonel, tapping them emphatically after he'd laid them on the desk. "This needs your attention, now, Walt."

"This those reports you were talking about, Ev?"

"Copies of reports from Mac's files," Scarborough said, getting up and crossing to a large bookcase. He scanned the displayed spines—bound *Congressional Quarterlies*, military

publications, a copy of *Pentagon* by Allen Drury—until he
found what he was looking for. A leather-bound volume of *The
Abridged Report on Project Blue Book*. He pulled the large
tome from its place and hefted it over to the desk. Quickly, he
found the pages he'd found in his own copy yesterday, opened
the volume to the first appropriate passage, and proffered it to
the air force officer.

"I'm supposed to read these?" said Dolan, taking out
half-frame reading glasses.

"I'll summarize. You can read later. What you've got there
are some significant changes of information. Particularly on the
Iowa business. The Blue Book report is very different from the
investigation report. Mac found a few more large discrepancies
like that, so he asked me to check them out as well. I didn't
think it was all that important—"

"Well, shit, Ev, it's not! This bullcrap is twenty years stale!
This is UFO stuff, Evvie, and you know that the Air Force
closed the whole investigation with Blue Book. You helped us
do it! Now, we're keeping a hand in helpin' people like you
disseminate our information to the public. We figure we owe it
to people to remind them that all this stuff about people from
other planets is hog pucky! But that's about the extent of our
present involvement. You know that, pal! You've written about
Air Force involvement with UFOs!"

Scarborough regarded the officer for a moment. All of
Dolan's body language seemed involved in some symphony of
sincerity. His eyes never veered to the floor, the expression all
rang true—but that Southern accent! Dolan always had a hint of
it, but never had Scarborough heard it poured on so thick. The
colonel was acting like some kind of Ocean City time-sharing
condo salesman. And Scarborough wasn't buying.

"If you could just examine this information, Walt—as soon
as you can—and report to me, in writing, an official explanation, I'll include it in my next book." Scarborough sipped at
the brackish coffee and cleared his throat. "Of more immediate
concern to me, though, is the matter of my missing files."

"Yeah, you mentioned something about that on the phone."
Dolan gave a dismissive gesture. "Those files are twenty years
old, fella. You must've either lost or misplaced them."

Scarborough shook his head. "No. I checked. And my late
wife was the person who organized my files, and she specifi-

cally created folders for those documents.'' Scarborough leaned forward, frowning. ''Walt, I think those files were stolen!''

Colonel Dolan held his hands out in a helpless gesture. ''Why would anyone want to steal some yellowing old reports on sightings of aircraft that don't exist!''

''My question exactly.''

''Now hold your horses a moment, boy. I'm starting to get the drift of your insinuations.'' He flapped the Xeroxes contemptuously. ''These reports don't match the Blue . . . Cousin Mac sees a nigger in the woodpile and comes bellowin' to his buddy the UFO expert. The doc thinks his are *stolen*. Sounds like you guys have been chewin' on some paranoia for breakfast!''

''Maybe,'' said Scarborough. ''And when you wouldn't talk to me this morning—well, that didn't help.''

''Cripes, Ev! I'm a busy man! Sorry about that, but I *am* talking to you right now, aren't I?''

''True.''

Dolan shook his head and ran his fingers through his shock of white hair, leaning forward in a confidential manner. ''Hell, Ev. You know that the bozos in this business can't even pull off a decent procurement-contract cover-up. Big business gets the crafty sorts—the military is lucky if the new officers can wipe their asses and pick their noses at the same time.'' Dolan snorted. ''So you think that we sent over one of those James Bond sorts to lift a stupid *UFO* report. Sheesh, maybe there *is* something weird in the drinkin' water out in Bethesda!''

''I'll admit, it does sound farfetched. But the fact remains, you've got this discrepancy here—I want you to tell me who wrote up that part of the Blue Book report. And I want to know why my report wasn't followed.''

Dolan shrugged. He examined the bent documents for a moment, then scanned the open book in front of him. ''Hmm. Yes. I see what you mean. There are differences. Green lights in the report, red in the book . . . Yeah . . . well, maybe you're right, Ev. I'll get to work on this. We do go back a long way, so I figure I owe that to you. But as far as these disappearing files of yours go . . . well, I think you're barking up the wrong tree on that one.''

''Could be. Nonetheless, thanks, Walt. I hope you'll be equally cooperative on my next request.''

Dolan rolled his eyes. "Lordy help me! He wants the keys to the officer's massage parlor!"

Despite himself, Scarborough chuckled. "Not quite. This whole business with the gunman at my lecture has postponed my tour. I've got some time on my hands. I'll be leaving tomorrow for a trip to Iowa. I'm going to reopen the investigation on UFOs out there with my friend Captain MacKenzie. I'd appreciate Air Force aid and support where and when necessary."

Dolan's cheek filled as he probed the inside of his mouth with a tongue thoughtfully. He gazed down at the rumpled report a moment, then looked back up at Scarborough. "Twenty years is a hell of a long time, Ev. What do you hope to accomplish?"

"I want to get the record straight. I pride myself on correct research for my books. I want to make sure that the facts are correct. Also, MacKenzie wants me to visit—maybe we'll do some fishing."

"So I take it that I can send you anything I find to his address—you don't happen to have it on hand, do you?"

Scarborough got up. "He's a retired air force officer, Walt. I should think that you've got his address and his phone number on a Rolodex *somewhere*."

Dolan smiled softly and bobbed his head. "Yep. Yep, I guess we do at that."

"Fine." Scarborough stabbed a finger at the copy of Mac's files. "You get someone on that, Walt. Right away. There's no way that I can prove those files of mine were stolen. In all probability they weren't. However it's a *fact* that there's some serious discrepancy between that report and *Blue Book*. Explain it or correct it. Good day."

He turned and marched for the door.

"Ev!" said the colonel, just as his hand touched the knob.

"Yes?" Turning.

Colonel Walter Dolan stood up and leaned against the desk, a broad smile on his face. "Ev, I do believe you are upset."

"I *am* upset," Scarborough said, annoying the attempt at ironic humor.

"Doctor Ev! How long have we been working together. What, almost twenty-five years now? Hell, I bounced that little baby girl of yours on my knee, we've burned tons o' barbecue, and we must a' put away a hundred cases o' beer and maybe a few kegs of that fine Scotch liquor o' yours. Ev, we're *friends*! And now, you come in here like a firehouse on fire, bangin' my desk and makin' demands. What gives?''

"Just do what I ask, Walt. We'll work this out later, okay?''

"No, it's not okay. You've been under *pressure*, friend. That business Friday night must have put you over the edge. You're flirtin' with a nervous breakdown, I can see it in your eyes. And hell, you're twitchin'!''

The colonel was right, Scarborough knew. Not about the nervous breakdown—but with this past weekend's problems, he did feel the strain. Nonetheless, it wasn't time to talk about it—especially not when Dolan was talking like some used snake-oil seller.

"Must go, Colonel. Just get me what I want, and I won't barge in on you anymore.''

"Sure, Ev, sure. You take care now, hear?''

Scarborough closed the door behind him and left, ignoring the dirty look from the corporal.

He had to go home and make that phone call to Mac.

And then he had to pack for his trip to Iowa—and, God help him, to Kansas University.

Colonel Walter Dolan waited three minutes after Scarborough left for his blood pressure to go down.

Then he made the phone call.

"Richards?'' he said, his voice low and slightly trembling.

"Yes.''

"We've got to talk. Scarborough was just here. Big problems.''

Dolan didn't get specific. It wasn't good to talk on the phone about specifics in matters involving Brian Richards. The man was absolutely top-level, with clearances up the wazoo—but with the era of technology the way it was, phones could not be trusted to be untapped.

"Okay. I'm still in town. Think you can make it up the George Washington Parkway in about twenty minutes?''

"Yeah, I think so.''

"This Scarborough guy—are we going to have continuing difficulties with him? He's a cornerstone of the whole operation!''

"I don't know,'' said Dolan. "We'll talk when I see you.''

"Right.''

The phone hung up at the other end.

Colonel Walter Dolan tapped onto another line. "Transportation? Colonel Walter Dolan here. Think you can have a chopper ready for me in about five minutes?" Dolan fumbled out a cigarette from a stale pack in his desk. He'd quit smoking for the nth time two months ago. But it was time to start again. "I only need a quick hop. Where?" He lit the cigarette. "Just up the road. Central Intelligence Agency building."

He sucked in the smoke and coughed violently.

CHAPTER SEVENTEEN

"Fuck me," she said, making small provocative motions with her hips, her new jewelry of love jangling. "Fuck me, lover. Do it good."

"Sure, baby. Sure," Justine said, pulling off his jockey shorts, standing buck naked on the side of the bed. "Lemme just check one thing." He leaned over and took the key out of the handcuffs attaching her right arm to the solid brass of the backboard. "Don't want it to fall out," he explained. "Might lose it."

He placed the small silver key by the muted light on the nightstand.

The woman stopped squirming sensuously, and lay back limply, mouth set in a cynical sneer. "C'mon, Woody, you wanna get on with business?"

He slapped her full in the face, and her head swung back, throwing a spray of blonde hair over the pillow. "Shut up, bitch."

Her voice was low and monotone. "That'll cost you a hundred extra, Wood. You know the rules."

"Oh, yeah. The rules." He vaulted over and landed between the V of her legs, which were handcuffed to the frame at the base of the bed. The scent of her snatch and her sweat, however, did not excite him as it usually did. He hovered over her, squatting, looking at the way her big breasts oozed down her rib cage. He needed this one, needed it bad, after that business in D.C. But for some reason, the usual rush of excitement wasn't coming. His cock hung limp just inches from a sexy, naked woman, which was about like Old Faithful deciding to stay put in the ground and not gush out of Yellowstone Park. A few preliminaries were needed. Yeah. He began to kiss her knees, working his way down her thighs. "Sorry, babe. I'm a little uptight. You'll get more, I promise."

"Okay, hon. Just don't forget the raincoat when you go drilling."

He picked up the cellophane-wrapped condom from beside her and whacked her left nipple playfully. Her name was Candy and she was a low-priced call girl, but she let him tie and handcuff her and that's what he liked, so he put up with her nasal, New York accent and snide comments. He'd gotten back that afternoon, and had been restless as soon as he'd walked into LAX. Women relaxed him. Women who knew their place, anyway.

He began to kiss her big, dark nipple, began to rub himself against her. A small tingle answered in his groin. Hey, maybe we got something cooking after all, he thought, untensing a bit.

Control. Woodrow Justine felt in control again, and slowly he began to forget the terror that had hung on him since D.C. like stink. This chick was his 'cause he had money. Afterward, he'd do some push-ups, take a long soak in his hot spa, and then crash into some deep sleep. Tomorrow morning, he'd hit World's Gym and drip about three hours of serious perspiration.

Yeah. He could feel his penis beginning to stir, stiffen. The sight of Candy, stretched out and helpless began to do its old magic.

He could do anything he wanted to her, now, if he pleased. *Anything.*

"Woodrow!" a voice whispered from the shadows. "Tell us about the UFOs. Tell us!"

Justine's head shot up. "Who's that?! Who said that?"

The shadows seemed to stir by the window. He thought that, or a moment, he could make out the dim form of a man.

"Who the hell are you talking to?" asked Candy.

Justine jumped off the bed and dived at the shadows. He camp up with fistfuls of curtain, and nothing more. There was no one there. "Christ," he said. He could feel something unhinging in his head.

"Go to church and talk to Christ. How about finishing up and then getting me out of here."

He realized that his hands were starting to shake, and his breaths were becoming ragged and uneven. *Get on top of the bitch and screw your brains out and you'll feel better,* he told himself. "Yeah, yeah, yeah," he said crawling back onto the bed.

He tried, and tried again, but it was no good.

Candy snarled contemptuously. "Face it, Wood. You can't get it up. Now let me go. I got other things to do."

Justine was shuddering as though a blast of frigid air had just swept through the room—but his face and chest were sheened with perspiration. *Gotta get outta here,* he thought. *Get out!*

He got off the bed and got dressed.

"So let me go, lover," said the call girl, rattling her cuffs.

Justine barely heard her. He turned and walked toward the door.

"Hey! Where you *going*? You walk out of this room, I'll scream my head off, Woodrow Justine!"

"Shut up!" he yelled, grabbing at his ears to cut off the noise. "Just shut up!" He ran back and stuffed her mouth with balled-up sheet. She struggled, but the cuffs were secure.

Her muffled yells followed him out of the house.

Gotta get outta here. Gotta get some air.

He walked down Grand to Venice Avenue, heading through the brisk night air toward the beach. When he had troubles, he walked on the beach. The salt air and the crash of the breakers helped him usually, and he needed it now, bad.

Venice Beach's boardwalk has no boards. It's just a strip of asphalt with cheap concession stands and bars on one side; and a bicycle path, a long stretch of sand, and the beach on the other. Justine passed the famous Muscle Beach workout bin, where old weights rusted quietly. He never worked out there. Unlike many weight lifters, Woodrow Justine was not an exhibitionist. The routine of strength training was just as important as the results.

It was late, and there were only a few stragglers on the beach. The strains of an electric guitar wailed from a bar nearby. The smell of rancid gyros and popcorn, dead fish and decaying seaweed, marred the freshness of the breeze coming off the white crash of the waves. Palm trees lolled listlessly, as though exhausted from the constant daytime sun. A half-moon hung over the Santa Monica mountains like a dead, ruined eye.

Rubbing his arm, Justine walked out onto the white, trash-littered sand ten yards, and then dropped to his knees, moaning softly.

They'd said it was harmless, those doctors. The needle had only left a tiny prick, and the solution that he'd brought back had been tested Sunday. Tap water, the lab had announced. "You're in absolute top physical form," the doctors had told him, and he'd been shipped back home to rest for a while. He'd been debriefed, and the powers-that-were listened to his tape stolidly, pronouncing Klinghoffer a solo agent, with no contacts to other organizations. He was thanked, given the usual bonus for the extreme-prejudice job. "The guy was a total schizo," they'd told him. "Don't worry about it. Good job."

Why was he hearing these voices then? Why was he seeing things, lurking in the shadows at the corners of his eyes? Why did his arm throb from time to time? They didn't have to tell him that Klinghoffer was a certified kook, that the only orders he was receiving were from some diseased corner of his own cerebellum. Why, then, did the images, the sounds, the wretched *smells* of that desiccated house haunt him still? Why did he feel as though Klinghoffer hadn't just injected water in him—he'd shot him up with something far more sinister. Like maybe his soul.

Justine had taken his medicine as usual that day, hoping it would calm him down. No luck. But now, kneeling before the mighty Pacific Ocean as though in supplication, he began to calm down. The familiar lulling scents and rhythms of Venice Beach made him feel better, and he felt that he was getting a grip back on things.

Yeah. Sit here for awhile, get steady. Then go back, let Candy out of those 'cuffs.

The thought of the whore spread-eagled there on his bed amused him. He chuckled a bit, and watched a seagull pick at a MacDonald's Big Mac Styrofoam box near an overstuffed litter basket.

"Jesus," he said to himself, shaking his head and laughing as the breeze scuffed a napkin in front of him. "I've got to get out of this UFO business. Like, maybe they'll assign me to somewhere safe and *sane*, like a marine barracks in Beirut."

He heaved a sigh and closed his eyes, concentrating on pleasant memories. Art shopping in Carmel; riding Route 1 down the California coast in a convertible, being startled by the aquamarine water embracing the rugged rocks. Feeling free, feeling *alive*, feeling in *control* . . .

It started as a sigh of the breeze, and slurred into the vague beginnings of a whisper: "Jusss . . . Jusss . . ."

He looked up, every muscle in his body clenching again.

"Jusss . . . Jusss . . . Jusss . . . tine"

At first the sound was as omnipresent as the air, and then it found a location. Justine snapped his head toward where it was emanating.

Twenty yards away, ten behind him, a public lavatory and changing-room stood, whitewashed cinder blocks perched on a foundation of raised cinder blocks. The front of the structure was surrounded by a fence, which was locked at this late hour. Behind this, a figure leaned against the wall, outlined in the pale moonlight. The figure wore a long black raincoat.

"You're . . . one . . . of . . . ussssss . . . Now." The voice said. "Justine. One of us!"

He hadn't noticed anyone there before.

Woodrow Justine shot to his feet, a desperate rage filling him. Kicking up a spray of sand behind him, he ran to the figure. The man in the black coat did not move, nor did he say another word.

Justine grabbed the man by the throat and threw him to the ground. He squeezed hard, banging the man's head against the sand, anger filling his entire world. "Stop it!" he cried. "Stop it! Who are you. WHO ARE YOU?"

The man groaned and gagged, and an effluvia of unwashed clothing and Thunderbird wine washed up. "Ugghh . . . get off me . . . You're crazy, man. Get offa me!"

Justine dragged the man to where the moonlight shown the brightest, and regained enough control to pull his hands away. Below him, the man gasped and gagged, coughing. A bottle sloshed in the pocket of the long black coat, and its long neck glinted in the moonlight. "What's wrong with you, man! I'm callin' the police!" He was a dark, bearded man with a broken nose.

"What's my name," demanded Justine in a dead voice.

"Your name! What, you crazy! I'm just mindin' my own business, havin' a drink, watching the sea . . . I don't know you, man!"

Justine rose. The anger and the fear were still there, but his control was back, confronted by the realization that this was just some derelict bum, overlaid by his imagination. Justine staunched an urge to kick the man hard in the side.

"Lee' me alone . . ." said the man. "I got friends . . . I'll call the fuckin' cops." The man's words were slurred with drink.

Justine pulled out a roll of bills from his pocket. He peeled off a ten and let it flutter down to the wretched figure on the sand. "Sorry. I thought you were someone else."

The man grabbed the bill, got to his feet, then vomited into the sand. As Justine walked away, the bum's curses followed him.

He knew now what he had to do. There was one person who could help him, the woman who'd straightened him out before, the CIA shrink who'd diagnosed his biochemical imbalances and prescribed the medicine that kept him straight. Cunningham. She was back on the base in Iowa now, and all he had to do was call her, let her know some of his pistons were misfiring, and then get out there, quick, for a tune-up.

Yeah, thought Justine, trudging off the sand and onto concrete, nervously avoiding the deep shadows of the shabby buildings where other imagined phantoms might lurk. That was the ticket. Cunningham would bail him out. Maybe he just needed a new prescription. A dash more thorazine, or a touch more zinc. Cunningham would do a quick computer analysis, mix together the right drugs, and voila! Woodrow Justine would be right as rain.

But as he negotiated Venice back past the snoozing bars, the still Penny Lane record shop, and the garish signs of the health juice-shop, a fear, unvoiced and barely thought, sat like a horned lizard in the pool of his consciousness. Justine had thought long and hard about his visit to that bent soul last Saturday night, thought about the car in the driveway, the garb the man wore the night he had shot at Scarborough. Although Woodrow Justine was no intellectual, he was an alert man who kept his ears open. These past two years, working on the Project, he had absorbed a great deal of fact and lore that had sprung up around the phenomena of UFOs. The whole affair was becoming nothing less than a new American mythology. And an oft-repeated story, a kind of underpinning to the sightings of flying saucers hovering and scooting about beneath the stars, concerned men—men with strange eyes, perhaps vaguely oriental; men who would arrive in black Cadillacs or black Pontiacs; men who would often interview those who had seen the saucers, and just as often harass them. Men who came at dusk with the long shadows, wearing clothing of all black.

A twitch of this notion caused Justine's entire body to shudder just as he reached Grand Avenue.

A grey cat leaped out of the shadows, ran across the road, hiding under a Toyota Celica, colorless beneath the moon and street lamps. The twitch-shudder of fear became a tremble and a shaking in Justine, causing him to stop and forcibly halt his line of thought.

Goddamnit! He knew the truth behind the whole fucking UFO business! He knew the facts, the hard cold data that underlay the CIA operation to which he was attached. For these past three years, it had provided him with such a source of power, such a feeling of superiority over the gullible fools who had bought the pseudoscientific nonsense dished out by the crackpots and swallowed by the credulous. This peripheral business was just folklore! The equivalent of ghost stories told around the campfire. They were just ridiculous nonsense... vague, unfocused snatches of paranoia.

He straightened and used every ounce of control in his sinews to make him continue walking home. If he brought up these thoughts to Central, they wouldn't modify his drug prescription—they'd just lock him up and throw away the key!

Still, once in the open, his thoughts continued, nagging and leering and laughing at him.

What if they *did* exist, these modern spectres of tall saucer-tales. What if they existed—and what if they were out to get him!

Justine swallowed down the thought like regurgitated bile,

but still it sat in him, grinning poisonously in the back of his mind.

Out to get him . . . out for vengeance!

The Men in Black.

CHAPTER EIGHTEEN

On the Tuesday morning following his confrontation with Colonel Walter Dolan, Scarborough rose early, packed some luggage, got in his Mercedes, and drove to Dulles International Airport. He parked in one of the satellite lots, not knowing how long he'd be away, and loathe to pay the premium prices for closer parking. He caught an 8:30 Eastern flight to Chicago O'Hare, where he caught the connection to the Iowa City Airport.

Waiting for him in the terminal, wearing his epauletted hunting jacket, jeans, a red-checked flannel shirt, a Met's baseball cap, and a huge grin, was Captain Eric MacKenzie.

"Ev!" he cried, waving his hands wildly. "Ev, buddy! Am I glad to see you!"

The big, red-cheeked man caught up Scarborough in a bearhug. People stopped, looked, and pointed at this amusing sight of two mature men acting like long-lost lovers, and Scarborough found it all slightly embarrassing. "Mac, uh, it's not like I was lost at sea or anything," he said, after getting a noseful of MacKenzie's Old Spice aftershave.

MacKenzie's expression turned suddenly mournful. "My friend, I'm just trying to show you how *bad* I feel about the way I acted the other night."

"Mac, we already talked about that yesterday. We were both out of line. I'm sorry, you're sorry—apologies accepted all around. And look...here I am in Iowa, on the great UFO-mystery hunt. No need for the histrionics.''

MacKenzie stepped away, but swung a big hand around to slap Scarborough on the back, a blow that almost put the scientist onto the floor. ''That's right. Heck, if you can't yell at a friend, who *can* you yell at?''

Recovering his balance, Scarborough said, ''You ever think of getting in the ring with Mike Tyson, Mac? You've got a pretty powerful right there.''

''Thanks, Ev. What say we go get your luggage, and head out for the old homestead?''

They got Scarborough's bags. Mac insisted on carrying the Jordache luggage, and Scarborough did not object. The big man hefted the bags easily out into the parking lot, where he threw them in the back of a red Ford Bronco, complete with a gun rack and dried blood in the back.

''Deer,'' explained Mac apologetically. ''Needs a comprehensive cleaning. With the old lady gone, not everything gets scrubbed up as well as it used to. Take warning, Ev. Serious bachelor condition back at the ponderosa.''

Scarborough strapped his seat belt on. ''Hop Sing's on vacation?''

Mac gunned the engine and the four-wheeled vehicle jerked toward the exit. Mac smiled over at Scarborough. ''Nope. Ran off with Hoss and Little Joe. Always thought those three were into weird sexual perversions.''

The big man paid his parking bill, then wheeled onto the highway toward his house on the outskirts of town.

Iowa City was a college town, and a quite nice one at that. The university was the shining jewel of a state famous for its high rate of literacy—one of the best schools in the nation. After he'd left the air force, Mac had decided that he'd get a Master's Degree. He chose the U. of I. because of its famous writing program, and because of its access to open territory and fresh air—prerequisites for an outdoorsman like Eric MacKenzie. Privately, Scarborough had doubted that his friend would last out such literary boot camp, but he'd been proved wrong. MacKenzie had immediately scoped out the territory, found the kind of counseling he needed, and worked damn hard. He received a great deal of help, for example, from Professor David Morrell—who advanced soon to fame for creation of the

Rambo character made famous by Sylvestor Stallone. Before long, Mac could turn out quite serviceable prose. Even before he'd graduated, he'd sold his first men's adventure book: *The Eagle's Claw*. Morrell had helped him find an agent, and the agent found him instant work in the burgeoning field of guns-'n'-guts action-adventures. "Blue-collar blood-porn," Scarborough called it, but secretly he read absolutely every word that his friend wrote, astonished at the clumsiness of the prose, as well as the energy and vitality and fun it contained. At first, Scarborough had tried to encourage Mac to set his sights higher, but the man was having far too much fun pounding out his fifteen pages a day to think about reforming. Mac liked Iowa, and he liked the university, so he and his wife had settled nearby in a large house. He taught the occasional undergraduate course, chased the occasional undergraduate skirt, hunted in the Midwest fields and woods, fished the freshwater streams. And he was a happy man—and even happier when his wife left him, unchaining him from a roller-coaster marriage.

Scarborough had to admit, Iowa City and its environs were very pleasant. As they rolled along toward Mac's home, Scarborough again admired the Hawkeye State's wealth of fields. The most fertile state in the Union, 95 percent of its land was farmable. This was Grant Wood territory, the home of American Gothic, the simple, clean lines of farm houses and barns rising up from the gently rolling or flat land, like natural growths of the green and brown land, not architecture.

Mac and Scarborough chatted affably as the Bronco ate up the twenty or so miles to Mac's house, making small talk before they had to tackle the larger task before them.

"I'm just tickled pink you're going to go down to Kansas, too, and check up on Diane," said Mac, downshifting and turning off the highway, driving onto a dirt road upgrade toward wooded hills. "She's a good girl. She may have a few screws loose—"

"But they're quality screws, right, Mac?"

"You betcha."

The Bronco rumbled up a hill, then turned onto a private road, rattling over a loose gravel driveway.

"Well, she's part mine, so I guess I'm responsible." Scarborough sighed heavily. "I've just got a dreadful feeling about it, that's all."

Mac pulled up in front of a two-car garage so filled with junk and gadgets there was no room for a car. He stopped the Bronco beside the house, a large two-story brick affair covered with ivy and surrounded by hedges and gardens and rich green grass—all Iowa rarities, but specifically introduced by Mac, who liked green overgrowth.

"Don't you worry your little pointed head," said Mac, getting out and going to the back to collect the bags. "We'll call the little darling later. Shit, you're helping me with this file business—maybe I'll take you down to Kansas myself, help you dig up the facts."

"Thanks, Mac," said Scarborough. "We'll see what happens."

Eric MacKenzie's house was not exactly a wreck. It was clean enough, thought Scarborough, just disheveled. Clothing lay strewn all over the early American furniture. Books and magazines were propped precariously on the dining room table and the TV. Packages and cans of food lay all over the place.

However, there were no dirty dishes in the sink, the bathroom was clean enough and smelled of Comet cleanser. And Mac's study, which he devoted to his sports, fairly sparkled with wax and polish. The guns and fishing rods were stacked neatly, the bookcases ordered, the trophies on the mantlepiece bright and dusted.

"Not bad, Mac," said Scarborough after depositing his bags in one of the guest rooms. "Better than when I was here last year."

"Yeah! I guess it is. But say, it's about lunchtime. How about a sandwich and a brew, and then we can dig into the dirt."

Mac made sandwiches that would cause Dagwood to drool, so Scarborough, who'd refused the plane snack, readily agreed. Old MacKenzie couldn't fry an egg, but he could make a mean sandwich. The jolly man first set a big bottle of Grolsch beer in front of Scarborough, then pulled out several Tupperware containers from the fridge, along with a section of bread and a tray of condiments.

"Any particular combination you favor today, Ev?" The burly man waved a hand over a deli's worth of supplies. Fresh-cut ham and lebanon bologna, tongue and roast beef, turkey, chicken, mortadella, salami, summer sausage . . . And the cheeses! There must have been twenty kinds to choose from, and not just midwestern bland stuff, but European camembert and brie, English stilton and cheddar—and real Swiss cheese.

"I think I'll just take the chef's special."

"You got it. We got some fresh rolls this morning. Man, since you were here last year, they opened a wonderful place in Iowa City. Combination bakery and deli. One-stop shopping for old MacKenzie! Rye rolls, with caraway seeds. How's that sound, Ev?"

Scarborough just drank his Grolsch and smiled.

"You got it! Listen, you ever try Bermuda onion on a sandwich? I've been reading this Lawrence Sanders guy. He's got a hero in the 'Deadly Sin' books after my own heart. Makes some nice sandwiches, and then eats 'em over the sink. Can you imagine? How's he gonna read and eat, over a sink?" The stack of magazines and books on the table testified to MacKenzie's own solitary eating habits. "Anyway, this guy, Captain Edward X. Deleney—he likes to put Bermuda onions on his sandwiches. It's pretty good. You wanna slice?"

Scarborough agreed, and watched as his friend built him a truly magnificent sandwich of sliced Danish ham, Swiss cheese, some pepperoni, a smear of braunswieger, a touch of caviar, a feathering of alfalfa sprouts, a slice of Bermuda and a generous ladling of imported Dijon mustard.

"Sorry," he said. "I forgot the tomatoes yesterday."

"Curses. I guess I just can't eat it then, Mac."

Mac sliced it in half and presented it to his friend on clean china. "Choke it down, bud."

He got himself a Grolsch and then made himself a similar sandwich. "So, old Ironpants won't cop to stealing your files, huh?" he said finally, after half the big stuffed roll had been wolfed.

"He probably didn't do it. Who's to say? Good sandwich."

"Thanks." Mac thoughtfully munched on his for a couple of moments. "So I can't figure it," he said, dripping green-and-brown flecks of sprouts and mustard onto his plate. "Why would Dolan and the air force change the facts we turned in—and then want to destroy the evidence of the truth?"

Ev put down his sandwich. "Whoa. Just a minute—I definitely think something odd is going on, but I'm not ready to go whole hog and buy the conspiracy theory like some silly UFOol. You seem all ready to jump on *that* bandwagon."

"Scarborough! What you want them to do, kick you in the head with a fifty megaton bomb? Wake up! We worked for a corrupt government! Old Dolan's 'bout as straight as a Confederate three-dollar bill. Now, I don't know what's going on, but I do wanna find out!"

Scarborough shook his head. He pushed his sandwich away. He wasn't hungry anymore. "No, I really can't buy that. That gives the air force too much credit for intelligence." He leaned forward toward his friend. A burp brought up the taste of pepperoni to his mouth. He covered his mouth and excused himself. "What started off all the secrecy with Dulles's CIA and the Air Force was legitimate concern, in the late forties and early fifties that the UFO sightings were caused by the Russians. That's why everything was classified—and continued to be. I've read the documents. Those old Geezers knew they'd be starting up some paranoia, but you gotta also remember, those guys weren't stupid either, they were veterans of the biggest war of this century. They were in a new world, filled with new technology and strange fears, and so they had to be *careful*. Who knows, the way the military and government works, all this business with the files might just be following some kind of obscure rules or codes. Names were mentioned that shouldn't have been mentioned. There *are* reasons for top-secret and classified materials, you know. I'll give you an example. You know that Stanton Friedman guy, right?"

"Sure, the UFO investigator who's the physicist."

"Now, I like Stanton, although we've locked horns a few times. I hear that he's trooping around the UFO conferences with a copy of a government document about UFOs he dug out, thanks to the Freedom of Information Act. He holds it up and says, 'Take a look at these pages and tell me that the CIA isn't covering something up.' Then he shows a document that's largely blotted out with black magic marker. And looks smug and pronounced Q.E.D!"

"Sounds pretty damning to me!"

"Mac! Mac! Fools jump in! Can't you see, *this* is the kind of jump-to-conclusions thinking that has spawned the whole UFO lore! You know as well as I do about the codes on these documents. Just because something is blacked out doesn't mean that it's covering up a record of President Truman playing Parcheezi with beings from Betelgeuse! There could be records of an agent's dealings that could be deleted because he officially did not work for the CIA then! Or because he was using a secret kind of ballpoint pen! That whole business in the 70s, with the disclosures of those documents that went through court? Did you see the stuff the CIA wanted to keep out, due to their classified nature? Weird stuff, harmless stuff, *odd* stuff. You read it, and you say, why did they *care*? I'll tell you—because the whole thing's a bureaucracy, and bureaucracies are far stranger than flying saucers.''

Mac shrugged. "Too true. But how does that explain your missing files, to say nothing of the discrepancies?''

"The colonel could be right. I might have misplaced them. They could have also been stolen, true—but that doesn't mean that it was because of some cover-up. See what I mean? Let's not jump in too far. This could all be explained.''

"I don't understand. If you think that, then why did you blow your stack at Dolan? Why'd you come out here?''

"I demand accuracy, Mac. I demand facts. Facts are the soul of any religion I serve. Facts are the basis of my exisistence. Facts are the rocks I kick, like Dr. Johnson when the illusory nature of reality was presented to him. 'Thus I refute thee,' he said, and thus I refute the believers. But if my facts are wrong, I need to straighten them out. Just because facts need to be straightened out, just because 'old Ironpants' Dolan is not being cooperative, and maybe just because there are things they don't want me to know, does not mean that the saucers have landed!''

MacKenzie pursed his lips. "Yep. Got me, pal. But you are going to help me check this stuff out, aren't you?''

"I said I would, and I will, Mac. And you know that I'm a man of my word.''

"You bet I do.'' MacKenzie got up and hauled out two more bottles of Grolsch. He handed one to Scarborough. "So you've been fed and watered. Come on up to my den of iniquity. There's work to be done.''

Mac's office was on the second floor. Two months after his wife, Tama, had left him, he'd had a weekend-long party to which he had invited Scarborough, as well as other male friends from around the country, and male friends from the town and the university. Student crashers were welcome. During this party, Mac produced gallons of booze and played Charlie Parker records nonstop—Tama had hated jazz. At the height of the bacchanalia, he'd revealed to the attendees his plan. With their help, they'd dragged the king-size nuptial bed of the MacKenzie's, mattresses and sheets and all, into the backyard. The guests were then charged to scour the premises. Anything they found remotely feminine—perfume, scented toilet paper, tampons, makeup, etcetera—was tossed onto the bed. At midnight, Mac doused the bed and its occupants with gasoline, and a lit wooden match was tossed into its center, producing a marvelous bonfire.

The next day, the remaining guests helped move Mac's typewriter, desk, filing cabinets, and chairs into the master bedroom. "My writing is my life," he'd said that day, as they toasted the new digs with a magnum of champagne. "And now it's my wife!"

He immediately broke his new office in by writing one of Scarborough's favorites, *The Immolator #53: Death to the Matchmakers*, in which Harry Diggs, the detective-cum-mercenary-cum-vigilante, uncovers a crooked dating service operated by the Mafia and the KGB, and firebombs an entire New York City skyscraper's floor that's filled with adulterous wives.

"Hey," said Mac, "since you were here last, I've got myself a new rug." He ushered his friend in and pointed toward the floor, where a lovely maroon-and-blue-and-gold Persian rug lay, supporting most of the room's furniture. "From India! Hand woven!"

"Quite nice," said Scarborough, admiring the weave and the intricate almost mandala-like patterns.

Mac's office was unquestionably the most comfortable room in the house—and certainly the neatest. It was the place, after all, where he spent most of his time and energy. The big bay windows afforded a pleasant view of the countryside, framed by tasteful drapes Tama had bought, which had somehow survived the purge. A couch and two Eames chairs sat on the rug, surrounded by filing cabinets, a desk, and, of course, Mac's new pride and joy, the latest-model IBM PC, which he used almost entirely as a word processer, along with a Hewlett-

Packard laser printer. Against the walls were bookshelves overflowing with books, both hard- and soft-bound. One whole case was devoted to Mac's work. Above this was an acrylic portrait by Boris Vallejo of Harry Diggs, The Immolator himself, a trademark flamethrower in his hand, his Clint Eastwood teeth clenched around a cigar, his veins popping from bare traps and delts, and a face in profile so that only a hint of the spiderweb burns which covered half his face could be seen.

Harry Diggs was a Vietnam vet, who'd been burned by napalm in the war. With no more Vietcong to fight when he returned, he turned to fighting other bad guys, book by book, when he returned to civilian life. These conflagrations were the subject matter that Mac dealt with or plotted—he didn't write *all* the Immolators, he farmed some out to other writers—in a series that had lasted a dozen years and spanned over a hundred titles. Oh, Mac wrote other books, but "Ol' Firebug" Diggs was his bread and butter. Scarborough kept and read only the ones that Mac had written himself—autographed of course—a stockpile of them on the back of his commode for toilet reading. They were entertaining little hunks of mayhem, their garish covers depicted explosions and weapons amidst running screaming men, with Diggs in the foreground, puffing on his stogie. Smoke and flame were usually in the illo somewhere— indeed, with the new string of re-issues, the graphics proclaiming the words The Immolator sprouted tiny fires themselves.

Appropriately, Mac kept his pipe collection, matches, and tobacco atop his Immolator books. It was to this that he repaired immediately, taking down a fairly new briar and stuffing it with fragrant leaf. "Park your butt over there," he said, nodding at the couch. "I'll haul down the stuff in just a minute." He struck a safety match and puffed, sending the aromatic smoke pluming into the room.

Scarborough noticed the pile of quality paper stacked on a shelf near the IBM. He examined the title page—*Until The Dawn*, it said, by Eric Landon MacKenzie. Most of the times that Mac used his own name, he just kept it to Mac MacKenzie. But *Dawn* was special—he'd started it two years ago, with Scarborough's assistance. It was going to be his "quality breakout" book, a carefully written book based on his experiences in the Air Force as a young man. Scarborough was gratified to see that it was thicker than when he'd last seen it.

He desperately wanted to read it, but Mac insisted that he had to finish the whole thing first, before he let *anybody* read it. He returned to the sitting area, not wanting Mac to know that he was snooping.

Scarborough recapped his Grolsch and set the bottle on top of the copy of *Guns and Ammo* that lay atop a carved Spanish coffee table. Copies of *Soldier of Fortune* peeked out from gun catalogues and almanacs, all part of Mac's steady stream of research material, most of which he kept on a bookshelf close to his word processor. He could just scoot his wheeled chair over on a whim, and pull down a volume of the *Encyclopaedia Britannica* or a copy of *Jane's Ships*. "Hardware!" the big man had growled once. "My readers demand hardware. They want to know the details right down to the millimeter measurement of the slugs that rip through the viscera of the bad guys and spray gouts of blood across the walls!"

"You have a discerning readership," Scarborough had commented.

"Naw, not really. It all has something to do with men's penises, did you know that? This gun stuff."

Scarborough had grinned. "No!"

Now, he watched as his friend went to the bank of stolen file cabinets, opened a drawer, searched for a moment, ahhed, and pulled out several tattered folders jammed with documents and notes. "Here we go, pilgrim," he said, putting the stuff on the coffee table. "We just have to cross Red River here, and get the cattle safe to Dodge City."

"You've got the copy of the Blue?" asked Scarborough.

"I sure enough do, partner." Mac feigned a bowlegged, spur-jangling walk to a bookcase. He pulled out a dog-eared copy of the Government Printing Office's edition of *The Abridged Report on Project Blue Book* and plopped it onto the table beside the files. "A yellow copy of the *Blue Book*," said Mac. He sat down beside his guest, and opened the file. He lifted his oversized beer bottle, bubbled it, and then put it down again. "I was looking over this stuff last night, Ev, and some other interesting stuff came up about that Iowa farm we investigated in '68."

"I'm all ears, Mac," said Scarborough, ready to dig in and work.

CHAPTER NINETEEN

When Diane Scarborough and Tim Reilly picked up Jake Camden, Diane regretted their call to him immediately. Camden came off the Piedmont flight smelling of gin and cigarettes, wearing a loud Hawaiian shirt and jeans. His handshake was damp and cool, and his greetings were glib and phony. The only thing genuine about him was the Leica camera that bounced on his chest—and Diane had doubts about that.

Tim, however, took to him right away.

"Kids, ya gotta feed me first," Camden said, after picking up his luggage—a patched brown leather carryall—off the treadmill. "We'll get your story down on some tape, and then we'll go out and click off some shots of the spot where you saw this UFO."

"Well, we've got a nice Denny's down the road," said Tim, grinning, knowing that that wasn't what the journalist had in mind.

"Ah, c'mon—treat me to one of your famous Kansas City strips. I hear that the best place to get 'em in these parts is in a *bar*." He winked at Tim, who nodded and allowed that he knew the kind of place that Camden wanted. Tim, a drinker himself, instantly saw a kindred spirit here. Tim was also the kind of guy who was fascinated with *characters*. He was at his happiest when life was a Dickensian feast, filled with broad and fascinating people, gilt-edged with drama. And lo, here before them was a veritable Mr. Macawber with a press pass.

They took Camden to a dark hole named The Hideaway that had a bar dating from the Gay Nineties, genuine slate pool-tables in the backroom, and steaks as thick as a brick.

When they were ushered into a booth by the waitress,

Camden took out his Sony tape recorder, lit a Camel, and ordered a steak, baked potato, and a boilermaker.

"Might I say what a handsome couple you two make. You look like you are definitely in love. And Diane—you truly are a bee-u-tee-ful woman." Camden smiled at her a bit whimsically, lust sparkling in his rheumy eyes. "Yep. I'm so happy you called," he said. "You know, I guess maybe the *Intruder* has got a bad rep amongst you intelligentsia. But did you realize that *all* the reporters have college degrees? Shit, I've got one myself! Look, let's face it—we all got to make a buck. And what the *Intruder* is, is a rag . . . A tabloid meant primarily for entertainment. Okay, so we stretch things a bit! Our readers know that, and fuck everyone else if they can't take a joke." He tapped the damp formica topped table with a forefinger. "But I ask you, how many papers with our circulation and our resources actually are investigating this kind of phenomenon? Zip . . . I mean, seriously—*something* is going on. It's gotta be checked out." He looked at Diane and she could tell he noticed her skeptical expression. "Look, I just want to say thank you for entrusting me with this story. I have years of experience in this kind of thing, and I'm going to do my damndest to help find out what the hell you saw last week." He smiled, showing yellowed teeth, then reached under the table and gave Diane's thigh a reassuring squeeze that lasted just a moment too long to be chaste.

His boilermaker arrived. He took the shot of whiskey, dropped it, glass and all, into his mug of beer, sipped, and sighed. "Ah. That's good. So let's start at the top. Tell me just what happened."

They ran through the story for him, Tim doing most of the talking, since Diane was suddenly feeling a little nervous about the whole thing. This guy was a *sleaze*. All her alarms were going off around him. No wonder Daddy got so upset when he heard that they were thinking of bringing Jake Camden into the story. She really hadn't checked out the *Intruder* at all—the man's book had looked reasonable enough, if slightly sensationalistic, and Tim had assured her that he was tops in the field. Jeez, if this was the top, she'd hate to look at the bottom! She'd assumed that her father hated Camden just because he was on the *other side*. Now she knew different.

Three boilermakers and a saucer-story later, Jake Camden

emitted a burp redolent of the onion rings he'd been munching. "You'll pardon me," he said, "Gotta water the old porcelain with me one-eyed trouser snake." He winked at Diane. "That's Australian you'll never hear in a Crocodile Dundee movie!"

The reporter stumbled back toward the john.

"Wow!" said Tim gleefully. "What a character! This is *great*!"

"Ti...im!" she whispered between her teeth. "This guy's a sleaze-ball of the first water! This guy *groped* me underneath the table! This guy make's yellow journalism seem like the *New York Times*!"

"Ah, so he had a few drinks on the plane. Did you hear the questions he asked? Did you hear the comments he had? This guy knows his UFO stuff all right. We're going to get some-place with him. And jeez, what a *character*. And I saw it, he didn't grope you, he just squeezed your thigh."

"Like a prime piece of meat! He smells like *sperm*! Tim, he'd been drooling all over me. Can't you see the way he looks at me?"

"Look, you're beautiful! I look at you that way all the time! I can't stop other guys from doing it. But c'mon, Diane, we're just going to deal with this guy a short time, he's going to help us investigate—and that's it! So just grin and bear it." Tim chuckled and sipped at his beer. "Whew, though. What a character. Whew!"

"Yes, well, just stay between me and him, okay, Tim?" she said. "And I don't want my real name used in any story in his newspaper."

"What—you think I got into a psych graduate program by being *stupid*? Give me *some* credit." He patted her hand placatingly, but when Camden came out, dragging a length of toilet paper sticking to his heel, Tim was lost again in mirth and admiration.

Jake Camden plopped down beside them again, zipping up his fly. "Yo! What do they have in this dump in the way of after-dinner liqueurs?"

She had to give him credit. Just as soon as he got out into the field, Jake Camden seemed to sober up. He darted about the field and forest where they'd seen the hovering lights like some bloodhound trailing spoor. He checked exact angles, took rolls of photographs and made Diane and Tim retrace, as precisely as they could, their path from the car through the woods, and pinpoint exactly where they stood in their last moments of consciousness.

"Yep," Camden said finally, nodding to himself as he pocketed a finished roll of Kodak film, and pulled a fresh one from his camera case. "What we have here, my friends, is a classic. A veritable *classic*."

"You believe us then?" said Tim.

"Look, if you were pulling some kind of hoax, guy, you'd have a hell of a lot more proof." Camden chuckled. "Shit, you got nothin'. Absolutely zip! No photos, no footprints, no burned spot where a saucer could have landed. But I'll tell you what you two *do* have. You've got *sincerity*. And you got pedigree. That counts a lot with me." Camden filled his camera with the fresh film, keeping up his monologue. "Like Diane here—I can hear the gears clicking in her head. Geez, here comes a guy in a cheap suit, snapping photos and sucking down juice like there's no tomorrow. Cripes, she's thinking. My daddy warned me about losers like this. Looks like a demoted paparazzo! Well, listen, I gotta tell you kids, I'm a *good* newspaperman. And the field that I deal with may be unorthodox, but I'm dedicated to dig out the truth. And listen—I'm an ambitious motherfucker." He grinned and clicked the back of the camera closed. "When and if the aliens actually choose to land officially, I'll be there, lens cap off. Meantime, though, I gotta dig. Lots of stuff I dig up turns out to be bullshit, but that's just a part of the game."

"What's next?" asked Tim enthusiastically.

"Well, I've just about leached you clean of information about what happened. Stuff you remember, anyway. And I'm no psychologist and I don't mess with hypnosis. When did you say that you're supposed to go in for a session, Tim?"

"We've got an appointment on Thursday."

"That may break the case. In the meantime, I'd like to ask you a few more questions."

They piled back into the car, and drove back toward Tim's apartment, tape recorder running and questions firing from the back seat.

"Okay, Diane, here's a whopper for you. Do you think that

having an old man like Everett Scarborough influenced this whole business?''

Diane was nonplussed. "What do you mean?"

"Well, there have been flying saucers buzzing around your ears all your life—I mean metaphorically. I know enough about the business to know that a large percentage of what people see in the skies starts out in their heads."

"Are you saying I'm lying to you, Mr. Camden?" Diane said, getting angry.

"No. I told you, I think you're telling me the truth."

"He's got something there, Diane. Kind of a mini-mass delusion between you and I—like maybe you conjured it all up in your head and projected a psychoimage that night," Tim said.

"Tim! How can you say that! You know what happened to us . . . And it wasn't any fantasy that I conjured up!"

"Don't get your panties on fire, Diane," said Camden. "I'm just covering possibilities. I told you, I'm a serious UFO investigator."

"He's right, Diane. Think it over."

"I'm turning this recorder off. What comes up next is just between us and the gearshift."

She thought it over, while Camden smoked his foul-smelling Camels in the back seat. Could it be possible? Was she some kind of psychic Carrie, troubled by a relationship with a father obsessed with proving the nonexistence of flying saucers? She knew exactly what Camden was suggesting here, and she was surprised by the intelligence it revealed in the man—there was a dimension to this whole flying saucer/Visitor business that ranged much further than the one in which most people cared to dabble. Certainly, her father only touched upon the psychological factors briefly, and merely scoffed at the farther-fetched philosophical theories put forward by such men as Jung and Strieber. He much preferred stomping fallacies with hard cold facts and logic.

Her father. Yes, perhaps there *was* something there.

"I guess that is an interesting suggestion, Mr. Camden," she said coolly, not looking back at him in the rear. "My father and I do have our differences, but I don't think it would cause me to see flying saucers and undergo an abduction experience."

"Good. I'll go with that, and thanks for giving it some

mental waves, Di.'' Camden slapped the seat and lay back, chuckling. ''Wow. I think we're onto something *big* here. I feel it in my gut! I can't *wait* to get hold of the transcript of your hypnosis session . . . You will let me have a look, won't you? Privacy guaranteed, of course.''

''Sure,'' said Tim. ''But what do you think you'll find there?''

''I think, kids, that if you *were* abducted by something or someone—that this may actually be a legitimate contact with something very strange and wonderful.''

Diane caught a glimpse of the tatty man in the rearview mirror, and there seemed an actual glow of wonder in his eyes.

On the way back, Camden explained.

''It's simple enough, kids. Virtually all the abduction stuff that I've dealt with that seems remotely sincere has got big black bands of paranoia running through it. We're talking deep psychological trauma. Now, who knows if this stuff really happens. If it does, we've got some pretty stupid aliens we're dealing with.'' Camden laughed to himself. ''This Budd Hopkins and Maximillian Shroeder stuff makes for great press copy— Christ, it's my bread and butter. But as your father has doubtless pointed out, if alien races are developed enough to travel the trillions of miles, they're surely bright enough to realize that they're dealing with civilized beings here and not lab rats!''

''But what about the observations *we* do to dolphins and park animals and such?'' noted Tim. ''You know, marking them, tracking them.''

'''Jesus, Timothy! Do dolphins drive cars? Do bears build skyscrapers? This isn't a Gary Larsen ''Far Side'' cartoon, this is real life! For one thing, if this abduction-stuff has been going on as long as we experts in the field would have you believe, then you'd think they'd realize that we humans have got long memories and we're into heavy things like retribution and revenge. The way some of these poor slobs talk, if one of these almond-eyed little guys chooses to walk into a saucer convention of abductees, it's Bela Lugosi time. He'll get ripped limb from limb. Personally, I don't buy most of this shit. I exploit it, sure, it's my job. But I don't buy it.''

"What do you think, Mr. Camden," said Diane, a little of the starch coming out with the man's disingenuousness.

Camden laughed, leaning forward and tapping his head. "I think that most of these bozos have got something loose in their noggins."

"I thought you said you honestly thought there is something behind the whole UFO business," said Tim.

"Oh, I do, I *do*! And I'd like to find out, really and truly I do. But let me put it this way, there's very little evidence that we're being visited by aliens from another planet." His voice became suddenly small and introspective. "On the other hand, there's a great *deal* of evidence that the human mind is subject to extreme—er—aberrations."

Diane had to smile. "Mr. Camden, that sounds like something my father would say."

"Well, you can give the quote to him, because in my business, *I* sure as hell can't use it! No, actually, to get back to why I'm excited about you two: This appears to be an abduction experience you've had—UFO sighting, missing time and all—but you're normal, well-adjusted human beings and you don't have any sense of foreboding or emotional upset on the matter. Man, this is unique! I really do hope we do have actual contact here!"

Tim dropped Diane off back at his place. She all but lived there, and she had some mundane matters to take care of, like bills that were due, and a quick shower. He would take Camden to check in at his Motel 6, and then would return. He and Diane needed something to get their minds off this business, and they decided that a movie this evening would do the trick. As for Camden, he just asked to be directed to the nearest strip-joint, where he could "celebrate this latest terrific development."

It was late afternoon when Diane got left off. She decided that a short nap would do her a lot of good. She flopped onto Tim's big bed, and tried to doze off, but so much swirled in her head that she had great difficulty.

This Jake Camden guy—maybe he'd work out after all. True, he was a bit seedy, but her first impression had not been entirely correct. He did seem honestly interested in helping them, in uncovering the truth.

The hypnosis session was on Thursday. It was their one hope

to discover what had happened, the key to dig out those
memories. She lay on Tim's bed for a long time, wondering
just what those memories were, feeling unanchored and adrift,
but not overly concerned. Camden was right. There seemed no
undue *fear* and *dread* here, which were keystones to other
abduction cases.

She had just decided to get up and take that shower, when
the phone call came.

It was from her father.

CHAPTER
TWENTY

There are no degrees in UFO Investigation from colleges.

There are no late-night TV commercials or ads in magazines
regaling consumers with "Your Opportunities in the Exciting
Field of Unidentified Flying Objects—Acme Technical Training!"

UFO investigators tend to be hobbyists and aficionados and
just plain kooks, fascinated with the phenomenon and eager for
knowledge and truth on the subject. Unfortunately for the field,
though—and this was something that Scarborough would point
out constantly—was the "quantum mechanics effect," which
was what he called the effect of enthusism on the scientific
study of the subject, an analogy to the recent discovery in
physics of the "Viewer-Participant" syndrome, wherein merely
observing things below the cause-and-effect level influences the
events themselves. In other words, because they tended to be
so enraptured by the thought of discovering real vessels from
outer space—real aliens—the investigators influenced the data
they dug up, to say nothing of wrongly interpreting it.

The only actually legitimate UFO investigators were those
employed by Project Blue Book in the fifties and sixties,
whether they were military and government personnel, or just

specialists brought in to consult. Everett Scarborough was one of these. His exemplary work in astrophysics at MIT would probably have gone unnoticed if not for the appearance of several articles on such subjects as the "Aerodynamic Unfeasibility of Flying Saucers" and "Atmospheric Delusions" in *Astronomy Magazine* in the midsixties. These articles were so lucid, interesting, and amusing that they were reprinted in larger magazines, including *Reader's Digest*. Perhaps that was when some high mucky-muck read them—probably, Scarborough always suspected, while sitting on the crapper—and decided that this man was necessary for Project Blue Book, a so-called "investigation" on the part of the air force, in which, according to a later article by Charles Corddry, military correspondent for the *Baltimore Sun*, "as little as possible" was done.

Into this malaise stepped the eager and serious young scientist, Everett Scarborough, who rapidly discovered how spotty and supercilious the UFO investigatory methods were. One of his colleagues at the time was Dr. J. Allen Hyenk, a distinguished astronomer who'd been working with the Air Force since the fifties. However, Hyenk and Scarborough had never gotten on. Not long after Scarborough had started work on investigations, Hyenk had been dispatched to Michigan to investigate some sightings, which he later attributed to swamp gas. This statement was skewed enough by the media to make it sound as though Hyenk was describing *all* sightings as swamp gas, a notion that was met with derision by the pro-UFO factions. Clearly upset and disgusted, Hyenk was never the same. He'd become, with good reason, discouraged with the air force investigations over the years, and began to change his skepticism to credulousness. Later, of course, he was heralded as the key scientist-expert on the matter—a man who actually believed that these UFOs could contain extraterrestrial life. Hyenk was the man who consulted on Spielberg's *Close Encounters of the Third Kind*.

Scarborough immediately detected this change of heart in Hyenk, and opposed it. His attitude toward the shoddiness of the Air Force's efforts toward investigating the UFO sightings was not to assume that something was being *hidden*, but rather, that the air force, hopelessly burdened with silly bureaucratic rules and attitudes, just didn't take that much interest in the subject, and was bungling along in the matter purely on the momentum from the early fifties, when they *had* been concerned.

With Scarborough's help, the investigatory methods were revised and honed to strict measures. Under his guidance both the O'Brien Report of 1966 and the Condon Committee from 1966 to 1968 were presented with the hard, cold facts, thus allowing Project Blue Book to wrap in December 1969 with the statement that there was insufficient evidence to conclude that extraterrestrials were buzzing the country in flying disks.

Scarborough's investigation methods were simple but effective, modeled on various literary detective methods, including those of Sherlock Holmes. He more than realized that these could not be strict scientific investigations, because the scientific method demanded not only specified conditions, but also such aspects as *controlled* subjects. A UFO report was usually so jumbled by the human interactions involved that it had to be first taken apart and examined bit by bit. To do this, *all* information available was necessary. Routinely, in the field, Scarborough would interview all the people who'd seen the object, and several in the same area who had not. He obtained precise meteorological information for the time involved, as well as any radar reports for the area. He researched the location for local power sources, power wires, and such. He became fully apprised of geological and geographical facts about the area involved. Any photographic evidence was thoroughly examined under strict scientific conditions. Soil samples were taken of so-called "landing spots." Scarborough told all those involved that if there indeed had been flying saucers or aliens in the area, *he* was the one who most wanted to prove that they had been there. Of course, he never did— quite the opposite.

The UFO generally turned out to be local aircraft which had reflected local light oddly, weather balloons, Venus, a bright star, a sun dog, a moon dog, a cloud formation, drifting spiderwebs, an odd weather condition refracting ice crystals in the sky—and sometimes, even "plasma" formations, an electrical phenomenon pointed out by one of Scarborough's more respected colleagues, Philip Klass, that was caused by power lines or power-generation plants.

It was this attitude that he and Captain Eric MacKenzie had brought to that Iowa farm in Johnson County, in 1968. The case had seemed simple enough then: a silvery vessel sighted cruising through the sky by a farmer. Who knew, thought Scarborough, as he studied the files on the case, that it would snowball into *this*, over twenty years later?

"Charles Higsdon," murmured Scarborough, tapping the files with a pencil. His ever-present field notebook for scribbles lay by his side at the coffee table. He looked up from the swath of cheap paper to Mac, who was making notes in the air force book with a yellow magic marker. "I only remember him vaguely. Younger guy, with a family. Kids didn't see the saucer, wife didn't see it either. He was out late, plowing—and at twilight, he made the sighting. The wife *did* concur that there were electrical problems in the house for hours afterward. And several other people in the neighboring town did see something strange scooting in the sky. But that was all. A simple enough investigation, a simple enough case."

Mac spread open the book for him, and pointed the tip of the marker at the sentences he'd underlined. "Now look. Green and red lights here . . . and in *our* report, red and blue . . ."

"Yes, a simple enough mistake."

"Wait . . . according to the Blue Book file, the thing landed. There's nothing about landing in our files on the subject."

Scarborough shrugged. "So what if it did an Immelmann roll around a crow? We established that there was insufficient evidence in this case."

Mac forged on. "There are other seemingly insignificant disparities. I realize that most of this stuff is pure apocryphal. But it made me go back and check other stuff. There's a homogeneity to the whole Blue Book file reports, which I think is very strange, considering the number of different consultants and investigators they used. Like in the sixties, they used entire university science staffs—and yet there's a similarity in the reports. Now we can't possibly go back and check on the other reports, but we know *ours*. And we know it was changed."

Scarborough nodded. "A little unsettling. On the other hand, you and I well know the way the subject was treated—pretty loosely. The write-ups were done by a staff of career air force bureaucrats who were probably dropouts from *Stars and Stripes* and wrote air force manuals on latrine-digging specs."

"The whole megillah is available if you want to go down to an Alabama air force base to go over it—which maybe I will, one day. But I know what I'll find. Scrubbed up, standardized reports. *Altered* reports.''

''That could very well be, but, like I say, what difference, really, are the colors?''

''Suppose there is something you wanna hide. What do you use? I'll tell you—camouflage. If all leopards have spots, you won't see the lion that's been dabbed with paint. One or two genuinely puzzling sightings of UFOs are going to look a hell of a lot less puzzling amidst many other easily provable hoaxes and optical illusions cobbled up.''

''Wait just a minute, Mac. You're saying that the air force *deliberately* manufactured UFO sightings, and modified details about actual sightings, to obscure the meanings of *genuine* sightings.'' Scarborough shook his head with disbelief.

''It all spells out clearly enough to me, Ev.''

''Yeah. It spells out p-a-r-a-n-o-i-a!''

Mac ignored the jibe. ''Here's something else, and the one thing that we can truly check up on, whether or not we get hold of Charles Higsdon again. Look here at the address of Higsdon's farm in the report.''

''2319 Hillcrest Street,'' Scarborough read.

''Now look at what *we* put down.''

The address was plainly spelled out: 1352 Ludlow Road.

Scarborough mulled that over for a moment. ''Okay, so maybe Higsdon didn't want his correct address printed.''

''Weak, Ev. Weak. When so many eggs are busted, you look for the fox, right? So okay, maybe you're right about all this—but I say, we go out to Johnson County and we see if Higsdon still lives there. If he's there, we interview. Harmless enough, right?''

''Yeah, I guess so,'' Scarborough said, unconvinced.

''That's the boy!'' Mac got up and clapped him on the back. ''Here, I'll go down and rustle up some more brew. Then we'll wade into this report some more, and cook up some possibilities. I've got a shitload of theories to dump on you.''

''I bet you do.''

They worked on through the afternoon, drinking beer and plowing through notes and ideas. Old Mac had a pretty feverish imagination, Scarborough had to admit. Maybe if they went out to see about this farm and it was all harmless enough, then the man would finally settle down and get back to what he did best: fiction writing.

"So then," said Mac, happily closing books and re-sorting the files. "When are you getting around to dealing with Diane?"

"I guess I should give her a call or something, shouldn't I?" Scarborough mused, feeling a little light-headed from the beer.

"Right. Tell her you'll be down there soon as you've dealt with the old fool in Iowa." Mac mimed neon lights on a marquee. "Doc Scarborough—UFO Exorcist!"

Scarborough chuckled. "I'm going to need something stronger than Grolsch to wash this one down, Mac."

Mac grinned. "You got it. Straight from the land of my forebears."

"Mac, I always suspected that you were descended from bears!"

Mac winked and went to get the Scotch.

Scarborough pulled out his address book from his briefcase, and looked up Diane's Kansas phone number. He dialed it and got no reply. Mac was bringing up a half-empty bottle of Dewars from his wet bar on the first floor when Scarborough cradled the phone.

"Well, so much for that. No answer."

Scarborough poured several fingers of Scotch into a smudged bachelor glass, and handed it to his friend. "Don't give me that bull, Ev. Hasn't she got that graduate boyfriend or something?"

"Yeah. Tim." Scarborough spat the name out, not hiding his disgust.

"So, you try Tim's number. She's probably there, doing his laundry or something."

Scarborough paged through his address book. Diane had made him take Tim Reilly's number as soon as they'd started seeing each other a lot. He strongly suspected it was just her subtle way of hurting him, possibly suggesting that the couple were living together.

He dialed the 913 number. A female voice answered on the third ring.

"Diane. This is your penitent father," he said. He took a quick hit of the Scotch, but the crow didn't taste much better.

"Dad!" she said, excited. "Hi! I'm so happy to hear from

you! You actually called me at Tim's! You've never done that before.''

"Right. Well, I should have called before. I'm sorry I lost my temper. We're a real pair, aren't we?''

"Where are you, Dad?''

"I'm visiting the Iowa hermit, Diane. He's got me on a wild-goose chase. Soon as I shoot down his goose, I'm going to come and shoot down yours.''

There was a pause at the other end. Then: "You mean, you're going to come down . . . and investigate?''

"Yes. That's all right, isn't it?''

"Dad, of *course* it is. It's wonderful.. It's just that . . . Well, sure! Come on down whenever you can.''

"What's wrong, Diane? Are you all right?''

"Oh, sure . . . We're just trying to figure out what happened, Dad—Tim and I. Just, uh, hanging in there . . .''

"You left so quickly . . . I've been worried about you.''

"You know I pretty much fall on my feet.''

"Yes. Your catlike abilities . . . When you were small, you *thought* you were a cat.''

"Yes, and now I know it. No problem. How's Uncle Mac?''

"Oh, he's fine.''

Mac took his cue and hollered, "Hello, Diane.''

"Bastard knocked some sense into me, I guess. I'm up here doing some reinvestigation out in Johnson County. Mac thinks there's some kind of sinister doings there, UFO-wise.''

"No kidding. How exciting!''

"And I'd like to come down and see you too, Diane. We're going up tomorrow to Johnson County—but Mac says he can drive me down on Thursday. You'll have two UFO investigators for the price of none!''

"Oh, I'd love that, Dad. I have an appointment during the day, but if you come later in the afternoon . . . I'll have everything all cleared up!''

"That would be splendid, hon. Now, would you like to talk to Mac. Maybe you can give him directions. I—''

There was a sudden disturbance at the other end of the line. Scarborough could hear a door opening, then the sounds of steps and voices, and a muffled "Shhhh! I'm on the phone,'' from Diane.

"Hey!'' said a distant voice. "It wouldn't be that distinguished, brilliant father of yours! Tell him he's got a wonderful, classy daughter.''

Scarborough felt as though someone had shoved a railroad tie directly into his solar plexus. He recognized the way that voice squeaked over the occasional vowels, and slurred on the odd consonant. He'd heard that voice on television and had talked to it on the phone. He'd even participated on an interview show with that voice once—a show that had erupted into a red-faced yelling match between the pro and anti-UFO camps. And he'd heard that voice on ''Entertainment Tonight,'' denying that the UFO debunker character in a certain sleazy movie was based on Dr. Everett Scarborough.

It was Jake Camden's voice.

''I'm sorry, Dad,'' said Diane a little stiffly. ''Tim and a friend came in. I have to go now, but I'll call later with directions. Okay? Dad, are you still there?''

Scarborough managed to get the words around the hurt. ''Diane,'' he said. ''Diane, that's Jake Camden...He's *there*!''

A long awkward silence. ''Uhm...well, yes...He wanted to get our story and he's been helping us investigate. But we still need *you* and—''

He felt a swelling of emotion, he felt on the verge of tears, and the only way he knew that he could stem that emotion, those tears, was anger. ''God *damn* you, Diane! God damn you to *hell*! How could you *do* this to me?''

''Dad! Dad, we needed *somebody*! And don't worry, Dad, this is all going to be confidential!''

''Diane, you and your no-account bedmate have got the brains of a peanut to share between you. Camden's about as trustworthy as a *snake*!''

''Look, let's not argue, Dad. What's done is done. Come on down, and we'll talk about it,'' Diane said in a tense, weary voice.

Another male voice spoke in the background. ''Boy, he doesn't have a bug up his ass, he's got an *ant colony*!''

''Tim!''

''Diane, we'll call Thursday, okay. Maybe this trip down isn't such a good idea. Good-bye.''

''Dad, I—''

Scarborough slammed the phone down. He looked up at the startled expression on Mac's face.

"Mac," he said, "You know, if I ever *do* meet an ET, the little fucker's gonna have a lot to answer for."

CHAPTER
TWENTY-ONE

Neither of them were able to rouse themselves very early, so they got a late start for Johnson County, not leaving until almost ten in the morning.

The country ham, eggs, and biscuits churned uneasily in Scarborough's stomach, as they sloshed about in Mac's grim coffee. A Thermos of the stuff sat between them, but Scarborough ignored it, keeping his eyes either dead-ahead, or on the map as the Bronco bucked up the highway.

Uncharacteristically, Mac didn't say much. He knew his friend well enough not to bring up the subject of Diane. Scarborough suspected that he, too, was pretty horrified at the idea of Jake Camden getting into the Kansas UFO picture. There was no question about what Camden wanted. A banner headline reading "Debunker's Daughter Romances UFO Pilot!" or some such nonsense. For Diane to call in a sleazoid like Camden was probably the stupidest thing she'd ever done, and she'd done some *crazy* things.

The day was a springtime dream: light cumulus lacing a vault of purest blue sky, sunlight accentuating the golds and greens and flower-colors of the Iowa fields. Through the open window, Scarborough caught the scents of young corn and wheat and honeysuckle in the mild air, and, of course, manure. By the time they made a turn off the highway—about one in the afternoon, Scarborough felt a little better.

The highly detailed map took them past a small town named Tipville, and then out into deep farm countryside. Ludlow was little more than two parallel cow paths, fringed with overgrowth and undergrowth. About five miles in, the fields looked totally neglected—as though they'd been on fallow-duty for a long, long time.

"There it is," said Mac, pointing to a tilting mailbox, labeled with the appropriate address. "Remember all this?"

"I sure don't remember the barbed wire!" said Scarborough, as the Bronco stopped. A fence of rusty, nasty eight-foot-high barbed wire stretched to either side, presumably to the limits of the farm's acreage. A narrow lane snaked through a copse of trees toward the farmhouse, then out of sight over a ridge. Between them and it, stood a gate, holding a sign that read, in crude hand-painted letters: No Trespassing. A metal chain was wrapped around the braces of the gate, and locked with a padlock.

Mac regarded the gate for a moment, then turned to Scarborough. "I got a handyman's box in the back."

Scarborough smiled for the first time all day. "Well, we have come an awfully long way today to be turned back by a silly little hardware-store toy."

"We'll make financial reparations to Mr. Higsdon," said Mac, coming out of the back of the car with a hacksaw.

Mac made short work of the lock, and soon the Bronco was chugging up the hill. From the crest, Scarborough could see the farmhouse, two barns, and several sheds in a complex at least half a mile distant.

"Looks bigger than I remember," said Scarborough, scratching his head.

Mac pulled out a set of binoculars from the dash. "Yep. And I don't see much going on either—no animals or anything. There's an old Volkswagen van, of all things, sitting by the farmhouse. I guess we should go knock on the door, huh?"

"That's what we're here for."

The absence of animals and activity in the fenced-in areas was rather eerie, thought Scarborough, as the Bronco eased up behind the VW. In fact, there were no farmhouse sounds or smells at all—no clucks and scratchings of chickens, no smell of hay and pig manure. A lonely tractor sitting by a silo was the only sign of farm machinery. In fact, if the buildings themselves were not so clearly well maintained and recently painted, Scarborough would have called the place a ghost farm.

They disembarked from the Bronco, and went to the front

entrance of the farmhouse. Mac opened the screen door, and knocked hard against the wood. The knocks echoed through the house hollowly. Mac knocked again, but there was no answer.

Mac tried the door, but it was apparently locked from behind with a deadbolt; Mac's credit card proved a fruitless tool. Scarborough went to one of the side windows and tried to peer past the blinds, but everything seemed thoroughly wrapped in darkness.

"Let's go try one of the barns," said Mac, gesturing toward the nearest of the hunkering, red-sided, blue-shingle–topped buildings. "Maybe there's someone working out there."

On their way over, they noticed something quite unusual for a farm. In the back of the farmhouse but before the barn was a basketball court. But the basketball backboards held hoops without nets, and the asphalt was not white-lined.

"Look at these marks here," said Mac, examining long scuff marks. "I've seen marks like these, back in 'Nam. Looks like choppers have landed here."

"So?" Curious, true, but no reason to get excited. "I hear they've been using helicopters lately for crop dusting."

"Yeah." Mac beckoned him to follow. At the barn, he stopped and tried the door. It was not locked. Mac turned the knob and peered in. "Yo! Hey, Ev, come have a look in here!"

Scarborough expected the usual hay, chicken-wire-and-dank loft in one big room, reeking of animals and moldy vegetation. Instead, the door pushed open on what appeared to be an office reception area with a linoleum floor and unadorned drywalling.

"Decidedly odd," said Scarborough. "Let's go through and see what's in the rest of the place."

They passed through the opposite door, and found themselves in a hallway that led to a series of larger rooms, empty but for workbenches and evidence of some kind of electrical work. The most unusual aspect in the rooms was the wealth of industrial-duty, three-holed electrical sockets in each, and the low-hanging banks of fluorescent lights.

Scarborough shook his head. "Unless I miss my guess totally, these rooms must have been used as some sort of laboratories."

"Yeah, that's what I was thinking. What do you think—a farm-animal experimental station? Doesn't look like good ole Charlie Higsdon lives here anymore though, does it?"

"Maybe we should have called first," said Scarborough doubtfully.

"Uh uh," said Mac, scratching. "I got this hunch, Ev. This stuff *means* something."

"Yeah? Like what?"

"Well, I guess we'll find that out when—"

Suddenly, from outside, came the sound of a rifle shot, and the squeal of a ricocheting bullet. "Get the hell outta here, buster!" came a cry. "You don't belong here!"

"Wait a minute! You got the wrong guy," answered a voice.

"Your ass is over the fence. You're a goddamn trespasser and I'm within my legal rights to shoot you! Now get out, or I'm gonna do it!"

Scarborough and MacKenzie raced outside the barn to see what was going on.

Parked behind the Bronco was a Lincoln Continental. Standing beside the Bronco was an unkempt-looking man, wearing a floppy golf hat and a Hawaiian shirt. "I'm not the trespasser! The guys in this four-by-four are and—"

The rifle cracked. The man in the golf hat grimaced and raced back to the blue Lincoln, opening a door and using it as a shield. "Can't we negotiate or something? I'll help you bring these hooligans to justice, and you answer some simple questions!"

The man with the rifle weaved a bit, his aim unsteady. He looked as though he'd just climbed out of bed after a long drunk, his flannel shirt wrinkled, his faded jeans stained. He squeezed off another round, and the bullet smashed through the Lincoln's windshield, spiderwebbing the whole right side.

"Holy shit! This is a rental car, man! And I waived the insurance!"

"Tough luck, bozo. Now vamoose!"

Mac had given Scarborough a significant look, and was creeping up behind the man with the rifle. Scarborough followed, ready to bolt and run for cover at the slightest provocation, but he was also fascinated with the violent scene unfolding. He recognized the man in the golf cap now, with his faintly sunken cheeks and protruding ears and sharp nose.

It was none other than Jake Camden.

Scarborough half wished that the guy with the rifle would *shoot* the little weasel. How the hell had he gotten up here?

Camden seemed so rattled at being fired upon that he didn't

notice the two men sneaking up behind his attacker. With a curse, he jumped into the Lincoln and started the motor. The next bullet tore off the side mirror. "Shit!" cried Camden. "Stop that!"

The man with the rifle chuckled and lifted his weapon again. But by then, Mac was close enough to pounce. He jumped on the man from behind, his two-hundred thirty muscular pounds pushing the slighter man down to the ground. The rifle skittered off over the gravel.

"What the—" said the man. The two struggled on the ground.

"Get the rifle!" barked Mac, clearly surprised at the struggle the man was putting up. Scarborough gingerly dodged the rolling pair, and picked up the rifle, a battered Winchester breech-loader. Fists flailed beside him. Then there was a solid thunk and a moan, and the flannel-shirted man wilted into unconsciousness.

Mac stood up. "We probably broke the law here, but I don't like to see the likes of this dork firing weapons." He wrinkled his nose. "Whew. Smells like he's been living in these clothes for some time, and showering in cheap whiskey."

Meantime, the Lincoln's motor had stopped, and Camden had hopped out, all smiles. "Wow! Hey, thanks, fellas. This guy's a *maniac*! Good thing I distracted him, heh?" He trotted forward, a hand held out. "Doc Scarborough. Good to see you again. We've got *a lot* to talk about! I just missed you at the Iowa City house, so I followed you up here. Whew, what the hell is goin' on, anyway?"

Scarborough just glared at the proffered hand, refusing to shake it.

"Who's this, Ev? He seems to know you."

"It's Camden. Diane must have given him your address," said Scarborough wearily.

"What a great lady, I'm telling you!" Camden interjected, "I told her, soon as you and I talked, everything would be fixed up. She's *extremely* bummed out that you're upset with her, Doc. So I had some time on my hands, and thought I'd hop up here and make it all better!"

"You just wanted to see what I was investigating, Camden. You're just looking for a story."

"Well, hey. If something pops up, I won't kick it out of

bed.'' He stepped over to MacKenzie, and offered to shake
hands with him. ''And you must be the great writer, Eric
MacKenzie. We're all writers here—we got to stick together!''

Mac stared knives at the reporter, who immediately lowered
his hand. ''So, what's the scoop, anyway? Diane said something about you opening an old Blue Book case? What gives?
You can trust me!''

''About as far as Mac here can throw you. Mac, why don't
we just check the distance of trust out!''

Camden backed away, holding up his palms. ''Wait a minute, guys. Do I sense hostility? Yes, I *definitely* do. Now,
maybe I can sort of understand why the Doc is a mite peeved at
me, but I'm here to make it all better. And Captain MacKenzie—
well, we've got no quarrel. Besides, you know, I could well
have information that can help you in this investigation.'' He
looked around, as though making sure no one else was listening
and then leaned over toward them confidentially. ''Yeah. As it
happens, I've been doing some digging up here myself, and I
can tell you some mighty peculiar stories.''

Mac turned to Scarborough. ''I'll leave it up to you, Ev. You
give me the word, though—'' He cocked the Winchester.
''—And we'll have 'im out of here soon enough.''

''Now, now, now,'' said Camden, still smiling. ''I'm sure
that the Doc here knows there's stuff to gain by keeping me
around. Besides, I think he'd much rather have me reporting on
moldy old Blue Book cases than his *daughter's* run-in with a
UFO.''

''You slimy turd!'' said Mac, lifting the rifle. ''Get out!''

''Not that I'd actually mention her real name!'' said Camden,
still staying cool.

''Let him stay,'' said Scarborough. ''We're wading in deep
shit here, banging up a private citizen like this and trespassing.
I've got the feeling that Mr. Camden just might be able to help
us out in this particular situation, Mac, in case we have some
problem with the law.''

''You know it, Doc! I know every trick in the book!''

''I bet you do.'' He turned and saw that the front door of the
farmhouse hung open. ''Come on. Let's get our unconscious
host in the house and nurse him back to health. He might be
more willing to answer questions without a gun in his hands.''

* * *

The farmhouse proved to be empty of furniture and fittings, except for an apartment-sized area in the back. With spartan furnishing, it was clearly where the man with the gun lived, sleeping on little more than a mattress on the floor and apparently living mostly on bottles of Old Grandad whiskey. The empties choked the trash bin.

Mac propped the unconscious man in a chair by a dining-room table filled with old newspapers, magazines, and an old Sylvania black-and-white television set. He poured some of the Old Grandad into a metal cup he found by the sink, and then splashed some tap water into the man's stubbly, sallow face.

The man spluttered awake. Mac poured some whiskey down his throat, and the man calmed down immediately.

"Sorry to take you out that way, Mister," said Mac, turning on an affable but authoritarian charm. "We just didn't want you to murder anyone."

The man blinked, looked around at Scarborough and Camden, and then back at MacKenzie. "Who the hell are you? What are you doing here?"

"Well, I guess we're trespassers, Mister. And we're sorry to disturb you. We've just got a few questions, and then we'll be on our way." He pulled out a couple of twenty-dollar bills, which he placed on the dining room table. "We hope this will pay for any harm done."

The man just stared blearily at the money.

"First of all, I'm Mac and this here's Ev and Jake. Now, what's your name?"

The man shrugged. "Clyde. Clyde Evans. I'm the caretaker here. Lot of good I've done . . . 'Sposed to keep out trespassers."

"Well, now, there's no reason that anybody but us has to know we've been here, right?" Mac put another twenty on the pile.

Clyde Evans licked cracked lips. "No. Guess not."

"Good," said Scarborough, taking up the inquisition from there. He used his friendliest, most persuasive tone. "Mr. Evans, have you ever heard of Charles Higsdon?"

"Nope."

"Well, let's just say that he used to live here on this farm about twenty years ago. We visited him here then, helping him out—let's just say with a little problem."

"Yeah! Flying saucers spooking the pigs!" said Camden, grinning.

Evans grunted. "Flying saucers, huh? You guys flying-saucer people?"

"In a way," said Scarborough. "We're just making a harmless routine investigation, Clyde. You say you're the caretaker here. Who pays you to watch this place?"

"Lawyer in town. Name of Brookings."

"Does he own this land?"

"Hell if I know. And I ain't seen no flying saucers either."

"How long have you worked here?"

"Couple years, maybe."

"Has it always been like this . . . empty?"

"Yep."

"Have you got any idea, Clyde, what people used those barns for? We had a look at them—they're *not* normal barns."

Clyde got suddenly stiff. He picked up the metal cup and knocked back the rest of the whiskey. "Hell if I know. Maybe you guys had just better go now. And keep your mouths shut, huh? I'll lose my job if . . ."

"If what?"

"Nothin'. Just go."

"Sure, Clyde," said Scarborough. "Thanks very much for your help, and we're sorry about the inconvenience."

"Oh, by the way," said Mac on the way out. "The chain on your fence is busted. Might wanna get a new one."

Scarborough turned and saw Clyde Evans stuffing the twenty-dollar bills into the front pocket of his red-plaid shirt.

"And we'll just leave your gun right by the gate, okay?"

Evans grunted. Scarborough thought the man looked very troubled and frightened indeed.

Outside, Mac said, "So, what next? We go talk to this Brookings guy?"

"You gotta be kidding me! A *lawyer*?" Camden chuckled derisively. "You'll get nothing from a lawyer. So anyway, come clean, guys? What's the mystery?"

Scarborough looked at the man, puzzled. Camden seemed generally curious, not just professionally. He shrugged. "Well, I don't think anything's going to come of it actually—but we'll tell you, since we're not really worried about you scooping us. We just want to find out the truth here."

Mac nodded. "Damn straight we do. Yeah, maybe you *can* help us, Camden. But let's not stand around here like sitting ducks. Ol' Clyde might have another Winchester in there. I noticed a roadside cafe called Hungry Joe's on the highway just outside of town. Let's have some lunch, and we'll tell you."

Camden grinned. "Yeah, let's! I'm starved. Getting shot at is hard work."

Scarborough shook his head. "And maybe you can tell us what's going on with my daughter in Kansas."

"That I will, Doc," said Camden. He seemed immensely pleased with himself and Scarborough felt a surge of hatred well up, and the desire to pop the man a good one right on the chin, which he immediately quelled.

No, he told himself. Not now. Maybe later. Meantime, maybe the loathsome yellow-journalist really *could* help them, and heavens knew, they needed all the help they could get.

"Wow, oh wow," said Camden around a mouthful of chicken-fried steak. "Am I in the clover this week. That's some story, Mac. And Doc—the fact that you're helping out here just speaks volumes to me. Volumes! You got some weight with me, pal." Camden shook a greasy fork at his UFO-ological adversary. "You may not realize it, but I've always respected you a *hell* of a lot!"

Mac raised an eyebrow. Scarborough shrugged. He couldn't deny it; this rumpled bad excuse for a reporter had a certain rank charm to him, like old familiar moldy cheese.

"Thank you, Mr. Camden. I'm sorry, but I'm afraid I've never respected *you* very much."

Camden laughed, showing a mouthful of half-chewed food. "Doctor Scarborough, you show an incredible amount of restraint! But so what if we work different sides of the same river. I bet you that not a lot of people in this world know what goes on in that brilliant head of yours the way I do." Camden pushed the plate away from him and leaned back in the booth. "Besides, Doc. If people like me didn't throw your skeet up in the air, how would you shoot 'em down?"

MacKenzie laughed. "He's got a point, there."

Scarborough gave his friend a "Who's side are you on?" look.

"Anyway, we both stand to gain from this little adventure. I get a story and you get to dig up whatever truth you're looking for. We can help each other out, like I say.'' He lowered his voice. ''If you ask me, chums, what we got here is just one more example of the great cover-up. Doc, Mac—you were Project Blue Book dupes. It was all just a scam to cover-up what the Air Force was *really* up to.'' He slid off the blue-patched plastic-covered cushion. ''Now if you'll excuse me, gentlemen, I've got to water some porcelain.''

Joe's was a classic-style diner that had seen better days, but served decent road-fare. From the streamlined metal-and-neon design, Scarborough estimated it was from the late forties or early fifties. As he contemplated the remains of his BLT on toast, and considered ordering another iced tea, Mac tapped him on the shoulder.

''What gives, friend? Yesterday you're gnashing your teeth about this guy, and today we're in cahoots with him?''

Scarborough nodded. ''A little strange, yes. But logical.''

''Oh, pardon me, Mr. Spock.''

''No, really Mac, think about it. I'd like to sock him, yes. But what would happen? At best, I'd get arrested for assault. At worst, he'd write about it in his rag—and disgorge the whole story about Diane and her UFO. The devil you know and all that—if we shake him off, there's nothing stopping him from following us and finding out what we've uncovered anyway. This way, we might actually get some help from him—and strange bedfellows that we make, we might actually create a temporary ally.''

''Whatever you say, Ev. I got no problem with the guy.''

Scarborough smiled slyly. ''Besides, this way, I can plan a devious, painful murder for the scum-sucking bastard!''

Mac did a double take on that one, but when he saw that Scarborough was just kidding, he guffawed.

Camden scooted back into the booth. ''Too bad they don't have cocktails in this place,'' he said mopily.

''So guys, next stop the county-record's place?'' said Mac.

''Hell no!'' said Camden. ''How do we know the records aren't fixed? Look, two things you want to know here: One, what the hell happened to this Charles Higsdon character. Two, who owns that farm? Now if there's a lawyer involved, you can bet that something shady is going on, so chances are damn good that we gotta look someplace other than the record's office for the truth."

"Oh? And pray tell, where might that be, Mr. Camden?" asked Scarborough sarcastically.

"The local newspaper!" said Camden. "Where else!"

The *Tipville Chronicle* was a weekly paper, with an office in the center of town that looked like something out of an old movie based on a Sinclair Lewis novel.

The middle-aged man in round spectacles who was the managing editor regarded the strangers with suspicion until Camden showed him his press credentials and put on a slick "We're all brothers in ink" show. "We just want to look at your morgue, Mr. Hawkins. I'm trackin' a real interesting story about a farm west of here, and we need some background on it."

The editor shrugged and allowed that it was a public-service paper and that Camden and cronies were certainly "public." He showed them down to a dusty basement, filled with filing cabinets, warning them that the paper was seventy years old and had a lot of records.

"That's okay," said Camden. "I'm like Br'er Rabbit in the briar patch among newspaper records, Mr. Hawkins. To show our appreciation, my companions here will make a significant contribution to your favorite local charity."

A smile appeared on Hawkins's pinched face, "Well fellas, I reckon that'd be my newspaper!"

Fifty dollars changed hands.

"I don't understand," said Scarborough. "Are we supposed to go through every edition of the *Tipville Chronicle*?"

"Doc, baby, this is a *small* town. It's very easy for small-town newspapers to keep some sort of records on *everything*. Now, let me see—what was the name of the road that farm was on?"

With professional speed, the reporter found the appropriate file cabinet. A plume of dust rose as he pulled open the drawer, but he successfully found the right file. "Good thing this stuff isn't on microfiche. I'm all thumbs with microfiche," he said, thumping the thick folder under an old-fashioned lamp. "Let's see what we've got here."

Camden whipped through the clippings, pulling out the

appropriate ones, along with several typed pieces of paper which were dense with information. He clucked and hmmmed over these for a time, until MacKenzie grew impatient.

"Well?" the burly man demanded. "You got something?"

"Gentlemen, you're surely familiar with government programs to regulate farm production; Department of Agriculture, and all that. Well, it would seem that in the fifties, a certain governmental office did more than just pay a few bucks to farmers to not plant corn or beef up their soybean crops—they bought a few farms that were going out of business. One of these was the farm we were just on today."

Scarborough was aghast. "That place . . . it's owned by the government?"

"Since the fifties."

"That's right, gentlemen. In fact, your friend Higsdon, according to this information here, was just a government employee. He and his family apparently moved to South Dakota, oh, about fifteen years ago."

"Any kind of hint about what the government has been using that farm *for*, since then?"

Camden waved the appropriate clippings. "Department of Agriculture soil-experiments is the official word, but lots of neighbors got upset in 1980 about all the helicopter activity— the noise, you know. They formed a coalition . . . and then, up and dissolved themselves."

"Paid off," whispered Mac.

"That's my guess."

"Those labs didn't look like agricultural labs to me," said Scarborough.

Camden had produced a special lens attachment, and was busy laying out the clippings under the light to photograph. "Gentlemen, there's something rotten in River City . . . and it ain't pool."

He turned and began clicking off his shots.

CHAPTER
TWENTY-TWO

It was late at night when the helicopter touched down, swirling up dust, landing neatly between the netless basketball hoops.

You shouldn't have called them, the man said to himself. You should have just kept your damn mouth shut and full of booze. But he knew, in his heart of hearts, that they would have found out sooner or later.

Sooner, he had a chance for grace.

Later, he was a dead man.

Clyde Evans watched nervously as the government agents in their grey suits and ties disembarked. He was surprised to see a woman, wearing a lab coat, exit last. But not as surprised as he was when he realized that the man leading the group was the head of the whole operation. Brian Richards.

The man walked toward him, the wind from the copter blades flapping the ends of his coat.

"Evans," said Richards. "First, what did they see?"

Desperately wanting a drink, the man swallowed dryly. "I don't know for sure. Two of them must have been exploring out back—the ones that got me from behind when I was trying to scare the other one off."

"Okay. What did you tell them?"

"That I was the caretaker, of course. Hired by a lawyer from Tipville."

"Describe the trespassers."

Evans described them, and Richards nodded.

"Now, how the hell did they get past you?"

"Uhm—I was taking a nap."

"The alarm didn't wake you? The hidden surveillance cameras didn't alert you?"

"Look, I'm *sorry*, okay? Hey I reported in, didn't I?" Evans pulled out the money they'd given him. "They took my gun and they were going to use it on me. They thought they were bribing me."

Richards took the money, examined it, then threw it in the man's face. "When they busted you out of the Agency, man, it was me, *me*, who picked your ass out of the garbage can and gave you a job." He grabbed Evans by the collar.

An agent came out, shaking his head. "Whew. This place *reeks* of whiskey."

"I thought we kicked you of that nasty habit," said Richards.

"God, it's just so *boring*! It's *hell*! I thought a little drink now and then wouldn't do any harm."

Richards pushed him back contemptuously. "I'm afraid that we're going to have to relieve you of duty here, Evans. We've lost our need for third-rate grounds-keepers."

"Yes, sir."

"Get in the helicopter. We'll send your things along after you. You're going to dry out in a security arrangement for a time, and then we'll decide what to do with you."

Evans's shoulders slumped. "Yes, sir."

Another agent rejoined the group, flicking off his flashlight. "Looks like someone's been in one of the barns, all right."

"Damn!" said Richards. "Scarborough, of all people—Fucking Sherlock Scarborough! Damn!"

The woman stepped forward. "Don't worry too much. They're pretty well cleaned out."

"Yes, but its not exactly animal farm in there. It's pretty obvious they weren't being used as *barns!*"

Evans started to trudge toward the copter. "Wait a minute, Mr. Evans," said the woman in the lab coat. She pulled Richards off to the side and they talked in whispers.

Evans couldn't hear them, and he didn't want to hear them. He hunkered back in the shadows, miserable beyond words. Dry him out—he'd get the DTs again. He couldn't stand the thought, so he just turned his mind off. Maybe he could just sneak back in while the two talked. Sneak a bottle. One more drink . . . one more drink for the road. Already his hands were shaking.

Suddenly, he realized that Richards was regarding him with a peculiar expression. Richard—Mr. Fucking Sleaze-IA, some of the agents used to call him back in the old days. There was a hint of a smile on his face. "Yes, it's a thought," Richards was saying to the woman, whom Evans did not know. "You think it would help him?"

"Without a doubt," said the woman. "I've got him on a different chemical mix, and he seems to have calmed down a bit. But he needs some kind of release."

Richards nodded. He turned and yelled back at the copter, whose rotors were only slowly spinning now. "Mr. Justine. Would you come out for a minute, please?"

A short-haired man wearing a plain grey suit like the others stepped from the plane, walking toward them just a little unsteadily. "Yes, sir."

"How are you feeling, Mr. Justine?"

"Much better, sir."

Richards smiled at the woman. "I like it—he's getting a 'sir' drug now? Not feeling so cocky anymore, huh? A little under the weather. Maybe you need a nice long rest, Justine! Maybe we should retire you for a while!"

"I'm fucking okay, Richards, you torturing bastard!" The short-haired man Richards had called Justine said.

"*That's* the attitude I like to hear." Richards walked to Evans and put a hand on the man's back. "We're pretty much your family, aren't we, Mr. Evans?"

"Yes, sir."

"Good. I hate to do this, Evans, but we just don't need you anymore. Tell you what, though. In the way of a going-away present, we'll forgo the gold watch. Instead, you've got a thirty-second head start on Mr. Justine here. Oh, by the way, Mr. Justine is the division mechanic." Richards stepped away. "Good-bye, Evans. You've got half a minute from—now!"

"What . . . ?" Fear and confusion gripped him.

"Twenty-eight seconds, Evans." Richards turned to Justine. "Mr. Justine, I do hope you're up to it."

Justine's face was stone. "Sure thing."

"Jesus!" said Evans, more prayerfully than blasphemously. "You can't *do* this. This is the U.S. government! We obey the law! We have *rights*! We're not savages!"

"As John Stuart Mill said, Mr. Evans: 'The greater good for

the greater number.' But *somebody* has to be the judge of what's best for everybody. What's best for our nation, now, I fear, is that you be put out of the picture. Fifteen seconds.''

Evans turned and ran. He didn't think about what he was doing or where he was going, he just ran as hard as he could. His pulse pounded in his ear and the air whisked by his sweating face. He saw the fence up ahead, and then the open gate. If he could just get through the gate, maybe he had a chance.

He was only a matter of yards away from the fence when the flashlight beam struck him. With a whine, he jerked away from it, heading for the gate. The beam found him again. Something hard and stinging struck him in the shoulder, and, almost as an afterthought, he heard the sound of a gun. He was hurled straight onto the mesh of barbed wire, and the sharp, rusty ends gouged at his face and chest, clinging at his clothes and puncturing his skin, pinning him in place. He hung on the wire, crucified and whimpering.

''You will forget about what you saw,'' said the man named Justine, coming up behind him. ''You will forget about the UFOs. Or you will pay the price.''

What was the guy talking about? ''Sure!'' Evans spat through his pain. ''Just get me off here, let me go! I won't say anything to anybody about this place . . . or about UFOs!'' He added hastily.

Footsteps. Evans sensed the man was very near. ''Stop it!'' the man growled to himself in a tortured voice. ''What's *wrong* with you, Justine! Get a fucking *grip*!''

There was a period of silence, and, for a moment, Evans thought that maybe the man was going to lift him off of the wire, tell him that this was all just a new form of punishment, and that he'd be sent along for detainment, detoxification, and then reassignment.

But then the bullets tore through his head and chest, and Evans's final neurological activity was nerve spasms.

When Justine came back, he was smiling a private little smile.

''Feel better?'' asked Richards.

''Much.''

''Okay. Sit in the copter till we're ready to go; take it easy. I'll get the other two guys to take care of the body.''

'''Yeah—Richards.''

"That's the old Woodrow Justine we all know and love." Richards watched as the hit man stepped jauntily into the helicopter cabin. He took Cunningham by the arm, and led her toward the farmhouse. "Just a quick word, Julia," he said. He looked over and saw Jenkins and Marshall carrying Evans's corpse toward one of the barns. When he judged they were out of earshot, he said, "Okay. He still seems operative. But it looks like we're going to have to ask a great deal of him in the very near future. Should I call up another agent?"

Cunningham looked at him, her Nordic features cold, her eyes piercing. "As I assured you, Mr. Justine performed this evening. He will perform, on-call, in the future. He is the *best*."

"I dunno, Julia. He's getting awfully twitchy."

"Justine is *my* creation, Mr. Richards," the woman said in tones of ice. "If not for me, he'd be in some prison for the criminally insane by now."

"Well, what's all this Men in Black stuff? God, talk about karmic backlash!" A moth beat its wings against the back porch's light-casing.

"Mr. Justine merely suffered a traumatic experience. Coupled with a need for adjustment in his medication, the experience in Takoma Park affected him adversely. You should have had him sent to me immediately. As it is, credit his intelligence and instinct for survival that put him on the jet to Iowa so quickly."

"You haven't answered my question. This Men in Black stuff—you're saying he picked it up from the Klinghoffer crazy who shot him up with a hypoful of water?"

"It follows, doesn't it? You did read the clean-up report on Klinghoffer, didn't you?"

"I'm a busy man."

"The guy was obsessed with saucer lore. I mean, you should have spotted it from the assassination attempt on Scarborough! Dressed in black . . ."

"I don't credit any of that stuff." The gossamer insect against the lamp fluttered down onto the concrete. Richards stepped on it, smearing the moth like a chalk mark.

Dr. Cunningham looked away. "And the guy apparently drove an old model Pontiac. A *black* Pontiac. Woodrow Justine was injected with more than water. He was injected with very strong *suggestions*. These are potent archetypes we're dealing with. Acid occasionally spills on the chemist's toes, Mr. Richards.''

Richards shook his head and leaned against the building, taking out a pack of cigarettes. He offered one to Dr. Cunningham who looked at him as though he were holding a handful of shit. ''That's right, you don't smoke. I don't much anymore myself. Just once in a while.'' He shrugged and lit up, blowing the smoke away from his associate. ''Well, I'm the executive branch of this operation, Cunningham. I do my job and I do it well . . . I'm pretty well-versed in the UFO facts by now, natch—'' He chuckled ruefully. ''Too much for my personal taste. But I pretty much ignore the apocryphal nonsense.''

''You shouldn't. It's all part of the fabric. The Men in Black phenomenon is a little-known but significant side effect of the UFO mythos.'' Like a pedagogue speaking to a recalcitrant student, she spoke tersely. ''Sometimes, witnesses of Unidentified Flying Objects are visited very soon after by men dressed in black who claim to be from the CIA or FBI or some other government agency; they warn the individual to be quiet about what they witnessed, and often threaten them. These men are notoriously weird and awkward, often they have dark skin and Asiatic features—men who don't seem much familiar with the American language—or sometimes speak it too precisely, as if it were a second language. These figures merely harass—they do not actually carry out their threats of violence. All of which causes the theorists to assume that they are mere wraiths of the imagination.''

''Men in Black. Like Satan or demons or something . . . only modern.''

''Excellent, Mr. Richards. Which is exactly my mythic point. The collective unconscious may ride around in jets and sports cars, but it still has its dark phantoms. They are just clothed in trench coats.'' She smiled at him without humor. ''Curious how they're often CIA agents, eh?''

''I do my job, and I do it well, Ms. Cunningham. Just like you. And we both reap the rewards. I'm in no mood for the casting of aspersions. And though I can't speak for you, *I* serve a cause *I* believe in, my *country*!'' He looked at her defiantly and blew smoke in her face.

She coughed. ''You needn't parade your patriotism. I wave

the same flag. Let's get back to the matter at hand. Justine. He's clearly somehow been affected by these stories—on some subconscious level. But I have spoken to him, and adjusted his drugs. He is back in control now, I can assure you. I stake my reputation on it.''

Richards grunted. "Good. I'll remember that.'' He looked around at the grounds and the barns. "We might need this place in the future again—we've got to contain Scarborough's investigation. But without hurting the bastard, and without giving anything away. A tricky business.''

"This has been a delicate operation from the very beginning.''

"Yes, but we've made some mistakes. It's that MacKenzie guy—we didn't realize that he'd kept the originals of his reports on Blue Book. That's how they got this address.''

"Well, count your blessings. They didn't catch us *flagrante delicto*.''

"Yes, but what *other* addresses are in that man's files? Scarborough's files were dealt with years ago. Now we've got to take out MacKenzie, before the two of them turn up the other bases.''

"It's dumb luck they found this one. Besides, that's one of the reasons we took it out of service temporarily. Questionable security background.''

"I don't know, Julia. Scarborough isn't dumb. He's stubborn and he seemed to adore the blinders we've had on him all these years. But I think they're starting to chafe. If I had my way, we'd just terminate the jerk. But of course, the Publishers—''

"The Publishers know what they're doing, Mr. Richards. We are but lowly Editors, taking joy in the creativity expressed in our careers.'' She smiled for the first time. "And of course, we get paid more than your average editor.''

The other agents were walking toward them from the barn.

"You two will stay here,'' Richards ordered. "Relief will be arriving tomorrow, and the body will be dealt with then.''

"Yes, sir,'' they said.

"Oh, and get rid of all that whiskey—without drinking it yourselves.''

They smiled. "Yes, sir. I think we've learned our lesson here, sir,'' said one.

They went into the farmhouse, and Richards and Cunningham turned and began walking back to the waiting copter.

"I can't take out Scarborough, but it's open season on the people around him, if necessary. That's why we need Justine. He's going to be my man in this."

"Count on him, Mr. Richards."

"Good. When we get back, we'll call the Pentagon." He ducked under the slowly turning blades, even though they were far above his head. "We're going to need MacKenzie's address. Or rather, Woodrow Justine will need it."

CHAPTER
TWENTY-THREE

At eight-thirty in the morning, there was a knock on the door. Scarborough heard it first since the guest room was nearest the front door. He'd gone to bed early, and Mac had stayed up writing; he figured the man deserved his rest, so he hoisted himself out of bed and went to answer the knock.

"Yes?" he said, yawning as he tugged open the oak door by its brass handle.

"Captain MacKenzie?"

There was a woman standing outside the front door, dressed in sharp air force blues. She wore her hair up in a bun under a cap. Thick black-rimmed eyeglasses magnified her eyes slightly.

"Uhm—no, he's asleep. I'm Dr. Everett Scarborough."

"Excellent. I'm Lieutenant Marsha Manning. You're the man to whom I've been assigned." She stuck out a slim, matter-of-fact hand. "Good morning, Doctor. I look forward to working with you."

Baffled, Scarborough shook the woman's hand reflexively. "I don't recall asking for help from the air force."

"You didn't. Colonel Dolan requisitioned my services. May I come in?"

"Oh—of course, Lieutenant. Please excuse the state of this

place, to say nothing of the state of *me*." Scarborough wrapped the tatty bathrobe tighter around his nightclothes.

The corners of the woman's severe mouth tugged upwards, but she suppressed the smile immediately. She surveyed the living room. "Bachelor-base central, eh, Dr. Scarborough? Don't worry, I've dealt with bachelors before."

"A woman of the world. How about some coffee, Lieutenant? Then we'll call Colonel Dolan and get to the bottom of this business."

The woman nodded and accepted a seat at the dining-room table while Scarborough rustled up some coffee.

"In the meantime, let me supply you with my background, Doctor," she said in an officious monotone. "With an ROTC scholarship, I attended Duke University, obtaining a B.S. in engineering, and an M.S. in computer science. I am thirty years old, and have field experience in jet crash investigations in Japan, Alabama, California and West Germany. Otherwise, my days in the air force have been occupied with training programs for technicians and pilots on various bases in the continental U.S. Recently I was stationed at Vandenberg in California, but I've just been transferred to Ohio, with an administrative position in pilot education in the works."

"Impressive," muttered Scarborough, trying to figure out Mac's Mr. Coffee machine. Since his wife's death, he'd devolved to instant coffee in the morning, a habit his tastebuds loathed, but one which he found quite efficient schedule-wise. "I take it you're here to help Captain MacKenzie and myself with *our* investigation. That's very thoughtful of the colonel— but I'm afraid we really don't need help."

She made a noise like squelched laughter. Scarborough poured water into the top of the drip-machine, and then turned, frowning.

"What was *that*?"

"Nothing, Doctor. I'm sorry." Again, she was a statue.

Scarborough regarded her. She sat stiffly, green eyes straight ahead as though in a form of attention. Her legs were slim and well formed. She filled her uniform out in the right places. She was a handsome woman. She wore no makeup, but Scarborough realized that with some eyeliner, some mascara, and those vibrant green eyes, she'd be a very striking woman. And the murmurings of amusement beneath the military ice-show were most intriguing.

"I take it, Lieutenant, that Colonel Dolan dispatched you personally, along with a few negative comments on our investigation abilities?"

"Well, Doctor. He mentioned that you might need some—help."

"And you think it's all pretty amusing. I bet you think all this is a lark. A UFO investigation with a couple of kooks."

"Well, sir, Project Blue Book *is* rather a joke around the barracks, so to speak, sir." She turned and looked at him with great sincerity. "But I'm a dedicated investigator, Doctor. I intend to do my duty."

The glint of those eyes. An Irish green field, encapsulated. Scarborough was startled by their beauty, and he turned away, mumbling. "Well, the colonel's gesture is appreciated, but I don't think you'll be staying, Lieutenant."

He looked back at her and could read neither disappointment nor gratification in her expression. Statue time again.

He poured the coffee and got on the horn to Dolan: it was well into the morning, eastern standard time.

"That's right, Ev. If you're going to open up air force business, I want an air force official there. Take her as a helper, take her as an overseer. Take her anyway you damn well please, but you're going to take her, like it or not."

For a moment, Scarborough was tempted to demand an explanation for the whole government-owned farm business. But he must have been *slightly* touched by Mac's paranoia, because he didn't. He still didn't buy the whole conspiracy bullshit that Camden mouthed. They'd argued long and hard about that last night, and Scarborough wouldn't budge. He didn't care for the secrecy involved, and he'd never liked the CIA much—but, so far there was nothing malevolent in what they'd found. Could be the farm had simply been a secret station for the Department of Agriculture or the EPA. Maybe it wasn't even *secret*—the time elapsed just made it look that way. Anyway, there was still some more digging to do before any alarms were pulled.

All the same, he didn't tell Dolan where they'd been yesterday.

"Walter, you talk to me as though I'm one of your military

flunkies! I'm an independent citizen, not some lowly corporal who shines your shoes!''

Dolan softened his tone. "Sorry, Ev. You just kinda pissed me off the other day. You're right, of course. But you can't just take matters into your own hands like this, on potentially classified subjects. Look, you're reopening an official government investigation, and I'm going to give you an official okay on that—if, and only if, you're accompanied by an air force officer. Namely, Lieutenant Manning.''

"Are you threatening to *arrest* me or something, Walter?" asked Scarborough defiantly.

A deep sigh issued from the receiver. "Okay, look at it this way. Just think of the access you'll have to things—I guarantee you, the lieutenant can cough up facts and dates and what-the-hell-have-you with her portable computer, and her modem, and her priority access faster than you can shake a stick. Can't you see, pal? I'm trying to *help* you—not hinder you. This is my way of saying, gol' damn, you're right, boy. Go ahead and stick your nose back into old Blue Book. 'Fact, here's some *help!*" Significant pause. "Between you and me, Ev—I'm *not* supposed to be doing this. This is Walter Dolan's way of saying, 'Sorry, I've been a real asshole.' ''

"Priority computer-access, you say," said Scarborough. "I don't see any computer here.''

"20 mega hard-disk Hewlett-Packard, 2400 baud modem," said Manning, putting her coffee cup down. "Back at the motel. Not far. I can go back and get it, if you like.''

Scarborough turned back to his phone conversation. No, it would look very bad if he turned this aid down. Besides, the lieutenant might actually be able to help some, and damn if he was going to get sucked into the conspiracy-paranoia about the whole thing. "We'll see how it goes, Walter," he said.

"Wonderful. You have any problem, you let me know, but I tell you buddy, Lieutenant Manning comes highly recommended for just the kind of work you insist on doing. Now, just let me know if there's any other way I can help you.''

Scarborough hung up and fixed himself some coffee. The first few sips cleared his head some, and he felt better—especially now, in the clear light of morning, with that crazed sleazoid reporter Camden gone. After they'd gotten back, Jake headed for the bathroom, and came back wired and coke-eyed, insisting on hitting the road again. Important business, yes, yes. He'd be back in touch. Soon. Sniff, sniff.

"Looks like you're on the team." Scarborough shook her hand, and, for the first time, realized that she was wearing a slight trace of perfume. Cinnabar. One of his favorites.

He sat down across from her and quickly outlined the situation. He told her about the visit to the Higsdon farm yesterday, but did not mention the discovery of government ownership. He did, however, give her the address when she requested it. She said she'd do some research on the missing farmer and the land, utilizing her computer access. Scarborough was intrigued at her willingness to delve into government computer-files—but he honestly wondered about their value in this situation.

About a half hour later, Mac wandered down, looking bleary-eyed, wearing only his BVDs. "Smelled coffee," he murmured, scratching his big, hairy belly.

"Uh, Mac—" said Scarborough, grimacing.

Mac stopped, gave Lieutenant Manning a low glance, belched, and went to get his coffee.

"You know, Mac, I realize that this is your house, but could you exercise some decorum? We have a lady visitor."

Mac poured the black stuff into a mug. "That ain't no lady, that's an Air Force officer." He slogged his way to the table and sat down. "Howdy do, Lieutenant."

"You must be Captain MacKenzie," she said coolly.

"'Tis my duty every day of the week to be me, aye." He tilted the coffee and swallowed. Immediately, he grimaced. "Christ almighty! What is this mud?"

"I must have fixed it wrong, Mac. Sorry."

Mac shrugged. "Oh well, the caffeine's still there." He gave Manning a closer look. "You're not an MP. We're not getting arrested."

Lieutenant Manning blinked. "Why ever should you get arrested?"

"Mac is paranoid. Thinks there's a government-air force-CIA conspiracy to stop us from looking into this UFO business."

"Captain MacKenzie, do you believe that earth is being visited by little green men in flying saucers?" The derisive chuckle was back in her voice.

"Lieutenant," said Mac, putting his coffee cup down onto

the table with finality. "I've been on this planet fifty-five years now, and each of those years just gets weirder and weirder. I'm hoping that when I get to be about ninety-four, I'm gonna die of weirdness."

"Sounds like wishful thinking to me, Captain," said Manning. "I prefer to stick to facts. Facts, logic, science—they've never steered me wrong."

"Hey, Ev. Your long-lost identical twin—minus about twenty years and a sex-change!" Mac rumbled with amusement.

Scarborough studied the cool woman in the Air Force outfit. No, she wasn't like him at all—there was something that rang hollow in that last sentence. Something off-key in the whole Ice Queen facade. It both intrigued and annoyed him.

"Well, Lieutenant," he said, "I'll change, and we'll go over and get that computer and modem of yours. I hope you have your access codes ready, because we're going to use them."

"No, Dr. Scarborough. *I'm* going to use them," she said with an almost haughty demeanor. "My eyes only, I'm afraid."

The words and her attitude rankled, but he let it go. It might be worthwhile putting up with her. Old Ironbottom might have given them just the tool they needed to get to the truth in this whole business.

He got up to leave, but paused at the door.

"Have you ever seen *Guns of Navarone*, Lieutenant Manning?"

She blinked, astonished at the non-sequitur. "No. Is it about UFOs?"

Mac laughed heartily. "Don't worry, Ev. I'll keep my M-16 square on her back when we storm the Germans!"

Scarborough shrugged off the paranoia worming into his mind and went upstairs to change clothes.

CHAPTER
TWENTY-FOUR

"Now, Diane," said the psychologist, "Relax a little more." The soft, soothing tones waved over her like warm Mediterranean waves in the shallow waters of a beach. "Re...lax. Re...lax."

Diane Scarborough was sitting in a reclining chair in a darkened office that smelled of pipe tobacco and old books. Her lids seemed very heavy now, as she stared at the top of a small potted palm by the shuttered window, while Doctor Raphael Mistone patiently lulled her into a hypnotic state. Nearby, she could hear the faint whirring machinery of a cassette tape, recording the session.

Tim sat quietly on the other side of the room, on a couch. The condition for him being here at all was that he not say a word while Dr. Mistone put Diane into the trance. He had been given a pad and a pencil to record any jarred memories that might come to him as Diane remembered what had happened to them that night. He would be next to go under.

"Excellent, Diane," said the small, dark-haired man in the sleeveless sweater after she had obediently counted backwards from one hundred to eighty. "You are now in a deep, restful place. It is very peaceful and calm. Tell me, Diane, do you feel peaceful and calm?"

The muscles in Diane Scarborough's arms and legs felt liquid, almost nonexistent. But she felt aware and alert, not at all in any kind of trance. "Yes," she found herself saying, not elaborating.

"I want you to go back in your mind, Diane. Go back deep into your memory. There's a blank spot there now, but when you go back, deeply, very deeply, it will come back to you. I want you to tell me what you see and hear and feel as you relive the experience. Do you understand me?''

''Yes,'' Diane said.

''You are back at the night when you and Tim saw the lights in the sky while you were parked by that field. Do you remember that night, Diane?''

''Yes, I remember,'' she said.

''Do you see the lights?''

''Yes—yes, I see them,'' she said, and she saw the object again through the windshield of the car, cruising over the Kansas field, shutting out the stars and the moon.

''You're following it now, walking across the field. You're in the trees. You see a bright, enveloping light.''

''Oh yes, yes. I see it.''

''Tell me what happens next, Diane. Describe it as it happens again.''

The floor of Diane Scarborough's mind seemed to open up beneath her, and the memory flooded back, moment by moment . . .

The light ebbed away, and she found herself standing in the woods, clutching Tim for dear life, frightened and yet filled with awe and wonder.

Ahead, there was a break in the forest, and through that break she could see a field; in it there was a large disk-shaped object about the size of a bungalow, sitting in the field like a new-grown mushroom after a rain shower. A string of multicolored lights pulsed along it, muting and brightening subtly, like luminous breaths across its mottled metallic skin.

''I don't believe it,'' said Tim, regaining his tongue. ''Would you take a look at that, Diane? Incredible!''

Diane stood transfixed, staring at the thing. Oddly, she felt no fear, no impulse to run. She merely felt a deep curiosity. ''Come on, Tim. We need to get closer to see it properly.''

Tim agreed, and they walked slowly through the prickly underbrush, eventually emerging out from the trees and into the clearing.

''A flying saucer. A real fucking flying saucer,'' said Tim, absolutely beside himself with glee. ''Look at this thing, Diane!

This is no practical joke! This is no movie special effect! This is real!"

The reality of the thing could not be questioned. It had the heft and feel of reality, the texture. Up closer, Diane could see the hull through the parade of lights, and the scuff marks and the seared spots from ablation. Nonetheless, the skin had a definite alien look, with no sign of the seams and bolts terrestrial aircraft showed.

"I knew it!" she said, expressing a long-held suspicion. "I knew they would choose me!" She was brimming with excitement.

"Hey, you," said Tim. "How do you know they didn't choose me, and you just happened be along for the ride!" Timothy Reilly could joke with her at the most incredible times.

At that moment, there was the shush of machinery, the whir of gears, a cracked-seal sound, the sussuration of depressurization. The outline of a door became visible at the base of the large craft, and a door opened, settling onto the grass with the wheeze and shush of hydraulics. There came from within the sound of footsteps, headed their way.

"So what do you think, Diane?" said Tim. "Almond-slanted eyes. Skinny limbs. Telepathic languages."

"I don't know. All I know is that I thought you're supposed to be scared out of your mind at times like this. I'm not scared . . . I'm thrilled!"

That was the truth, and it surprised her. She felt an absolute inner glow of warmth, anticipation and well-being. She knew that somehow the vessel before her was radiating the feeling to her, but she didn't care. It just felt too good, too real, to care about where it came from.

They watched patiently as feet appeared at the door of the saucer. The feet stepped down, revealing legs clothed in jumpsuits, and the jumpsuits continued on up the bodies.

Diane stared at the two creatures, astonished.

They didn't seem alien at all.

They looked just like two ordinary men, in well-pressed tan overalls.

One of the men seemed to be in his fifties, his hair nearly silver, and very human wrinkles around his eyes. The other looked to be in his twenties, with pure black hair, a handsome face, and a dimpled chin. They both wore professional smiles of relaxed corporate executives.

"Hello," said the older one. *"I hope you're not experiencing fear presently."*

"No," answered Diane.

The younger man's smile turned a little brighter and the older one nodded at him, as though acknowledging some job well-done. *"Excellent,"* said the older. *"This kind of experience could potentially be quite unsettling. Strange craft dropping from skies, a pair of odd people disgorging from a flying saucer . . ."*

"But you're . . . you're humans!" said Tim, aghast.

"Well, possibly. Aren't you relieved?"

"I don't know. We hardly expected people like ourselves from another planet." said Tim. *"It seems so . . . prosaic!"*

The senior of the two chuckled. *"Oh, hardly, believe me, Mr. Reilly."*

"You know my name."

"Yes, and your companion is Diane Scarborough."

The younger turned and spoke to his companion. *"It's best not to linger. We hardly need other witnesses at this point."*

"Yes, you're right." The grey-haired man turned back to Diane and Tim. *"Come on aboard awhile, won't you. We won't keep you long. And there are matters of grave importance to discuss."*

Diane did not hesitate. She started walking forward, but was held back by Tim. *"Wait,"* he said. *"This could be some kind of trick to lure us aboard."*

"Tim," she said. *"Don't you think that if they wanted us there, they could just take us?"* She had a peculiar but thrilling feeling of well-being. Intuitively, she knew she could trust these creatures, human or not.

Tim nodded. *"Yeah, I guess you're right."*

Diane took his hand. *"C'mon,"* she said reassuringly, *"Everything is going to be all right."*

His hand was cool and his grip was firm. They walked under the overhang of the great vessel, toward the ramp that led into the heart of mystery . . .

Then, suddenly, there was a void, a nothingness . . .

And Diane woke up, with a gasp, from her trance.

"Are you all right, Diane?" asked Dr. Mistone.

Diane blinked. *"Yes . . . yes, I'm fine. And I remembered it, didn't I. That incredible ship . . ."*

"Yes, you did. Now, I'm going to put you back under, and I want you to try to remember the rest."

But it was as though her memory was striking a brick wall. She could remember nothing more. The psychologist gave a significant look to Tim, but Tim drew a blank on everything; he remembered no saucer, no men in jumpsuits, and certainly no entering of a spacecraft.

Dr. Mistone put Diane back under. "You have entered the ship, Diane," he said, after the preliminaries. "What do you see?"

Not only could Diane see nothing, but she popped out of the hypnotic trance like an unleashed jack-in-the-box.

"Remarkable," said Mistone, stroking his mustache. "I've never seen anything quite like it! As you know, I *have* dealt with abduction cases before. That's why Mr. Hopkins's group put you in touch with me. But *never* have I encountered a situation like this. Why, it doesn't even seem like an abduction, if it really happened. It seems more like an invitation."

"Do you want to try again, Doctor?" asked Diane, impatient to know the truth, straining with all her faculties to remember, but coming up blank.

"No, if you don't mind, I'd like to try with Mr. Reilly. Please linger, though, Diane. And I want you to take the tablet of paper and jot down notes."

Tim handed her the tablet. All it held were doodles. But one of the doodles immediately caught her attention—it looked like a simple Vendanta mandala, a circle with cloverleaf-like figures enclosed. It struck something in Diane, but she wasn't sure what.

Tim was a more difficult subject for Dr. Mistone. It took awhile to get him into something resembling a hypnotic state. And when Tim did go under, there was absolutely no recollection past the blinding light in the forest.

The psychologist brought his subject back to normalcy, and sighed, running his fingers through his thinning black mane. "Well, that's it for now, then. We not only have a block here, the whole experience seems blotted out. Perhaps we can try another session next week, eh?"

"Dr. Mistone—you do believe us, don't you?"

The man went back to his desk and fiddled with a pen. "You must realize, Diane—there is the possibility here, that this is a shared illusion. My experience with abductions has convinced me that there is *something* going on. Whether it has any empirical basis in consensus reality—Hopkins of course thinks it does, but sometimes I'm not so sure."

"I see, Doctor," said Diane. She got up, and started away, and then turned back toward the man. "Just because they didn't look like something out of a Steven Spielberg film doesn't mean they don't exist! And it doesn't mean that we didn't experience what we experienced!"

"You're quite right, Diane. I'm sorry for my seeming doubt and callousness." He opened up his appointment book. "Now then, how about another appointment for the same time next Thursday?"

"I'll think about it," said Diane, a bit huffily. She turned and marched from the office.

"Count on it, Doctor," said Tim. "We'll be back."

"Thank you for coming," said Mistone. "A most peculiar case!" he called after Diane. "I look forward to exploring it further!"

Diane, feeling confused and upset, was already out in the waiting room, where the receptionist, doing dictation memoes, studiously ignored her. A man stood up from the couch and stepped forward expectantly toward her. It was Camden, looking if anything more disheveled and bedraggled than before. His eyes were bloodshot, and it looked as though he'd been up all night.

"Well, how'd it go?" he asked eagerly.

Diane hesitated. She didn't want to tell him *anything*. Camden noticed this hesitancy and took pains to reassure her. "Diane, don't worry! Your father and I—we've got a truce. I was just up in Iowa, working with him on that investigation. And look, I talked to him. He's not so upset anymore."

"Mr. Camden, I'm sorry. I just don't know if I can trust you."

"For God's sake, call him if you want to! I smoothed everything over, I'm telling you. I came all the way back last night, just so I could get the scoop—I mean, get the news on how your hypnosis session went!" He looked hopeful, threadbare and not a little pathetic, somehow vulnerable in his weariness, as though he'd just driven miles and miles to ask about a sick aunt.

Tim was out by then, and he said, "Jake! Hello!"

Tim's greeting seemed to hearten the man. "Timothy Reilly, me boy. Your brain all shrunk now?"

Tim glanced at the receptionist. "Maybe we better go back to my apartment to talk."

"Yeah, sure kid! Great! I'll see you two there!" he rubbed his hands together eagerly. "Right! We're going to get to the *bottom* of this business, I can tell." And he left.

"I think Jake Camden is pretty accustomed to the bottom of every business," Diane said acidly.

"Come on, Diane, it's not his fault I brought him in while you were talking to your old man. We've been through all this. The thing we've got to talk about is this hypnotic session." He escorted her out of the office and to the elevator, where he hit the Down button. "I just don't remember what you remember, Diane, and it bothers me."

Diane realized that she was still hanging onto the tablet of paper that Dr. Mistone had given her. She held it up to Tim and tapped the doodle that had attracted her attention. "Tim—why did you draw this?"

Tim looked at the mandala-like rendering. "You got me, Diane. I was just fooling around."

Diane looked at it, at the curlicues and the squiggles, swirling round and round and round, and suddenly she felt dizzy. "It reminds me of something, Tim," she said, the elevator going out of focus, all fuzzily. "Something—"

She lost her footing, and Tim grabbed her. "Diane! What—"

Whispers and echoes. Voices and not-voices.

She didn't lose consciousness, but merely touched on the hypnagogic dream-state for the barest breath of a moment. She saw those men again—the young one, the older one—and they spoke to her, clearly and plainly.

Behind them, on a wall, she could see the thing that Tim had drawn. An emblem that looked like a Hindu mandala: circles and loops.

"Diane, you will forget this now," said the older man. "But it will float back into your mind within a week. We will meet again, Diane. And this is where we will meet." And he told her.

"Diane!" Tim said, shaking her a little. "Diane, what's wrong?"

The lines and shadows of the reality of the elevator car filled in around her. She looked at Tim Reilly and she smiled. "I'm going to meet them again, Tim," she said, taking his hand in hers and clutching it warmly. "And now I remember exactly *where* and exactly *when*!"

Dr. Raphael Mistone pored over his notes again, line by line. He didn't have to replay the tapes of his last patients—their words were frozen in his mind. *Unique* was the word that kept popping up in his head. *Unique*. Mistone had been doing this work with alien abductees for five years now, and nothing remotely like the Scarborough-Reilly case had ever cropped up before.

Human beings, in a saucer?

The couple seemed sincere enough, certainly. In the business of the human psyche, reality and illusion mixed in every warped fashion imaginable and unimaginable. Sincerity was no measure of truth. Nonetheless, Diane and Tim's story had a peculiar ring to it, and merited further exploration.

Mistone sipped at his lukewarm coffee, and brooded. It also *could* be the kind of case worth reporting. God knew, he cashed those people's checks fast enough when they came, regular as clockwork. *"Just a regular report on your abduction cases, Doctor, that's all. Quarterly. Written. Specifics, and psychological affects. We're most concerned about this phenomenon, and despite our public poo-poohing and skepticism of such cases, we must constantly be kept abreast of the situation in the interests of both national security and the psychological health of our citizens. However, if you find anything remarkable or unusual, please report immediately. Such cases will merit increased compensation."*

It all seemed to make enough sense, Mistone thought, leaning back in his chair and studying the display of his diplomas behind his desk. If they copped to actual concern about what seemed a small phenomena, then what was merely a limited hysteria could well become a *mass* hysteria. Phantom aliens would be popping up all over the United States.

Besides, he rationalized. His divorce settlement on his wife and kids was costing far more than he thought. He could use a little spare change underneath the table. *Untaxable* spare change.

Mistone reached out and pulled in his personal rolodex. He

spun through the cards, selected the appropriate one, and dialed the number on his phone.

A secretary answered at the other end, and Dr. Raphael Mistone said, "Hello. I'd like to speak to Mr. Brian Richards please. It's urgent."

CHAPTER TWENTY-FIVE

"Cute," said Scarborough.

"What, you don't have one of these?" said Lieutenant Marsha Manning, looking up from her tinkerings with the portable computer on the table.

Scarborough shrugged. "I suppose I should. I travel enough. On the other hand, I need to really concentrate when I write, and I can't seem to do that on planes or in hotel rooms."

"You get used to it," said Manning, switching the thing on and watching as digits danced across the backlit orange LD display. Her fingers tapped the keys for a while, calling up her communications program. "Okay, Doctor. You wished information from government computers? We now have access."

A bluff voice called from the kitchen. "Hey, beautiful. How 'bout a brew!"

"No thank you, Captain MacKenzie. No drinking, I'm afraid; not while I'm working." She sat stiffly at the dining room table, near the keyboard. Scarborough thought she looked like she wanted a cigarette, but he didn't know her well enough to pry. Besides, their trip back to her motel to get her Hewlett-Packard had not exactly been a gabfest. Indeed, what few words they spoke seemed to be slightly abrasive. For whatever reason, he and the Air Force lieutenant were *not* getting along particularly well. In fact, he rather wished she weren't around, access or no access.

Still, he had to find out some important things about this
plant that Dolan had made: Was she legitimate, or was she a
CIA dragon-lady or its air force equivalent. If she wasn't
legitimate, she'd be a bit smoother operator, certainly. Lieutenant Marsha Manning acted as though she had a broom up her
ass at times, stick-end south. That was, when she wasn't
tripping over her shoelaces.

Like now.

"Damn," she said. Her mug went sailing over the edge of
the table, spilling coffee onto the rug. "I'm so sorry."

"No problem," said Scarborough. "I'll just go get a wet
rag. You burrow your way into the Department of Agriculture
files, like you said you could."

He could almost hear her teeth grinding as she swung her
glasses toward the display screen and began hitting the keys.
As he left, Scarborough heard the electronic bleeps of the
modem, dialing numbers.

"Lieutenant Calamity Jane just flavored your rug with coffee, Mac," said Scarborough, grabbing a fistful of Big Job
paper towels from the roll.

"No shit," said Mac through a mouthful of pickle as he put
the finishing touches on their lunches. Sandwiches, of course.
"Strange broad. Nice legs, though, huh?"

"No fraternization with the enemy, pal."

Mac distributed iceberg lettuce on top of slices of Havarti
cheese. "Hell, no, Scarborough. Wouldn't think of getting in
your way."

"In my—" Frown lines angled down on Scarborough's face.
"Mac, what the hell are you implying?"

Mac winked. "Let's just say if I wanted a hot lunch, I'd
only have to put frying pans on your laps."

"What absolute drivel! I admit the woman seems to be put
together interestingly—but that doesn't mean I want to hop into
the sack with her!"

Impassively, Mac put the tops of the caraway-seed rye on the
sandwiches, sliced them, and placed them on plates. "Nothing
unusual about it, Ev. Suave and charming as you are, chum,
and as many women who would like to butter your toast,
you've *always* had to call long-distance to keep in touch with
your gonads."

For some reason, Scarborough was infuriated with Mac's

lewd suggestions. If he wasn't his best friend, he probably would have let loose with an angry barrage and stalked from the room. True, Marsha Manning had nice eyes, and her perfume stirred something in him. But Mac was way offtrack about this strong attraction business—and Manning acted as though she'd sooner drink hemlock than touch him. No, the fiction-writer's imagination was running far off course.

"Mac, we're delving into some serious matters here. There's no time for male horseplay and obscene, off-the-wall remarks."

Mac put down the knife. "Is that muffled buzzing coming from the bug that seems to have crawled up your ass? Gimme a break, young Master Scarborough! You just seemed a little agitated in the lady's presence, and, understanding the logic of testosterone, I assumed that you wanted to drill for oil! So, am I forgiven if I admit that your tender feelings for the damsel are chaste and pe-ure!"

"Feelings? I've known her for about two hours, and she's been sent here by a guy whom you claim has been pulling the wool over our eyes for twenty years! I—" He sputtered a bit, and realized he was getting red in the face. "The hell with it, MacKenzie. The fucking hell with you, too. This is serious business, and unlike one of your silly male fantasy books, there isn't necessarily copulation in every other chapter!" Scarborough spun on his heel and stalked from the kitchen.

"Methinks thou dost protest too mucho!" MacKenzie called after him in a leering Mexican accent.

Scarborough banged through the swinging door, muttering to himself. Marsha Manning was sitting in front of her computer, engrossed in her telecommunications. He bent down and began to wipe the coffee spill. That ham-brained lummox! he thought as he blotted up the coffee. Just because *his* temporal lobe occupied his scrotum didn't mean that Scarborough's did. Everett Scarborough enjoyed women very much, but he knew that A: He'd never be in love with anyone in the way he'd loved Phyllis, and B: Dalliances with the weaker sex were strictly for fun, and very low on his list of priorities. The last thing he needed now was a stupid love affair, and besides, he wouldn't touch this starched blue creature even if she were the deciding judge for the Nobel prize for science.

He heard a soft sigh from above him. A gentle feminine sound of satisfaction. He looked up from his work, and found himself staring at the gradual part of her thighs, the soft length of pale curved skin slinking up to shadowy, frilly pink undergarments, a soft mound of mystery breathing a subtle perfume from beneath the crisp skirt.

"Yo!" a deep male bellow came from behind him. "Grub's on, partners!"

The cry startled him so much that he jerked up, striking his head on the bottom of the table. Pain drove through his skull like a spike.

"Oh ho!" said Mac, putting the tray of sandwiches down onto the table. "Caught you peeking up the lady's dress, Scarborough!"

"That's ridiculous!" said Marsha Manning. "How could you say such a thing? Dr. Scarborough was cleaning up the mess that I made on your rug, Captain MacKenzie!"

Scarborough got to his feet, rubbing his head sorrowfully, saying nothing.

Mac just laughed it all off. "Well, whatever. Dig in folks, before the mustard burns the mortadella!"

"Can it wait for a minute," said Marsha with barely suppressed excitement as she returned her attention to the monitor. "I'm onto something here."

"Sure," said Mac picking up half of his sandwich and inserting it into his mouth. "Whatcha got there, sweet stuff?"

Scarborough slumped into a chair and grabbed a cold Watney's Red Barrel from the tray. He contemplated dumping it directly on his scalp, but opted instead on the alimentary path to the source of his pain.

"You did ask me for the Department of Agriculture files, didn't you? Specifically, government-subsidized or -owned land in the state of Iowa?"

Scarborough nodded. "That's correct."

"And you gave me an address in Johnson County. Well, it fits—the government has owned that land since 1953. Now, you also mentioned a certain Charles Higsdon, who worked on the farm from 1966 to 1972—looks like he's bought his own farm in South Dakota. I've got the address here, if you want it. Even the phone number." She beamed at them and took off her glasses. "How's that for fast work, huh?" she said, pointing to the screen.

Scarborough and MacKenzie exchanged surprised looks.

"Wonderful," said Scarborough. "That's very good, Marsh—I mean, Lieutenant Manning." He stepped beside her and looked down at the screen. Sure enough, there was the information, in bright orange letters. "My, you *do* have access, don't you." He'd totally forgotten the pain in his skull.

"You needn't patronize me, Doctor. I have bouts of clumsiness, true, but I'm a competent career officer of the U.S. Air Force!"

Mac took a swallow of his beer and grinned. "So tell me, kiddo. Who's working that farm now?"

She clicked a few buttons and hit the Return control, staring intently at the screen. "I'm afraid there's no information on that, Captain MacKenzie."

"I shouldn't wonder," said Mac, with a self-satisfied smile.

"Wait a minute. Something else is coming up. My goodness, it appears that that area had some significant work done to it in the mid seventies. The nature of the work doesn't show here—but it was contracted by the air force! Here it is—we've got a stated reading of 'Experimental Agricultural Lab' here—present status, moribund." She looked at them both inquiringly. "Well, is that the kind of information you wanted?"

The smile left Mac's face. Scarborough put his beer down onto the table, and began to pull their host back to the kitchen. "Pardon me, Lieutenant. We've got a private discussion to deal with here. In the meantime, could you access the air force construction files for the exact information on what was done in the seventies?"

"Surely," said the woman, who returned to her pecking.

Out of her earshot, Scarborough said, "Well, what do you know. We didn't have to make that trip out to Johnson County after all, and we didn't have to bribe that newspaper for information. We could have just called the air force."

"I don't understand," said Mac, getting another beer from the fridge.

"Well then, let me spell it out for you. Your conspiracy theory goes up in smoke! If the government cared about who knew that that farm was owned by the government, why would they send Manning out to place the info right in our faces?"

"Snafu? Wouldn't be the first time. Maybe they didn't know the information was there."

"Come *on*, Mac. Face up to it! There's no conspiracy! It's

just a trail of *dead* herrings We're reading too much into far too little!"

Mac considered this a moment, swishing a mouthful of beer thoughtfully. "Okay, okay. That's a possibility. But as long as we're here, as long as we've got Manning and her modem, let's get all the information we can. If for no other reason than for you to use the wild goose chase as comic relief for your next book, huh? And anyway, we should call up that Higsdon guy and find out why the hell we got the wrong stuff in our reports."

"Okay, Mac. I'm going to have to hang around in the middle of the country anyway. I should go down and check on Diane. But you've got till next Tuesday, and that's all. Then I'm *gone*!"

"Fair enough," said MacKenzie. "You know, Ev, there's still the matter of those files—and why the *wrong* address was in the Blue Book version."

"Have you ever heard the word *snafu*, Mac—how about *mistake*? History is riddled with them, and God alone knows how much *erroneous* information is on file."

"Well, I should warn you, I'm still not convinced. Manning could be a ruse—maybe they *know* we've got that information, and they're just trying to belittle us by letting *her* dig it up!"

Scarborough shook his head. "I give up, Mac. There's always got to be something for you, doesn't there!"

Mac feigned a "who me?" expression.

"Mac, it's just a—oh, to hell with you. I'm going back to see what else the lieutenant's got on her computer."

"Maybe she's got time for some other kind of interfacing later, eh, Ev? Nudge, nudge. Wink, wink."

Angry again, Scarborough ignored him and went back to speak with Marsha Manning.

CHAPTER
TWENTY-SIX

Timothy Reilly met Jake Camden at the Eight Ball Saloon at nine-thirty, exactly on time. There, the graduate student told the reporter what little he could, while they drank mugs of cold Milwaukee beer.

"They're going to meet here again at Hoover Dam, this week, huh? Makes sense," said Camden, knocking back a shot of Old Grandad and then licking his lips.

"Why's that?"

"Power source. UFOs seem to like to hang around power sources."

"Well, whatever. All I know is that we've got to fly to Nevada. Diane's keen on going." He shook his head. "I wish I could remember. It kind of troubles me that I don't. I mean, between you and me, Diane's got an incredible imagination, and sometimes it gets the better of her."

"You're telling me that you doubt you were on a UFO?"

"Look, I know what I *saw*—but I don't know exactly what happened afterwards, and I'll tell you, Mister, between you and me, I love Diane dearly, but I wouldn't exactly take total stock in what she has to say. I mean, this damn business could have come out of an article she read recently. That's what happens with her. She free-associates, you know what I mean."

Camden nodded, looking stone cold sober. He hit the bar with the flat of his hand. "Damn! And I thought this was for certain. I thought maybe there was some grain of truth." He turned to Reilly, a kind of strange fervor in his eye. "Look, Tim. You've been straight with me, and you've trusted me. I don't know why, but I appreciate it. I gotta tell you, what I want most now, more than money or anything, is to be a good journalist. I want to break an important story. I want some kind of legitimacy!''

Reilly backtracked a bit. "Well, you don't know what will pop up here, do you.''

"Where is Diane, anyway?'' Camden said, declining an offer of another beer from the waitress.

"Tonight's her yoga class. She says she really needs it to relax after all that's happened—and all that's going to happen. But you better leave her be, Jake. If she had her way, you'd be out of this.''

"Even with the alliance with her father...?''

"I guess she just doesn't trust you. You don't exactly inspire trust, I suppose, working for whom you do, acting like you do. Not amongst the educated, anyway.''

"And what about you, Tim m'boy.''

Tim grinned. "Hell, I'm Irish. I can see past the blarney. Camden, you got something that haunts you. And I believe you when you say you're looking for legitimacy. My old man was a stringer for a newspaper in Boston in his early days, and even after he did well in business, the lust for print never left him. He even eventually bought a paper, but that didn't quite satisfy him. He sometimes gets that crazed glint in his eyes that I see in yours.''

Camden nodded and reached into his pocket. He pulled out lint. "Hey, Tim, you got enough blarney in you to stand me for these drinks?''

Tim raised an eyebrow. "I guess so, Jake. But this is going to be the last round. I think I'm going to go dry until I see this whole thing through. You'll be there, won't you—I mean, the dam.''

Camden slapped Reilly's back. "With bells on me toes, Tim. Thanks for the info. This story is going to save my life.'' He knocked back the rest of his beer and winked at his new friend and spoke in a soft whisper. "And just maybe what's left of my soul.''

Tim Reilly tilted his way up the garden apartment stairs, fumbling at his collection of keys for the strip of metal that would unlock his apartment. He felt more than a little light-headed from the alcohol he'd consumed with Camden. Drunk

vas what they called it now, in the dry late-eighties, though it
vas not a state that Reilly was unfamiliar with, so he'd
navigated his way home reasonably well. Maybe just one more
peer, and a hit off the bong as well, and that would be it. He'd
hit the hay and then keep his promise. No more cold ones until
his business was laid to rest.

Tim Reilly was basically a solid sort, who just dreaded the
idea of growing up and taking on responsibility. This was why
he had lingered in college, avoiding the completion of his
Master's Degree like the plague—but he had a very hard time
of it, since his curiosity concerning his studies often got the
best of him, and he had gotten so absorbed and fascinated that
he aced the courses despite his best efforts to stall himself.
Thus, a Master's Degree hovered over his head now, along with
its attendant responsibility. He knew he wouldn't like that—
back to Boston, to take his place in his father's megaheaded
business ventures and face the Big Bad World.

Actually, he thought as the keys jingled against the metal
door of the apartment and he was vaguely aware of the beer
fumes that surrounded him like an olfactory shroud, what he
wanted was to stay near Diane. He never realized how much he
loved her until all this insane business started. Amidst strangeness
and uncertainty, one clung to comforting emotions—and the
one that loomed strong and vital now was his feeling for Diane
Scarborough. Life with her had never been boring, certainly,
with her enthusiasms and constant monologues and self-
dramatizations. But he'd never before known any woman
who'd owned such a heady combination of intelligence, beauty,
sexiness—and such a unique character. Not that Tim Reilly was
short on individuality—he was fiercely individualistic, a fiery
combination of Irish and American qualities. But Diane
Scarborough kept him on his toes. There of course was the
possibility that he had become so obsessed with her that he
even shared her delusions—and that was okay with Timothy
Reilly, just as long as he could share her bed and her life as
well.

The apartment smelled of old marijuana smoke and funky
strains of incense and Hercules's cat box. And something
else . . . A strange uneasiness invaded Tim, rippling along his
spine like a wet feather. He turned on the lights and looked
around. Nothing *seemed* wrong. But then again, the place was

usually such a disheveled jumble of this and that—from Tim's antique train-collection to the piles of playing cards and Tarot cards Diane had brought over, along with the various musical instruments that Tim diddled on, it was difficult to say if anything had been tampered with. Certainly nothing seemed stolen—the 25-inch Mitsubishi color TV draped with a couple of Diane's bras was still sitting on the orange crates which housed part of Tim's record and CD collection. And the stereo was in place, and the computer stocked with papers Tim was working on now. No, he thought, it must be my imagination.

What *wasn't* imaginary, though, was the pressure he felt in his bladder. He went to the toilet to relieve himself.

While he was inside, he thought he heard a door opening and closing—but then, in an apartment house consisting of sixteen units, sound carried, and creaking doors were not unusual.

When he was finished and the apartment reverberated with the sounds of the flushing toilet, he went to the icebox and had a look. One more beer, yes—well, there were a number of varieties available, but as long as there was only *one* he was going to allow himself, it might as well be that invitingly large Foster's. Tim grinned to himself as he pulled the can out, wiped some of the condensation off the metal, and popped the top. "G'day, mate," he said, toasting his choice. "Here's a good movie for you! *Crocodile Dundee meets the Flying Saucers*."

He took a pull of cold brew and instantly felt a lot better about everything. Now all he needed was to stuff and fire up the old bong. Maybe turn on the stereo, strap on some head-phones, and listen to some speed-metal like Motorhead or Metallica. Metal was a private vice, unshared by Diane. Their musical tastes generally dovetailed nicely, from a predilection for baroque to an appreciation for electronic pop. But once in a while, Tim felt the need for some head-banging, some juiced-up hormonal power-chords rumbling through his synapses. Metal did the trick, even though he had to suffer the slings and arrows of Diane's outrageous cracks on the musical form.

So he was looking forward to cranking up the new Voivod CD when he stepped out into the living room, toting his huge beer can. The last thing in the world he expected to see was a man standing by the coffee table, training a gun on him. He was so startled he let the Foster's drop. Beer spurted and spumed onto the floor.

"Don't move," said the man. He was slender, well built with short, businessman's hair and pitted cheeks. He was dressed in a grey silk suit and a tie.

"Who—who the hell are you?" Tim managed to say.

The man stepped forward carefully but confidently. "I got the gun, I ask the questions."

"You don't look like a burglar."

"No, I'm no burglar." He looked down toward the bedroom. "Your girlfriend here, Reilly?"

"I don't know what you're talking about," said Tim. With immediacy and certainty, he knew that his fears had come true. This whole UFO business was leading someplace dark and dangerous, and here was that darkness in flesh and gunmetal.

"Don't fuck with me, bozo," said the man, eyes flashing as he grabbed Tim by the shirt. He drew Tim so close that he could smell the peanut butter on the man's breath. Tim could feel the tensile strength in just the guy's arm, and fear made his bowels feel all liquidy. But he said nothing. "Where's Diane Scarborough?"

Tim swallowed. "Diane. Well, I guess Diane's at her apartment."

"She's not there, shithead, I've just been there. *Where* is she?"

"I'm not her keeper," said Tim. The man brought the gun across Tim's face, and he felt a momentary splash of stars. Throbbing pain poured in with returning consciousness. Something thick and wet dripped down from his nose and mouth. Tim tasted blood. The man kept him upright.

"You wanna live, asshole? You tell me where she *is*!"

"Hey! I don't know, okay?" Blood bubbled from his lips. "Who wants to know?"

The man flung Tim across the room. He fell over the coffee table, hard, onto the floor. The man leaped easily over the table, put a knee into Tim's chest and stuck the automatic into his mouth.

"I'll tell you who wants to know. My fucking *gun* wants to know." The man thrust it further down, so that Tim started to gag. Then he pulled it out, rattling the metal hard over his teeth. "Diane Scarborough. You tell me where she is, asshole," the pockmarked man said, moving the gun-bore down to Tim Reilly's crotch. "Or I'm gonna make sure you don't fuck her or any other woman again!" The gun dug painfully into his groin.

Instinctive terror flooded Tim Reilly, and he almost spouted out the truth, that he knew where Diane was, she was at the Y, doing a long yoga session, and then she was going to go visit a girlfriend for the night and cool out over the day's events. But he bit down on his fear, and called up all his Irish anger and stubbornness. There was something about this man in an expensive suit that was off kilter, that was unhinged. He was a professional, no question, clearly used to interrogation. But there was a fury at the back of his eyes that was Tim's chance to save Diane before he pried the information out of him.

"You want to know about the UFO, don't you?" whispered Tim.

The gun moved away from Tim's jeans and the man turned and stared down. "Yeah."

"I can tell you what you want to know. You don't need Diane," he said in a croaking rasp.

"You can, huh?" the man pulled off his knee and lifted Tim up. "Yeah, I suppose you can, asshole. You were with Diane Scarborough, weren't you?"

Tim nodded, wiping blood from his face. "Yes, that's right. What happened to her, happened to me." As he talked, his right hand reached out in the direction of the base of a stained-glass lamp on the side table.

"You might as well tell me where she is, Reilly. I'll get it out of you one way or the other."

"Okay," he gasped, feigning weakness. "Okay, I'll tell you." He leaned over as though to communicate better. "She's—" Next from his mouth were not words, but a glob of spit and blood that splattered into the man's eyes.

"Wha—" said the man, and Tim quickly grabbed the lamp and flung it against his head. Then he leaped on the man and bore him down on the ground, pummelling his face with blows. The man dropped his gun.

Unfortunately, Tim was still weak from his own beatings and the blows were not as strong as they might be. Within moments, the suited man recovered from his "stunning" and lifted Tim off of him and hurled him hard against the coffee table.

Tim Reilly barely felt the blow on the back of his head as he struck the edge.

A curtain of black fell over him, and it was the end of this particular act.

When the curtain rose again, Timothy Reilly sat in a small room. His consciousness had not been seamless. He dimly recalled nightmarish images of being carried to a car, of banging off tarmac, of the whirl of what could have been helicopter blades, of the sensation of flying, and the fear of falling, falling ... .

Now things seemed steady enough, if quite a bit blurry and smudged about the edges. The taste of blood was still heavy and salty in his mouth, and he ached like he never had before. But he was still alive, something he wasn't entirely sure he'd be after pulling that little stunt with the man in the suit. True, he seemed securely strapped in a chair, but he was still alive, which was something.

He had the impression of a doctor's examination room, and he was able to turn his head far enough to establish the presence of a metal cabinet; a padded examination table, complete with disposable paper-covering; a magnifying lamp; and a rolling tray, its stainless steel instruments peeking up from sterile gauze. There was the smell of disinfectant, too; the scent of needles.

The fear in him now hung like icicles. He had no sense of what the time was, and the place was a total mystery. Still, he knew the longer he kept his mouth shut, the safer Diane Scarborough would be, and that seemed to be his main priority. The extent of his nobility and courage surprised him, but he was far too upset to pat himself on the back.

He was awake and aware only a few minutes before the door opened. The man who had broken into his apartment entered, wearing a bandage over his left eye, and a short-sleeved white shirt. He had a mean little grin on his face, and Tim could tell in this better light that the man was a sadist. Following after him, was a woman in a lab coat, carrying an electronic machine, which she placed on the examination table.

"Hey, asshole," said the man who'd brought him here. "Glad to see you're up and about. Hope you're rested, because you're going to need all the energy you've got."

The woman in the lab coat was frosty and pretty, even though she wore no makeup. She plugged her machine into an electrical outlet, and then started fiddling with the controls. An oscillating wave began whirling; needles twitched.

"Me, I have other methods of digging information out, but the powers-that-be have decided they don't want any scars." The grin grew wider. "On the outside, anyway."

The woman turned and looked at Reilly without expression.

"Mr. Reilly, you have absolutely no control in this matter, so just relax and take what pain you must. You may save yourself a great deal of trouble and concern by answering our questions truthfully. However, there are things that we wish to know which have been screened from your conscious memory, and we must probe for them." She nodded toward the device she had brought in. "This is just one of the machines we will use for the inquest. Others will follow."

The man with the large biceps that stretched his short sleeves leaned over Tim. "Yeah. So tell us where Diane Scarborough is, and save yourself some grief."

After working his jaw a bit to make sure it was still operational, Tim said, "Let me guess who we have here. Either it's the Daughters of the American Revolution or the goon squad of the CIA."

"How do you know its not the KGB or the IRA, or any other group?" asked the short-haired man. "How do you know we're not from another fucking planet?"

Tim tried to smile. "All those other groups don't hire scum of your low caliber, Mr. Sphincter."

The man raised his hand to slap Reilly, but stopped as the woman shot him an icy glare. "Please! You'll knock him unconscious again! We don't want that."

The man reluctantly lowered his hand. "That's okay, fellow," he said in a calm voice. "You'll get yours."

"Mine? What did I do to get you Nazis so upset?"

The woman looked at Tim curiously. "All you had to do was cooperate, Mr. Reilly. To tell us where Diane Scarborough was. Now, I'm afraid we're going to have to attempt to obtain the information from you that we wanted from her. Only I'm afraid that it will be more difficult with you, Monsieur." She sighed and looked back at her machine with a glint of fascination in her eye. "Of course, on the other hand, I shall have the opportunity to utilize some new methodology, some new gadgetry. And since you have already categorized us in 'goon' territory . . . well, we can just dispense with subtleties.'' She turned to the muscle. "Thank you. You can go now.''

The man kissed a fingertip and laid it on Tim's forehead. "Have a good time, Mr. Reilly.''

"Oh my God,'' said Tim, looking at the woman as the man left. "I know what this is about. Look, I'm sorry about that undeclared income last year! You're the IRS, aren't you?''

"Please,'' said the woman, rubbing conductivity solution on the ends of electrodes. "The IRS uses far more barbaric methods that you're about to undergo, Mr. Reilly. But they told me to tell you that you've been given fair warning.''

Timothy Reilly closed his eyes and said a soft prayer under his breath.

The man named Woodrow Justine felt good.

No, he felt *great*, he realized as he made his way from the lab and tech buildings hidden in the South Iowan farm, through the smell of grass and hay and trees under the starry Midwest sky, to the farmhouse that served as headquarters and living station for the technicians of Project White Book's Beta Station. The phantoms of his brain had been summarily booted out by Dr. Cunningham, her machines, and her lovely drugs. His confidence had been returned to him by the sweet pressing of a trigger. And now his enthusiasm had returned, singing with the elation of adrenaline, after a job well done. He felt on edge and alive now, as he entered the office and went to the phone to report in to Central. The clock on the wall said 1:15—it was not too late to call Richards directly.

The Editor-in-Chief listened to his report without comment.

"Good work, Justine. Too bad you couldn't get Diane Scarborough, but actually, this may work out for the best. We're still in a delicate state in regards to her father, but things are getting close to critical there, and we can't take chances. How are you feeling?''

"I'm feeling fine.''

"Good. I want you to get some rest, because you've got to do tomorrow what you were going to do today when this other business sidetracked. And it's even more important, Justine, because I've been doing some homework and if Captain Eric

MacKenzie has got the files he may have, then chances are he's also got the address and location of the very spot where your tight little buns are seated.''

"Damn!"

''Yes, indeed. And if Scarborough and MacKenzie show up there—well, there's no time to evacuate. No, Justine, we're going to have to destroy those files. With maximum prejudice. You've got the address and the map?''

"Yeah."

"You get some rest, eat a good hot breakfast, check yourself out some guns and explosives, and drive down to Iowa City tomorrow morning."

"And what if Scarborough gets in my way?"

There was a pause at the other end of the line.

"Fuck the Publishers," said Richards. "He's getting to be too much of a problem. We can't afford him or MacKenzie finding Beta. If he gets in the way, kill him."

"With pleasure," said Justine.

CHAPTER
TWENTY-SEVEN

The call came at 8:15. Scarborough was already up, looking at the printouts of the information that Manning had gleaned from government computers. Manning had been up since 6:30, and was working with some air force files on her Hewlett-Packard, running up Mac's phone bill. Captain Eric MacKenzie was still rumbling the top floor of the house with his snoring.

The call was from Diane. She was very upset, but she was able to relay the situation. Tim was gone, there was blood on the floor of his apartment. The police were on their way. What should she do?

"Blood? How much?"

"Just a spot—but Dad, the living room was a mess."

"Diane, now calm down. Tim's a bit of a carouser, isn't he? And you say he went out with Camden last night? Well, there you have it. I bet there's spilled alcohol and everything..."

"Just a beer..."

"They had too much to drink, maybe they got into an argument... who knows. But there's no real indication of an actual *kidnapping*!"

"His car... it's in the garage."

"Yes, but think this out logically, Diane. If he was with Camden, they could have used *his* car. Am I right? Look, I've met Tim, and I know what he's like. And I can surmise what Mr. Jake Camden enjoys. They went out, they picked up some women and they went back to Camden's—"

"*Daddy!* Tim loves me. Tim would *never* do such a thing!"

"Tim's a male, Diane. A male who drinks a good bit. You don't know what—"

"Daddy, I *feel* it. He's been taken... I can't describe it to you. And I'm in danger too. My intuition..."

"Okay, okay. Just calm down."

"Daddy, can you come down here?"

"Look, I was planning on coming down tomorrow. There's some stuff that's come up here... I can't get away from it."

"Well, I can't stay here. I've got to talk to you, Dad. Any reason I can't come up there?"

"No... no, in fact. Yes, that would be fine, Diane. You come up... there's room here at Mac's."

"Okay, Dad. I'm coming up. I see the police coming now, and I'll deal with them. I'll get a plane reservation and then call you back. And Dad—you're dead wrong about Tim! You just don't know him, and you shouldn't jump to conclusions!"

"Me! Jump to conc—"

She hung up.

Bemused, he went out to the dining room, dragging his cup of coffee with him. Lieutenant Marsha Manning, looking pert and professional as ever, glanced up from her computer. The dot-matrix printer they'd rigged up for her last night was zapping and jigging letters onto computer paper.

"Yes?" she said.

"Hmmm?"

"You look like someone put something sour into your coffee."

"Oh. Just talked to my daughter. She's coming up here today."

"You don't look terribly excited at the prospect, I must say."

"You're a daughter. Do you be-devil your dear father with nonsense? Do you speed the greying of his hair, teeter his chair further over the chasm, speed his dimming days toward the grave?"

"No. Actually, my father and I see each other on holidays and we get along famously."

"You're a good daughter then. Well, I happen to be gifted with a twenty-year-old as stubborn as I am, who's like night to my day."

"Or day to your night?"

"Hey, who's side are you on?"

"I'm a card-carrying member of Daughters Amalgamated, Incorporated. You fathers can be pretty tough sometimes, you know."

"They say that daughters just want to seduce Daddy. I think mine wants to lobotomize me."

"I take it you share different philosophies."

"Yes, she's a total flake. A proselyte of the New Age. A dingbat of the first water."

"You sound like you're very proud of her."

He sighed and looked at Manning. She had an inquisitive expression on her face, open and curious. He felt strangely trusting of her. "She's a lot like her dead mother." Funny how you come out with private things like that when the person you're talking to is a relative stranger, mused Scarborough.

Marsha was respectfully quiet for a long moment. "I look forward to meeting her. May I come out with you to the airport? I think I'm going to need a break about midday."

Scarborough examined the new pages of print out. "Sure, why not. We'll have lunch. I'll explain the situation on the way out. So, what have we got so far today?"

"Nothing much, I'm afraid. The problem with a lot of the computer files for the air force is that they're just as confusing as the paper kind."

Scarborough picked up the sheaf of paper, and just stared at it for moment, not reading but considering. "Lieutenant— Manning..." he said. "Have you ever met Colonel Dolan?"

Manning did not look up from the monitor.

"No, I can't say that I've had that pleasure, Dr. Scarborough."

Scarborough nodded. "Everett," he said. "Call me Everett . . . or Ev, if you like."

"Only if you call me Marsha . . . Ev."

"How very unprofessional sounding, eh?"

"Sometimes that's the professional thing to do, Ev." she said, and when he looked at her, she was smiling a secret smile into the monitor.

Captain Eric MacKenzie stared glumly into his computer monitor, examining the last part of chapter ten of *The Immolator Number 121: Contra Flareup*. Ten chapters was all that New York writer had turned in at deadline time, and now it fell to MacKenzie to finish the sucker in less than two weeks' time, so that 100,000 hungry readers in 7-Elevens everywhere could get their slurpee-stained paws on this latest lava-and-gunlust epic! Wasn't it just his luck to have the thing fall into his lap, when things were finally starting to get exciting with this UFO investigation?

"Goddamn you, Lou," MacKenzie muttered beneath his breath. He picked up his Tabasco-sauced Bloody Mary—his "hacking fuel"—and swallowed a gulp. Well, less than a hundred pages to go. Even if there were a few more field trips in the next few days, if he pounded out twenty pages today while Manning and Scarborough pored over those computer files, he'd be able to squeeze out a few pages everyday for ten days, and then lock himself up with a couple bottles of Popov, some limes, and lots of Snappy Tom mixer, and bash out the rest in a couple of days. By this point, he could write Immolator books in his sleep—but he found that he was farming more and more out to other professional writers who needed extra money and were willing to put aside a few weekends from their regular work to grind out some tasty and manly violence. It was a damn shame about Lou Hilton—Lou was a good writer, and the Immolator books that he did burned with the snap and authority of the Old Pyre-lighter himself. But Lou just wasn't a very fast writer.

MacKenzie sipped at his drink, enjoying the bite of alcohol after the kick of hot peppers, and then commenced to tap at the keyboard and get his hero out of the Nicaraguan jungle. It was a sad and moving scene—to survive the long trek, Harry Diggs had to abandon one of his prized weapons, a Peacemaker Colt. MacKenzie smiled to himself as he described the touching, manly scene of a man abandoning a gun. Yep, there wouldn't be a dry eye in the house.

MacKenzie paused for a moment, and took another drink. He was near the end of the chapter, and he wanted to power his way through at least a page or two of the next one before he stopped for some lunch. The thing he'd learned pretty quick about writing day after day was that you had to prime the pump for the next foray into prose consciousness. A cold start on a chapter or even a scene was the hardest thing. MacKenzie had learned to write books like a chain-smoker smokes—light one from the fire of another, don't get outta that fuckin' chair till you've got the next one cookin.' It was a variation on Hemingway's rule to leave a little water in the well to start the next day's draw, and it helped keep that darkest dread away from MacKenzie's door: writer's block.

MacKenzie drank the last swallow of his Bloody Mary and grinned at the monitor. Yep, he may be the despair of Alcoholics Anonymous, but he'd copped their motto and bent it to suit his needs. "One day at a time" became "One *word* at a time."

Harry Diggs was nearing the end of a chapter, hacking away at a boa constrictor with a dull Swiss army knife, when MacKenzie heard the sounds from below. They weren't huge sounds, but his ears were good, and he recognized the sounds of the back door opening, and closing. Funny, because Scarborough and Lieutenant Breasts had gone to the airport just before he'd sat down at the word processor, and weren't due back for another hour yet. Maybe something had gone wrong.

MacKenzie hit a function key—F10, since it was the Word Perfect program he used—and saved the new paragraphs. He got off-line and went downstairs for a look-see. Everything looked fine downstairs. He checked the back door. Locked. He looked out into the driveway. Manning's rental car was still gone.

Must have been his imagination, he decided. Still, as long as he was down here, maybe he should get another drink . . . He nixed the idea immediately. A little vokda or beer singing through the brain greased the wheels of his writing machine; too much jammed them. The day he was too drunk or too hungover to sit down at his IBM and *write* was the day he quit drinking. And since he had no desire to quit drinking, he exercised iron control on the stuff. Instead, he poured himself some coffee and went back up the stairs to finish off that monster snake.

When MacKenzie stepped back into his office, he immediately saw a man, sitting in his typing chair. The man wore a silk suit, and his hair was cropped short. There was a Band-Aid on his brow, and a sprinkling of acne scars colored a livid red against the man's fading tan. But the most distinguishing characteristic was the H-K Automatic that the man held in his hand. The H-K was probably the finest modern handgun that money could buy. Efficient, accurate, reliable, and very, very deadly in a skilled marksman's hands. After his initial shock passed, MacKenzie looked up into the man's eyes, and he saw something even more chilling than a skilled marksman with a superior weapon.

He saw a professional killer, who enjoyed his work.

"Good afternoon. You must be Captain Eric MacKenzie," said the man, flexing his shoulders a bit beneath the silk. MacKenzie could see taut, well-hewn muscles flow—this guy worked out.

"What the hell are you doing in my house! You want me to call the police, or should I kick your butt out myself?" MacKenzie yelled, his outrage at the trespass overwhelming his sense of danger.

"I've just been reading your little masterpiece here," said the man, tapping the computer. "Fun. Oh, I added one little line that I really dig: 'The snake strangled the Immolator to death and swallowed him whole.' You like that, MacKenzie? I do."

MacKenzie started toward him, and the man waggled his gun in warning. "Hey, dude! Are you blind? I can connect your belly button with your spine with this little gun here! And don't you think I can't—or won't—shoot."

"Fuck me . . . You're with the goddamn government, aren't you? CIA, I bet. Those assholes. I was right. We *are* onto something here. That farmhouse business . . . it did tug some bigwig's nuts, didn't it?"

"Look, I'm not here to explain anything, Mr. Author. I'm here to do a job, and if you care to help me out, maybe the snake won't swallow *you*." The man eased out of his chair. "The files, MacKenzie. The Blue Book files you so stupidly kept. Where are they?"

Yes, that was it, then. The files. They'd triggered a nerve deep in the Great Monster, and its reflexes were much faster than MacKenzie had expected.

"So, there must be more correct information, more problem-addresses in my notes, huh?" MacKenzie casually stepped forward a few paces.

"None of your business, man. So tell me, where are the files?"

"Those old cabinets over there, fella. They're in the second one from the left. Say, why don't you just take lunch now and I'll parcel-post them to you, huh?"

The man looked over toward the cabinets MacKenzie had indicated and the author knew that he was going to lose his chance at his big story if he didn't do something quick. Frustration overcame common sense, and he tossed the hot black coffee directly into the man's face.

The man screamed, and fired his gun, but MacKenzie was already dodging, ducking down and then firing his girth directly into the man's midsection. The force of the blow knocked the man back hard against the computer table, and his wrist hit the top of the IBM, knocking the gun out of his grasp and onto the rug.

MacKenzie was able to get one good roundhouse against the trespasser's face, before the man's superior training took over. He shot out a leg, and pushed MacKenzie; the bigger man tripped and fell. But not before grabbing two handfuls of silk jacket, pulling the man down with him.

Over and over they rolled, and when they stopped, they traded hard, stunning blows to one another's face and midsections. For a moment, MacKenzie was on top and had his meaty fists around the man's neck. As MacKenzie squeezed, he thought he had the man—but then rock-hard sinews snapped into action, and MacKenzie was heaved over and flattened on his back, like some wrestler slapping the mat. The man did not stop to fight more, he scrambled for the rug and his gun.

MacKenzie caught the man's foot and desperately held on. But the man kicked him in the face, sprang over, scooped up the gun, and trained it on his opponent.

Painfully, MacKenzie got to his feet, holding his hands up in surrender. "Yo! Great fight, pal. You're the winner and champeen." He coughed, exhausted. "Couldn't let you go without at least a little tussle, huh?"

The man's pockmark scars glowed a livid red as he stood up.

"Fuck you, author!" He turned and fired a slug into the IBM, and another into the hard disk.

It was worse than any blow. "Shit! I got a novel in there! I didn't have any backups!"

Sparks snapped and sputtered from the computer. The man spun on MacKenzie, his silk jacket belling with the action.

"Yeah, Mr. Author. Well, let me just deal with your troublesome software too, then."

He fired a round into MacKenzie's midsection.

The shock kicked MacKenzie back a yard and a half. He felt as though someone had split him in half with an axe. He went down hard onto the floor, with a splatter of blood; blackness came oozing down on his mind like dead, cold rain.

When he came to, he realized he was spitting up blood. He took a deep ragged cough, and everything rushed back. There was the sound of falling papers and clanking drawers. MacKenzie craned his neck painfully around and saw the man in the silk suit dumping the files from the cabinets—*all* the cabinets—into one large pile in the center of the floor.

"No," croaked MacKenzie. "Stop!"

He tried to crawl forward, but the pain instantly severed his action.

"Oh, you're still alive, huh?" said the man, dumping one last handful of paper into the huge pile. "Just as well. You get to watch a little pyromania in action." The man looked around, and spotted the large lighter on the coffee table. He picked it up, twisted off the flint and wick head, and dumped the lighting fluid over the papers. "A little foretaste of hell, you asshole!"

The man took out a book of matches. He lit one, then flared the other match heads with the small flame. The light washed a diabolical glow across the man's tight little grin as he held the flames above the mound of paper.

"My mother always told me never to play with matches, Captain MacKenzie. And as you can see, she was quite right."

With a laugh, he tossed the flames down onto the drenched pile of paper. With a whoomph, the fluid ignited, coughing up a gasp of heat and conflagration.

MacKenzie watched the pyre grow with horror, forgetting his pain.

The man stepped from behind the bonfire he'd created.

"There we go! That should take care of the files. And now to take care of you!"

He aimed his gun, and MacKenzie thought, *Jesus Christ. I should have had that Bloody Mary after all.*

The man in the suit squeezed off a bullet squarely into MacKenzie's big chest.

The last sound Captain Eric MacKenzie heard before he again dipped into unconsciousness was the second-floor's First Alert fire alarm screaming to life.

CHAPTER TWENTY-EIGHT

When she came in on the 11:54 Braniff flight to Iowa City, Diane Scarborough found her father waiting for her along with a woman dressed in air force blues, whom Dr. Scarborough introduced as a Lieutenant Marsha Manning. Diane, not merely unafraid of intuition but wholeheartedly accepting her own, liked the woman immediately and sensed a kind of romantic friction between her father and the officer. But she was far too immersed in her own troubles to take much note of either of them.

"Dad, we've *got* to talk," she said.

"Well, we'll have lunch and you can say what you want Diane. You can trust Lieutenant Manning. She's shown me that I can trust her." He smiled at the woman. "Within certain limits."

The air force officer nodded curtly. "I'm overwhelmed."

Scarborough took them to a nice roadside tavern, dark, with a nice electric fire in a pseudo early American hearth to match the pseudo early American interior decor. They ate thick hamburgers, which could have been cardboard as far as Diane was concerned. She took two bites, and nibbled at the cole slaw and french fries that came with the meal while she talked.

For Lieutenant Manning's benefit, she explained what she had experienced over a week before. Scarborough had explained the situation to Manning already, and the woman appreciated the problems that Scarborough had with it—but she wanted to hear Diane's version anyway. Diane then described their visit with the psychologist, and the results of the hypnosis sessions, all of which was news to Scarborough.

"Hoover Dam?" he said, his voice tense with total disbelief. "Why the hell do they want to meet you at Hoover Dam!" He shot an upset glance at Manning. "Not that I think 'they' are more than some faulty neurochemical spark in Diane's hippocampus."

"Dad, I don't know. I don't know anything. I just know that that's what I remember." Her face was drawn and her color was pale. "So will you just listen and stop interrupting?"

"You really aren't being fair, Ev," said Marsha.

Scarborough shot her a scathing glance, but quieted. She was right. And he respected the way Manning was able to stand up to him despite himself. He just grunted and chewed on his hamburger.

Diane said, "You were right about the police, Dad. There's no real proof that Tim was kidnapped. They say to give it a day, and then call if he hasn't showed up. I'm telling you, though, I *know* that Tim was abducted . . . and not necessarily by aliens. I just feel it in my heart."

"You see my dilemma," said Scarborough. " 'Abducted by aliens'—it's like a line from a comic book or something. Not real life."

But Manning paid no attention. "Intuition isn't always right. As your father points out, Tim Reilly is a young man, and young men do go on escapades."

"No, not Tim! Dad thinks he's just some drunken Irishman, but he's wrong. Tim's a smart man. He may not exactly have the most solid reputation yet—but he's destined for a real solid career of helping people. Dad, Tim has done a lot of fine things that you don't even know about. He's a good, honest, worthwhile person!"

Scarborough sighed. "Okay. Assuming all this—what can I do about it?"

"I thought you could answer some questions, maybe. I don't know . . . that's why I needed to talk to you. Assuming that the aliens didn't take Tim . . ."

"Easy assumption!" said Scarborough.

"And assuming that he's not on a bender or whatever— which I *know* he's not . . . Then there's no real reason anyone would want him! That *I* know of, anyway. But I was thinking on the plane . . . our experience with this UFO *was* unique. There might be people who want to know more about it . . . or people who don't want us to spread the story."

"That doesn't pan out," said Scarborough. "Why would they take Tim? *You're* the one who claims to remember meeting the saucer people." The last two words almost stuck in his throat.

"No, wait a minute," said Marsha. "Diane, where were you before you went to stay with your girlfriend?"

"A really long yoga class."

"Did you stop by your apartment at all?"

"Just for a few minutes in the afternoon."

Manning tapped Scarborough on the shoulder. "Could be that they wanted Diane and couldn't get her. So they settled on Tim."

"Tim knew where I was!"

"Maybe he wouldn't tell them."

"But if they could kidnap him . . . they'd be ruthless enough to torture. And . . . oh my God."

"Ladies, ladies!" said Scarborough, arms lifting in supplication. "Please, this isn't some cheap spy movie! This is real life! Diane, why would anyone want you because of a UFO experience you had? There's absolutely nothing like it in the annals of UFO investigation! My God, even the fabled Men in Black just make empty threats!"

"It's logical, Dad! It makes sense!"

"Down to a point. And that point rests on damn shaky ground. Look, Diane. You stay with us the evening. We'll go back down to Kansas together tomorrow. If Tim hasn't shown up, we'll notify the FBI. We'll get his apartment dusted for fingerprints, we'll do everything forensically and humanly possible to find him. And no matter what happens, I will personally look into your UFO experience."

Diane seemed satisfied enough, so they left it at that.

* * *

They heard the fire sirens miles away.

As they got closer, they saw the smoke rising in a tilting black column from past the trees.

When the rented Chevy Cavalier pulled off the highway onto the road to the house, there could be no doubt—Eric MacKenzie's house was on fire.

Two bright red old fire trucks from the local volunteer fire department stood by the burning house. Firemen in steel helmets and thick coats were pumping streams and gusts of water onto a smouldering roof, where flames chewed at blackened shingles. The acrid stench of burnt wood hung in the air as a stunned Everett Scarborough jumped from the car and started toward a knot of gathered men, supervising the firefighting. Let him be there, thought Scarborough. Let Mac be okay.

But he could see no red-haired man amongst the group.

"Stay here," he told the women.

Halfway there, though, he heard a faint voice calling his name. "Scarborough! Ev! Over here . . . behind the tree."

Some thirty yards from the side of the house, far from where the firemen doused the flames, there grew an old oak, blooming now with a wealth of spring leaves. In the shade, by the thick bole, Scarborough could see a form sitting, with his back against bark.

Closer, he recognized the red hair. "Mac! What the hell are you doing here! What happened to the house! I—" And then he saw the blood. "Jesus, Mac!" He stared down at the man, whose entire front was matted with dark red.

Captain Eric MacKenzie was staring off as though watching the water spouts draping over his burning home, but then Scarborough could see the faint glazing of those eyes. His left hand was hooked around a bottle of Glenlivet Scotch.

"Mac, I'll get help!"

"Have to—talk—to you," the words were halting and filled with pain. "Can't—last—"

"Uncle Mac!" The horrified words came from behind him. Scarborough turned and saw his daughter behind him, staring at the man by the tree with horror and disbelief.

"Get those men over there to call an ambulance!" Scarborough ordered coolly. Diane scurried off to obey the order and Scarborough kneeled by his friend. This close, he could see the ragged entry paths of the bullets in Mac's abdomen and chest. Rivulets of whiskey-diluted blood streamed from MacKenzie's nose and mouth. Half-opened eyes turned to Scarborough.

"The files. Came to destroy—files," Mac whispered.

"What . . . your Blue Book files?" Scarborough said in disbelief.

A nod. "Acne scars—short blond hair. Fucking pro—" A cough spewed up more blood. "One of ours—CIA, I think."

"No, no it couldn't be."

The eyes opened wide, anger filling them. "Wake up, Doctor!" The eyes looked away. "Shit. Sorry—Ev. Can't lift damn . . . bottle." The eyes gazed down longingly at the bottle of Scotch. Scarborough took the bottle and carefully tilted it into the dying man's mouth so that he could get just a sip. Mac took the sip, then asked for more. He took a gulp, coughed, and sighed.

"You're going to be okay, Mac. Just hang on!"

"Get—real," said Mac. "Fucking miracle—I need—here."

Scarborough looked back and saw Diane with the group of men, pointing. Two of the men ran for the truck, while another hurried back toward the oak with Diane.

"We're getting you an ambulance. A doctor, Mac."

"Ev, I have to—to tell you. Watch . . . your ass. I didn't— know what big . . . artillery we . . . were sticking our—heads into . . ."

"Yes, Mac, yes. Now quiet. Save—"

"Ev—something else." Mac's right arm moved, trying to pick up something. Scarborough saw that it was a pile of bloodied paper. A tattered manuscript. He reached over and took it, seeing immediately the familiar title page. *Until the Dawn*, it said. By Eric L. MacKenzie. On the title page were scrawled in letters of blood the words: PRO. BLUE BOOK FILES. POCKMARKS. A last message—just in case.

He must have dragged the manuscript all the way out of the burning house, from his office. Scarborough was overwhelmed.

"Only copy . . . now," said Mac, looking at Scarborough with fading eyes. "Almost . . . finished. I was gonna—dedicate it to you, pal."

Diane and the fireman arrived, along with Lieutenant Marsha Manning, who hung back respectfully. The fireman was hardly into his twenties, with freckles and long brown hair. He looked down at Eric MacKenzie and he said. "My God—this man's been *shot*!"

"No shit, Sherlock" gasped Mac.

"We've got a first-aid kit coming," said Diane.

"Don't forget the Band-Aids," said Mac.

Scarborough put his hand lightly on MacKenzie's shoulder. "You've made it this far. Hang on!"

"The book—Ev. It's good."

"Of course it's good, Mac. You wrote it."

"No—I mean it . . . It's really good."

His head lolled onto his chest.

Five minutes before the ambulance arrived, Captain Eric MacKenzie, USAF, Ret., died with the taste of good whiskey in his mouth. As he watched the ambulance men wheel the body into the back of their long vehicle, Everett Scarborough sipped absently at the bottle that was flavored lightly with the blood of his friend, feeling his world falling apart.

CHAPTER TWENTY-NINE

Diane and Everett Scarborough stayed that evening at Lieutenant Marsha Manning's motel, a Holiday Inn with all the generic trimmings. It took all afternoon for Scarborough to deal with the ruined house, the police, and make arrangements for MacKenzie's body. With the help of his friends and associates at Iowa University, a simple funeral was arranged. Mac could have been buried in Arlington Cemetery, but Scarborough nixed that. He arranged for an Iowa grave, close to the fields and forests Mac loved to prowl . . . besides, in light of the situation, Scarborough felt quite ambivalent, at the very least, about the U. S. government. If it *had* been a CIA agent who'd killed Eric

MacKenzie, he doubted that Mac would have wanted his bones planted down the river from their headquarters.

They took a late, somber and sober dinner, where Scarborough tersely instructed his daughter to fly back to Kansas the next day. If Tim Reilly had not returned, she was to report the disappearance to the police, and then contact the FBI concerning the possibility of kidnapping. She would do this, and then *not* return to her apartment, but rather go to a hotel, asking for police-supervised protection.

As for Scarborough and Manning, they would fly back to Washington, D.C. tomorrow for a pre-arranged meeting with Colonel Walter Dolan. Dolan had been horrified with the news about Mac, when Scarborough had called—he immediately agreed to the meeting, though it was doubtful that he knew what was in store for him.

Scarborough then would fly to Kansas, ask the police where Diane was staying, and stay there as well. The next day, they would fly to Arizona, where he would personally escort her to the Hoover Dam for the supposed meeting with the alleged extraterrestrials.

That was the plan, and Diane agreed to it.

None of them had any idea how wrong these plans would go.

There was a knock on the door of Scarborough's motel room.

Scarborough stood up from the desk where he sat, filling out the necessary forms for Mac's arrangements. Ted Allbury, an associate professor at Iowa State, had agreed to deal with the rest of the business while Scarborough was away, and notify friends. What little family Mac had were not in Iowa. Mac's address book had burned in the fire and it would be difficult to notify them, but Allbury claimed he would try.

Marsha Manning stood at the door. She wore jeans, a dark blouse, and Reebook shoes instead of her normal severely creased Air Force blues. Her hair was unpinned, and fell naturally around her makeup-softened face.

"Hi," she said. "I thought you might need some company."

Scarborough nodded and stepped aside to let her in. Marsha had a paper bag in one hand, and she lifted a bottle of Kentucky whiskey from within, putting it onto the table. "I thought you might like a drink too."

"No thanks. We have to get up early tomorrow. Besides, I'm not in the mood."

"Mind if I help myself then?"

Scarborough shrugged. "Ice and glasses over there. Disposable plastic glasses—makes whiskey taste terrible."

"I drink it so seldom, I wouldn't notice," she said, scooping out the ice. She poured a little whiskey in, sipped, made a face. "I think I need some water."

"I've got a couple cans of Coke here."

"That would be wonderful." She popped the top, and it sprayed over her blouse.

Scarborough chuckled softly. "Must have dropped one."

"No, it's just my karma." She poured the fizzy stuff into the glass. "You know, I haven't had a major car accident and, I've never had stitches or broken bones. I figure all the little things kind of release the accident pressure. So what if I'm a klutz. I survive."

He sat down on the bed, and leaned back onto the pillow. "Thanks for coming. It's all just starting to sink in."

"You and Captain MacKenzie seemed very close."

"We were good friends, yes."

"Who would have done such a thing to him?"

"Someone who didn't want us to know something."

"You mean about the old UFO cases? I'm sorry, but I find that difficult to believe."

"Yes, I can't blame you. But Mac is dead, and he told me, before he died, that his killer burned his Blue Book files. So what am I supposed to think?"

"Colonel Dolan'll be able to help us. He'll get to the bottom of this."

"He'll need some explanations for me, or I'm going to go to higher authorities than Dolan, I promise you that."

"I'm glad I'm going. I'll do what I can to corroborate your story." She sat on the bed by him, the ice cubes rattling in her cup. This close, he could smell the gentle ambience of perfume and her natural scents.

"Thanks," he said feeling himself relax and soften at her closeness. "I'm going to need all the help I can get."

She took a sip of her drink, and then got a curious expression on her face. "Something puzzles me though. I mean, here I am, an employee of the Air Force—sent by an official of the government that Captain MacKenzie was so wary of. And you're not suspicious of me?''

"No."

"Why not?"

"You had opportunities to go through Mac's files. All you had to do was to take the offending ones out, steal them, or destroy them—without our even knowing about it. You didn't even ask where they were. No, the only reason why I trust Dolan at all now, is that he sent you to me—and you have proved to be a help. That business with the government owning the Higsdon farm—we knew that. Camden uncovered that news for us at the local newspaper. If you worked for the people covering that information up, you wouldn't dig it up for us, now, would you?''

She sipped at her drink thoughtfully, then put the cup down at the nightstand. "I'm not arguing, Ev. You don't have to persuade me I'm not some Mata Hari."

"Rhetorical phrasing, Marsha." He lapsed into silence, staring off at the cheap beige polyester drapes above the temperature control unit.

"You don't really think MacKenzie was right, do you? You don't seem the paranoid type who subscribes to conspiracy theories."

"I'm not. And what I want from Dolan is proof, an explanation, or whatever he has to offer me. I'll weigh it, consider it, do some of my own probing and research, and make a judgment. That's the kind of man I am."

"What if he was right? What will you do then?"

"I'll cross that bridge if I come to it. I doubt I'll have to. Mac assumed that he had information some people didn't want him to have. There's no proof that the people who sent that killer were associated with the U.S. government or *any* government. There's no proof that what they were after has anything to do with UFOs—the UFO factor could be a coincidence."

She picked her drink back up. "That's true. I personally don't see any conspiracy here. But aren't you bending things a little? Seems to me, you're twisting things to avoid even the *thought* that you might be wrong." Pause. "I sense this obsession with UFOs—well, it's almost a personal thing with you. You campaign with the fervor of a former smoker, or a recovered alcoholic."

"Nonsense!" He said fervently. "I'm a scientist! I seek the truth! If there's any emotion involved, its anger at the effrontery of the pseudoscience involved with the so-called saucer invasion."

"Whoa, fella! I came to comfort, not combat! Like, I thought maybe you could use a hanky or a back rub, not a sparring partner!" She got up.

"Wait. Sorry. I'm guess I'm little tense—I shouldn't have snapped at you. Maybe a back rub would be nice."

"Roll over," she instructed.

He obliged. He felt her sit and begin to slowly massage his back. After just a few moments, it was clear that the woman had "the touch"—that sense of just the right pressure to exert with the fingernails on skin to engage nerve response. Some women didn't have it at all—it seemed more an instinctive talent than anything learned. Coupled with the right pheromonal presence, the right visual presentation, the right personality behind the fingers, and "the touch" transformed from the merely pleasurable to the erotic. After a couple of minutes of Marsha's ministrations, Scarborough found himself thoroughly aroused; he was aware of his heart beating faster, of all his senses coming alive. Her musk and her presence were almost like an electro-chemical mix hanging in the air between them.

"Do you want me?" she whispered huskily.

Yes, actually he did. Very much. Physically, sexually . . . what have you. Yes was the word on his lips, but a deep-down knot of tension brought him up short, making him think. And the more he considered it, the worse the idea got. For *lots* of reasons.

"That's a fairly loaded question, Marsha." He turned over and looked at her warmly.

She leaned over and kissed him. He could not help but respond for a moment—her warmth was so relaxing, so arousing. But he pushed her gently away.

"Is something wrong?"

He tapped his head. "Yes. I'm thinking. I do that a lot, you know."

"Too much, Dr. Scarborough. Entirely too much. Don't think that I proposition guys every day. It just seemed . . . appropriate."

He shook his head, smiling. "Some serious sensual pleasure.

A nice little romp in the sack to take our minds off what happened today . . . And in turn you'll feel like a good little Girl Scout, turning a sad camper into a happy camper.''

She stiffened, moved away from him. "Maybe."

He grasped her by the arm, pulled her back. "Marsha, don't get in a huff. Yes, I want you, dammit! You're just about the sexiest thing I can imagine at this moment."

She looked down, moping a little. "I am?"

"Oh, yes. No lie. But Marsha . . . I've fouled up *far* too many relationships by having sex too soon. Especially amongst women with whom, more than anything, I want to be *friends*. I don't have too many woman friends, Marsha. I think . . . I think maybe I want one."

She smiled slightly. "Namely me."

"Nobody else in this room."

She nodded. "Yeah . . . that's happened to me too, Doc. I guess sex can gum things up a bit."

"I *know* it would be great with you, Marsha. I honestly do. But I want you in a different way. I want you to be close to me, where it *really* counts for now."

She turned away from him and laughed. "God! This is maddening. This just makes me want you more."

"Bear with me, Marsha. I'm kind of unglued inside. I need you—but I need to know I have a friend more."

"Oh, no. Don't apologize." When she turned back to him, Scarborough saw that a pair of tears were creeping down her cheeks. "I think it's wonderful. Yes, I'll be your friend, Everett."

"Thank you, Marsha. Well, maybe we'd both better get some sleep."

She smiled softly at him, looking at him as though she'd never properly seen him before. "This means I can still insult you, right?"

"Only if you do it with your usual odd wit, Marsha."

"I'll do my best. One more condition of friendship, Ev. We get to hug each other once in awhile. Like when we both need it." She reached over to him. "Like *now*."

"Hugs? I don't know if I'm very good at *hugs*."

"It's just like whistling, silly man." She moved to him and put her arms around him and held him tight. "Only you don't put your lips together, and you don't blow."

Feeling a little awkward, he put his arms around her as well. "How's this?"

"Not bad, Doctor. But we'll just have to practice to perfection." She leaned her head against his chest. "My new buddy."

He sighed and surrendered himself to what he could accept from her. "Pal."

CHAPTER
THIRTY

"Everett, Everett," said Colonel Walter Dolan, immediately responding to the buzz of his corporal-secretary. "Come in, come in! You too, Lieutenant Manning." A liver-spotted hand patted Scarborough's back solicitously. "I'm so sorry to hear about the death of Captain MacKenzie. I'm shocked and saddened. He was a vibrant and worthy man, and I know what good friends you were."

They went into the office, with its prosaic view of Shirley Highway, the Northern Virginia suburbs, and the huge Pentagon parking lot. The colonel closed the door behind them.

Scarborough and Manning sat down in straight-backed chairs, and Dolan settled attentively at his desk. Scarborough related the events which had occurred the previous day as best he could, without commentary, and watched the colonel's reactions carefully. When he described the assassin, and what happened, he thought he noticed an almost imperceptible lifting of eyebrows, an exhalation of breath—but it could have been his imagination. He wanted to give the officer the benefit of every doubt, before coming down hard on him.

It was three o'clock in the afternoon. Scarborough and Manning had arrived early at National Airport, and he'd taken her to a favorite Georgetown Restaurant, Clyde's, for lunch. Then they'd strolled amongst record and book shops, peeking in at art galleries along the way. The previous night had left an afterglow that lingered through the splendid spring day; but the moment the monolithic Pentagon appeared through the taxi windshield, the bubble burst. Mac's blood shone bright in Scarborough's mind—his purpose here overwhelmed every other thought.

Now, as he sat in Dolan's office, relating the last details to the colonel, he could feel the anger and frustration and grief surging back up, like bile, bitter in his throat.

"There will be a full investigation," Dolan promised. "I promise. We've already scheduled an air force military-police official to work with the local authorities. For whatever reason that Captain MacKenzie was killed, we'll bring the culprit to justice." Dolan pounded on the desk with a too-studied conviction.

"Whatever reason! I *told* you—the guy wasn't there to kill Mac . . . Mac just happened to be in his way. The killer wanted to destroy Mac's files. His files for Blue Book. That's why there was the fire, Colonel Dolan. He *burned* them—and almost everything else. I didn't tell you this on the phone, Walter—but Mac pegged him for a CIA man. Enforcement division."

The colonel turned to Lieutenant Manning. "Did you hear this from Captain MacKenzie as well, Lieutenant?"

"No, sir. He only told Dr. Scarborough."

"Hmm. Well, we'll make a report of this to the appropriate authorities," said the officer glibly.

"You don't seem to understand, Dolan." Scarborough leaned forward emphatically. "Something is going on here! Mac thought it was government suppression, a cover-up, and he lost his life. So that's why I'm here. I want *answers*. You were the man who knew what kind of information MacKenzie had . . . knew because I showed it to you. Now, I've worked with you for a long time, Walter, and I'm loathe to think that you're mixed up in any way with this sordid business. So you tell me—did anyone else, besides Lieutenant Manning, know what Mac and I were up to . . . namely, investigating irregularities in the Blue Book reports, checking into the disparities?"

"Now let me get this straight, Ev. You're saying that someone in the military, or perhaps in the government, purposely altered Blue Book, and is now *killing* people to keep certain facts suppressed. That's a pretty wild accusation, my boy!"

"Who else knew what we were doing, Dolan!"

"I made a report of it—God, a dozen officials and administrators here, I guess."

"Can you ask your secretary to give me a list of names, then?"

"No. I did the informational transference myself," said Dolan.

"Your—I'm sorry, Colonel. I find it hard to believe that you'd Xerox and address the interdepartmental mail on your own. That's just not your style. You're holding back on me, Walter. What's going on?"

"I'll make a fully study of it," said the colonel, sitting up straight and acting officious. "In the meantime, because of the clear danger involved, I am going to cease your official involvement in the case, Ev. We'll of course call upon you to consult on the matter, and you will be paid your usual fees for such . . ."

"What the hell!"

"Lieutenant Manning, I shall expect a full report from you next Monday morning. You may use local Air Force facilities and accommodations in the meantime. After that, you will be relieved of your duties in this matter. You may return to your previous post."

Lieutenant Marsha Manning looked stunned. She did not respond, just looked to Scarborough.

The scientist stood up and leaned on the desk, glaring at the colonel. "I wanted to give you the chance to explain, Dolan. It looks to me as though you've explained quite a bit! I'll just have to take this to a higher court. Won't your superiors be interested in knowing that you've played a part—big or small, I don't know—in defrauding not only the public, but the law! I smell a court-martial here, Colonel, and I'm going to enjoy it!"

Dolan stood as well, veins standing out at his neck, wagging a thick forefinger at Scarborough. "I'll not be talked to in that manner, man! I'm a full colonel with forty-five years service to my country!" He stopped and flapped his jaw a moment, seemingly unable to speak. "Are you calling me a traitor?"

"I don't know what you are, Colonel. But you're not telling

the truth. And I'm beginning to get the feeling that this has
been the situation for a long time between you and me."

"Ev! How could you say such a thing?" But the laconic,
good-ol'-boy-Chuck-Yeager phrasing was leached from the colonel's words.

"Quite simple, Walter. I open my mouth and enunciate the
truth! So, are you going to tell me what the hell is going on? Or
do I march out of here and pound on the appropriate door?"

A look of pure fear suddenly invaded Colonel Dolan's eyes.
"Scarborough," he barely whispered. "Just leave it alone.
We're both out of our depth here." He looked away, growing
pale, as though he were about to vomit.

"You set us up, you bastard!" shouted Scarborough, a dark
film growing in his vision as the anger began to grow more
fiercely inside of him. He leaped around the desk, and hovered
over the colonel threateningly. "How long has this been going
on, Dolan! Since 1965 when I was hired?" The implications
were so astounding, that Scarborough didn't dare to consider
them. He let himself go in his fury, if only to keep himself
whole. He grabbed two fistfuls of military cloth and shook the
colonel.

"Ev!" said Lieutenant Manning. "Stop it!"

The violence seemed to rally Dolan, shaking him out of
whatever funk he'd fallen into. His eyes came alive again,
aware and awake. "Get your hands off me! What are you
talking about? You're making absurd allegations, Scarborough!"

"You can't get off the hook this time, bastard." Scarborough
lifted the older man from his chair forcibly and slapped him
hard across the face. "You're responsible for Mac's death,
aren't you—directly or indirectly—you're responsible!"

Dolan reached out for his intercom. "Help! Corporal. Get
me help!"

Scarborough could only see the dying face of his best friend
before him. He pulled the colonel away from the intercom and
hurled him across the room. Dolan staggered, struck a table,
with a potted azalea, and fell onto the floor. The plant teetered
on the edge of the table a moment, and then fell, cracking on
the floor and splattering Dolan with dirt.

"Degenerate!" cried Scarborough. He put a knee against the
colonel's chest and pinned him to the floor. "*You* had him
killed, didn't you? And if *I* had been there, I would have been

killed." Scarborough punched the man hard in his soft, round gut.

Lieutenant Manning ran to the pair and tried to pull Scarborough off. "Ev! Ev, don't do this."

The haze lifted partially, and Scarborough was suddenly aware of Dolan looking up with an expression of pain and pure terror in his wrinkle-wreathed eyes. Scarborough rose, shaking off the insane anger that had so abruptly and uncharacteristically filled him—astonished and numb at his lack of control.

As Dolan was picking himself up from the floor, the Colonel's secretary walked in. "Colonel, I heard—"

"Would you please order up some MPs, my dear?" Dolan said, recovering. "We have a little discipline problem here."

"That won't be necessary. I'm under control now," said Scarborough. But the secretary was already gone.

The terror and upset that the anger staved off suddenly rose up in Scarborough like a flood. He collapsed in his chair, weary and shaken. "He was my best friend," he muttered. "And my role for you, my place in science, was my *life*. And now you're telling me it's a sham!"

"Nonsense!" said the colonel, brushing himself off. "You're having mental problems, it's clear, Scarborough. Just hold yourself steady awhile. Get yourself together, man."

"No, Colonel, I'm going to find out why my friend was killed! I'm going to find out why the government keeps secret bases on farms in the Midwest. I'm going to tear off these goddamn blinders you've put on me, and I'm going to uncover the truth—even if it destroys all that I've built up, all that I've mouthed in the past."

"You're insane, Scarborough!" whispered Dolan harshly.

Two privates with MP bands rushed in.

Colonel Dolan pointed at Scarborough. "I want this man taken away and incarcerated at Fort Meyer, immediately!"

The two burly men immediately grabbed Scarborough's arms and yanked him out of the chair.

"Wait a minute, you can't do this to me!" said Scarborough.

"He's right!" said Lieutenant Manning. "He's a civilian!"

"He's been in the employ of the United States Air Force for many years," said the colonel with a smug look of satisfaction. "He signed the appropriate forms that turn over disciplinary matters to *us*!" Dolan went up to Scarborough. "Cool off tonight, Ev. Think about your position. I'll deal with you tomorrow."

As Colonel Dolan turned to deal with Lieutenant Manning, a stunned Everett Scarborough was dragged away by the military police.

CHAPTER THIRTY-ONE

Lieutenant Marsha Manning went to one of the Pentagon's commissaries, where she drank three cups of coffee, and thought the hardest she ever had in her entire life.

The drab decor, and the dour-looking people who milled through the dim, table-filled room which was lined with Macke food-machines and faded photographs and smelled of cheap floor-wax, only served as a reminder to Marsha about how frustrated and trapped she felt in her position in the military. She sipped the bitter coffee and stared bleakly into nothingness. She could have gotten out last year. Instead, she'd re-enlisted. It wasn't the mere ten years to go before a nice pension—she just didn't know where else she could go. She stayed in the air force more because of momentum than anything else—and of course, because the traumatic breakup with Phillip had left her a walking basket-base for close to a year.

The trouble was, the military was like a mutant family. They fed you, clothed and trained you, gave you a warm place to relieve yourselves, sure—but it was more than that: all your recreation tended to be on base, under control. All your exposure to life was laced with their brain drugs of commitment for "the Life," from Officers Club, to softball teams, to commissary-cheap tampons. And to keep you from getting too attached to any one locale, they kept moving you around the country, around the planet. Two years at Andrews in Maryland, two years at Vandenberg in California, two in Japan, two in Frankfurt, Germany...

Follow orders. Yes, sir; no, sir: the binary system of that computer of the ages, the soldier. She'd turned into a robot, she realized; dead in the head, free from choices.

Until she'd met Everett Scarborough.

Somehow, he'd made her feel tingly. She had a new, valuable friend ... and he made her feel very special. Last night, today, they had gotten on so *well*. In conversation, in silence, in sharing a meal. They meshed, they sparked, he could make her furious, he could make her feel like a Madonna, a Venus ... like Albert Einstein. In just over two days! And there was the promise of something more between them ... something that had been denied last night so that it could grow and be richer for the future ... And now, she was drinking black coffee at the commissary, assignment over, Scarborough put away.

A kind of aloofness engulfed her as she thought the whole thing out step-by-step. She had absolutely no idea whether MacKenzie's theories were correct. Certainly, it seemed that the man had bumbled into *something* nasty. But the way Colonel Dolan had acted ... what he had done, throwing Scarborough into a military detainment-cell. She'd never heard of such a thing, though she supposed that there must be some kind of precedent. A colonel just didn't go about taking civilian law into his own—*The laws. The rules*.

Of course! Marsha could have kicked herself. There *was* something that she could do for Ev. Rules were written down, even military laws. And where else would they be, if not in the middle of the goddamn Pentagon!

She chucked the rest of her third cup of coffee into the trash bin, and hurried to find the Pentagon library.

It took her awhile, but she found it, an obscure section of the civilian codes in some thick tome of military law, hidden deep in the stacks of the reference section of the library.

She dug through her purse, found some change, and Xeroxed the relevant passage proving her case—Air Force colonels simply could *not* jail civilians. At least not in this kind of white-collar situation. Any disciplinary action of this sort had to be coordinated with the local civilian authorities. When the machine had finished flashing, and she was satisfied that the copy was legible, she returned the book to its shelf, and checked the time.

5:40.

It was her hope that she would catch Dolan in his office, confront him with this matter, and have Scarborough released. Surely, Colonel Dolan, in his anger at Scarborough's roughness, had overreacted, and would see the error of his ways.

It was ten before six when she reached the colonel's office.

The front office was empty. The secretary had apparently left for the evening. But the colonel's door was closed. Maybe he was still there. High-ranking officers tended to linger until six or seven, relieving their workload, doing paperwork maybe.

She walked toward the door, clutching the Xerox copy in one hand, raising the other to knock at the door.

But she caught herself in midstride. She heard voices in the room. She paused a moment, and she listened.

"...out!" One man was saying. "We're getting in over our heads, and I don't like the operational procedures that I see you exhibit!" She recognized Colonel Walter Dolan's voice, heavy with upset and anxiety.

"Look, Dolan! You can't! You're up to your bald scalp! You were here years before I took over Enforcement, and look how ineffective the programs were. The Publishers were not pleased. That's why they got new Editors!"

"I don't like it . . . Cold-blooded murder. I've had my fill of it, I tell you!"

"Dolan, how many times do I have to tell you . . . Justine said it was an accident! He didn't mean to kill MacKenzie. But you've got to agree, he's done his job. No more phantom files to haunt our nights!" The man's voice, a civilized tenor, chuckled ruefully.

"I don't care. I'm out of it."

"Dolan, you know that's impossible! You've been with Blue Book from the beginning! Now, I realize that you didn't start White Book, and God knows you've avoided Black Book . . . But you've got a responsibility to your country, to the Publishers . . . And most of all, to me. We can't afford to lose you. We're so *close*! Look, you're almost at retirement age. Hang on a little while longer, drop out gracefully. Otherwise, I'm afraid the Publishers will want harsh action taken."

"You mean . . . kill me!"

"I never said such a thing, Dolan."

"Okay, okay. I understand." Dolan's voice was petulant, but accepting. "Damn! And it was working...Lieutenant Manning was doing just fine! I'd planted all the right information in the computers. They would have been misled! And Justine had to go and pull *this* one! He's a maniac!"

"A useful maniac."

"But what about Scarborough?"

"Every man has his price. You certainly do!"

"You don't know Everett Scarborough. He'd *die* first."

There was a pause. "Well, Colonel, the Editors will take that into consideration."

Manning stood there, unable to move, understanding the conversation just enough to be horrified. White Book, Black Book—were these *legitimate* government programs? Or were they as covert as North, Poindexter, and Reagan's Iranscam? She had to linger and find out as much as she could.

"Okay, okay. But please, after tomorrow, I'm just a coordinator. An interface here."

"That will be more than sufficient. I'm sure the Publishers will see that Everett Scarborough is of no further use to the Cause. We had hoped to use him for a long time, worked hard to keep him bamboozled, but of course we did not forsee these events." Another rueful chuckle. "He certainly isn't going to be able to so blithely brush off accusations of government cover-ups now, is he?"

"What's the news on his daughter?"

"She's still managed to stay out of our grasp. But we've managed to pry the information from her boyfriend. We know where she'll probably be, and we'll be there as well. My goodness, the time has just flown. And I have a dinner engagement with the Attorney General."

Steps coming this way? They would catch her! There was no hope of running out of the door into the hall—they'd see the door closing, and they'd know that someone had been there, listening to this damning conversation.

But where could she hide?

Her eyes swept the office. The only possibility was the desk. Quickly and silently, she strode to it, moved the chair, and ducked beneath just as she heard the click of the door. She squeezed underneath the desk as far as she could, trying to control any telltale rasp of breathing.

"Thank you for coming, Richards. I had to tell you about this. And I'm waiting here for an important dispatch, so I couldn't leave for our usual meeting place. I feel a little better."

"Don't worry. Everything's under control. I personally will deal with our man in the brig first thing tomorrow morning. Good evening. We'll talk again soon."

Steps echoed down the hallway. The front door closed. Marsha watched as the black, spit-polished shoes of Colonel Dolan clicked back toward his office.

The shoes suddenly stopped.

Dolan stood still for a moment—then the toes about-faced. And the shoes began walking her way!

He's found me! she thought. He knows I'm here! She had to bite her tongue to keep from screaming with alarm.

The shoes stopped in front of the desk. She heard hands rummaging through some papers on top of the desk. There was a grunt of satisfaction and a crinkle of bond, then the shoes swung around again, and walked back to the open door of the other office. The door closed.

Manning heaved a sigh of relief. She waited for a moment more, then quickly crawled out from under the desk and as quietly as she could left the office.

She knew what she had to do, now. And she had to do it quickly, before it was too late to do any good.

CHAPTER
THIRTY-TWO

Diane Scarborough pounded on the motel door marked 134.

"Come on, Camden! Open up, man! I know you're in there! I see the light, your car is parked below."

No answer. Diane looked around on the open second-level, but saw no other signs of activity. The sun was low on the horizon, causing the automobiles in the tarmac parking-lot to cast deep shadows. Cars whooshed by on the highway in the eternal drone of modern transportation.

"Camden, I've got the story of the century for you!"

"Go 'way!" The voice was slurred. The goof was drunk. *Shit*!

"Camden, let me in, or by God, I'm going to call your publisher and let him know what is slipping between your fingers!"

A pause. She heard the uncertain skitter of steps, and a hard whump on the door as Camden overshot his mark. The knob turned, and the door opened. Diane smelled him before she actually saw him; whiskey exhaled from the doorway like pickled halitosis. A disheveled blot against a single lamp's light hung before her, weaving. "Don' do it. Please. You call my boss, my ass is cooked."

She pushed past him, and he closed the door and swung around squinting at her uncertainly. She went to the table, where a number of whiskey bottles stood. She picked an empty one up. "Jake! How long have you been in here?"

"Since ... last night," he said, leaning against the door, struggling to keep his eyes opened. "This happens sometimes. Reilly disappearin' ... MacKenzie *murdered*." A shudder visibly went through him. "God. Jus' too much. Went out for a drink las' night. Went a little overboard. Yeah."

His notes were scattered all over the desk and floor. The TV was on, volume off. Vanna White turned letters as the Wheel of Fortune twirled.

"Okay, Jake. I understand," she said softly, turning to him with a friendly smile.

"You do?"

"Yes, a lot of pressure here. A guy has to have a way to take off pressure, doesn't he?"

"Yeah! Thas' right! You're not so bad, you know?"

She took him gently by the arm, in an almost solicitous manner. "I'll let you be, Jake. But first, I'd like to show you something in the bathroom."

He seemed on the verge of falling to the floor, but Diane

managed to support him, guiding him toward the bathroom. "Yeah?" said Camden. "What?"

She flipped on the light and he flinched back., "Come on, Jake. It's in the bathtub. I've got this thing for bathtubs. They turn me on. I thought maybe that you and I . . . well, you know!" She tugged suggestively on his belt, half unlatching it.

The alcohol-drenched eyes lit. "Yeah! I always knew you had a thing for me, Diane," he said, clearly using high-proof logic.

"Oh, yeah," said Diane, maneuvering him so that he faced away from the tub. "I've had a thing for you, Jake."

Camden grinned woozily, and leaned drool-flecked lips, puckered and working, in her direction.

"Total disgust!" she said, pushing him back hard, the back of his legs hit against the porcelain and his knees buckled. Arms flailing, he fell back into the tub. "Ouch!" he cried, hitting his head against the tile, and collapsing ass-first into the basin. Diane leaped forward and turned on the shower. She put a foot onto Camden's chest, and then she turned the faucet all the way to C. Freezing-cold water slapped down onto Jake Camden's face and body. He flapped like a fish, gulping and gasping, spitting out water. Diane kept her foot levered on him for a full thirty seconds, then let him go. He struggled out of the tub, then slipped and splashed back in.

"What did you have to do this for?" he said, clambering out, dripping, his mouth working like a landed fish.

"To try and sober you up so I can talk to you, Camden. Has this dump got room service?"

"Uh uh."

"How about a coffee machine?"

"Yeah. Downstairs by the soda machine."

"That's going to have to do."

She marched the sopping man out of the room, down to the coffee machine, slammed two quarters into the slot, and made him drink the stuff on the spot.

"Urgh. This is awful!" But he drank it.

"Good. You'll want another one then."

She bought him another, then took him back upstairs, setting him down on the bed. She took the remaining bottles of whiskey, one full, one half-full, and dumped them down the sink, then returned to the man, who was wide-awake and stunned, sitting on the bed.

"Wow," he said. "You're a handful, aren't you?"

"Good. Half-sober is better than nothing. Are you listening to me, Camden?"

"Yeah."

"My father sent me here to deal with Tim's disappearance. I've notified the police, I've notified the FBI. I've done all I can. I'm supposed to stay here. But I can't."

"That's right. You've got to meet those ETs or whatever."

"How do you know that?"

"Tim told me."

"Good. Yes, that's right, Jake. And I'm going. But I'm not going to go alone. You're going to go with me. Sober—and with your camera. I've got two tickets for a flight to Las Vegas leaving at midnight. Guess what, Jake. You're going with me!"

Finishing his coffee, Jake choked a bit. His face grew red and Diane slapped him on the back a few times, harder than necessary.

"Me?" he said. "Why me?"

"I've been giving it some thought. I need backup, Jake. Tim was going to be my backup. I want *proof* this time. A photo, tape rolling, maybe even a Super-8 or videotape."

Jake sat down wearily, a droplet of water hanging from the end of his nose. "Diane, I work for a questionable newspaper. I'm a questionable journalist." He sighed with self-disgust. "I can't even handle my liquor. Get someone else. For your own sake."

"Sure, I'm going to go to the local TV and say, 'Come out with me! I'm going to meet a flying saucer.' Can't do that, pal. Not with who I am. I can't let it get any farther than it's gotten, this whole biz—for my father's sake. But I need someone to come along with me."

"Your old man, huh? Guess you're a good daughter after all."

"Not really. He wants me to stay here and wait. I can't. I can't miss out on this opportunity! And neither can you, Jake!" She squatted down beside him, a sincere hand on his arm. "Jake, remember—this is your chance. The big story, Jake. Now for God's sake snap out of it! You're no coward! You just drink too much."

"Big story," Camden mused slowly emerging from his funk. "Yeah, that's right. I really need that big story. I really need to keep my job, make some money . . ."

"And don't forget—become respectable!"

Bloodshot eyes cast a tired glance her way. He drank some more coffee. "Yeah. Sure." He snorted. "Leopard spots, and all that."

"We're talking redemption here, Jake. Renewal . . . a second chance. We're talking maybe Pulitzer prize time! And you've got to be straight and sober, so drink that coffee up now. Let's get you changed and packed."

She went to his closet, and opened the door. Camden's loud and tasteless floral shirts hung there like thrift-shop rainbows.

"Remind me, after we get to Vegas and rent a car," said Diane. "We're going to *have* to buy you something more subdued."

"Oh yeah. I can just see the headlines: First Fully Documented UFO Contact—A Black-Tie Affair."

She threw him some dry clothes. "Come on, Mr. Hotshot Reporter. Get changed. We've got a plane to catch."

CHAPTER THIRTY-THREE

It was still dark when they woke him up.

"Scarborough," said the brusque soldier, shaking his shoulder. "Hey, chum. Wake up."

Awareness settled around him in shades of black and white. He was lying on a metal cot, with only a wafer-thin mattress between him and its wire-mesh bottom. A joke of a pillow supported his head. The smell of industrial-duty disinfectant hung everywhere about him, making his stomach turn. He lifted himself up on the cot, rubbed the back of a hand across his eyes. "What's happening?" he muttered.

"You're outta here, Scarborough. Don't know what the hell you were doin' here, anyway."

The words jolted him awake—but then wariness crept in. "Who . . . who's taking me?"

The soldier—a sour-faced young private with short hair and a clear distaste for guard duty and late-night shifts—grunted. "Come on up to the front desk and find out."

Groggily, Scarborough obeyed, getting up, finding his coat, putting on his shoes, and staggering out the door of the room where they'd locked him up; no bars, just reinforced walls.

Their treatment of him had been totally illegal. No phone call to his lawyer had been allowed. They'd simply stuck him inside the cell and thrown a little food and water in just after sunset. How much sleep had he gotten? he wondered as he traipsed down the corridor. Not much, his weary joints and the ball of cotton in his head answered.

The military guard unlocked the door at the end of the corridor and ushered Scarborough out to the front desk, where a crew-cut man in wire-framed glasses sat, filling out a report in a cranky, humming typewriter. The clock on the wall said 4:35. Sitting in a wood chair by the desk was Lieutenant Marsha Manning, looking tired but determined.

She brightened when she saw him. "Dr. Scarborough," she said. "Are you all right?"

"Nothing some coffee won't help . . ." he said. "But how the hell . . ."

The sergeant behind the desk looked up at Scarborough, then pulled the form from the platen of the typewriter.

"Would you please sign this, Lieutenant?" As she signed, the sergeant gave Scarborough a disinterested examination.

"Don't know what you were doing here anyway, Doctor. Sorry about this. Just following orders."

"Well, thank God there were no showers or ovens, that's all I can say!" Scarborough spat out sardonically.

Manning grabbed his arm. "Come on, Ev. We've got to get you out of here. My car's outside."

Scarborough glared at his former keepers, but allowed himself to be led out into the predawn night. The military barracks and nondescript buildings, separated by tracts of macadam and grass, stretched out toward lamplit highways. Manning had a Chevy Sprint this time. "On my own card this time, Ev," she said, unlocking the door for him. "Hurry. Explanations in transit."

Bemused, he got in, automatically buckling the safety belt.

Silently, Manning drove the car off of the base. It was only when she got on Route 1, headed away from the base toward Washington, that she said anything.

"I'm taking you to National Airport, Ev. There's bound to be an early flight to Kansas and you've got to be on it. Your daughter is in danger."

"Whoa there! Just a second! Start at the beginning!"

She took a deep breath and told him how she'd gotten the legal information to get him out of confinement before Colonel Dolan could do anything else to him. She told him about her trip to argue with the colonel, to show him how he had erred. She told him about the meeting she had overheard between Dolan and the man he had called Richards.

"Project White Book! Project Black Book!" Scarborough whispered between clenched teeth. "Publishers? *Editors*?" He felt so overwhelmed he could say no more. A deep nausea churned at the core of his being as he looked away at the vague mists rising up from the edges of the Potomac River. And Diane! Merciful God, *Diane*!

"It took me awhile, but I finally got hold of the commanding officer of the base. General Watkins. I had to go to his house, Ev," she chuckled humorlessly. "I dragged him out of bed. You should have heard me. I *made* him deal with the whole business—but still, the paperwork took a few more hours. God, I don't know how I did it, but I cut through about an acre of red tape!"

"Dolan had no legal right to incarcerate me. I knew it, he knew it—but the bastard did it."

"Ev, I don't know what's happening, but it doesn't sound legal to me at all! Have you got any kind of idea, after what I told you, what's going on?"

"Looks like my friend Mac MacKenzie was more right than even his paranoid mind could imagine. What we've got here is a conspiracy within the halls of power," said Scarborough. "A conspiracy and a cover-up. God alone knows how far, how deep it goes, but for twenty long years I've been its dupe. And mean to make up for those years. I want to see Dolan hanging from the masthead of the *Washington Post* by his balls!''

"I'm doing the right thing, heading for National?"

"Yes. I have to get to Diane first, get her out of this. Somehow, I get the feeling that Dolan and company—White Book, Black Book, whatever, are behind this sighting she's made. Marsha, you've been a savior. Thank you. Yes, you've done exactly the right thing."

She put a hand on his knee. "Ev. Are you going to be okay?" she said, concerned. "You look pale as a ghost."

Scarborough nodded and squeezed her hand. "Yes. Yes, thanks. But what about you? Colonel Walter Dolan is not going to be thrilled when he finds out it was you that sprung me!''

She smiled to herself. "No, he's not. But he doesn't know what I heard between him and that Richards guy. I'm positive of that, Ev. As for the rest—well, I've got over ten years experience with the air force. I think I can handle myself. But I'm going to have to keep my nose clean. No more putting it where it's not supposed to be, or I don't know *what* will happen!''

"Yes. Yes, of course," said Scarborough, preoccupied.

They drove in silence the rest of the way to the airport, Scarborough thinking furiously. Diane was his first priority. He had to make sure she was safe. He'd hide her somewhere, then he'd take them on, the bastards. For MacKenzie, yes . . . it was more than apparent that Dolan and this Richards man were behind his best friend's murder. But now, it was bigger than that—he had to find out the *truth*. This was for *himself*. The enormity of what he'd stumbled across was too much to take all at once—he just had to concentrate on action, or he'd turn into a useless puddle of spineless Jell-O.

Dawn was just paling the horizon as Manning essayed the winding curves of the approach to National Airport and pulled up to the passenger drop-off point.

"I wish I could have coffee or something with you, Ev. But I've got to get some rest before the shit hits the fan."

"I understand." He leaned over and they shared a meaningful kiss. For a moment, Scarborough was back in bed with her in Iowa, and felt as though he just wanted to tell her to take them some place far away, away from this insanity, just the two of them.

"I can't thank you enough, Marsha," he said, after breaking
off the kiss.

"I . . . I . . ." she said, then stopped herself, and started
again. "You're a wonderful, good person, Ev. I wish you
luck."

He was getting out of the door when she called him back.
"Ev! Wait a minute!"

She was busy scribbling on a card. "If there's anything I can
do for you . . . any kind of help. Here's my phone number back
home." She gave it to him, then she touched his cheek with a
finger tip. "And Ev . . . maybe you'll call me anyway, if you're
ever in my neighborhood."

He touched her hand, nodded, then hurried off into the
terminal to get a ticket for Kansas City.

Somehow, Everett Scarborough managed to get a few minutes' more sleep on the two-hour flight. When the Braniff 737
landed at Kansas City International, he rented a car and drove
out to the motel where he'd told Diane to stay.

The hotel clerk reported that Diane Scarborough had checked
out last night.

"What about Jake Camden?"

The clerk looked at the records. "Hmm. He checked out
about the same time."

Baffled, Scarborough called the local and state police of
Diane's community. They reported to him that yes, they were
investigating the matter of the disappearance of one Timothy
Reilly; yes, they had worked with Diane yesterday; but no, they
had not heard from her today. Scarborough thanked them and
hung up.

He had one more lead. Kathryn Rashone, Diane's girlfriend
with whom she'd been on the night Tim had disappeared.
Scarborough had met Kathryn, an anthropology student who
shared a rambling old Victorian mansion with a group of other
students on the edge of town. A bit fey for Scarborough's
tastes, but pleasant enough. Maybe Diane had left a message
with Kathryn.

There were no private lines in the house, and Scarborough
had to wait at the telephone stand outside a 7-Eleven while the
male student went to knock on Kathryn's door.

"Oh, hello, Dr. Scarborough," said Kathryn, breathlessly picking up the phone. "I thought I might hear from you."

"Hello, Kathryn. Yes, I'm looking for Diane, and she's not where she's supposed to be."

"Where are you?"

"I'm here at the university."

"Well, Diane said she didn't want to leave a message with anyone she didn't trust. She sounded kind of freaked. I mean, with Tim disappearing and everything, and all this strange UFO stuff, who could blame her. Dr. Scarborough, *you're* the UFO expert. What do you think about all this weird stuff poor Diane's been going through?"

"Kathryn, I don't have time. Could you please just tell me the message that Diane left?"

"Oh, sure, Dr. Scarborough. Sorry. She says she's sorry, but she has to go where you told her not to go. She can't take the chance of missing out on an experience of a lifetime. But she wouldn't tell me where, Dr. Scarborough. She said it might be dangerous to tell me exactly where. Do you have any idea of what she meant?"

Scarborough watched a little boy push through the glass doors and walk past him clutching a cherry Slurpee, sucking it up through a straw.

"Yes, Kathryn," he said, feeling a tingle of adrenaline shoot through him, feeling his heart pound harder with dread. "Yes, I know exactly where."

CHAPTER THIRTY-FOUR

When Colonel Dolan called Brian Richards's office in the morning at the CIA Building in Langley, Virginia, his secretary informed him that Mr. Richards was not in today. No, he wasn't on field duty—he was at home.

Richards lived in Great Falls, on the Virginia side of the
Potomac, a woodsy and expensive area, a rustic bedroom
community favored by many of the elite of the executive-end of
government. Dolan had been to Richards's house. It was a
beautiful colonial on twenty acres of woodland. Deer could be
seen in the morning at the salt lick that Richards kept in the
backyard. The man had three kids, all in high school or
college, and his wife was active in community affairs, just now
serving in a county government position. When Dolan called
Richards on his private, high-priority line, the man picked up
almost immediately, his voice sounding irritated. As soon as
Richards discerned that it was Dolan calling, he said, "I know
why you're calling. We have to talk. But not here, and not
there. Meet me at our rendezvous Point 5 at exactly 11:15
A.M."

Dolan didn't argue. Unquestionably, Richards knew the situation. Scarborough had somehow gotten himself released from
incarceration, despite Dolan's precautions.

Dolan, who commuted to the Pentagon from his home in
East Falls Church, got his Cadillac from the huge parking lot
quickly, and was soon on the northbound George Washington
Parkway. When Richards specified a meeting time to the
quarter-hour, he insisted upon prompt arrival. Rendezvous
Point 5 was within easy access to both of them for this time of
day: Great Falls Park.

How the hell had Scarborough gotten out? They had plans
for him today. His escape spelled big problems. Dolan drove
the whole way along the scenic ride that skirted the Potomac
River valley, which was wearing its spring green finery, so
tense his teeth were clenched. Damn the man! How could such
a good thing for, lo, these twenty-plus years suddenly turn so
sour? Well, he just prayed there was a way that Richards had
worked out to deal with it, because Dolan hadn't the faintest
idea.

Great Falls Park was a few miles north of the Washington
Parkway's intersection with the Washington Beltway. Dolan
pulled his Cadillac Seville into a parking space shadowed by
trees; he walked past picnic tables and the Central Office which
housed the Men's and Women's rooms toward the expanse of
reinforced concrete edging the cliff that overlooked the rock-
filled falls and waterways. This early, there were only a few

people milling about, enjoying the fresh air and scenic beauty the falls provided. There was the taste of mist in the air, and the smell of a nearby barbecue firing up charcoal to broil an early lunch. The roar of the falls was a steady, comforting sound.

Richards was leaning against the railing, looking out at the white spray of the main waterfall. He was wearing his regulation spook Burberry raincoat, but Dolan was gratified to see that beneath it was a red flannel shirt, jeans, and tennis shoes. Dolan himself had changed to civilian clothes, and removed his tie. For these kind of meetings, you didn't want to wear your official blue, no sir.

Dolan leaned on the railing two yards from Richards, and pulled out a pack of Doublemint Gum, offering it to the man.

"No thanks," said Richards.

"We okay here?"

"I've got a couple men as backup. You're right though. From now on we've got to be careful." He pulled up a Nikon from where it hung by a leather strap and clicked off a shot of the rushing white water below them. "It was that Lieutenant of yours that got him out. I checked."

"Damn."

"Scarborough was right. You had no legal right to put him here. But that's neither here nor there. Actually, in the long run, it may work out for the best. I talked to the Publishers this morning. They agree with me. Where Scarborough was once a strong asset, the events of the past week have made him a liability. And I think that my men can deal with him better on the loose, if you get my drift."

Dolan shuddered. "I didn't want it to come to this."

"I think that you're going to have to let loose some of these scruples, Colonel, if you want to retire safely and happily. Things are charging ahead on several fronts."

Dolan silently chewed his gum, feeling ill but not offering any kind of objection.

"I'll deal with Scarborough. He's fully my problem now. Understood? You're going to have to do some serious sandbagging for a while. God knows what kind of shit's going to hit the fan. But that's the totality of your involvement until I say different. Just guard Blue Book. White Book and Black Book will proceed apace. They are too important not to."

Dolan nodded silently. He wasn't enjoying the gum at all; in fact, somehow, it was making his stomach feel sour and upset. He took it out and wrapped it up in a length of handkerchief, which he stuck back in his slacks.

White Book. Black Book. God, what they'd developed into! Even now, even though he'd been involved with both of them since the late forties, the very thought of their importance staggered him.

From the very beginning, Project Blue Book had been a cover-up. A form of lip service paid to quell the demands of the public. And to think, from the very beginning of it all, certain key members of the air force, of the government, had known the truth. Including Walter Dolan.

Simple enough in the beginning. But then, in the beginning it had just been high echelons of the U.S. government, principally defense personnel who had been involved. But then, the organization known as the Publishers slowly had gotten involved, subtly and inextricably—and things had gotten complicated.

At first, the young and ambitious and starry-eyed Walter Dolan had no moral qualms about what he was doing. It was for the benefit of his country. Now, though—God! What a morass! He wanted out, but he was in too deep. Far too deep. If he even made a peep about getting out now, he knew that one of the Junior Editors would be paying his East Falls Church home a surreptitious visit. It would be Dolan and family at the wrong end of the gun, and not poor Scarborough!

"I understand," said Dolan. "You know you'll have my full cooperation, Richards."

"Good. That's what I had to be sure of, Colonel. We can't hazard unloyal constituents. Not at this stage of the game. We're too close to our goals."

"Scarborough will go looking for his daughter, you know. His daughter is very important to him."

"Yes. Our ministrations with one Timothy Reilly have proved most revealing."

"You mean, you know where she's gone?"

"We certainly do. Which means we know exactly where Scarborough will go as well. This business will be tidied up thoroughly by the end of the week, I promise you." He turned to Dolan, and poked him in the arm. "But there's going to be fallout. The Publishers had hoped to protect Scarborough—and now they're going to have to remove him. This is going to attract attention!''

"Can't he just—disappear?''

"Oh, sure! Can't you see the headlines? UFO Debunker Abducted? No, we have to try to make it look like an accident, but without any harm done to the incredible amount of anti-UFO propaganda generated by his books and appearances. This is where you come in, Colonel. To begin with, you're going to have to stonewall on Scarborough's air force connection.''

Dolan nodded. He'd stonewalled so much, he felt as though he'd invented the word.

"Then, we need some kind of replacement. Someone to take up the slack—a new debunking spokesman, as it were. Now, he doesn't have to have been with Project Blue Book.'' Richards cleared his throat. "In fact, from recent experience, I'd say maybe it would be best if he *wasn't* associated. At any rate, he has to have an unimpeachable scientific reputation, just like Scarborough, with attendant respect, etcetera. Media-ready, a nice smile, a man who knows his way around a *bon mot* and who'd look good on the Carson show.''

"That's a big order to fill.''

"Don't worry. This is really the Publishers' area—but I figure they might want your input.''

Dolan felt relief. "I'll send a list of candidates from my end, yes.'' He shook his head. "Damn shame we have to write Scarborough off. He's the best.''

"Exactly. Which is why we don't want him appearing on Ted Koppel's 'Nightline' anytime soon. Savvy?''

Dolan let go an expulsion of breath. "Boy, *do* I! But what about Diane? You can't...''

Richards glared at Dolan with a coldness that frosted the colonel's spine. "Don't tell me what I can and cannot do, man! You forget who's in *charge* here.''

Dolan looked away. Down below, the sun had placed a small rainbow into the mist that hung over a convergence of white, roaring water. Killers and hooligans, that's what Richards, his men, and the Publishers were, for all their high-minded and vaunted ambition for this country, this world. Killers and hooligans, maybe even madmen on a level with Adolf Hitler or Napoleon Bonaparte. No, it had all been very simple at first, back in the old days of Project Blue Book, when Walter Dolan had *lived* to serve his country. Now, he served his country's secret masters, to live.

"I understand," he said, and turning away from the water-filled chasm, he walked back to his car.

CHAPTER
THIRTY-FIVE

"Well, what do you think, kiddo?"

Camden stepped out from the dressing room of the Vegas Cut-Rate Clothing shop and preened for Diane, showing the sartorial splendor of a pink-and-yellow flowered shirt with green nylon trimming. "More subdued than my usual threads, huh?"

Diane Scarborough stared aghast at the ugly thing. Not even a nice jacket would cover up this atrocity. Diane's intellect may well rove the cosmos, all time and space—but her tastes were purely Fifth Avenue. She simply could not deal with a travelling companion who looked like a refugee from "Don Ho's Hawaii Goes to Hell."

"Pretty cheap too!" said Camden fluttering the price tag at her.

"I'll *bet* it is!" said Diane, grimacing. "Jake, you look like a party favor in that thing! It's *awful!*"

It was the middle of the afternoon, a bright sunshiny Vegas sky shining beyond the plate-glass windows of the shop. She'd let Camden sleep late while she went out and bought maps and information on Hoover Dam and the surrounding area. He'd be absolutely no use to her tired and hungover. As it turned out, it had been a good idea. After she'd pumped some Denny's twenty-four-hour breakfast into him, he was the old Jake Camden again, rarin' to go, eager to chase those "bogies," as he called them. He even bought new Kodak film for his camera, and new SKC tape for his cassette-recorder. Now they were buying him some new, subdued clothes.

"I still don't get it! Hell, don't you want me to fit in with the tourists?" Camden said. This was his second swipe at her taste in clothes.

"Jake, you don't understand. I don't personally care what you look like. But whatever happens, there may be pictures involved. As my father would be certain to point out, Jake, this sort of subject material would look shoddy and questionable if it had pictures of you in it looking like a two-bit LA con-artist. *Comprende?*"

Jake shrugged. "Okay, tell you what. You've got my size, now, you go and pick out something that will match your outfit for this evening, suitable to your sense of taste and decorum for the occasion of contact with aliens from Planet Xenon!"

"Jake! Shhh!" She put her finger to her mouth and looked around the room, past mirrored racks of clothing and clerks with tape measures hung around their necks. "You don't have to broadcast what we're doing tonight."

"Okay, okay," said Jake, calming down. "You're right. I'm sorry, I guess I'm just a little jumpy, a little edgy. Yeah, you're probably right. But you gotta help me, you gotta pick something out. I'm a forty-Regular, thirty-three waist, thirty in the leg. You find me something, I'll wear it tonight. But *only* tonight." He looked at his watch, then out the window across the street at the Rexall Drug Store. "I'm gonna hop outta these things now, and go get some more batteries. I don't want to get caught with duds in my machines."

"Okay, Jake." She looked at him sternly. "But no stopping in any bars. You promised me, no drinking until this is over."

"Don't sweat it! I touch a drop, and the way my system is now, I'll puke! I swear!"

"Okay, Jake. I'm counting on you." He disappeared back into the draped changing rooms, and Diane set about finding something suitable for him to wear. Not that it really mattered, she supposed. She was like this with Tim, too, always choosing his clothing. Maybe it was the Scarborough in her—she had elements in her personality of a control freak.

Anyway, Jake was right about one thing. They had a few hours to spare. The time she remembered being given for the rendezvous was nine o'clock, and it was now only a little after five. Still, she wanted to get to the dam early. As she'd thought about it, it seemed a damn public place for an encounter—but at the back of her mind, there was the thrilling thought that maybe this was going to be IT—the first public contact of an earth citizen with extraterrestrial visitors.

That was just the way Diane Scarborough thought. Tim Reilly called her the Meryl Streep of self-dramatizers.

Immersed in a cloud of brooding, she went to the men's jacket section. She would have just settled on something simple, like a nice Izod shirt, and some tasteful grey golf slacks, but the temperature was supposed to go down to the fifties tonight and she didn't want Camden's hands to be shaking on the camera.

She was going through the jacket and suit section, in the size forty-R selection, pondering this whole business, when she stopped still, feeling a little faint.

Suddenly, as she was fingering the fabric of a nice linen jacket, things became *very* wobbly.

The floor seemed to drop out from beneath her feet. . . .

She was back on board the ship again.

Before her were the two men. Normal looking, in their jumpsuits. The sensations and exhilaration and awe at being where she was swept through her again. The moment seemed encapsulated in eternity.

"Hoover Dam, at nine. You will be more prepared to accept what we have to tell you at that time."

But the man with the grey hair and the fiercely intelligent eyes did not stop there.

"But not on the dam itself. Two miles away, off the highway, there is a valley formed of small hills, out of sight of the road. Here, there is an old rock quarry. A small lane veers right as you approach the dam, heading southeast from the town that is called Las Vegas. That is where we will meet at nine o'clock, after the sun has set."

The clothing shop swirled back into existence around her and she had to grab a stand of clothing to prevent herself from falling headfirst onto the floor.

"Are you okay, Miss?" asked a balding clerk.

"Oh,—er—yes. Yes, I just felt a little dizzy for a moment."

"Can I get you a glass of water?"

"No. No, I'll be okay."

"Can I help you choose something then?"

"No, I think I've already made my choice." She had to get out of here quickly, had to talk to Camden. Things were getting complicated—this altered the plans! She quickly thumbed through the forty-R suits, and found a cheap cotton one, not exactly stylish, but far from bad taste, and it wouldn't draw unfavorable attention tonight, wherever they ended up—on the front cover of *Time* magazine, or in an interstellar craft headed at faster-than-light speed for a private audience with an alien princeling. She hoisted it off the rack and handed it to the clerk. "Do you take VISA?"

Sitting in a blue Buick half a block down from the discount clothing store, Woodrow Justine spoke to the other team members via a cellular phone.

"Okay, she's coming out of the Cut-Rate with a package and she's crossing the street. She's going into the Rexall Drug Store where that other guy went."

"Should we take them when they come out?" The voice was from the red Oldsmobile with tinted windows down the road, yet to communicate from less than a block, the signal first had to be relayed to the phone company, and bounce off at least one satellite. The notion tickled Justine.

"Negative."

They'd had a man stationed at the Las Vegas airport last night, he'd tailed Camden and Diane to their motel. They'd followed their movements all day.

"We're going to follow them to the dam. We don't do anything till after it's dark, and not so obvious. You got me?"

"You betcha. Sounds good to me. That's about when Scarborough should be showing up, right?"

Justine grinned. "You better believe it."

CHAPTER
THIRTY-SIX

Hoover Dam was not always called Hoover Dam.

One of the largest concrete dams in the world, the arch-styled behemoth had been built on the Colorado River during Herbert Hoover's presidency, from 1928 to 1932, to generate electrical power for the Southeast, as well as to control flooding, improve navigation and river regulation, and provide water for the very dry areas surrounding it. It had been dubbed "Hoover Dam" in 1931 to honor the President, but after Hoover left a depressed economy behind him, the Department of the Interior began to call it Boulder Dam or Boulder Canyon Dam, after the nearby town of Boulder, Nevada. In 1947, though, with memories of breadlines and hard times behind them, the dam was dubbed "Hoover" by congress itself.

Hoover Dam was on the Arizona-Nevada border, approximately twenty-five miles southeast of Las Vegas.

Scarborough landed at the famous gambling city in the early evening of a typically hot sunny day. The flight had been delayed, partly by an afternoon storm in Kansas, partly by the usual vague human/technical foul-ups apologized for by the pilots in the Chuck Yaeger drawls adopted to calm frayed nerves. By the time Scarborough checked out a rental car from Avis, he wasn't sure he'd make it to Hoover Dam in time to get Diane the hell away from there before Richards's people swooped down on her.

He wouldn't have minded some kind of police backup. But what was he going to tell them. "Officers, you see, my daughter is waiting for a spaceship from another planet, but actually she's going to be kidnapped by a secret government conspiracy!'' Yeah, sure, and officer, Godzilla is at the Sands chomping quarters from the one-armed bandits as well!

He bought a map, and received directions from a Shell gas station. A highway—Route 93—used Hoover Dam as a bridge, and the attendant informed him that evenings held a small to moderate amount of traffic. The moon was full tonight, the sky clear, which was supposed to cast a beautiful light over the dam, the surrounding rough and rocky land of the El Dorado mountains, the desert it helped irrigate, and Lake Mead, the reservoir it created—a tourist attraction in itself.

A hazy sun was sinking over the horizon as Scarborough drove down the highway, his map accordioned out on the passenger seat. He wasn't entirely clear on what would happen after he yanked Diane away from the place—maybe stay the night in a Las Vegas motel and fly out in the morning, maybe just point the headlights west and head for California. The latter wasn't a bad idea. He had a close friend in L.A. they could stay with. On the other hand, driving in open spaces might not be such a great idea—they could easily be cut off in open spaces. Scarborough wished he knew the extent of the corruption indicated by Colonel Dolan's cooperation with this Richards guy. A tremor of paranoia gripped him. God, this could extend *everywhere*! But, no—Marsha had sprung him from that brig, using legitimate measures. Clearly the conspiracy— whatever it constituted—was limited.

Scarborough had gleaned what information he could about Hoover Dam from a Nevada tourist manual he'd picked up at Kansas International. The irony of the location had not been lost upon him. Arizona was perhaps the number one state for UFOs—the mystical UFO people in particular, channellers, and such, fancied that the aliens favored the rugged landscape and desert of the state, and were attracted by power nodes of crystal buried in the earth or some such nonsense. As for the dam— well, a hell of a lot of hydroelectric power was generated at that dam. It powered much of Arizona, Nevada, and Southern California. UFOs were notoriously attracted to power sources. Nonetheless, Dr. Everett Scarborough did not for a moment consider that there was any truth to Diane's story. He considered it merely coincidence. Other, more mundane powers were at work. There was proof enough of that.

He wished he had a gun, he thought as the cactus and the

hills swept by along the unwinding road. But he couldn't have taken one on board the plane and he didn't have the faintest idea where to get one in Las Vegas. Not that he really knew how to use one. Mac had always been after him to learn, but he never had. Still, in this kind of situation, it would be nice to have some kind of effective weapon in his hand. He had his wits—his wits and his intelligence would just have to do.

The sun had not gone down by the time Scarborough reached the dam, but it was very close to setting. The light cast swatches of strange colors from the jagged rocks on either side, and danced into the depths of Lake Mead, swelled now with runoff from a snowy winter. The view of Arizona was quite spectacular, all reds and browns and shadows tilting toward sundown. The sound of the coursing water, where the base of the huge arched dam became a river again, mixed with the faint throb of the mighty engines hidden within the structure.

Scarborough parked in the lot for tourists and sightseers. He went to the Nevada Tourist Information booth, which was closed. A sign proclaimed hourly tours of the dam's interior, but the last one had been at five o'clock. He bought a can of Pepsi at a soda machine, then he went back to his car. With the sun dipping over the horizon, the evening was cooling. He saw no sign of Diane, nor had he necessarily expected to yet. She'd said the meeting was supposed to be at nine, and it was only a little after eight.

Now that he was here, though, with the adrenaline of his efforts wearing off, he began to have doubts.

I should have brought somebody else. Anybody else. Here I am, unarmed and relatively defenseless, waiting for who knows what?

He'd jumped into this half-cocked, and now had the extra time to ruminate. Still, he didn't know what else he could have done, and he had no time to veer from his course. So he stopped damning himself, and tried to concentrate on something else for the time being. He reread the material on Hoover Dam in the Nevada tourist booklet.

Hoover Dam, Scarborough had read, was 1,244 feet long and 725 feet high. Elevators descended forty-four stories into the dam, and stopped short of the base. The base itself was 660 feet thick, containing over 4,400,000 cubic yards of concrete; sufficient concrete to pave a two-lane highway from West Coast to East. The power it generated from the water running through the huge turbines could reach up to 1,344,800 kilowatts.

It was a big fella, all right, thought Scarborough.

He waited for the dusk to level off into night, then got out of his car. Sodium lamps along the top of the dam had faded on, lighting the two-lane concrete highway atop the dam. Scarborough pocketed the keys, but left the doors of his car open—a quick escape might be necessary. He took a deep breath of the dry, clean air, and strode toward the dam.

Okay, Diane, he thought. *Now where the hell are you?*

From where he was, he could see the entry port for the elevators, its lights standing sentinel in the bunkerlike hub of concrete. He could see a security guard, sitting just inside the door, with a view of the whole top of the dam.

When he reached the door, he found it was locked. He knocked, and eventually a monotone answered from a speaker grate. ''Yes?''

''Pardon me, I'm supposed to meet my daughter here. Have you seen an attractive blonde woman, twenty years old walking hereabouts?''

''Nope.''

''Are you positive? This is very important.''

''Your daughter, huh? Mister, we don't get too many young blondes walking along Hoover Dam at night. This ain't exactly a pickup spot, you know. If I'd seen her, I'd remember her. And I ain't seen her.''

''Right. Thank you. By the way, is it okay if I walk along the sidewalk at night?''

''Free country, and that's a national highway you're lookin' at. Just be careful, huh?''

''It's a beautiful night.''

''Yeah. Nice view. Have fun.''

''If you see her, would you tell her that her father's here?''

''Sure. But if she's as pretty as you say, can I ask her for a date?''

''It's a free country!''

The security guard laughed, and Scarborough stepped away and crossed the highway to the sidewalk. Traffic had slowed from moderate to a mere occasional car whooshing along, its sound dopplering as it passed, its wake kicking up the odd bit of litter. Scarborough walked out onto the dam. No one else was walking on the sidewalk. His steps clicked and echoed faintly against the concrete abutment to the right. There was a metal guardrail between the two-lane road and the sidewalk. A short metal railing overlooked the dam itself. Scarborough, a third of the way across, leaned against the rail and gazed down from the dizzying height onto the angled spillway. The bright moon reflected off a sheen of moisture against the concrete. The dam's operator must have let some of Lake Mead's water go this way. Normally, in a hydroelectric dam, the penstocks— the pipes—conveyed the water from the reservoir on through the turbo-system, creating the electricity. Scarborough remembered he'd read that the main penstocks to Hoover at this point were thirty-foot diameter plate-steel pipes with a maximum thickness of almost three inches. Far below, at the base, he could see the white water churning out from the ends of these pipes.

He walked a little ways farther, to the middle of the bow of the arch. The dam was engineered in this manner so that much of the water-weight in the reservoir could be distributed to the abutments to the side and the base, which were anchored to hard bedrock. Still, as he walked on top of it, Everett Scarborough marvelled at the technological wonder of this dam, and how it built so much upon the science of engineering throughout the ages.

He stared awhile at the moon with its attendant speckles of stars, rippling in the dark blue desert sky. He closed his eyes, and drank deep of the smell of the water and the power in the air, trying to calm himself. Peripherally, he noticed a car coming along the road. However, he was so wrapped up in his attempt at meditating, that he did not notice it stopping.

Scarborough opened his eyes, took one more deep breath, and was about to start back, when he heard steps. Puzzled he turned around. With the speed and skill of an athlete, a man wearing a grey suit leaped over the guardrail and was on Scarborough in a twinkling. Before Scarborough could do a thing, he was aware of the bore of a gun digging into his abdomen.

"Hello there, Mr. Scarborough," the man said. He smelled of expensive cologne and sour sweat, and of the Juicy Fruit gum he chomped in his mouth. "I've been looking forward to meeting you for a while, and what a spectacular staging for our meeting."

They stood in a shadowy area between two lights, but enough illumination shone for Scarborough to see a portion of his attacker's face. Short hair, chiselled features—and a cheek speckled with acne scars. Pockmarks.

Scarborough backed up against the cement behind him, and a breath of desert wind blew his hair. The jacket of the gunman flapped. ''You're the bastard who killed Eric MacKenzie!''

Woodrow Justine had been waiting on the Arizona side of the dam for over an hour. He had not noticed the car pull into the visitor's parking lot on the Nevada side—he had been using the public toilets—and he did not know that Scarborough had arrived until he noticed the solitary walker approaching the elevator entrance during a sweep with his field glasses. By the time his car had navigated the road on the dam, Scarborough was already walking along the sidewalk.

Justine had turned off the road and considered. The other boys were following Diane Scarborough and her companion, and damn if they hadn't shown up yet. Justine wanted to deal with Scarborough himself. It struck him as a move of elegance and economy—a gesture to Richards illustrating his competence. But then he had to decide whether to wait until the man came back to his car, or to just apprehend him in the middle of the dam.

At first, Justine opted to wait. Scarborough had to come back, and it would be a hell of a lot easier to take him in the parking lot. But then the bastard just squatted out there like he'd fallen asleep, so Justine had cursed, started his car and zoomed out. No real prob, he reasoned. Just a quick stop, a jump from the car with the engine idling, and then he would pull Scarborough in (or shoot the son-of-a-bitch if he resisted) and ride off toward Arizona.

And it was all working well enough until Scarborough started to talk to him. He'd pulled the car's tires up along the curb enough so that there was plenty of right-lane left, and was out in a flash, his gun trained on the man leaning over the edge, as though he were contemplating a jump. But then, surprise! The man looked Justine square in the eye and told him that he'd killed Eric MacKenzie. Which was true enough, but how the hell did Scarborough know that? He'd left MacKenzie dead in a burning house. No one else in Iowa City had seen him come or go. The statement threw him for a loop.

"That's right, Scarborough," Justine said, hiding his surprise with admission. "And now it's your turn. Hard to believe. You had such a good thing going, and you *blew* it. Shit, I protected your ass once. Now I'm going to blow it away—unless you cooperate."

A car passed by on the other side.

Scarborough's thoughts were unreadable. "Okay. I'll cooperate. But who are you, and where do you come from?"

"None of your business, pal. Now I want you to get in the car!"

"Whoa. Just a moment here! Can't we talk this over? Who do you work for, and how much are you paid? I'm sure we can make some kind of financial arrangement."

"Get in the car, asshole, or I'm going to spray you all over the Colorado River!"

"You don't want to do that here, not really. I'll come. But first, do you have my daughter, Diane?"

"I've got a short temper, Scarborough. You're right, this is not the best place and I want to get out of here. And if I have to drag your bleeding body in the car, that's the way—"

A car approached them on their side of the road. It slowed and stopped directly behind Justine's car. Jeez! thought Justine, who the hell is this? He couldn't see who was behind the wheel, but he couldn't take any chances. He moved closer to Scarborough, shielding his gun from the view of the newcomer. "Now keep your mouth shut, or you've had it," Justine whispered.

He heard the door open and the sounds of a man getting out.

"Now move around so that your back faces the car." Justine shoved the hard gun into Scarborough's back to punctuate his demand. Scarborough obeyed. This way, Justine could watch them both. He directed his eyes to see who it was that was getting out of the car.

The car was large and black, with fins. An older model Cadillac. The man getting out seemed spotlighted by the lamp from the other side of the highway, revealing straggly hair and a face totally in shadow, unrecognizable. The man wore a suit that was a little too big for him, with baggy pants.

And the suit was entirely *black*.

"Hey, guys," said the man. "Seen any UFOs hereabouts?"

Black. *Black!*

A violent seizure swept through Woodrow Justine's brain.

"We've come for you, Justine," said a voice inside his mind. *"You must answer to us. You must join us!"*

His arm where Klinghoffer had injected him with the hypodermic throbbed painfully.

Woodrow Justine lost his composure completely.

"No!" he cried. "Get away! Get away from me!"

He pulled the gun away from Scarborough and fired at the Man in Black.

CHAPTER THIRTY-SEVEN

The man with the gun fired, his eyes wide with a wild, inexplicable fear.

The man who had just arrived yelped a surprised curse, grabbed his arm, and ducked behind his car. Everett Scarborough knew that he wouldn't get a second chance—the gun was pointed away from him; the pockmarked man had let go his grip on Scarborough's arm, and his right hand was extended in firing position. Almost instinctively, Scarborough swiveled, joined his hands together, and brought his linked fists down hard on the wrist. A grunt of pain. The man's hand was shaken loose of the weapon. The gun dropped and skittered along the sidewalk into a large pool of shadow.

For whatever reason the new arrival had freaked the gunman, the man's training took over at this point. With great strength and a savage cry, the pockmarked man hurled Scarborough back against the cement wall, then pummeled him with hard and determined fists. Scarborough scrunched himself into a ball to protect himself, but, finding the blows so fierce that his consciousness was threatened, he burst from his position and hurled himself upon his attacker. The man was driven back against the opposite railing. He slipped and fell down with a curse.

"Scarborough!" came a cry. "Scarborough, that *is* you, right? What the hell—"

Everett Scarborough recognized the voice. "Camden! Get the gun—"

Scarborough kicked at the man on the ground, striking him in the face and knocking him back. But on the second kick, the man caught his foot, his hands clamping onto it like the jaws of an alligator.

"I'm wounded! He'll shoot me again!"

"I knocked the gun away. It's over—" But the man in the grey suit twisted Scarborough's foot, throwing him to the ground. Scarborough turned so that he landed knee-first in the man's abdomen. There was a whoosh, an expulsion of air. But the man grabbed hold of Scarborough's shirt and threw him down. They traded more blows, which made Scarborough acutely aware of just how much more powerful the man was.

The next thing he knew was that Camden was standing over them, bright blood on his shoulder, kicking the pockmarked man as hard as possible, trying to get a shot at the groin.

"No, Camden! The gun!"

"I don't know where—" His foot connected with the attacker's groin. The man on the ground cried out in pain, but in the same moment he also managed to lift himself off of Scarborough; he grabbed a fistful of Camden's coat and hauled him off his feet.

"Shit!" cried Camden, but somehow, the wounded man managed to turn his fall into a hard blow against the pockmarked man. Scarborough scrabbled away from the man on the ground.

"Keep him down, Camden!"

Camden was clinging with all his might on top of the man, who was attempting to get up. "What do you want me to do? Drown him with my blood?"

Scarborough didn't stop to answer. He scrambled back to where the gun had been dropped. That was their only hope— the gun. But where was it?

He fumbled about in the shadows, hands reaching for the gun, finding nothing but cement and empty air. Where the hell was it? Behind him, he could hear cursing and the sound of fists on flesh. The groans of pain seemed to be mostly Camden's.

but the man was hanging on for all he was worth, like some terrier on a postman's pants leg.

His heart pounded in his ears. The gun! He had to find the gun. If he didn't, Camden would be thrown off at any moment and then—

His foot struck something. Metal skidded on concrete. Something glinted in the light. He'd found the thing, but he'd kicked it away.

"Damn!" He heard Camden's cry. "He's shaken loose, Scarborough! He's getting up. He's—"

Scarborough looked around. The man was standing up, and reaching behind his back, for something stuck in his belt. He was going for another gun

His heart in his throat, Scarborough turned and leaped for where he hoped the gun had been kicked. There it was! He fell onto the ground, and fumbled it up into his hand, just as he heard a gunshot. A bullet tore a divot of concrete up just inches from Scarborough's face. With the same motion he'd used for picking the gun up, Scarborough rolled under the metal barrier-ence and scurried behind one of the cars for cover.

He fitted the gun to his finger, and came up from behind the trunk of the car. The pockmarked man was running his way, gun out in front of him.

This was it! thought Everett Scarborough. His last chance. He aimed wildly and squeezed off a shot in the general direction of the assailant.

A splash of blood sprayed from the man, and he was kicked back hard against the metal fence, his gun clattering into the ground. He was a tall man, and his back struck the barrier railing. So hard was the force of the bullet that struck him—apparently in the chest—that the man's torso was flung over the railing, pulling his legs with him. The result was a spectacular somersault.

Somehow, though, the man was able to reach out and grab the edge of the concrete, where he clung precariously.

Scarborough took a quick deep breath and hurried over. The man dangled by one hand over the drop, his fingernails digging at the cement, scraped, bloody and raw.

Scarborough put the gun down on the ground and reached over to pull the man back over the railing before he fell. He was badly wounded and couldn't hang there much longer—

maybe he had the information that Scarborough needed. He leaned out and grabbed the man's wrist and was immediately struck with revulsion and vertigo over the depth of the dam spillway.

The man had swung in such a way that he had a grip with both hands, but he couldn't last long. Scarborough was going to have to pull him up so that he could get a leg over. "Okay, you're a strong bastard. You can do this."

There was fear and panic in the man's eyes, but he said nothing. Scarborough pulled on him, but it was hard going.

"Camden!" he cried. "Hurry. I need some help."

"What! I'm dying here!"

Nonetheless Camden in his black suit joined him, weaving a bit.

"Grab his jacket! Help me haul him up!"

"The bastard tried to kill me!"

"Just do it, dammit. We need to know who's behind this!" cried Scarborough. He turned back to the man and strained to prevent him from falling. Sweat hung in beads from the man's forehead. Blood flowed freely from the man's wound, dripping down to splatter against the cement of the spillway. "Where's Diane?"

"She's back at some rock quarry about three miles away!" Change of interpretation of message. "She's okay."

Scarborough tugged. "Okay, who's your boss? We can let you drop right now, or you can tell us who you're working for!"

The man's eyes were glassy and they looked up at Scarborough with pure hatred. "Get me up!" It was a demand.

"Geez, how did the guy know that I was a Man in Black!" quipped Camden as he reached down to grab hold of the man's jacket.

The effect of the statement was immediate on the man hanging from the wall. His mouth opened and closed like a beached fish gasping for water. "Man in Black! No! Get— away—"

A spasm seemed to strike the man, and his fingers lost their grip. For a moment, Scarborough was able to hold him, but so strong was the attacker's spasm that the man was wrenched free as well. Camden did not even try to grab hold at all.

The man fell.

"Shit!" cried Scarborough.

Screaming, the man dropped in what seemed like slow-motion. He hit the spillway, and rolled down, leaving narrow smears f blood on the cement. Down and down he went, rolling and mbling, until he stopped screaming, as the mists and water wallowed him up in their hungry, roaring maw of night.

Scarborough watched in horrified fascination, and then put is hands on his arms.

"I think I said the wrong thing," said Camden. "Oh well. o big loss."

Scarborough sighed. "Are you okay?"

"Oh yeah. Flesh wound. Stings like the very devil, but it's ot serious."

"That was the man who killed Mac."

"Are you sure?"

"Sure enough. He had pockmarks, which fits the description lac gave before he died, and he acknowledged it."

"Bastard." Camden sighed, and held his wound. "Diane ent me back to pick you up."

"How'd she know I'd be here?"

"She called her girlfriend back in Kansas, who reported ou'd gotten the word that she'd flown the coop. Diane knew ou were aware of her destination. But by then that destination anged . . . Say, why was that guy so upset when he saw me?"

"That's something we'll never know. Why are you dressed a black suit?"

Camden rolled his eyes. "Long story."

"We can't stand here gaping. You've got to lead me back to here you left Diane. A rock quarry, you say?"

"Yeah, about three miles northwest of here, just off the road, a the Nevada side."

The scream of sirens was suddenly on the air. Scarborough hirled around and saw a stream of flashing lights coming their ay.

"I think, though, it looks like we're going to have to answer few questions first," said Camden.

"There's no time!" said Scarborough. "They'll *get* her! ome on! Back in your car." He hurried Camden toward the ntal car and they were about to get in, when another blast of shing lights appeared from the other side of the dam.

"Everett, old buddy, it's time for the old mouth here to go

into high gear.'' He patted the man's back and they waited for the police to arrive.

CHAPTER
THIRTY-EIGHT

As she stood in the abandoned rock quarry with the cooling desert night settling in like the black satin from that Moody Blues song, Diane Scarborough for the first time doubted herself.

The place was like something out of a science fiction movie. God, it felt like an alien planet here, thought Diane as she surveyed the rugged, ragged landscape. The quarry was like a crater, cut in the face of granite, surrounded by straggles of desert growth, swathed here and there with sand. The stars were out now, bright pinpoints pricked into the hard sky, and they looked down mercilessly onto the bleak rock holding its tiny bit of humanity in its palm. The only sweetness about this place was the suggestion of desert flowers; the rest was the hard, nasty flavor of sand and rock and survival.

Maybe she shouldn't have sent Camden back.

Maybe she needed him more than she realized.

She checked her wristwatch. He shouldn't be much longer and then he'd back. She'd just wanted him to check the dam anyway, to make sure her father wasn't there.

Why ever had she called Kathryn, anyway? If she hadn't she'd have remained in blissful ignorance, could have just gone through this experience with Camden—if there was even *going* to be an experience. The longer she waited, the more she doubted that this ''vision'' of hers was anything more than a mental defect, a brain-flicker.

And if that was the case, maybe she could just forget this whole thing and get on with her life . . . but at least for now

Diane Scarborough had to humor herself. She had to know. If these were alien creatures who had summoned her, she had to meet them.

"Goddammit," she said, pacing by the large hunk of rock that thrust up from almost the very center of the quarry. "Hurry up, Camden. I don't *like* it here!"

Who she really wanted, though, was her father. That she'd checked up with her girlfriend and made her spill the beans meant chances were pretty good that dear Doc Scarborough was on her trail. That was all right, but now he was on the *wrong* trail... A trail that might get him in trouble with whatever group of sickos had kidnapped Tim Reilly. Besides, if there *were* aliens trying to contact her, and her father could be there when they did... Well, that would indeed be wonderful.

Somewhere in the distance, a coyote howled. A breath of night wind came and flickered the scarf around her neck. It was a red silk scarf, edged in gold thread. One of her favorites. Her father had bought it for her in Italy. She buttoned up her jacket now, shivering with the surprising chill that the wind brought with it.

Instead of decreasing, the wind hissed up into a stronger gust, carrying with it a spray of sand.

"Dammit!" she gasped. Before she had been able to cover her eyes, a blast of grit had blown into them. It was painful too, and she bent over, struggling to remove the stuff.

It was then that the noise began.

It started as a low hum, and Diane Scarborough thought at first that it was the sound of this new and sudden wind, pushing through cracks in the stone-rise near the roadway. She had her eyes half-closed as she worked carefully to remove the sand so as not to scratch the corneas or anything. But then the noise got louder, and kind of strange.

It was a roaring sound, rising to a low hum, and soon it started to congeal into *thrumming*.

Wasn't that the sound helicopters made? wondered Diane as the roar crescendoed and rolled through the quarry. She didn't know, she'd never been around helicopters that much. Her tear ducts were working like hell, her eyes were tearing up, and even though she was managing to get her eyes open a little, she couldn't see much.

That was when the light hit her.

It could have been a spotlight or a searchlight; she wouldn't have known. To her, it was just a blazing blast of brilliance, filling her eyes and, seemingly, her whole being.

Now she could hear something slowly crunching ahead of her, but she could see nothing but the brilliance in which she was bathed.

She had a bad feeling about it. This was nothing like the experience in Kansas. Nothing at all. There was nothing mystical, nothing wonderful or hypnotic here.

Suddenly she was very frightened, and the only thing that seemed right to do was to turn and run.

She faced away from the light, but things were just as bright away from the thrumming sound.

She started to run ... And then something struck her from behind. Abruptly the lights seeped away, and she felt herself slowly falling down onto a rock, and into oblivion.

CHAPTER THIRTY-NINE

After Camden's flesh wound had been treated and bandaged at the local hospital, Scarborough and Camden were detained for over two hours at the local police headquarters, answering questions, filling out forms and begging to be let free. They were not charged with anything, but they had to stay in the area and come in the next day for further interrogation. The first thing Everett Scarborough requested was that a patrol car be sent to the Mitchell Quarry, where he felt his daughter was in great danger. The police sergeant, a young and alert man named Ferrer who recognized Scarborough and had read one of his books, agreed.

A half hour later, though, when the patrol car reported in, it was with the news that no young woman of Diane's description could be found in the quarry, or in the surrounding area.

Scarborough filed a missing persons report, and asked that a search be undertaken immediately. Sergeant Ferrer was very sorry, but no such search was possible until an appropriate number of hours had passed.

Before they were released, the results of the search for the body of the pockmarked man in the grey suit came in: no body had been discovered in the Colorado yet.

Then the keys to Camden's rental car were returned, and the odd duo were released under their own recognizance, with orders to report what motel they were staying at the next day. There would be more questions then.

As soon as Everett Scarborough got into the passenger seat of his car, he said, "Camden, drive me to that quarry."

"Ev, pal——she must have given up on us and hitched back to the motel in Vegas. Maybe she's there by now."

They stopped by a gas station and Camden used the pay phone.

"Well?" demanded Scarborough.

Camden shrugged. "They haven't seen her."

"The quarry," said Scarborough tersely, and then he fell into a sullen silence.

"Camden," he said softly. "I can't shoot a gun."

Camden said, "Huh? Oh——yeah, you mean with that killer on the dam. That was a damn lucky shot you pulled off. You saved our lives there, Scarborough."

"Luck," said Scarborough, puzzled. "Yes."

Camden had some difficulty finding the place again in the dark, past midnight; but after a few wrong turns, he found the road and drove past the rocky upthrusts that hid the large indentation in the ground from the view of the highway.

"Yeah, right. She was sitting on that rock just over there," said Camden, pointing.

"Drive there, but stop about ten yards short and turn on your brights," Scarborough said.

Camden obeyed.

Scarborough got out of the car and looked around. The cliffs of the abandoned quarry had turned into slopes over the years, and they surrounded an expanse of perhaps three hundred yards in diameter. Patches of desert vegetation grew here and there, and Scarborough could see the gleam of smooth rock rising up from sand and dirt blown into arroyos by the wind. The headlights of Camden's car illuminated a stand of granite beside a stretch of sandy dirt.

Scarborough strode to it, careful of where he stepped, and examined the loose dirt. Camden followed respectfully behind him.

Scarborough pointed. "This was where she was?"

"Yeah! That's right."

Scarborough nodded. His face was as pale as death. His finger pointed limply at the story etched into the sandy dirt and the twisted branches of the bushes. Tire tracks. Footprints that were smeared. Just to make sure, Scarborough examined the treads of Camden's car, comparing them to the outlines in the dirt. They did not match.

Jake looked at him. "Hey, it could have been the police car!"

Scarborough shook his head no.

They looked around a little longer. Camden found something behind the bushes. It was one of Diane's shoes. Nearby, was her purse. Scarborough took them, and examined them carefully using the light from the headlights.

"We'll have a look at the purse's contents later, at a motel," said Scarborough.

"Geez—" said Camden, looking up at the cloudless sky, dominated by a moon. "You think that maybe Diane was *right*? You think that maybe a spaceship came down and picked her up like she said it would?"

Scarborough shot Camden an angry glare. "Of course not, you idiot! The proof is right here before our noses! Whatever group that pockmarked man who killed Mac was with—the group that Colonel Dolan belongs to." His voice broke and became strained. "The people who have made a fool of me for over twenty years." A helpless sound cracked his voice. "They're the people who have Diane. Not aliens. Project White Book, Project Black Book! A conspiracy!"

"Evvie, chum, settle down. You're gonna bust an artery! We'll get her back. I promise you." He put a hand on Scarborough's shoulder, but the man shrugged him off. "Boy, though," said Camden in an awed whisper. "What a great story."

Scarborough felt as though the very cosmos had cracked beneath his feet. A pain he had not known since Phyllis had died began to well in his chest, and he had to turn away from Camden. He walked back to the car and leaned against a fender, taking long, slow breaths, trying to recover his equilibrium.

He had to hold himself together. For Diane's sake, he had to keep his head.

This was his fault that she'd been taken by those maniacs. His fault—and he knew that she was in very grave danger.

After a time, he turned, a look of pure defiance and determination etched on features suddenly very old.

"You bastards," he cried, shaking a fist at the sky, toward the darkness that hid the foul snakes who had stolen his only daughter away from him. "I'll get her back. And you're going to pay! Do you hear me! You're going to *pay*!"

Jake Camden lit a cigarette, took a drag, got Dr. Everett Scarborough in the car, and drove back toward Las Vegas.

"Something tells me," he said softly, as Scarborough stared out mordantly at the desert, "we're not in Kansas anymore, Toto."

EPILOGUE

The two men dressed in business suits, who looked like lawyers but were not, watched the black car leave the quarry from their hiding spot behind a large rock on the edge of one of the cliffs.

One of the men had grey hair; the other, much younger, held a high-velocity rifle with an extravagant scope set on the gun barrel.

When the black car had dusted away into the night, the young man turned to his elder.

"All has gone well," he said with a sigh. "I am glad."

"Yes. Scarborough has run the first part of his maze well," said the older. "His death has not been necessary, and this gladdens my heart tremendously." He turned to his partner. "But do not think that all is settled now. There are many obstacles yet for Everett Scarborough. Many obstacles for us, to achieve our goal."

The younger man nodded and put his rifle in the trunk of the car. He looked soberly at the other. "Yes, brother. How often I forget, as I have followed Everett Scarborough these past weeks, that much more is at stake than the life of a solitary man."

The older man looked up at the desert stars for a moment, and then heaved a long sigh.

The two men in black suits got into their Cadillac and drove away into the cooling desert night.